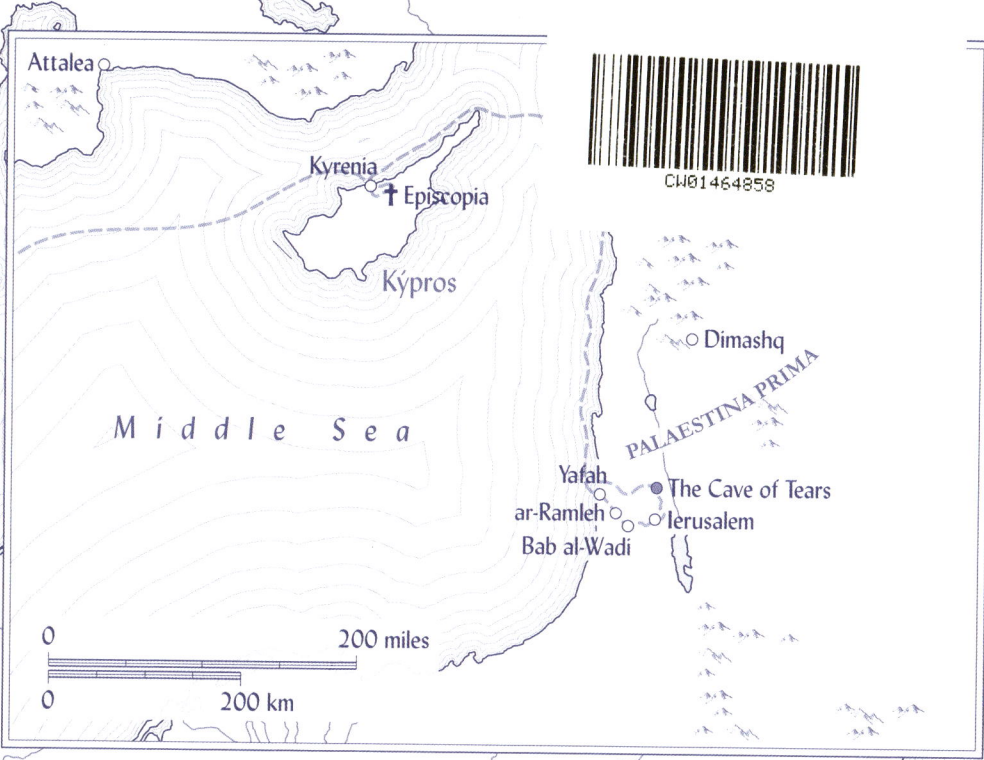

Praise for
MATTHEW HARFFY

'Harffy is the gold standard of historical action adventure.'
Theodore Brun, author of *A Mighty Dawn*

'Terrific white-knuckle action, absolutely gripping storytelling...
Can't wait for the next one. Highly recommended!'
Angus Donald, author of *Robin Hood and the Caliph's Gold*

'A breathless charge through Dark Ages intrigues and infighting
that brings the period to savage, bloody life. Masterful.'
Anthony Riches, author of the Empire series

'Nothing less than superb... The tale is fast paced
and violence lurks on every page.'
Historical Novel Society

'Harffy's writing just gets better and better... He is really
proving himself the rightful heir to Gemmell's crown.'
Jemahl Evans, author of *The Last Roundhead*

'A tale that rings like sword song in the reader's mind.
Harffy knows his genre inside out.'
Giles Kristian, author of *Camelot*

'Top class adventure writing, with action that
moves as fast and keen as a whetted blade.'
Ian Ross, author of *Battle Song*

'Visceral tales of battle, revenge, and honour.'
Graham McNeill, author of *False Gods*

BY MATTHEW HARFFY

The Bernicia Chronicles

The Serpent Sword
The Cross and the Curse
Blood and Blade
Killer of Kings
Warrior of Woden
Storm of Steel
Fortress of Fury
For Lord and Land
Forest of Foes
Shadows of the Slain

Kin of Cain (short story)

A Time for Swords

A Time for Swords
A Night of Flames
A Day of Reckoning
Dominion of Dust

Novels

Wolf of Wessex
Dark Frontier

DOMINION OF DUST

MATTHEW HARFFY

HEAD
ZEUS

An Aries Book

First published in the UK in 2025 by Head of Zeus,
part of Bloomsbury Publishing Plc

9 7 5 3 1 2 4 6 8

A catalogue record for this book is available from the British Library.

ISBN (HB): 9781035916467;
ISBN (ePub): 9781035916481; ISBN (ePDF): 9781035916436

Cover design: Simon Michele/Head of Zeus
Map design: Jeff Edwards

Printed and bound in Great Britain by Clays Ltd, Elcograf S.p.A.

MIX
Paper | Supporting
responsible forestry
FSC
www.fsc.org   FSC® C018072

Bloomsbury Publishing Plc
50 Bedford Square, London, WC1B 3DP, UK
Bloomsbury Publishing Ireland Limited,
29 Earlsfort Terrace, Dublin 2, D02 AY28, Ireland

HEAD OF ZEUS LTD
5–8 Hardwick Street
London, EC1R 4RG

To find out more about our authors and books
visit www.headofzeus.com
For product safety related questions contact productsafety@bloomsbury.com

Dominion of Dust
is for all the residents of Dorksville
(you know who you are)

DOMINION OF DUST

N

NORRLAND

HORÐALAND

✝ Lindisfarnae

○ Eoforwic

MERCIA

Aachen ○

ATLANTIC
OCEAN

○ Tours

Banbalūnah ○

ITALIA

Roma ○

Toledo ○   Balansiya ○

AL-ANDALUS   BALEARES   Cagliari ○

Qadis ○   Sicilia

Xiphonia ○

Legend

○ Settlements

✝ Holy sites

Hunlaf's voyages

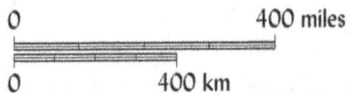

0		400 miles

0		400 km

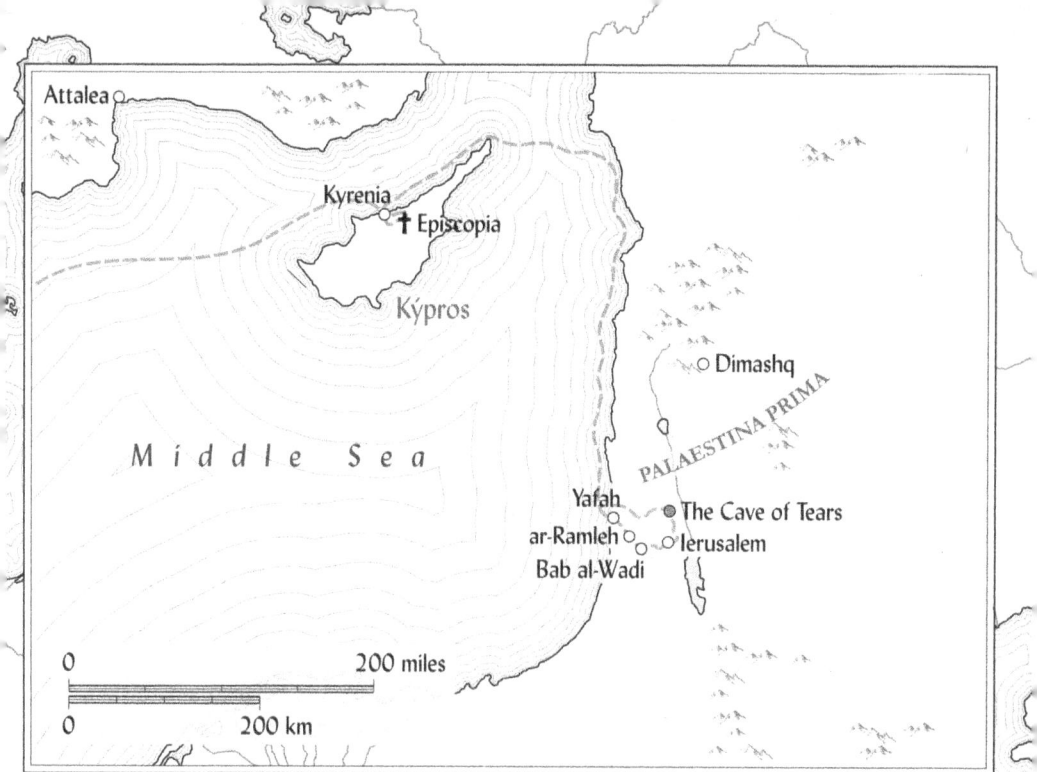
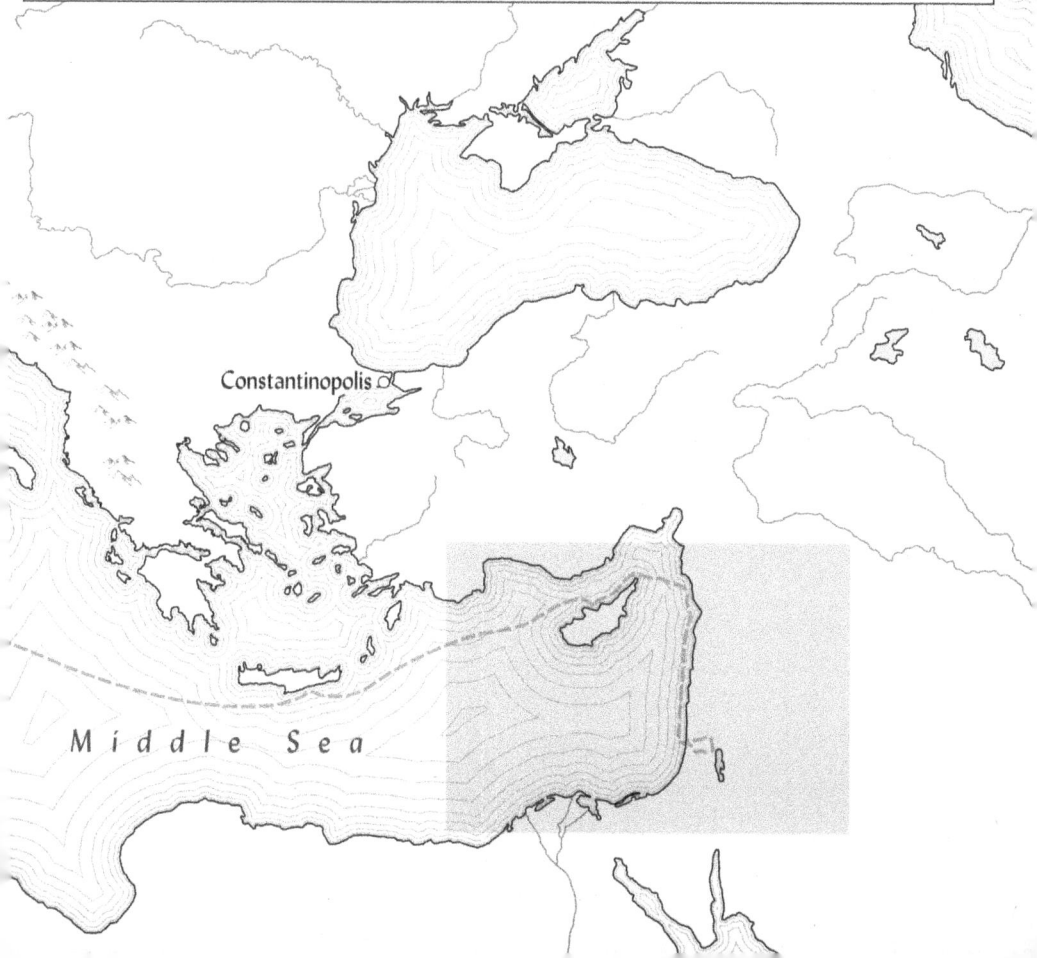

"And almost all things are by the law purged with blood; and without shedding of blood is no remission."

Hebrews 9, verse 22

"But one of the soldiers with a spear pierced his side, and forthwith came there out blood and water."

John 19, verse 34

Place Names

Early medieval place names vary according to time, language, dialect and the scribe who was writing. I have not followed a strict convention when choosing the spelling to use for a given place. In most cases, I have chosen the name I believe to be the closest to that used in the late eighth century, but like the scribes of all those centuries ago, I have taken artistic licence at times, and, when unsure, merely selected the one I liked most.

Some of the place names also occur in my Bernicia Chronicles novels with different spellings. This is intentional to denote that this is not part of that series and also to indicate the passage of time and the changes to language that occur over the centuries.

Æbbercurnig	Abercorn, Scotland
al-Andalus	The Muslim-ruled area of the Iberian Peninsula
al-Masjid al-Aqsa	The Al-Aqsa Mosque, Jerusalem
al-Wadi 'l-kabir	"The Great River". Guadalquivir River
ar-Ramleh	Ramla, Israel
ar-Raqqah	Raqqa, Syria
Attalea	Antalya, Turkey
Bab al-Wadi	Sha'ar HaGai, Israel
Balansiya	Valencia, Spain

Baleares	Balearic Islands
Banbalūnaĥ	Pamplona, Spain
Bebbanburg	Bamburgh
Byzantion	Constantinople (Istanbul)
Cagliari	Cagliari, Sardinia
Constantinopolis	Constantinople (Istanbul)
Dimashq	Damascus, Syria
Danapr	The Dnieper
Eoforwic	York
Episcopia	Minster at the site of Bellapais Abbey, Cyprus
Ğarundaĥ	Girona, Spain
Hálogaland	Hålogaland, Norway
Họrðaland	Hordaland, Norway
Ierusalem	Jerusalem
Ifriqiya	Area comprising what is today Tunisia, western Libya and eastern Algeria
Išbīliya	Seville, Spain
Italia	Italy
Kýpros	Cyprus
Kyrenia	Kyrenia, Cyprus
Lindisfarnae	Lindisfarne
Madīnat as-Salām	The City of Peace, Baghdad, Iraq
Malaqah	Malaga, Spain
Mercia	Kingdom in Britain centred on the River Trent and its tributaries. Loosely covering the region known now as the Midlands of England
Middle Sea	The Mediterranean
Norrlanden	The northernmost, largest and least populated of the three traditional lands of Sweden
Oguz il	"Oguz Land". Turkic state located in an area between the coasts of the Caspian and Aral Seas

Orkneyjar	Orkney Islands
Palaestina Prima	Byzantine province in the region of Palestine from the late fourth century until the Muslim conquest in the 630s
Papia	Pavia, Italy
Qadis	Cadiz, Spain
Qubbat as-Sakra	Dome of the Rock, Jerusalem
Quentovic	Frankish trading settlement. The town no longer exists, but is thought to have been situated near the mouth of the Canche River
Qurtuba	Córdoba, Spain
Roma	Rome
Roman Sea	Old Arabic term for the Mediterranean Sea
Rygjafylki	Rogaland, Norway
Sardinia	Sardinia
Septimania	Visigothic kingdom in modern-day southern France that roughly corresponds to the former administrative region of Languedoc-Roussillon (now part of Occitanie)
Sicilia	Sicily
Tours	Tours, France
Ubbanford	Norham
Uuir, River	River Wear
Uuiremutha	Monkwearmouth
Werceworthe	Warkworth
Xiphonia	Augusta, Sicily
Yafah	Jaffa, Israel

One

I have not written for weeks. And yet it is not the gnawing at
my guts, the affliction that has ailed me these past years, that
has held me back. Nor have I been prevented from my work
by an overbearing abbot. In truth, it was the newly appointed
minster-father, Godstan, who came to my cell this morning and
encouraged me to pick up my quill once more.

"It smells like a stable in here," Godstan said, stepping over
the detritus on the stone floor and swinging open the wooden
shutter that covered the window. The sudden draught of cool
air made the sour stench of the room more evident. There was
the faint scent of smoke and ash on the breeze, and the cries
of the gulls reminded me of screams of pain. "You must stop
this languishing," Godstan said, turning to face me. The wispy
hair around his tonsured head looked like cobwebs in the sun.
"Rise up from your bed and continue what you started. It is
what he would have wanted."

I felt a surge of my old ire, a spark of the passion that had
been all but extinguished with the passage of the years.

"Do not tell me what he would have wanted," I growled.

I cared nought what the abbot thought of me or the smell of
my quarters. I had barely roused myself from my mattress for
days, content to lie swaddled in the sweat of my self-loathing.
But now I pushed myself into a sitting position, groaning at

the aches the motion awakened in my back. I held a bony hand above my eyes, squinting at the blaze of early summer sunlight that pierced the gloom.

My throat was dry and my words rasped. I reached for the flask that rested beside my pallet. There should still be some of the cunning woman's draught from the previous night. I always made sure to have enough to dull my pain when I awoke. Not that the ache in my stomach had grown any more intense of late. If anything, it had abated somewhat, almost as if the Lord in His infinite wisdom wished me to have a clear head so that I might think of my actions and what they had caused.

Godstan moved quickly across the room and snatched up the flask. I lunged for the bottle with an effort, but the speed of my youth had long since vanished and the abbot was faster. Biting my lip, I leaned back against the wall.

He sniffed the flask's contents and grimaced.

"Tell me," he said. "And tell me true. How bad is your pain?"

I thought about lying, but Godstan's open gaze halted me. I had once been capable of subterfuge, but now I tried to maintain my vows, despite my weakness. I was feeble, but in this at least, I did not falter. The truth was not lost to me.

"My stomach aches," I said, "but the pain is not as sharp as it has been."

He nodded slowly and offered me a thin smile. I thought he was going to hand me the flask. Sweat beaded my forehead and my breathing quickened at the thought. But he did not relinquish his hold on the draught, instead he filled a cup with weak ale from a jug that he had brought with him.

"From now, you will drink of this potion only at night," he said.

I did not reply. It would be easy enough to drink some of the stuff once he had left my cell. I could already taste the bitter brew, and I sighed in anticipation of its warming effect, the dulling of my senses, the softening of the jagged edges of my memories.

"I will have the woman from the village bring more," Godstan said. "I will administer the correct dose to you after Compline each evening. You will sleep well and in the morning your head will be clear so that you may continue with your work."

"What if the pain grows?" I asked, my voice trembling in a way that disgusted me. That pleading tone spoke eloquently of the hold the concoction had on me and I imagined what Godstan must think.

"Then you will pray with me. And with the Lord's guidance, we will do what is best."

Admitting defeat, I held out a hand. Godstan gave me the cup of ale. I drank, suppressing a shudder as the cool liquid washed down my parched throat.

Still holding the flask, Godstan returned to the open window and stared outside. I could picture what he saw as clearly as if I was standing at his side, so familiar was that view to me. The herb garden with the constant drone of bees flitting over the rosemary and lavender. The scriptorium, with its high windows and steep, sloping roof. The chapel and chapter house, almost fully repaired now. The building bore little evidence of the fire that had threatened to engulf it just weeks earlier. Beyond that, the sloping fields of barley, peas and oats that ran down to the river, where the tall alders lined the bank.

Those trees had been tall enough to hide the masts of the ships that had slid onto the shore. The raiders, Danes, so Lord Osulf believed, had come up through the green barley in ordered silence. I clenched my jaw at the recent memory.

"Those Danes would have slaughtered us all without any remorse," Godstan said, sensing where my thoughts had wandered. There was a bleak shock in his voice.

"It was only luck that saved us," I replied, remembering how Osulf and his warriors had galloped across the minster's vallum before dawn. They had ushered the brethren into the chapel in the darkness, closing the doors and leaving us huddled there, the stink of fear oozing from our pores.

Godstan turned back to me, his brow furrowed.

"Luck, you say?" He rarely displayed signs of anger, but he was furious now. "This was not the capricious whim of wyrd. This was God's will and we should rejoice in it."

The bright sunshine picked out the lines of age and worry on his face. These past weeks had brought suffering to us all and I felt a pang of guilt at having allowed Godstan to bear the weight of it without offering my aid.

"You are right, Father," I said. "Forgive me."

I had not been surprised by the raiders' lack of compassion. But I had lived a very different life to that of Godstan. In my youth I had leapt over *Brymsteda*'s wale and rushed up a beach in search of adversaries. I had plunged my sword into the guts of any who had stood before me. I had done all this and worse in the service of the holiest of kings: the Emperor Carolus Augustus himself. I had killed countless foes in Carolus' service. In the name of God.

Godstan's anger vanished as quickly as it had come.

"There is nothing to forgive, Hunlaf," he said. "You have done nothing wrong." He looked away, unable to meet my cold stare. "You were not to blame for any of it."

"I should never have filled the boy's head with tales of adventure. If I had not done so, he might yet live."

"Perhaps," Godstan said, his tone soft with sorrow, "but only the Almighty can decide when a man's life should be ended. You did not wield the axe that slew Coenric."

I closed my eyes and, unbidden, I saw Coenric as I had found him, twisted and bloody in the doorway of this very cell. The boy's expression in death had been one of shock. Surprise perhaps that he had not managed to slay his adversary with the sword he had snatched up from the chest I kept under my bed.

My sword.

It was lying there now, in the darkness, sheathed and wrapped in cloth. I had cleaned and oiled the blade before putting it away, just as Gwawrddur had taught me. The thought of it made my stomach lurch. It was vanity to keep the weapon and I should never have shown it to Coenric.

I have lived a violent life, filled with blood and battle. I am a sinner and weak of flesh. I have revelled in the bloodlust of the shield-din and rejoiced at the death of my enemies. And yet, I know life is sacred. Death is never something to be taken lightly, and the demise of a loved one always cuts deeper than any sword thrust.

"I have seen so much death," I said. "Buried so many friends. But I never thought I would lose Coenric. He was so young and I barely cling on to this life."

"And yet God spared you once more, my friend."

"Why would He take Coenric and not me?"

"None save the Almighty Himself can answer that. But you are no fool, Hunlaf. Whatever else you may be. The reason you yet live is clear. God's hand was at work here."

"If only He had seen fit to save Coenric," I snapped. "He was only a boy!"

"Sadly he will not be the last innocent to die while sinners yet live. The Lord's ways are mysterious, but we must trust in Him. We must have faith."

"Faith?" I said. "What use was faith to Coenric?"

"Do not speak thus," Godstan said reprovingly. "Coenric is now seated with our Lord. His faith has been rewarded with everlasting life."

I shook my head. "If only he had run," I said. "He did not need to die. He could have saved himself. I should have been slain. Not him."

"And yet, in His wisdom, God saw to it that you would survive."

"What wisdom to keep me alive!" I scoffed.

"Do not question the will of God, Hunlaf." A hard edge had entered Godstan's tone. "You may wallow in self-pity and despair in this stinking cell, but do not blaspheme in my presence. I will not have it."

I fell silent, my cheeks hot. Godstan was right to rebuke me. I was behaving like a child.

"I have faith," Godstan went on, his tone mellowing. "It was His providence that brought sight of the Danish ships to the eyes of the sentinels. And it was God who gave Lord Osulf and his warriors the strength to defeat the raiders."

"I praise the Lord for Ealdorman Osulf," I said. "For his foresight and courage."

Godstan narrowed his eyes, perhaps imagining that I was less than honest in my approbation. But I spoke the truth. Things would have been very different for us if Osulf had not been warned of the approach of the ships. That he had led his guards to the minster at a gallop had surely saved most of the brethren from death or slavery. If I was dishonest at all, it was in my thanks to God for Osulf's intervention. It seemed to me that rather than the work of the Lord, the minster's salvation was due to the actions of a thoughtful ealdorman, who had inherited his father's canniness. Like his late brother, my shield-kin, Gersine, Osulf was steadfast, decisive and brave. There had been no Norse raids for decades and the men of Northumbria had grown complacent. But when he had heard of the recent attacks on the distant isle of Iona and the coast of Cantware, and even across the Narrow Sea in Frankia, Osulf had set sentinels and beacons all along the coast, ever vigilant for the sleek dragon-prowed vessels of the northern pirates.

"And I praise the Lord that you will be able to continue your work," said Godstan.

"I may have been spared from the axe and sword of the Danes," I said, "but I will be dead soon. What does it matter if I write or just sup of the cunning woman's draught and welcome death with open arms?"

Godstan sighed. He stared, as if fully seeing me for the first time.

"Death comes to us all, Hunlaf," he said. "If we're blessed, or as some would put it, lucky, we have great friendships and loves before the end." He walked across the room, careful not to step on any of the items strewn across the flagstones, and sat beside me. The ropes beneath the straw mattress creaked. Godstan placed a hand on my shoulder. "I have read your writings. You had many such blessings, Hunlaf. Old age is not something to hate. It is a treasure, bought for you by the sacrifice of others."

"I did not ask for it," I said, stifling a sob. My throat was thick and tears prickled my eyes.

"The gift is yours whether you sought it or not. Do not squander what you have been given."

I cuffed the tears away from my cheeks. Coenric's face swam in my mind and alongside him Lord Osulf's warriors who had fallen protecting the minster. I saw too the faces of the friends who had sacrificed themselves for me over the years.

"Perhaps you are right," I whispered. "Maybe I owe it to them."

"Coenric would have wanted you to carry on," said Godstan, rising from the bed. "I too would read the end of your tale."

"I know not if I have the strength to write more of it," I said, my voice thin and cracking. I recalled the screams and clash of weapons as Osulf's warriors had fought the Danes. The sting of smoke in my eyes, the odour of burning, reminding me of so many previous battles. I had trembled in the gloom of the chapel, listening to the fighting outside. The sounds and smells conjured up images from my past, a time when I was hale, strong and brave. I'd longed to snatch up the sword from its hiding place under my bed. But instead I had cowered with the rest of the monks, while Osulf and his guards faced our attackers, and Coenric – brave, foolish Coenric – had taken up my blade and been cut down. "There is too much death and sadness in my tale."

"Honour and bravery too," Godstan said. "Friendship and love."

"And sacrifice," I whispered.

"Sacrifice too. You alone can record the exploits of those who travelled with you. Would you deny them that?"

The ale had cleared my head somewhat and I pushed myself up from the pallet. My knees and ankles cracked like fresh logs on a blazing fire.

"I was fast and deadly once," I said. "Then I would have stood shoulder to shoulder with Osulf's hearth-warriors. I would have drenched the earth with the blood of those Danish nithings."

Godstan's face paled at my words, shocked by my sudden bitter rage.

"Age takes our strength," he said, "but brings wisdom."

I sneered at that.

"You think me wise? I am a fool. And now only my words are sharp."

"All men possess both wisdom and foolishness, Hunlaf," Godstan said. "Perhaps age allows us the time needed to distinguish between them."

I yearned for the astringent taste of the cunning woman's brew, but Godstan still clutched the flask, so I reached for the ale jug.

"Coenric will never have that time," I said.

Godstan's features were sombre. "No, he will not. But you do."

"Not much," I said, my tone gruff. "God must soon tire of keeping me alive while other, better men die."

"You live now, Hunlaf," Godstan replied. "And while you do, I say you continue the work you started. I can think of no better way to honour the memory of those who have fallen before you. You can give their deaths some meaning."

"Their deaths had meaning," I growled, my anger flaring.

"Then tell their story. You are the only one left who can. Finish it, for Coenric."

Godstan left me in my squalid cell and for a time I sat, wallowing in abject pity and sorrow. His words echoed in my thoughts.

For Coenric.

Slowly, the fog of grief lifted from me enough that I could think. The abbot was right. I am still alive and, while I am yet able to lift a quill and to make out the shapes of the letters on the vellum, I will continue to recount the tale of my life outside the walls of this minster. A time when I was headstrong, young and often foolish, just as Coenric had been.

Coenric will never again read the pages of parchment, leaning over my shoulder and irritating me with his incessant questions. I would never have believed I would miss his constant interruptions, but of course, even though I am old and should be wise, I am still a fool.

I will write for Coenric's memory and the memory of all the other men and women who died in the making of these stories. Too many have lost their lives and surely it will change nothing to write about their deaths. And yet I pray that, in some small way, the recording of it might assuage some of the guilt I bear for my part in each loss.

After Sext, Godstan sent a couple of the young novices to tidy and clean my cell. I sullenly watched them sweep and mop, feeling shame at the squalor of the room and envy at their youth. They brought me fresh sheets of vellum, newly cut feathers and a pot of encaustum, and not once did I do more than grunt in response. My head throbbed as it did whenever I went for a time without the brew Godstan now rationed for me.

The pain in my head went some way to explaining my taciturn anger at the novices, but then I imagined Coenric watching me disapprovingly, and grudgingly I thanked the young monks before they left.

And so it is that I take up my quill once more. I am alone in my cell, without Coenric's constant fussing, and I feel a pang of sorrow at his absence, at the silent space he had filled. The only sounds now are those of the daily life of the minster, and the wind rustling through the leaves of the trees by the river.

Time continues to pass as it always does and life goes on as it will until the Day of Judgement. One day, when the Lord Almighty has made me suffer enough on this earth, I will die, perhaps dropping dead over a sheet of ink-scratched parchment, or maybe cut down by heathen raiders from the sea.

I cannot tell the future, but until God calls me to His side, I can turn my mind once more to the past, to a time long ago when Carolus, king of the Franks, yet lived. To a time before he was known as Augustus, Emperor of the Holy Roman Empire. I cast the net of memory into the dark pools of my mind and pull forth recollections of that distant past.

I remember a scorching mountainside, where I climbed, drenched in sweat, hemp rope cutting into my palms as I swung precariously over a vertiginous drop.

Runolf, Gwawrddur, Hereward, Drosten and Revna were on that mountain with me. All of us were close to exhaustion from the heat and travel, but our spirits were high at nearing our goal.

Looking back now through the dark glass of time, I know our mood would have been less buoyant if we had known of the betrayal that awaited us, and that some of our number would not live to see the end of that long hot summer.

Two

Runolf Ragnarsson grinned down at me from the cliff edge, his mane of fiery hair framing his head. Beside him, I could see Drosten, his swirling tattoos giving his face a scowling aspect. The Pict watched in silence as I swung on the creaking rope. Hereward, his hair and beard dark with sweat, said nothing. The surly Northumbrian had been against this plan, but had eventually bowed to the pressure from the others. This was the fastest way to our destination and would save us half a day's travel in this broken land of rocky crags and splintered crevasses. None of us wished to be out there beneath the cloudless sky in these mountains for any longer than we had to be, so Hereward had finally grunted his approval. In an effort to distract from the fractious atmosphere that had built in the group, I had volunteered to be the first to go down.

I now regretted that decision.

"Not far now, Killer," said Gwawrddur, his tone both encouraging and slightly mocking.

The hemp rope tore the skin from my palms. I looked down and instantly wished I hadn't. The jagged rocks at the foot of the ravine were still a long way beneath me. If I slipped, my body would surely be broken on those shattered boulders.

"Hush, Gwawrddur," said Revna. "Hunlaf, don't look down."

My head was spinning. Looking beneath me was perhaps a worse mistake than descending on this rope in the first place. I pulled my gaze away from the jumble of rocks that I imagined were eager to welcome me onto their sharp edges.

"I wish you'd told me that earlier," I said, sweat stinging my eyes.

"I did," said Gwawrddur, "but as ever you would not listen."

"Then I am a fool," I said through gritted teeth. The muscles in my arms were screaming and I felt foolish for saying I could climb down without assistance.

"Hush," repeated Revna. Gwawrddur fell silent. I noticed that neither he nor Runolf were smiling now, as if they had realised the time for jesting was past. "Shall we pull you up?" Revna asked. "Someone else can go down first. And whoever that is, we should tie the rope about them and lower them down."

My face grew even hotter than from the exertion of the climb. I stared up at Revna's lovely face, surrounded by the golden cascade of her hair.

"No," I gasped, "I can make it." I would not turn back now.

She held my gaze for a moment, then nodded.

"Very well," she said at last, and I could tell she thought me a fool. "Careful. One hand after the other."

I did not look below me again. Keeping my eyes on Revna's face, I lowered myself down the rope. My hands were slippery from sweat and weak from bearing my weight. My shoulders, chest and back ached, and my kirtle was sodden. Nobody spoke. The only sounds now were my panting gasps, the rasp of my shoes as I pushed myself off from the rock face, and from time to time, the clatter of pebbles and scree dislodged by my passing.

I reached the bottom just as I was beginning to fear losing my grip completely. Leaning over, I took in great lungfuls of hot air. When my heart had slowed and my breath had steadied,

I shouted up that they should tie some of the provisions and waterskins to the rope and lower them down.

"Good idea, Killer," shouted Gwawrddur, his humour returned. "Just don't drink all the water before the rest of us get down."

I ignored him, too breathless and tired to continue the banter. The rope slithered against the cliff like a giant serpent as Runolf pulled it up. It would take them some time to secure the packs and lower them down, so I looked about me.

It was not as hot here as on the higher part of the rock face. Shadows filled the foot of the gorge and I welcomed the relative cool. Tiny thorny shrubs jutted from between the rocks here and there, and a couple of large flies buzzed around my head. Other than that, there was no life or movement. As we had climbed into the mountains much of the land we had passed through had been like this: barren, rock-strewn and arid.

We had arrived on the island of Kýpros three days before and this was the end of the second day of our journey into the slopes to the south of Kyrenia – the port where *Brymsteda* was docked. Most of the crew remained there and, if Theokleia was right, we would be reunited with them in a couple more days, along with the object we sought.

Theokleia was an interesting character and, though she was a nun, I would be lying if I said I had not noticed her beauty. She was dark where Revna was pale. The small wisps of hair that escaped her headscarf were as black and gleaming as a raven's wing. Theokleia's eyes too were dark, large and shining, hinting at secret depths within the sister in Christ. Her robes covered her body, almost completely hiding her feminine curves, but she was tall, lithe and moved with a natural assurance. It was difficult to judge her age, but I guessed she was perhaps ten years my senior.

We had met Theokleia in the hills overlooking the port, the vibrant blue-green of the Middle Sea spread out beneath us as far as the horizon. Those waters had borne us far and God had smiled on us. It was early summer and the weather had been fine, the winds favourable. We had made good time around Hispania, between the mountains that marked the entrance to the Middle Sea, which the ancients had called the Pillars of Hercules. Our pilot, Nicetos, had navigated a course hugging the coast before hopping between the Baleares, around Sardinia and Sicilia, and then on to Kýpros.

As we'd rounded the southern tip of al-Andalus, we had been approached by a large-sailed vessel. *Brymsteda*'s crew had grown nervous. I admit I too felt the scratching fingers of dread on my neck at the sight of the ship. Scarcely a year had passed since our adventures in the lands of Emir Al-Hakam and the memories of imprisonment in Qadis, the intrigue and horror of Qurtuba and the fire and blood of Aljany's fortress were fresh in our minds. We feared being boarded, but we needn't have been concerned. Runolf laughed when he saw our anxious faces.

"Trim the sheets," he yelled, "and watch as that wallowing barrel of a tub tries to catch *Brymsteda*."

We all knew the longship was capable of great speed, but Runolf trusted the ship he had built, and his own skill, absolutely. The men on the Moorish ship signalled for us to allow them to approach. When we did not slow, they lowered more sail in an attempt to match our speed. Runolf simply laughed.

"A pig would have more chance of catching a stag," he said. And he was right. Before nightfall they had given up the chase and disappeared beneath the horizon.

We saw other ships on our voyage from Tours to Kýpros. And we put in at the harbours of Cagliari and Xiphonia for supplies, but we were careful not to attract the wrong type of attention, removing the carved stallion prow beast before approaching land and keeping all of the crew on board.

This was not the time for whoring and partaking of the

delicacies of Sardinia and Sicilia. We were on a quest, on the orders of Alhwin, and what we searched for, he had told us, was of the utmost importance to his lord and master, King Carolus.

This was not the first such mission we had embarked upon. After giving us the silver he had promised on our return from al-Andalus, Alhwin had offered to pay us handsomely for retrieving his collection of books from Britain. I would have been pleased simply to have been able to read the tomes in Alhwin's library, but Runolf and the rest of the men had other considerations. They cared little for the wealth found in knowledge and holy artefacts, it was the more earthly value of silver and gold that spoke to them. Runolf, no good Christian despite having been baptised in Eoforwic, was all too pleased to accept the payment and remain in Alhwin's employ. The others were content enough to do likewise. Each had their own reasons to do Alhwin's bidding. Some, like Runolf, wanted riches; others, Gwawrddur chief amongst them, sought further challenges. Most of us looked for a mixture of riches, adventure, and even fame. But I was alone in my yearning to find holy relics and to seize the rare opportunity to peruse the pages of ancient tomes.

Hereward was the only one of our number who had been reticent to continue aboard *Brymsteda*. He saw it as his duty to return to Northumbria. His lord, Uhtric, had died, releasing Hereward from his oath as long as he agreed to see that Uhtric's son Uhtred would receive a portion of whatever fortune the crew of Runolf's longship should amass. When we had gone in search of Alhwin's books, Hereward had travelled north with silver for his erstwhile lord's son.

He had returned ashen-faced and dour. Uhtred had died of the pox the previous winter. Hereward, ever a man of honour, had given the wealth he had accrued to Uhtred's mother, ruler of the fortress until her youngest son would come of age. Hereward spoke of a hall devoid of light and laughter.

A stronghold of darkness and sorrow. He had not offered his oath to the sullen mistress of Bebbanburg or to her son.

Bebbanburg was not alone in experiencing shifts in power. Before our arrival in Britain we had learnt that King Æthelred had been slain, murdered by ealdormen enraged by his despotic nature. When we reached Eoforwic, we discovered the leader of the revolt and many of his allies were slain during the ensuing unrest. I was shocked to hear that one of those killed was Lord Mancas. It was inconceivable to me that Gersine's father, a man of cautious calculation, would have taken such a risky path and I wondered how desperate things must have become for him to gamble his life on the overthrow of the king.

On hearing the tidings about his father, Gersine had become withdrawn and subdued. I travelled with him to his father's hall, where we were met by his mother and brothers. It seemed all of Northumbria was under a cloud. A pall of sadness and fear hung over Uuiremutha, an atmosphere of despair that pervaded everything. I wondered how my own kin fared, but had no urge to seek out my brother in Berewic or my father at Ubbanford.

I felt sorry for Gersine at the cool reception he received at his father's hall. It appeared his mother placed much of the blame for Lord Mancas' death on Gersine. There was little sense in that, it seemed to me, but grief often leads to rage. Gersine's brother, Osulf, took him aside on the morning of our departure and assured Gersine he held no anger for him. Osulf was content to govern the hall and the estate, and Gersine – grim-faced and appearing older by several years – was glad to board *Brymsteda* once more and sail far from the shores of Britain.

We had been surprised that two others from Uuiremutha also wished to rejoin our crew. Cumbra and Arcenbryht were both stout warriors who had travelled with us aboard *Brymsteda* when we had sailed to Rygjafylki and Hǫrðaland. On our return, they had remained in Britain, held there by their oaths to Mancas. Now they were free to pursue a different path.

"You have not sworn an oath to my brother?" asked Gersine, when the two men rode out of the settlement after us.

"He did not see the need," said Cumbra. "He knew he had our loyalty. That is no bad thing. Osulf is a good man and I dare say he will be a fine lord. But things are dark in Northumbria, and we would see more of the world and be far from the intrigues and fighting that has blighted this land."

"The road we follow is rarely easy," I warned.

Arcenbryht laughed. "We will take our chances aboard *Brymsteda*," he said. "With luck we will find riches." He looked up at the gloomy, cloud-thick sky. It was raining that day, the air grey and dismal. "And I like the sound of the hot sun of those southern lands you spoke of in the hall."

Arcenbryht and Cumbra joining us went some way to lifting our spirits as we rode towards Eoforwic. Cumbra was right; Northumbria had become a dark place and we were all keen to leave it behind.

Alhwin's man, the mysterious Giso, had informed us of the death of the king of Northumbria. His tone, tinged with a perverse humour, had rankled with those of us who came from that kingdom, but Giso often seemed to take pleasure at others' misfortune. He prayed every day and professed a deep faith, but we had witnessed how callously he killed in order to achieve his ends and we were all wary of him, unsure of his true motives.

Just as when we had travelled to Qadis, shortly after arriving in Britain, Giso had vanished on some mission only he was aware of. He appeared once more as we were about to push *Brymsteda*, laden with Alhwin's library, off from the riverside jetty at Eoforwic. Giso made no mention of where he had been. Such was his way and while I did not like it, I had grown accustomed to his secrets.

So I was not surprised when Alhwin called us to his

chambers in the abbey of which he was now the abbot, to find that Giso had disappeared. When I enquired where he had gone, Alhwin shook his head.

"You are ever inquisitive, young Hunlaf," he said, pouring each of us wine from a finely crafted silver pitcher. "But you should know by now that Giso comes and goes as he wishes."

"As he wishes, or as you command?" I asked.

Alhwin chuckled. "Quite," he said, handing me a cup, then sipping from his own. "Giso's whereabouts are no concern of yours. All you need to know is that the information he has provided me leads to the island of Kýpros."

"Where is this Kýpros?" asked Runolf. "I have never heard of it."

"Far to the east, beyond Italia. Beyond Byzantion even. At the edge of the Middle Sea. Near to the Holy Land itself."

"You wish us to travel there?" asked Drosten.

"Perceptive as ever, my painted friend," Alhwin said with a smile.

"Such a journey will take time," Runolf said.

"I have faith that your vessel will make the voyage faster than any other ship. Is my faith misplaced?"

"Never," said Runolf. "*Brymsteda* will gallop us across the waves, and I can skipper the wave-steed over any sea there is, but I do not know the way to this island. I may be the best sailor that lives, but I am still merely a man."

Alhwin laughed at that. "Such humility," he said. "But I have thought of this. I will send with you a pilot. A seafarer who has traversed the Middle Sea and beyond. He will guide you to Kýpros."

"And what is it we seek there?" Hereward asked. "More books?"

"Books will always be welcome here," said Alhwin, waving a hand at the stacks of scrolls and leather-bound tomes on shelves and tables around the candlelit chamber. "And I will pay you well for any books you might find on your travels, but what I am sending you after is much more valuable. You are to find the Spear of Longinus."

The others did not appear to understand the significance of what Alhwin had said, but my breath caught at the mention of an artefact of such importance.

"The Holy Lance," I said, my voice filled with awe. "You know the whereabouts of the spear that pierced our Lord Jesus' side?"

"It was believed lost," replied Alhwin. "I now have it on good authority that it has lain hidden and undisturbed for centuries on the island of Kýpros."

He set aside his cup of wine and moved the leather-bound book he had been reading. From beneath it, he produced a folded scrap of parchment.

"Hunlaf," he said, handing it to me, "here are instructions for where the relic is located."

I unfolded the sheet of vellum, turning it so that the light from the candles fell on the faded ink markings. I had expected a map, but instead I found a list of incongruous items.

"The Lion's Head," I read aloud. "The Horns of the Minotaur. The Dragon's Spine." I looked up in confusion. "These are things of myth and legend. How can this help us find the Spear of Longinus?"

"Ah, they mean nothing to you or me," Alhwin said, "but I believe each of the items on that list refers to a location on Kýpros. Follow these instructions and you will find the most holy relic."

"But how will we know what these things represent?" I said. "None of us has ever been to Kýpros. It is a long way to travel in the hope we might stumble on a place called…" I glanced down at the list "…the Serpent's Maw."

Alhwin scratched at his tonsured head.

"Whoever wrote that list had an eye for the dramatic and poetic," he said with a smile. "But do not be concerned about a wasted journey. I have sent word ahead. There is one on the island who wishes to help with the cause. They will meet you at the minster of Episcopia."

"How will we know this person?"

Alhwin's smile broadened.

"I like this subterfuge. They will approach you and ask you, 'What makes bitter things sweet?' And you will reply, 'Hunger.'"

Gwawrddur had remained silent all this time, seemingly content to sip his wine and listen. Now he stepped into the brighter candlelight close to Alhwin. "We are to sail in search of a relic you say has been lost for centuries," he said. "Are you sure it is worth the risk?" He glanced at Runolf. "And the expense?"

Alhwin waved a hand as if swatting away a meddlesome fly. "The cost is of no importance," he said. "You will be paid well for your troubles – do not doubt that. As to the likelihood of finding the relic, who can say but the Lord Almighty? But know this: King Carolus is facing enemies on many sides. To the south are the Moors of al-Andalus. There are still rebellious Saxons and Avars to the north and east. Further yet to the east lies a greater threat, an individual who wishes to rule the Empire of Roma in their own right when that honour is destined for Carolus alone. Everything I do is aimed at seeing the Iron Crown placed upon his brow."

"You speak of Eirene of Athens," I said.

Alhwin sneered. "That Jezebel would see herself crowned Empress of Roma. Her lust for power is unbound. She has put out the eyes of her own son so that she might take his place. Can you imagine such evil? And now she seeks to draw unto her whatever allies and power she can. Be certain that where King Carolus has loyal servants searching for the holiest of relics and the knowledge hidden within ancient tomes, so Eirene has her own agents who will stop at nothing to secure those same artefacts for her. They will further her ends by whatever means possible, in the hope that she will eventually stand unrivalled for the crown of the Empire of Roma itself." He swept us all with his cool glare. "She must be stopped." With each word he thumped the leather cover of the book before him.

I had never before seen Alhwin so impassioned. His eyes glistened and his cheeks were flushed. I wondered how much wine he had consumed before calling us to his chamber. I had never known him to be so forthcoming with his plans or the reasoning behind them.

A thought came to me.

"Does not the island of Kýpros fall under the rule of Byzantion?" I asked.

Alhwin brushed aside my question.

"It is a distant island on the edge of the empire, and you will carry nothing that will mark you as men of King Carolus. You will be merchants from the north, hoping to find lucrative trade on Kýpros. You will find all manner of trade goods, from rare dyes to silver jewellery of the finest quality, that would make you wealthy men in the lands of the Norse."

A shouted warning from above snapped me out of my reverie. I looked up, startled. A rock the size of my head clattered down the cliff face towards me.

Three

After hitting a ledge, the rock bounced away from the cliff. Leaping back instinctively, I felt the rush of air as it hurtled past my face, missing me by a hand's breadth. The rock smashed into the ground, sending up a cloud of dust. Several smaller stones rattled around me. One landed a painful blow to my left hand.

"Sorry!" shouted Runolf.

The bags of provisions were lashed on the end of the rope and were halfway down the cliff. The rope creaked and swayed, and the bundle knocked clear another shower of stones. This time I was quick enough to jump back and they all missed me, harmlessly peppering the rocky ground.

I rubbed my hand. The stone would leave a painful welt, but the skin was unbroken. Fleetingly, I imagined what would have happened if the rock had struck me. I shuddered and watched as the saddlebags and packs touched the ground.

I untied them quickly, lugging them away from the base of the cliff. Finding a full skin, I unstoppered it and took a long draught. The water was warm as piss and sour from the leather, but I gulped it down, glad of the moisture.

Wary of more stones, I shielded my eyes to watch who would come down next. To my surprise I recognised the bulky form of Theokleia's companion, Artemis. Another nun, Artemis was everything that Theokleia was not. Where Theokleia was slim and pretty, Artemis was as broad and ugly as an ox. Her robes did nothing to disguise her hulking arms and stout legs and we had all seen how easily she lifted the heavy packs onto the mules. She spoke little and only responded to Theokleia. Truth be told, we were all somewhat in awe of Artemis and after our first meeting with the two nuns, Drosten had chuckled.

"If I were still fighting for money, I'd place a wager on Artemis over any man I ever fought."

I recalled how I had met him in Eoforwic, battered and bloody, betting on his prowess with his fists.

"Would *you* beat her in a fight?" I asked.

Drosten held up his large, scarred hands.

"I would not dare to face her," he said.

The rest of the men laughed, but when I looked at Artemis' broad shoulders and flat-featured face, I thought of how often there was truth behind words spoken in jest.

The huge nun reached the bottom of the ravine and untied the rope. She gave me a baleful glance and stepped over to stand beside the packs. She did not speak, but I could feel her gaze on me while the others descended.

Our meeting had been as Alhwin had foretold. We had moored *Brymsteda* at the harbour of Kyrenia. Hereward had sent Gersine and Nicetos, the diminutive navigator, into the town in search of supplies and possible trade goods. Most of the crew remained aboard the ship and Runolf gave Alf instructions to keep a strict guard and to only allow a small number ashore at a time. Then, a group of us had gone in search of the minster of Episcopia and the person who would help us locate the Spear of Longinus.

It had been searingly hot, painful to walk on the cobbles of the winding streets of the town. Runolf, Gwawrddur, Drosten, Hereward, Revna and I trudged along, moving between whatever scant shade there was on the dusty path that led out of the settlement and into the hills. We had been at sea so long that the ground itself felt unsteady and we walked with the rolling gait of seafarers. Cumbra was the only one who appeared undaunted by the heat. His face was flushed and sweat drenched his kirtle, so I could see he felt the same discomfort as the rest of us, but despite the long weeks of travel he was still as excited as the day we had left Britain. With each passing day of cloudless skies and blistering sun, Cumbra seemed to grow happier.

"To think I lived all my life in the dreary north," he said. "I cannot imagine returning to Northumbria. I shiver when I think of the grey skies and all that rain."

Arcenbryht was not so pleased with his own decision to join us. He had suffered badly from the sickness that sometimes afflicted sailors, and he did not enjoy the hot weather. On the first sunny day there had been a swell that made the ship yaw and rock. Arcenbryht had leaned over the side, puking and moaning pitifully. That night he had lain awake in agonised misery, his stomach empty and his skin burnt crimson by the sun.

When we had reached Kýpros, Arcenbryht was contented just to be on dry land and had remained at the harbour. Cumbra, seemingly oblivious of his friend's misfortune, had been eager to join us.

"You might miss the cold one day," said Drosten, wiping sweat from his brow. He wore a long scarf wrapped about his head in the way he had learnt from the Moors of al-Andalus. "I like a warm day as much as any man, but this heat grates on you after a time."

Cumbra laughed and shook his head.

"I've had enough rain and frost to last me a lifetime," he said. "No, I think I will live the rest of my days somewhere hot, where the sea is as warm as fresh milk."

In Kyrenia I had asked a group of fishermen for directions and we had arrived easily enough to the entrance of the minster. A twisted oak tree grew beside the gate and out of its shadow stepped the two robed women we came to know as Theokleia and Artemis.

"What is it that makes the bitter taste sweet?" said Theokleia in Latin.

"Hunger," I replied.

Beneath the shade of her wimple, her face displayed shocked joy.

"By the Blessed Virgin," she said in Greek, "I had begun to lose hope you would ever find us. We have come to this place every afternoon for weeks, haven't we, Artemis?"

The burly nun scowled and said nothing. She stared at us as if we were sheep and she had been given the task of providing the minster with mutton. For her part, Theokleia looked over us all, her gaze lingering for a moment on each of us. Runolf with his flame-red beard and shaggy hair, as broad as Artemis but nearly a head taller. Revna, her golden hair draped in a long plait down her back, her slim form belying her strength, the sword at her side marking her as a warrior. Gwawrddur bowed slightly as Theokleia looked him up and down. Hereward met her gaze without comment, his expression stern. Cumbra grinned at the nun, and she nodded in acknowledgement. Her eyes lingered the longest on Drosten, with his tattoos and Moorish headgear. Finally, she turned back to me, taking in the blade I wore on a baldric over my shoulder.

"Quite the unusual band of individuals," she said.

"What had you expected?" I asked.

She smiled and I saw then that she was beautiful.

"I know not who I thought would come," she said lightly, "but not you."

Her amused tone irked me.

"Well, we didn't expect a couple of Sisters of Christ," I said.

Her smile broadened at that. She led us out of the sun to a shaded hollow where several olive trees grew. It was away from the road and out of sight of the minster's gate. A spring trickled from the rocks, splashing over green-streaked stones into a small pool.

"The water is good," she said and we drank.

When we had slaked our thirst, we sat on rocks that seemed placed there for that purpose and she asked us of our journey and what we knew of the whereabouts of the Spear. She told me she could speak in either Latin or Greek. I was more fluent in the former, so we conversed in that tongue, with me pausing every now and then to translate for the others. We spoke for some time and my throat grew dry. I was glad of the cool water running from the crack in the rock.

I told her about the instructions Alhwin had given to me.

"May I see the parchment?" she asked.

I had memorised the words, worried that I might lose the written list, but I was still reluctant to hand them over to Theokleia. Since Alhwin had given me the scrap of vellum, I had shown it to nobody else.

She appeared to understand my nervousness and took the parchment carefully between her long, delicate fingers. I noticed her hands were smooth and unblemished and I wondered if she spent her days scribing. She could clearly read well enough. Her lips moved as she scanned the words on the parchment. She was silent for a time, biting her lower lip as she pondered what she had read. Then, without warning, she clapped her hands and her face lit up.

"You know where we will find the Spear of Longinus?" I asked.

"I believe I do," she said. "I have lived here all my life and I recognise some of these places from my childhood. Tomorrow I will lead you to the first."

"The Lion's Head," I said.

"Yes, I think I know what the author of this list refers to. From there I am certain I will be able to follow this trail as surely as if we had a map."

I translated her words.

"Ask how far," said Runolf.

"Two, maybe three days," Theokleia said, after I had relayed Runolf's question. "It is no wonder the relic has not been found for centuries. The land is harsh. Dry and hot. Two mules will be enough to carry water and provisions for us. I can procure them, if you bring the supplies. And it would be good to take rope. You can fetch some from your ship?"

Runolf grunted his agreement.

"Perhaps we should bring more of the crew too," Hereward said, "but we would need more than two mules for the provisions then."

Theokleia shook her head when I told her of Hereward's suggestion.

"We are already a large group," she said. "More will draw too much attention." She glanced in the direction of the road and lowered her voice. "There might be others on the island who are searching for this relic."

Gwawrddur went over to the spring. Cupping some of the water in his hand, he drank, then splashed some on his face and slicked it through his hair.

"I would know something," he said, frowning.

I waited for him to say what was on his mind.

"Ask her why she would give such a treasure to the king of the Franks."

Theokleia listened as I voiced Gwawrddur's question and nodded sombrely.

"This was not an easy decision for me," she said. "But there are many rumours of agents of Eirene *Basileus* searching for relics so that they can take them to her and give her the strength, the divine power, to be crowned Empress of Roma. Her servants seek to make her the most powerful woman in the world."

"And you do not want that?" I asked. "Are these not Eirene's lands? Are you not her subjects?"

Theokleia made the sign of the cross.

"Eirene has shown herself to be no good Christian woman. No holy mother would do what she did to Constantinus. To her own son." Theokleia scowled. "No, this evil woman must not be allowed to hold the most precious of holy relics. She already has many of them in her clutches. I have vowed to do all in my power to see that she gains no more."

True to her word, Theokleia had met us the following morning with Artemis and two mules. She had led us into the mountains and despite it being hot and the going arduous over the rocky terrain, we made good time. It soon became apparent that Theokleia did indeed know how to follow the instructions left by the nameless scribe in the coded list of locations.

From a jagged ridge that we all agreed looked like a dragon's spine to a pair of sharp outcrops of rock that could be said to resemble the horns of a bull, or a minotaur, Theokleia guided us unerringly ever further into the crags and ravines of the mountain range. At the bottom of the cliff we had reached the final item on the list.

"Somewhere along there," Theokleia said, pointing along the boulder-tumbled crevasse, "we should find the Maw of the Serpent." She had been lowered down after Artemis and now the three of us awaited the others.

"A cave, you think?" I asked, watching as Gwawrddur descended the rope quickly.

"Most likely," Theokleia said, wiping sweat from her brow. Despite the heat both she and Artemis wore their thick habits and wimples. "But the truth is, I have never been this far into the mountains."

"We are close though," I said. "I can feel it. And there can be little doubt you have led us well."

"Whoever wrote those instructions left a path that is easy to follow, as long as the first step is correct. Let us just pray that the Spear of Longinus remains where it was deposited all those years ago."

We waited as the others clambered down. The last one to

reach the base of the cliff was Runolf. Cumbra looked down from above.

"I'll watch the mules," he shouted down. "And soak in some of this glorious sunshine."

Hereward shook his head.

"The man is mad," he said. "The sun is hot enough to boil his brains."

"Perhaps it already has," replied Gwawrddur.

"Anything is possible," said Runolf.

Theokleia was already picking her way along the gorge, evidently anxious to continue. I did not blame her. We did not know what lay before us, and I would not wish to climb that cliff in the dark.

Unspeaking, Artemis followed behind Theokleia. I scrambled after them, excitement building within me at the thought of what we would soon hold in our grasp.

The ravine floor was narrow, clogged with heaps of jagged rocks, and difficult to traverse.

Using her hands to help her climb over a pile of sharp rocks deposited by some long-ago landslide, Theokleia slipped. With uncanny speed for one so large, Artemis caught her, steadying the slender nun and preventing a painful fall. Several rocks slid down from the pile, opening up dark gaps between the boulders.

"Careful where you put your feet," Hereward said. "We don't want to be carrying anyone out of here with a broken ankle."

Cautiously we continued. The ravine was in shade now, but it remained stiflingly hot, the air still and breathless. Sweat stung my eyes. I cuffed the perspiration from my face and paused for breath. Revna was close behind. Her cheeks were flushed and she was panting from the heat and exertion.

"Could someone truly have hidden the relic we seek down here?" she said. "It looks as though nobody has ever been here before."

"Let's hope nobody has been here since the Spear was brought here," I said.

"You truly think it is here?"

"I hope it is," I said, forcing a smile in spite of the anxious knot in my stomach. "Otherwise we have come a very long way for nothing. The instructions have led us this far. I have faith."

Revna looked up at the rocky cliffs looming above us. She blew a strand of golden hair away from her face. I found the oft-repeated gesture distracting, so looked away, focusing on how best to navigate the confusion of rocks.

"I still cannot fathom how Alhwin came to possess those instructions," Revna said.

"I know not," I said, pulling myself cautiously up the snarled stones. "Alhwin seems to have countless contacts and boundless knowledge. But who wrote the instructions, or how he came by the parchment, was not something he shared."

Runolf was scaling the heap of rocks Theokleia had disturbed. His voice was not unlike the grind of the stones shifting beneath his weight.

"Perhaps," he said, "this is the moment we discover Alhwin does not know everything."

I glanced at Runolf and followed his gaze. He was looking beyond Revna and me at Theokleia and Artemis. They had come to a halt and I understood at once why. The ravine ended in a sheer wall of rock.

"Perhaps I have made a mistake," said Theokleia, as we arrived at the end of the ravine. "Maybe we should have gone the other way."

"I don't think so," I said. "The instructions said west at the chasm and we would find the Serpent's Maw."

"I know that," she snapped, tension making her tone harsh. She took a calming breath. "Forgive me. I am tired and there is nothing here. Perhaps there never was and this has all been for nought."

Runolf moved past us. He squinted up at the rock face. High above, boulders protruded, bright and shimmering in the afternoon sun.

"You say we are looking for a cave?" he asked.

"That is what we imagined," I said. "But we do not rightly know. All we know is it says we will find what we seek in the Maw of the Serpent."

Crouching down, Runolf studied the rocks he was standing on.

"If this relic has been here for centuries," he said, "rocks might have fallen from the walls and buried it."

"Perhaps," I said dubiously. "But look at those rocks. If they have buried something, what chance do we have of moving them?"

Runolf scratched at his thick beard and smiled.

"You speak so freely of faith and the power of your god and yet you believe we are defeated by some rocks."

"Do you think you can move them?" I was incredulous. Some of the rocks were too big even for the strongest of men to lift.

"Anything is possible," Runolf said with a grin.

He began barking orders, sending Hereward, Gwawrddur and Revna back to the provisions and to where Cumbra waited.

While waiting for them to return, Runolf climbed over the rocks, pushing some aside, lifting others and throwing them down to crack at the base of the rock slide. Artemis joined him, lending her considerable strength to the effort.

Runolf strained for a time at one rock the size of a sea chest. The muscles in his arms bulged and flexed, but to no avail. I was about to offer my help, even though it seemed clear to me that the boulder was too big to shift, but before I could climb up, Runolf gave up and lifted a smaller one that rested nearby. This rock he lifted with ease, tossing it away. As he did, he let out a cry and staggered back, losing his footing and falling into Artemis' arms. The brawny nun grunted at the effort of catching him, then shoved him away from her.

"By Óðinn," Runolf exclaimed, pointing to where the dislodged rock had revealed a dark hollow.

There was movement there and my skin crawled as I saw what had made Runolf recoil. Out of the hole in the rocks slithered several snakes, stubby bodies writhing as they slid over the stones.

"Are you bitten?" I asked.

Runolf shook his head, his eyes wide.

"No," he said, a mixture of fear and exhilaration in his voice, "but I seem to have found the Serpent's Maw."

Four

"Vipers," hissed Theokleia. "Their bites are venomous."

"Then we shall need to be cautious," Runolf said.

"Aren't we always?" I replied, smiling in an attempt to hide my fear. The truth was the sight of the snakes had unnerved me. And I saw I wasn't alone. Runolf and Artemis had both abandoned moving the rocks with their hands and hurried down to where I stood with Theokleia.

The others returned with rope and spears. I still wasn't certain that Runolf would be able to move the largest rocks, but drawing on his experience of ship building, he put us to work.

Following his commands, we fashioned crude pulleys and levers, and soon, the sweat running down my back reminding me of the slithering movement of the vipers, we were dragging the rocks out of our way.

"Careful of the serpents," I said, as Revna inserted a spear haft between two boulders and used her weight against the lever. She gave me a withering look, but I could not get the thought of the creatures from my mind. The snakes had vanished, finding other hiding places within the rocks, and I imagined them springing from each dark nook and crack to strike at our hands and feet as we went about the work of clearing a path.

Without warning, Gwawrddur drew his sword and its blade flashed. Reaching down, he lifted the now headless form of a viper. The beast was about the length of his arm.

"Hard to make it out against the rock," he noted. "Difficult to see, but not as fast as I would have thought."

He tossed the body in Drosten's direction. Rather than flinching as I think I would have done, Drosten snatched the dead creature from the air.

"I wonder if they make good eating," he said, dropping it into an empty sack.

This exchange did nothing to set my mind at ease, but even nervous and cautious as we were, following Runolf's instructions, we were able to move aside enough of the rocks to expose a cavernous opening. Any doubts we might have had about the location vanished as we saw steps carved in the rock, leading down into the earth.

I looked up at the boulders jutting from the cliff above.

"Perhaps whoever built this place caused these rocks to fall in order to cover the entrance," I said.

Theokleia nodded.

"This place is remote, but even so, without these rocks covering the entrance, I wonder if some goatherd might not have stumbled on the place before now."

Praying that nobody had been here before us, I peered into the dark, toothless mouth in the rock.

"How deep is it?" I asked.

"Only one way to find out," said Drosten, placing his foot on the top step.

I shivered at the thought of following him. That I might be trapped in the darkness with all those snakes filled me with a terrible dread. And yet we had travelled so far, and my fingers itched at the thought of being the first person to touch the Holy Lance since it had been deposited here, hidden in the broken mountains of Kýpros centuries before.

I had not yet summoned my courage when Theokleia stepped forward.

"Look," she said, stooping to retrieve something from a ledge next to the steps. She held up a small earthenware lamp, blowing dust from it and turning it over in her hand. "Long dry. But I have some oil in my pack."

Artemis went for the flask of oil. Theokleia poured some into the ancient lamp, while Gwawrddur went about striking a light. It was windless down in the ravine and the spark caught in the tinder immediately. Gwawrddur blew on it gently until smoke became fire. He transferred the small flame to the lamp with a thin twig of olive wood.

The oil sputtered to life and Theokleia held up the guttering lamp.

"Who is coming with me and the painted man?" she said.

While we had waited for Artemis to bring the oil, I had made the decision that I could not bear to stand above ground while others discovered the secrets of the Serpent's Maw. Swallowing down my terror, I said, "I will go."

"There is not enough space in there for me," said Runolf, leaning over to squint into the gloom.

"You're just frightened of the serpents," said Drosten with a chuckle.

"Not frightened," said Runolf. "Clever enough to know they are dangerous. Something that doesn't seem to penetrate your thick Pictish skull."

Drosten laughed, but Runolf wasn't wrong about the size of the entrance of the cavern. The tall Norseman would have needed to crouch down to enter.

In the end, Drosten led the way, with Theokleia and me behind him. Gwawrddur brought up the rear. Hereward, Artemis, Runolf and Revna all remained on the surface.

I was acutely aware of Revna's gaze on me as we followed the steps down. As the shadows swallowed us, I wished I had ignored the voice that had told me to follow Drosten. But it was too late for that now and I refused to turn back and be shown to be a coward.

Theokleia held the oil lamp high, the small flame illuminating rough walls. Dancing shadows leapt and stretched over the rock. Despite his bravado, Drosten was no fool. Walking before Theokleia, the Pict moved carefully, a spear in his left hand, a long knife in his right.

"Careful," he whispered, halting. I held my breath. None of us moved and I wondered what the Pict had noticed. An instant later, he lunged with the spear. Peering over his shoulder, I saw that he had used the spear's blade to slice a large snake in two. Each half of the creature coiled and rolled in the dust, blood spattering the stone. After a time, the serpent stopped moving. With a deep breath, Drosten continued.

The air was stale. Our feet sent up clouds of dust from the uneven steps. The stairs ended and a tunnel opened out before us. There was nothing but inky darkness ahead. My mouth was dry. I longed for another drink of water but I would have to wait until we were out of that black hole. Up to that point, light from the entrance had filtered down. The sun's rays would penetrate no further into the depths. We would have no light now but the faint glimmer from the oil lamp.

We hesitated, each of us silently contemplating the darkness. I wondered if the others also imagined all manner of beasts and enemies lurking out of sight. I did not voice my own fears.

Without warning, Runolf's booming voice echoed down to us. I jumped at the sound. I think I noticed Drosten and Theokleia also start, which lessened my embarrassment somewhat.

"What do you see?" Runolf asked.

"Nothing yet," Gwawrddur called back. "Just more darkness. Let's hope no foe is lurking for us. Anything in there will be awake after your shouting!"

Gwawrddur's words did nothing to alleviate my anxiety.

"Lead on, Drosten," he said.

With a grunt, Drosten began to shuffle along the tunnel. Theokleia moved with him, holding the lamp aloft so that its pool of light shone a few paces ahead of us. We were all close enough to touch now, instinctively seeking the proximity of the others as the darkness wrapped tightly about us.

Moments later, a mixture of emotions flooded through me as we reached the end of the tunnel. There was no way onwards. No unspeakable evil lurked within the gloom and I felt foolish at my own fears. But my foolishness was washed away in an instant by a wave of exhilarated joy. For there, on a plain plinth of stone, rested a small box. In the flickering lamplight it appeared to be carved out of pale wood, or perhaps ivory. Its clasp was gold and even though dusty from centuries beneath the earth, the precious metal gleamed.

The walls around the casket were carved with symbols and I recognised them as Greek letters. Theokleia pushed past Drosten, holding the lamp high so that she could better see the carvings.

"*This Holy Lance Jesus' side pierced, and came out immediately blood and water,*" she whispered, her tone filled with awe.

"That wee thing is what we've come all this way for?" asked Drosten. "Doesn't look like much. Hard to believe such a small thing has any power."

"I would have thought," said Gwawrddur, "that you of all people would content yourself with the knowledge that size is not everything."

"You make a good point, Welshman," Drosten said, his tone flat, his eyes unsmiling. "Even the smallest of vipers can possess the deadliest of poisons. Just like the one on the wall by your head there."

Gwawrddur leapt away from the wall, pushing into me and causing me to stumble forward. Drosten let out a braying laugh that resounded in the subterranean chamber. Seeing there was no serpent, Gwawrddur snarled.

"Quiet!" snapped Theokleia.

Drosten and Gwawrddur did not need me to translate. The nun's meaning and anger were clear. The two warriors fell silent.

"Hunlaf," Theokleia said, her voice softer. "Would you care to pick up the box? It has been in the darkness these many lifetimes. Let us take it out into the light and open it there."

I swallowed my nervousness and licked my lips.

"Thank you," I said, stepping up to the plinth.

Gwawrddur's voice halted my reaching hand.

"You mean to take it?" he said. "Just like that?"

"We will carry it outside and open it," I said. "Theokleia has done me a great honour in allowing me to be the first to hold this most holy of items."

"Or she does not wish to risk touching it herself," Gwawrddur said. "Had you thought of that?"

"Aye," said Drosten, "there could be a serpent inside it ready to sink its fangs into your hand."

I glowered at them both. I had not considered such a thing, but now I hesitated, fresh fears rising within me.

"Bring the lamp closer," I said. "That I may make sure of what I am about to touch."

Without a word, Theokleia lowered the lamp down near the box. I examined it from all sides as she moved the lamp around. The casket was ivory, carved with depictions of the Passion of Christ. The most prominent of the pictures showed an armoured warrior stabbing a spear into the Son of God's chest as He hung from the cross. A fountain of liquid spouted forth from the wound. Another image was of women wiping Jesus' corpse free of dirt and gore.

The chest's golden hasps were intricately fashioned, reminding me of the binding of the *Treasure of Life*, the tome that had brought me such misery and dominated my life for several years. There were no openings on the box that would allow a serpent to slither out and bite me. The stone the box rested on appeared solid.

Drawing in a deep breath, I steeled myself and picked up the casket. It was cool and not as heavy as I had imagined it would be.

I waited to be struck down, anticipating searing pain and retribution for daring to take the artefact. Nothing happened. I let out a long sigh.

"Well," chuckled Drosten, "you can never be too careful."

There was nothing else of interest within the cavern, so we made our way back out into the daylight. A sombre mood fell on us as we walked along the passageway, the shadows swarming and swaying about us. There was no further jesting or light-hearted banter. We had traversed much of the world to find this relic and now that I held the ivory casket in my hands, the enormity of the achievement settled on me with the weight of a thick winter cloak.

Runolf and the others were conversing quietly as we climbed the steps, but they grew silent as we emerged, blinking into the afternoon heat. I wanted to open the box immediately, but I could not dispel the thought of the serpents, imagining them residing in the gaping cracks and holes between the rocks. So, holding the ivory box as carefully as if it were a newborn babe, I picked my way down the pile of rubble and onto the weed-tangled ravine floor. Finding a suitably sized boulder, I placed the reliquary upon it.

The others had followed me in silence, the same reverent sombreness enveloping them all. Now they stood in a ragged semicircle about the boulder, gaping at the chiselled ivory casket.

Runolf's deep voice broke the stillness.

"Are we going to open it, or just look at it?"

I glanced at him, annoyed at his lack of awe at what we had found in the cave. His eyes glittered.

"We've travelled too far not to check the contents of that box," he said.

I looked at Theokleia and she nodded.

"He's right," she said. "Open it." Her tone was hushed and she licked her lips nervously. Artemis moved to her side. I noticed the nuns were holding hands in anxious anticipation.

Taking a deep breath to steady my nerves, I prised open the lid and raised it.

Five

I pulled my fingers back quickly, frightened at what might be hidden inside the coffer. But there was no movement in the box's interior, just the dusty, crumbling remains of what looked like a silk-covered pillow. Atop that pillow, dull with the grime of centuries, rested the blade of a spear. The metal was dark and I wondered whether it might be stained with the very Blood of Christ. Or perhaps it was simply iron rot, the red rust of age that smeared and pitted the surface of the relic. Whatever caused the dark hue of the metal, there could be no doubt that this was the item Alhwin had sent us after.

The others crowded forward, trying to peer into the coffer. But I knew from their positions they would not be able to make out what I was looking at. Mine were the first eyes in generations to contemplate the relic. That sudden realisation made me giddy. I held out my hand above the metal, imagining for a moment that I could feel something akin to heat shimmering from it, a murmuring tremor in the air, testament to its immense power.

Unbreathing, I took hold of the relic, and lifted it up, turning towards the others so that they all might see this thing of wonder.

"Behold," I said, my voice catching, "the Spear of Longinus."

Of course, it was not the spear, merely its metal head, and it measured no more than two hands' lengths. I had expected it to be hot, or somehow pulsing with its holy power, but it was cool to the touch and I felt no jolt of energy. It was just a piece of old metal.

Theokleia and Artemis made the sign of the cross. Their eyes were wide and both of them murmured prayers in their native Greek. Drosten, Gwawrddur and Hereward gazed at the relic with open-mouthed amazement. Revna stared at the spearhead, a frown of concentration wrinkling her brow.

Runolf alone seemed unmoved by the sight.

"Is that it?" he said. "We have travelled the length of the Middle Sea and into these mountains for that?"

I raised the relic higher, as if I thought perhaps he had not seen it properly.

"This is the spearhead that Longinus used to pierce the side of our Lord Jesus Christ on Calvary," I said, unable to hide my anger at his disdain. "It is a thing of extreme holiness and immense potency."

Runolf shrugged, unconvinced.

"At least it is valuable," he said. "With what Alhwin says he will pay for it, we will be as rich as kings."

Theokleia looked up into the pale sky. From where we stood deep within the ravine, there was no sign of the sun.

"Store it safely," she said, handing me a leather bag she had brought for the purpose, "and let us climb out of here before nightfall."

Shaking off my annoyance at Runolf, I placed the spearhead back into the box and closed it. I accepted the bag from Theokleia and slid the reliquary into it. It was a snug fit, but that was a good thing and hopefully would help to protect it.

"Come on," I said, slinging the bag's long strap over my shoulder. "Theokleia is right. The sun will be setting soon and there will be time to celebrate, or—" I flashed a stern look at Runolf "—to count our silver, when we are out of this crevasse."

We hurried back to where Cumbra waited. Our provisions

were piled there where the rope dangled down from the cliff top.

"Whose idea was it to lower all of that down here?" grumbled Drosten. "We are going to have to carry it all up again."

"There's nothing to be done about that now," Gwawrddur said. "The sooner we start, the better."

"Cumbra!" bellowed Runolf, his thunderous voice startling a falcon into flight from where it nested on the cliff.

We waited, but there was no movement from above. I watched as the hawk flew high into the sky. Catching warmer air, it began to circle languidly far above us.

"Damn him," snarled Hereward. "The fool has fallen asleep in the sun. Cumbra! Get your fat arse up and help us with the rope."

Several more heartbeats went by before at last Cumbra's face appeared. Even from that distance I could see his skin was ruddy, his eyes bleary.

"You lazy toad," called up Hereward. "Were you asleep?"

Cumbra rubbed at his eyes and stifled a yawn.

"No, no," he said. "I was on guard. Of course," he continued with a sheepish grin, "I may have needed to rest my eyes."

Gwawrddur snorted and Drosten chuckled. Hereward growled.

"You know my feelings about those who sleep on guard duty," he said.

"I know, I know," said Cumbra, holding up his hands. "But no harm has been done and..." he gave a broad smile "...remember who is holding the end of this rope."

He shook the rope and it snaked out from the cliff, rippling down and slapping against the rock. A few pebbles, dislodged from the wall, showered around us.

"Careful," hissed Hereward, shaking his head at Cumbra's complacence. "Hunlaf, come. You have the relic, so you go first."

Seeing Hereward handing me the rope, Theokleia stepped forward.

"Perhaps it would be best if Artemis went first," she said. "She is strong and can help pull the others up."

I translated her words, but Hereward shoved the rope into my hands. He did not like to be contradicted and he was already irritated by Cumbra's behaviour.

"Get the Spear up safely," he said gruffly to me. "Artemis can go next," he conceded, "if she wishes."

Theokleia looked as if she might protest, but she nodded and stepped away from the rock and the threat of falling debris from the crumbling cliff. She stood close to Artemis, leaning in and whispering quietly. Artemis did not look at her, instead her severe stare lingered on me and I imagined I knew how a mouse must feel when caught in the gaze of a snake. Turning away from them, I took hold of the rope.

"Tie it about yourself," Cumbra called down. "Under your arms. Then walk up the cliff as I pull with the donkey."

Runolf tied knots with as much skill as he sailed and fought. I called him over, explaining what I needed. In moments he had expertly secured the rope around my body. Walking to the edge of the cliff, I shouted to Cumbra that I was ready.

I held the hemp rope in my sweaty hands, feet against the rock. Feeling the rope growing taut, I leaned back, allowing the rope to bear my weight. Without warning, the rope jerked, pulling me off my feet and into the air. I crashed into the cliff, and was dragged painfully up for a couple of heartbeats, narrowly avoiding smacking my head into an outcrop.

"Slow down," I shouted. I was swinging from the rope, my feet the height of a tall man above the ground.

The movement stopped and I dangled there helplessly for several heartbeats. I had clattered into the rocks with my shoulder. It hurt and I would have a bruise there, but I was conscious of the precious cargo in the leather bag on my back and pleased it had not been broken.

"Sorry," I heard Cumbra call down. "This blasted animal is keen to be home, it seems."

I looked up at the craggy rock face. Straggly ferns jutted from clefts in the cliff, and there were countless protuberances and cracks that would provide good footholds.

"I'll climb," I said, "and you take up the slack with the donkey in case I fall."

Cumbra's voice was clear, but I could not see him as he was hidden by a large ledge I had noticed on my way down.

"Let me know when you need me to take up the rope," he said.

I began to climb, quickly finding that it was easier than the descent. The rock was riddled with depressions and breaks, so I was able to use my feet and hands to heave myself up. After a short while I was about a quarter of the way, my feet safely resting on a narrow ledge and my hands gripping tightly to a straight-edged slab of rock.

"Take up the slack, Cumbra," I called up. "Gently!"

The rope began to slither up the face of the cliff. When I saw there was a little slack remaining, I shouted for Cumbra to halt. The rope stopped moving and I continued.

I carried on in this way, climbing for a spell and Cumbra reeling in the rope above me, until I reached the large ledge. The sweat was pouring down my back and my fingers and arms ached, but I was nearly there and making good progress.

Reaching up to the ledge, my hand brushed something that moved beneath my touch. Images of the vipers flooded my mind, and I recoiled. Snatching my hand back, I flung what I had touched out into the void behind me. I flailed for a time, in danger of slipping, before finally regaining my composure enough to grip the ledge. Below me Runolf was shouting angrily, but I was too focused on not falling to pay attention.

Pulling myself up so that my eyes were level with the ledge, I peered over. There were no serpents there, just loose stones. It was one such stone that I had unwittingly tossed down at my friends and now I could make out Runolf's words.

"Are you trying to kill us?" he roared.

Hauling myself onto the ledge and leaning against the cliff face, I allowed myself to take some much-needed breaths. Climbing was hot work and my hair was slick and plastered to my head, my kirtle drenched in sweat.

"If I had wanted to slay you," I shouted, "do you think I would have waited till now?"

"Perhaps, Killer," came Gwawrddur's mocking reply. "You may well be more dangerous with rocks than a sword."

I ignored them both and called up to Cumbra who took up the remainder of the slack on the rope. When I had regained my breath, I set off once more, reaching the top of the cliff without further incident.

Panting, I tugged the rope free of my body.

"Watch out below," I shouted and threw the rope and the makeshift harness into the ravine.

"You look done in," said Cumbra, pulling a waterskin from the back of one of the pack animals. He handed it to me and I drank gratefully, not caring that the water was warm and bitter.

"Don't you wish you had climbed down with us?" I said, smiling despite my breathlessness.

"In truth, I do not," Cumbra said with a grin. "I have enjoyed the peace and quiet. And the sun is very pleasant up here."

There was little shade. The sun, low in the sky, bathed the hillside in simmering heat. Cumbra was red-faced and sweating, but seemed genuinely happy.

"You did not worry about serpents while you slept?" I asked.

His face paled. "Serpents?" he asked. "Should I have?" He looked nervously about at the barren rocks and the scrubby patches of dry grass and wild thyme as if snakes were about to leap from every shadow.

I told him the reason for the name of our destination and he shuddered.

"I thought the Maw of the Serpent was like the gilded language scops use in their songs and riddles."

I shrugged. "Perhaps it was once so," I said, returning the waterskin to him, "but the maw is filled with vipers now."

"But you found the relic?" he blurted out, as if the thought had just occurred to him. "The Spear was there?"

I smiled broadly at him, struck once more with the amazing truth of it. We had found the fabled spear of Longinus. I patted the bag strapped to my sweaty back.

"I have it here."

"Can I see it?" Cumbra asked, his voice hushed and filled with awe.

Appreciating his reaction after that of Runolf, I pulled the leather strap over my head, shrugging the bag off my shoulder. It was a relief to remove it and my wet kirtle began to cool immediately in the soft warm breeze.

I was about to open the bag and remove the ivory reliquary when shouts echoed up from the ravine. I bit my lip, hesitating.

"There will be time to show you later," I said.

I leaned over the edge. Our friends were far below in the shade of the deep defile. Artemis had the rope about her and had already commenced climbing.

"Take up the rope," shouted Hereward.

Cumbra hurried to do as he was ordered, leading the donkey slowly away from the edge of the cliff. I guided the rope away from the rocks and gravel with my hands, watching Artemis' progress and relaying instructions to Cumbra, telling him when to halt and when to continue.

Artemis was tall and strong, but she was a surprisingly nimble climber. She scrabbled up the rock face, her hands and feet unerringly finding holds in the crumbling cliff. She looked to me more like a bloated spider than a nun and I watched her avidly, bemused at the ease with which she scaled the rocks. Her face was red, blotchy and drenched in sweat when she reached the top.

I held out my hand and she grasped it, allowing me to heave her up. Her hand enveloped mine and I winced at the strength of her grip. She offered me no thanks, but stepped out of the looped rope in brooding silence. Cumbra was watching, and now he brought the donkey back closer to the edge of the cliff. Without thinking, I coiled the rope as Runolf had taught me aboard *Brymsteda*.

Artemis peered over the edge, then nodded curtly at me. I checked below.

"Stand clear," I shouted, not that they needed to be reminded. The process was already familiar to them. After pausing for a heartbeat, I threw the loop of rope down. The rope uncoiled as it fell.

Moments later, Theokleia was tied into the loop and making her way up. She was lither than Artemis, so it was less of a shock to see that she too was a skilled climber. But I was still surprised that a sister in Christ had the strength and agility to leap from one rock to the next, on more than one occasion pulling herself up using the power in her arms alone. Perhaps Theokleia had climbed similar cliffs as a child, I mused. After all, she had told us that she was a native of the island and she clearly knew these mountains well. Theokleia made even better time than Artemis and I felt a ridiculous prickle of envy at their skill, and foolish shame that I had not been faster than the women.

Cumbra and I repeated the process from before, except that this time Artemis loomed over me, suspiciously eyeing my every move as if she thought I might cut the rope at any moment.

When Theokleia reached the top, I made to help her, but

Artemis grabbed her outstretched hand and pulled her up. Theokleia patted her massive companion on the shoulder and offered her thanks.

Cumbra had seen Theokleia and was already leading the donkey back.

"I will see to Cumbra," Theokleia said, her voice quiet and calm. She was barely breathing hard after her climb and again I wondered at her fitness and strength. "Give Hunlaf here a helping hand."

The slim nun had loosened the rope and stepped out of the loop. Readying myself for the next of our number to make the climb, I retrieved the rope and began coiling it, the roughness of the hemp as familiar to my hands as the motion of coiling the line. I had performed this task countless times as part of *Brymsteda*'s Aft crew, so I paid little attention to my hands, trusting they would do their job. I stepped close to the cliff edge once more, looking down and wondering who would be next.

"Ready below?" I called.

Hereward waved and I was half turning to check on Cumbra when I heard a strange sound behind me; somewhere between a gasp and a cough.

I am an old man now, a monk once more. Wise and studious I may be, but I have not stood in battle for many years, and I can barely recall what it felt like to be young. But all those years ago, in the mountains of Kýpros, I was youthful. And what I lacked in experience I made up for with the sharp instincts of a warrior.

Something about that sound had alerted me, even if I did not yet realise it with conscious thought. That animal that resides in all men perceived I was in danger. And all those long days training with Gwawrddur had paid off. My reflexes were sharp, and I was fast. And so it was that, even tired and distracted as I was, part of me sensed the threat even before I knew what it was.

Trusting my instincts, as I turned I flung myself to the side. Something hard struck my left cheek and I stumbled over the coiled rope, falling into the dust. I was confused and wondered how our attackers had reached us without warning. Had they crept up while Cumbra slept? Shaking my head to clear it and barely registering the pain blooming in my face, I scrambled to my feet, all the while aware of the yawning drop beside me.

As so frequently occurs in battle, my senses became heightened by the danger and everything seemed to slow around me, giving me time to consider the best course of action. With a sensation of calm washing through me, I looked about for signs of danger and the identity of my attacker.

There was nobody else on the hillside but Theokleia, Artemis and Cumbra. For a moment I could not comprehend what was happening. Then a bright splash of red caught my attention. It was Cumbra's blood blossoming in the warm air and I knew with a sudden certainty that it had been the man from Northumbria who had made the sound that had alerted me. And I understood, with a dreadful realisation, who our assailants were.

Six

Cumbra was floundering, eyes wide and arms flailing, as his lifeblood spurted from the deep gash in his throat. Theokleia, small knife glinting in her hand, stepped away from him to avoid the fountain of gore. The donkey, spooked by the stench of fresh blood, brayed loudly, kicked out and ran away from the nun and the dying man.

I took in all of this in a heartbeat, but I had no more time to contemplate the sudden violence and terrible betrayal, for Artemis strode towards me. I realised then it had been her meaty fist that had glanced against my cheek. Now, teeth pulled back in a snarl, she rolled her head on her shoulders the way I had seen Drosten do before a bare-knuckle fight, and – huge fists raised – she closed with me.

I have never been a brawler and I was certainly no match for Artemis' size, but I was quick and strong. My mind was still spinning from the suddenness of the treachery and attack, but I could not allow Artemis to get the better of me. Theokleia's cold-blooded murder of Cumbra had shown me the peril I faced, and there was nobody else on that hillside to help me apart from God, and there was no time for prayer.

"What are you doing?" I shouted, more in an attempt to distract Artemis than with any expectation of a meaningful answer. To my surprise, Theokleia snapped an order and Artemis halted her advance. I dropped a hand to my belt, but I carried no weapon. Casting a glance over to the remaining pack animal and the provisions we had left with Cumbra, I cursed silently, remembering I had left my sword with the rest of our gear at the bottom of the ravine.

"You men are so trusting," said Theokleia with a sneer. "To think we would aid that Frankish bastard Carolus to obtain such a holy relic."

"You are servants of Eirene," I said. It was not a question.

"Of course we are," hissed Theokleia. "She is the greatest woman who has ever lived and soon she will be crowned Emperor of all Romans, as is her right." Her eyes flashed with passion. "And we will be at her side. She will reward us well for bringing her the Spear of Destiny. With it she will be invincible! And truly, I must thank you."

I scowled. My cheek throbbed.

"For what?"

"Hurry up," came Hereward's cry from the ravine. "What is taking you so long?"

"One moment," shouted Theokleia in a sweet voice. Behind her Cumbra lay in the dirt, blood soaking the ground. Theokleia smiled, amused perhaps to know that Hereward and the others would be waiting for a long time. I said nothing, too stunned to speak.

"I found the nun who professed knowledge of the Spear's location," Theokleia said. She noticed a spot of blood on her hand and rubbed at it absently. "She told me all she knew. They always do. But without the instructions you brought from that accursed Alhwin, I would never have found the Spear." She frowned then. "It is a pity to kill you, Hunlaf. You are not as stupid as most men."

A white-hot rage swept through me.

"You used me to get the Spear."

Theokleia chuckled. "What are men for if not to be used?

Now, there is no more time for this chatter," she said, snapping her fingers. "Artemis, finish him."

With that, she turned away, dismissing me completely. Without a backward glance, sure of her companion's ability to dispatch me, she went to retrieve the donkey that had halted and now nibbled at the dry leaves of a spindly bush of thyme.

For her part, Artemis looked all too happy to obey Theokleia's orders. Without a sound she lowered her head and rushed at me. I barely had enough time to raise my arms, when her first punch hit me. It was a stunning blow to my left cheek. I had tried to turn my head, but her knuckles connected soundly, rattling my teeth.

My feet scraped in the loose gravel, sending stones tumbling into the ravine. I had to get away from that precipitous edge. I shuffled to my right, catching Artemis' next blow on my left forearm and sending a straight jab into her chin. It was like hitting granite. She didn't even flinch.

She came at me again, and this time I was able to dodge and avoid the worst of her attacks. Dimly, through the ringing in my ears, I could hear Hereward, Runolf and the others shouting. But I could not make out their words.

"Treachery!" I screamed as loudly as I could, hoping they would understand my word of warning. But I had no more time.

I stepped in towards Artemis, using my agility and speed to my advantage. Ducking under her punches, I rained a series of savage blows on her face. My knuckles split and I grunted. My blood speckled her cheeks and her nun's wimple. But she did not seem to feel any pain.

Shaken and increasingly desperate, I made to dart away, further from the deadly fall of the cliff and out of range of Artemis' slab-like fists. I was fast, but I had not reckoned on her speed and reach. As I pulled away, I realised my error too late. With horror, I felt her hands grab my kirtle and pull me to her in a savage embrace. She heaved me close, wrapping her arms tightly about my back and squeezing. She had trapped my right arm at my side. With my left I punched and scratched ineffectually at her face.

With a growl of rage, she renewed her efforts to crush the life from me. I could not breathe and I could feel my strength ebbing. I stared into Artemis' dark eyes and saw no compassion. There was nothing in her eyes but death. Terrified and frantic, I reached out to gouge at those cold eyes, but as fast as a hound, she opened her jaws and bit into my hand.

I howled with pain, trying to free my hand from her grasp, but she had it trapped, her teeth latched on like a terrier fighting a bull in a pit.

Frenzied with fear and seeing my death approaching, I pulled back my head and smashed my forehead into her nose as hard as I could. I heard and felt the cartilage crushed beneath the force of the blow. Blood gushed over her chin.

This had some effect on Artemis and she loosened her hold on me. Able to breathe once more, I drew in great lungfuls of air. The bright spectre of victory rose in my mind as I sought to free myself from her grasp.

But as quickly as the thought of triumph came to me, it was quashed. Artemis had loosened her grip, but had not relinquished her hold. She had merely shifted her balance, and now – with a sickening realisation – I understood what she intended.

With a bellowing roar Artemis lifted me into the air above her head. Blood dribbled from her broken nose and ran red into her snarling mouth. For an instant both of my hands were free, but I didn't even have time to renew my attack on her. The world spun about me and for a horrifying instant I could see the faces of my friends far below staring up with open mouths and wide eyes.

Then everything was spinning and I was falling, tumbling towards the jagged rocks in the ravine as Artemis threw me over the edge of the cliff.

Seven

Darkness.

A rushing sound like waves rolling up a shingle beach. Sensations returned to me slowly. My left arm was twisted painfully behind my back. My head throbbed. Far away I could hear shouting. I almost recognised those voices, but they were thin and distant, like barely remembered dreams. Something sharp and hard was pressing into my left cheek. The pain there was dull, but part of me knew that it would hurt more when I gave it my full attention. Had someone punched me? My memories were blurred.

Where was I? The voices came from beneath me. How could that be? Then, from above, more voices. I had a sudden, blindingly clear vision of lying somewhere between this life and the next, Satan and his devils below, calling for me, desperate to drag my soul down into Hell, while God and his angels called to me from heaven.

Was I dead then?

One of the voices from above me coalesced into an incongruous bellow of deep-throated laughter. That was no angel. The sound washed over me and, as if water had been splashed onto my face, I came to. In that instant, crashing back to wakefulness, I recalled what had happened and to whom the voices belonged. Still, I had no idea how I was not dead.

Opening my eyes, I looked about me to see if I could make sense of it.

My cheek was pressed against a ridge of stone. I could see bright drops of my blood on the outcrops below. My friends stared up at me with shocked faces. I lifted my head, groaning at the flash of agony in my cheek and left shoulder.

"Don't move!" screamed Revna. "You'll fall!" Her beautiful features were contorted by real terror. I knew how she felt. I did not want to fall, and yet I could not remain where I was. As my senses returned, so the pain increased, particularly in my left arm and shoulder.

Risking movement, I craned around to get a better view of where I was and how it was I had not fallen to my death. I was lying in an almost impossible position on the ledge I'd noticed earlier. I winced to see that all that had prevented me from dying was my left arm. It had somehow become lodged between two boulders, checking my fall.

My vision swam. I must have hit my head hard when I fell. It was difficult to concentrate, but I knew I had to focus. Nobody could help me all the way up here.

Nobody but God, whispered a small voice inside me.

So many times in my long life the Almighty has intervened, saving me from what seemed in that moment certain death. I know that He is all powerful, but my faith is often weak and I still find it hard to believe that God would work miracles for me. But that day, on the cliff in the mountains of Kýpros, could there truly be any doubt that God had a hand in my salvation?

The laughter from above emanated from the bloody and battered face of Artemis. She stared down at me, her eyes dark and incredulous. Beside her appeared Theokleia. She had removed her head covering and her angular features were wreathed by lustrous long black hair.

"It seems the Lord has other plans for you, Hunlaf," she said, shaking her head so that her hair wafted about her like wings. "I knew I should have taken you with us."

"Shall I kill him?" asked Artemis, her voice husky.

Theokleia stared at me for a long while. Revna and the others below had fallen silent, watching how this conversation would unfold, knowing they were unable to affect the outcome.

"Leave him," Theokleia said at last. "Who am I to defy the Lord Almighty? He has spared Hunlaf. Perhaps one day we will see why that is. But for now we have what we came for. Come, my dove."

Theokleia disappeared from view. Artemis glowered down at me and there was such hatred in her eyes I knew that if she could have done so, she would have squeezed the life from me. Finally, with a growl, she spat a gobbet of phlegm and blood at me and vanished.

The bloody spittle splattered the rock near my head. I turned back to look down at my friends. My shoulder was throbbing with each beat of my heart. I flexed my hand and was dismayed to find I could not feel the fingers. The blood flow was cut off by the rock. If left much longer the wound rot would set in and the arm would need to be amputated. Too long and that arm might yet claim my life. I shuddered.

Taking a deep breath, I raised myself up, cautiously reaching with my right hand to grasp the nearest boulder.

"Careful," Revna said.

I ignored her. I was in a twisted and awkward position. The ledge was narrow and crumbling and my left arm caught in such a way that I was unable to raise my body up high enough to prise myself free. I pushed with my right hand, straining until the sweat poured from me, stinging my eyes and the cuts on my face. At last I fell back, exhausted.

"It's no good," I panted. "I'm trapped."

I closed my eyes and prayed. Surely the Almighty had not saved me from the fall only to have me die like this.

"Hold still," shouted Gwawrddur.

"I'm not going anywhere," I replied with a thin smile.

The Welshman grinned, but I knew him well enough to see

the concern behind the veil of amusement. "I'm coming for you," he said, and, slinging a waterskin over his back, he began to climb up the cliff face.

It took him a long time and I watched him all the while, unable to move and terrified that I would see him plunge to his death at any moment. But Gwawrddur was strong and sure-footed and, after what seemed an age, he reached me, clambering up and pulling himself onto the ledge.

"I'll lose the arm if we don't free it soon," I said, wondering if it might not already be too late.

"And there I was thinking you might give me more of a welcome than that, Killer," he said. "Always so impatient."

Despite his jovial tone, his expression was grim and I could see he was trying to work out the best way to proceed.

"How bad is it?" called up Runolf.

"Not bad at all," Gwawrddur shouted down. Then, quietly enough that only I could hear him: "I hope you have been praying."

"I won't stop till we are safely away from here," I hissed.

He nodded, but said no more for a while as he examined my arm and the rocks that pinned it.

"I am going to lean over you and do my best to lift you up," he said at last. "But you are going to have to help me." He shuffled closer and leaned across me. I couldn't see what he was doing, but I felt his right arm wrap about my chest. I twisted again and reached over to grip the rock as I had done before.

"Ready?" Gwawrddur asked.

I nodded.

"I'll count to three," he said, "and then we'll pull that damn arm of yours free."

I clenched my jaw, preparing to apply all the strength I had left.

"Oh, and Hunlaf?"

"What?" I said, my voice strained and barely audible.

"Keep praying."

Under my breath, I whispered the words of the twenty-third psalm.

"One." Gwawrddur tensed and adjusted his grip.

"Two." I took a gulp of air into my lungs.

"Three!"

We both heaved and strained, grunting with the effort. For a dreadfully long time my arm did not budge. I thought we were going to fail, and then, with a wrenching pain and scraping sound, my arm flew out, released from the clamping pressure of the two boulders.

So suddenly did my arm come free that Gwawrddur lost his balance and collapsed on top of me. My left shoulder shrieked with pain and I began to shake as if caught in the chill of winter.

"Let the blood flow again," Gwawrddur said, carefully moving off of me. "Breathe deep and rub some life back into that arm, for you will need it soon."

The arm was numb, but even as I pushed myself away from the drop, my skin began to grow warm, to prickle and tingle. I was pleased about the sensation, but with it came a new concern and fresh agony.

"I'm not sure how much use the arm will be," I said. "I fear the shoulder was torn in the fall." It was true, the pain now was excruciating and as I had moved it back to a more natural position, I found my shoulder tight and swollen.

Gwawrddur glanced up at the sky. I saw with a shock that the light had taken on the golden tinge of sunset, the shadows in the ravine starker and darker than only moments earlier.

"Can you move to sit facing me?" Gwawrddur asked.

There was very little room on the ledge, and I was woozy, but I nodded.

"Best not to look down now," he said, smiling. "Just carefully sit like that. Thirsty?"

He took the waterskin he'd brought with him, unstoppered

it, and passed it to me. I took it in my right hand. While I drank, he shuffled closer and took my left hand in both of his.

"Let me have a look," he said, gently massaging my shoulder. It was stiff and painful. He nodded. "I've seen this before," he said, keeping his tone calm as if talking to a frightened animal. "Place your hand here on my shoulder." I did so, and felt some of the pressure relieved from my own shoulder. The prickling of my arm had grown in intensity as the blood flowed and I could feel the texture of Gwawrddur's kirtle under my fingers now.

"Have I torn the muscle?" I asked. My voice sounded small and frightened to my ears.

"I don't think so," he said. "But the bone has come free of the joint."

I tensed.

"Do not worry," he said. "Trust me. I can fix this." He offered me a smile. "But you might want to keep praying. I'm going to rub the muscles for a time."

He probed with his fingers, relaxing the muscles of my shoulder and upper arm. As he did so, he exerted some pressure on my elbow, pushing it gently away from my body.

Without warning, I felt something shift in my shoulder. It was still painful, but already less tense and I could move my arm more freely.

"There," Gwawrddur said. "The bone has slipped back to where it should be. That's good."

"What is going on up there?" yelled Hereward. "It will be dark soon."

"We are fine," replied Gwawrddur. "Better?" he said to me more quietly.

I nodded, tentatively moving my arm and taking another sip from the skin.

"Good," he said, his voice not much stronger than a whisper, then, loud again for the others to hear: "We cannot talk now.

We are going to need all our energy to climb to the top of the cliff."

"Climb!" I said, sputtering on the water I had been drinking. "I can barely move this arm, let alone climb with it."

"Then you had best get praying, Killer. For it will be dark soon and we cannot spend the night on this ledge."

I argued with him for a time, but in the end he convinced me of the foolhardiness of remaining where we were.

"We are going to need to climb eventually," he said.

"What about the others? Couldn't they climb up and help us?"

"How? I doubt those whores have left us a rope." He smirked. "I know I made the climb look easy, but do you think it worth the risk for the others to scale that cliff? The best thing we can do now is to get to the top and have the others walk out of the ravine and back to where we will be waiting for them."

"Theokleia said that would add a day to our journey."

"Then you will have time to rest and heal while we wait."

I glanced down at the faces staring up at us. My eye was drawn to the jagged rocks.

"I would rest and heal now," I said. "Not climb."

"And a feather bed, a warm bath and scented oils would be pleasant no doubt," said the Welshman with a lopsided smile. "Perhaps a young slave girl to rub your tired muscles."

Despite the pain I felt and the predicament we were in, I could not stop my mind from turning to Revna.

"That sounds better than this."

"Maybe when we return to Kyrenia there will be time for oils, baths and girls, but for that we need to get off this accursed ledge."

"Blessed ledge," I replied. "Without it I would surely be dead."

"Blessed, then," said Gwawrddur, carefully standing up.

"God saved you from near-certain death, now it is your turn to save yourself. With a little help from me, of course."

In the short while we had been talking, the sky had grown a darker shade of blue. There was no more time for debate. With a sigh, I offered him my right hand and allowed him to pull me upright. My head spun and Gwawrddur gripped me tight, pushing me against the wall.

"Easy now, Killer." He held me firmly until I had regained my balance.

"You know how I hate that name," I said, my voice tight with anxiety and emotion.

Gwawrddur's expression became serious.

"I give you my word that after you have climbed to the top of this cliff, I will never call you Killer again."

"You mean 'if'," I said.

"You'll make it," he said. "I know how stubborn you are. Come on. Lead the way."

"No," I said.

"There is no time for this, Hunlaf," Gwawrddur said, unable to hide the frustration creeping into his tone.

"No," I said again. "I mean you should go first. You should not go behind me. If I fall, there is no need for me to take you with me."

He stared at me for a couple of heartbeats, then nodded. "Very well," he said. "Follow me."

"I thought you had faith I'd make it to the top," I said.

"I have every faith in you," replied Gwawrddur, reaching for a handhold and pulling himself up from the ledge, "but there is no reason to tempt wyrd."

All these years later the only things I can recall of that climb are the stabbing pain in my shoulder every time I needed to use my left arm, the pounding headache that made my head spin, and the sting of sweat trickling into my eyes.

Gwawrddur went slowly, choosing the easiest route he could find. I focused on watching his feet, placing my hands in the holds he found and hauling myself up. I gritted my teeth against the searing agony of my wrenched shoulder, forcing myself onward.

We climbed for what seemed a long time, though the distance truly was not that far. I was lost in my own world of pain and determination. Just as I began to feel giddy, my exhaustion threatening to overcome me, Gwawrddur's strong hand reached down and clasped my wrist. He had made the summit and now pulled me up to safety.

We lay on our backs there, panting and looking up at the darkening sky. Two large vultures circled above us, and with a groan I thought of Cumbra, sure that the birds had come to feast on his corpse.

"Told you," said Gwawrddur, his breath ragged from the climb.

"What?"

"You're too stubborn to die."

"Perhaps it is as you said and God spared me for a reason."

"You know what that reason is?"

I turned my head so that I could see Cumbra's corpse. Theokleia and Artemis had not bothered to move him. There was no sign of the women or the pack animals. As breathless as we were, it was a good thing they had gone. The thought of facing Artemis again in my debilitated state made me shiver.

"I do not know why God saved me," I admitted. "But I hope to see those nuns again and retrieve what they stole from us."

Gwawrddur glanced over at Cumbra's body.

"You cannot bring Cumbra back," he said.

"No." I sighed. "But after we face those whores again, perhaps you will be able to call me Killer once more."

"Perhaps," he said.

"But not before," I said, rolling over and pushing myself to my feet with difficulty.

★

It was late the following afternoon when the others reached us. They were dusty and sweat-streaked. They threw the sacks and packs they had carried onto the sandy earth where we had made camp.

"Cumbra?" Hereward asked, pointing at a large pile of rocks.

Gwawrddur and I had nothing to dig with, so we'd spent the morning collecting rocks and fashioning a cairn over Cumbra's bloated corpse. It might stop animals from getting to him for a time, but already the air around the makeshift barrow was thick with flies.

"Theokleia slit his throat," I said. "He never saw it coming."

"None of us did," said Drosten. The skin of his face was burnt red between the coiling blue tattoos. "To think we trusted those nuns."

"So we have nothing to show for all the weeks of travel," grumbled Runolf, slumping down with his back to a boulder. In the morning that rock had been baked hot in the sunshine; now, with the sun in the west, it provided one of the few areas of shade on the hillside.

"We are not empty-handed," said Hereward, indicating the provisions strewn about the campsite. There was a small pile of twigs and branches Gwawrddur and I had accumulated during the day in preparation for another night out here. Despite the heat of the day, it was cool in the dark and we would all welcome the flames' light. "We do not have the relic we came for," Hereward went on, "but we have found it once. Perhaps we can find it again."

"Anything is possible," Runolf said grudgingly. "If those nuns have it, they will pay for what they have done."

"Before anyone pays for anything," said Revna, "we need to get back to the coast. We have some of our weapons. Some dry bread and a little cheese. A few blankets." She picked up a waterskin and shook it. It was almost empty. "But we have little water. I saw no rivers or streams on our journey into these mountains. Without water, we will perish as surely as if Theokleia had sliced all of our throats."

"God damn those women," said Hereward. "We should have known not to trust them."

"Why?" asked Revna. "Because they are women?"

Hereward scowled. "To think that nuns would risk everything to accompany us into these mountains. It was foolish beyond all reckoning."

"Foolish or not," I said, "the past cannot be altered and Revna is right. We will die of thirst before we have a chance for vengeance if we don't find water. I say we rest a while, then, when night falls, we head towards the coast. The going will be easier at night and with God's grace perhaps we will find a spring in the foothills."

There was much grumbling, but nobody had a better plan. We shared out some crusts of bread and thin slivers of hard cheese, and we each had a sip of the dwindling supply of water left in our skins. Then everyone sprawled out to rest before dusk and the time came to move once more.

Revna sat beside me. Her freckled cheeks were crimson from the sun, her hair unkempt. She was grimy, sour with stale sweat.

And she was beautiful.

I looked at her sidelong, as always unnerved in her presence. Gersine knew how I felt about her. I wondered how many of the others did too. Surely I had not hidden my desire so completely. Perhaps Revna herself knew. If she did, she had never given me cause to believe she felt anything more towards me than friendship. And I did not wish to risk that. It was chiefly my friendship with her father that halted me making any advance. That and what I imagined Runolf might do to me if I showed an interest in bedding his daughter.

"I was worried about you," she said.

"You were worried?" I replied. "Imagine how I felt."

We fell silent and chewed our bread. It was hard and stale,

but Gwawrddur and I had eaten nothing since the day before and I was ravenous. The dry bread sucked all the moisture from my mouth but I forced myself to chew, then swallow it down.

"I feared you had broken your arm," she said. "I could barely believe you didn't fall all the way down."

"It's the shoulder," I said, "but it isn't so bad now." I moved my arm gingerly. It still ached, but it was improving. "Gwawrddur was able to push the bones back into place."

She winced.

"Poor Hunlaf," she said, reaching out and gently touching my bruised and scabbed cheek.

My skin tingled at her touch and I forgot to breathe. Looking away, I saw that Runolf was not dozing like Drosten and Hereward. He was propped up on one elbow and glaring at me.

I swallowed at the dryness in my mouth.

"We'd best get some rest," I said, lying down and rolling onto my side, turning my back to Revna. "It will be a long night."

Revna didn't say anything. I lay like that for a long time, cursing my weakness as I pretended that sleep had claimed me. Eventually, Revna rose and went to lie in the shade of the boulder near her father.

Eight

It was two days later when we reached Kyrenia. We were battered and exhausted after the trek down from the mountains, but we were alive. There had been a moment when it seemed all too possible that we would die out there in those dusty hills. We had run out of water by the morning of the first night's walk and, as the sun had risen into a cloudless sky that promised another blistering day, things had seemed bleak.

Again, it was prayer that saved us.

We had decided to rest in a small valley that would provide us with shade for all but the hottest part of the day, but we had barely any food left and our waterskins were dry. We were all bone-weary and had decided there was nothing for it but to rest for a spell and then continue downhill in the hope that we might stumble on some water or perhaps a settlement, though we could not recall any in this area when Theokleia had led us into the mountains.

In spite of my tiredness, I decided I needed to pray. I missed the routines of the monastic offices and the calm they brought to my mind, so, on that barren slope, fearing that we could not escape death this time, I made my way from the camp to pray. I was drawn to a solitary rock that stood at the top of a rise, jutting high above the sandy ground.

Kneeling in the rock's shadow, sharp gravel digging into my

knees like a penance, I closed my eyes and effortlessly began to recite the liturgy of Prime, the office of the first hour of the day. A sense of serenity settled over me and I opened my eyes to take in the land beyond the boulder. On the far side of the rise was a steep-edged vale. The rising sun streamed into that valley, picking out the same familiar rocks and sandy earth. But it was not as barren as the rest of the land we had traversed. There were trees down at the bottom of that valley, and not the dry, gnarled mastic bushes and junipers that dotted the deserted peaks. These trees were green, their leaves shimmering in the sun.

I was already rejoicing, for where so many trees grew, there must be water. I saw movement and, a moment later, a thin bleating reached my ears.

"Goats," I whispered, awed once more at the power of prayer and angry with myself for my lack of faith. "Praise the Lord!"

I called to the others and with renewed energy at the prospect of water and possibly food, we hurried down the slope. Two large dogs barked as we approached, alerting the pair of goatherds. They were a boy and girl, neither older than twelve or thirteen summers. Both had the same tanned skin, pointed, angular features and thick crow-black hair.

Clearly frightened, the boy tugged at the girl's arm, pleading with her to run. I feared they would flee, but the girl was brave and shook off the boy, who it transpired was her brother.

"We mean you no harm," I said, holding up my empty hands. "All we seek is water."

Snapping at her snivelling brother to be quiet, the girl pointed down through the trees. "There is a spring there," she said. "Don't piss in the water."

I told the others what she had said and Drosten laughed. "I wish I had enough water in me to piss!" he said.

We made our way into the shade beneath the trees and found where a stream of water trickled from the rocks. The goats watched us from where they nibbled at the bark and low leaves. The dogs had stopped barking now, but they were observing us closely.

"I wonder how they stop the goats from pissing in the water," said Gwawrddur, "or is it just our piss they don't like?"

We filled our skins and drank deeply. The water was cool and sweet as only the truly thirsty can ever comprehend.

The flock of goats numbered perhaps a score of animals: scrawny beasts with ragged coats and protruding ribs. But we had not eaten meat in days and our bellies growled at the prospect of roasted goat.

However, when we asked if we could buy one of their animals, the siblings refused. Runolf was the hungriest of all of us and offered them the price of five head for their oldest, skinniest animal. The girl shook her head, rejecting the Norseman's silver. Runolf snarled at her stubbornness. The dogs, sensing a threat, growled deep in their throats, hackles bristling.

"These children are brave," Runolf said.

I had been listening to the brother and sister debating the way forward and I knew the truth of their steadfast refusal to part with a goat.

"They are more frightened of their father than they are of you," I said. "He will beat them if they sell one of his animals."

Runolf nodded. That was something he could understand. "Ask them how far it is to their father's house," he said.

I did as he asked and listened to the girl's reply. It was half a day's walk away. After a discussion with her brother she informed us they would be happy to lead us there.

We accepted their offer, and they began to lead us out of the valley, driving the herd of goats before them.

"This is the wrong way," Hereward said.

"I'm sure they know the way to their own home," said Drosten.

"Kyrenia lies to the north," Hereward said. "They are taking us south and east."

I asked them then in which direction their father's house lay and the girl confirmed what Hereward had surmised.

Runolf sighed.

"We cannot walk half a day out of our way," he grumbled. "Ask them what price they put on a beating. I will give them enough silver that their father will be happy with them, and if he is not, they will have enough themselves to accept any beating he might give them."

After some haggling, it transpired that for a silver *denarius* each, the brother and sister would be content to risk their father's wrath and, before the sun reached its zenith, the glorious smell of roasting goat filled the small wooded area around the spring.

We ate our fill and dozed for much of the long afternoon in the shade of the trees, surrounded by the occasional bleating of the goats, the burbling trickle of the spring and the droning buzz of insects.

Filling our skins again, we set off with full bellies, as the sun dipped towards the horizon. We halted some time past midnight after we crested a rise and saw the silver rays of the gibbous moon dappling the sea that spread out below us as far as the horizon.

It was midday when we reached the gate of the minster. Hereward had been brooding on Theokleia's and Artemis' betrayal and now he strode to the gate and hammered upon it with his fist.

"They won't be there," Gwawrddur said.

That much seemed obvious to us all, even Hereward.

"You are probably right," he said, "but mayhap they will know where they might have gone."

Gwawrddur shrugged and the rest of us remained silent. I went over to stand in the shade of the tree where we had first met the nuns. There was no movement from the minster. After a time, Hereward beat against the gate again, taking out his anger on the timber.

At last, a small grille opened and an old nun peered out.

"By all that is holy," she said in a rasping tone, "what is the meaning of this?" She glowered at each of us through the metal grating, taking in with disdain our travel-stained garb, sunburnt faces and the weapons we carried. She made no effort to open the gate.

"Ask her about Theokleia," said Hereward.

With a sigh, I pushed myself up and went to the gate. The old nun scowled at me. Her nose wrinkled at our stink after the long days of travel and hardship we had endured.

"We are looking for two nuns," I said.

"We don't sell them, you know?" she said, looking me up and down. "This is a minster, not a brothel."

Taken aback, I pressed on. "The nuns we seek are called Theokleia and Artemis."

"There is nobody with those names here," she said.

"Are you certain?" I asked. Her dismissive tone annoyed me. "One is young and slender, the other very large, almost as big as him." I pointed to Runolf.

"I think I would remember a giant sister," she said. "No, the nuns you describe are not here. Why did you think they were sisters at Episcopia?"

"They told us they were," I snapped, but then, casting my memory back to the day we had met them, I realised that was not true. Theokleia and Artemis had been waiting in the shade of the oak near the entrance to the minster, and of course, they wore the habits of nuns, so we had assumed they were sisters of this order. Feeling foolish, a sudden thought came to me. "Have any of the sisters gone missing recently?"

At these words, the old woman's expression became stern and drawn. She made the sign of the cross.

"What do you know of that?" she asked, her voice croaking.

"Know of what?" I asked.

"You are saying you know nothing of Metrodora?"

"I know nothing of any Metrodora. Is she a sister here?"

The woman's rheumy eyes narrowed as she stared at me, evidently weighing me up, searching for signs of guilt or duplicity. I met her gaze unblinking and it appeared she decided I could be trusted enough for her to continue talking.

"Loved the books in our library, Metrodora did. Always reading." Her demeanour had softened as she recalled Metrodora. "She was a bright, clever thing." Tears glimmered in her lashes. She brushed them away with gnarled fingers.

"What happened to her?" I asked, holding my hand up to silence Hereward and the others, fearful that they might interrupt the nun's tale. I sensed that what she had to say was important and that breaking the small amount of trust she had bestowed upon me would silence her.

"Evil," she spat. "The Devil. Metrodora wandered outside these walls where I could not protect her." She let out a ragged breath. "Now she is dead."

"What happened?" I asked again, keeping my voice soft.

"Who can say but the Lord?" she replied, her voice cracking. "Perhaps a sailor, or a young farmer in town for the market... Of course, we all know such things can befall a young woman if she is not careful." Her eyes flicked to Revna and she frowned to see she wore a sword at her side. "But who would do such a thing to a nun?" The old woman's voice wavered and trailed off.

"Do what?" I prodded gently.

"Abuse her body!" she said, anger and outrage lending her strength. "Violate her! Torture her! Tear at her flesh..." She shuddered and looked at me as if returning from a dark land I would never travel to, never comprehend. "Metrodora was killed by some man. Down by the harbour. They found her body discarded like an animal carcass. Butchered like one too. Whatever man did this has the Devil in him." She made the sign of the cross again. "Now begone from here before I call for the town militia. They have no fondness for strangers."

"My condolences for your loss," I muttered, even as she was turning away.

"All men have the Devil within them," she said, pausing. "Wickedness and evil. The man who did this to Metrodora must be as evil as Satan himself."

When she had gone, I told the others what she had said.

"You think there is a connection between Theokleia, Artemis and this Metrodora?" asked Revna, her expression haggard from tiredness and perhaps the thought of what had been done to Metrodora.

I recalled what Theokleia had said to me at the top of the cliff.

"I think the person, or people, who did these things to Metrodora were truly evil," I said. "But I do not think it was any man."

Weary and dejected, we trudged down to Kyrenia. The bright sunshine shimmered on the Middle Sea and the many ships and smaller vessels that dotted the harbour waters. My spirits lifted as I spied *Brymsteda* anchored several spears' throws from the dock.

We spoke little as we made our way through the sweltering tangle of streets, but the sight of the ship raised everyone's morale. I cannot say what the others were thinking, but my mood had grown very dark over the previous days, to the point I had almost expected to find our ship gone, perhaps sunk or captured by our enemies. After seeing *Brymsteda* safe, the thought of reaching the ship and our friends gave us all renewed energy and we hurried on in spite of the heat.

The scent of fish cooking wafted to us on the breeze. Runolf sniffed the air and followed the smell and billowing smoke to a small area behind a hut that looked as if the slightest wind would blow it over. An elderly woman dressed all in black was tending a small fire upon which she was roasting several sardines skewered on thin twigs, rotating them frequently.

Runolf did not speak Greek, but he quickly made himself understood to her, holding out a gleaming silver coin.

Moments later – our mood buoyed further by the warm, salty fish we nibbled – we continued on our way through the twisting streets of Kyrenia, always following the downward slope to the sea.

It was late afternoon when we reached the harbour. The sun was hot on our faces as we stared out to *Brymsteda*. There was no sign of life aboard and I could see that the sail had been rigged across the deck to provide shelter from the sun.

"They must all be asleep, the laggards," grumbled Runolf. "I thought they would have seen us before now."

Fishermen were fixing their nets and, down on a shingle beach, some were smoking fish. Several beggars were huddled in the shade of the harbour wall and watched us intently. Runolf ignored them and strode out along the harbour, his red hair aflame in the light of the lowering sun. Still there was no movement from the ship. An uneasy nervousness coiled in my gut.

"Ahoy, *Brymsteda*!" Runolf bellowed, startling the nearby fishermen and sending several black-headed gulls scattering into flight.

At last we saw a face peering at us from the ship. It was Alf, who had been left in command in our absence. The knot of anxiety in my belly loosened. Alf waved, then cupped his hands to his mouth. "Wait there," he shouted.

"Where else does he think we will go?" said Runolf. "I hope he has done a better job of buying supplies than he has of keeping watch."

As he was speaking, without warning, Drosten sprang past me and dived into the sea. I glimpsed his tattooed back and arms and bare legs before he disappeared into the water. Looking back at the wall, I saw he had shed most of his clothing and left his sword, pack and waterskin there.

Breaking the surface he shook his dark hair, a wide grin

on his tattooed face. "Why wait?" he said. "We need a wash anyway."

With that, he turned and swam out towards *Brymsteda*, his muscled arms pulling him quickly through the water. I imagined following Drosten and how good the cool water would feel on my skin. But even if I were able to swim, my shoulder still ached. Besides, the thought of pulling off my clothes so close to Revna made my cheeks burn.

Gwawrddur shook his head at Drosten's display.

"I'll wait," he said.

Like me, the Welshman could not swim. Unlike me, he had once fallen overboard and nearly drowned in the chill waters of the North Sea. It took all his resolve to shake off his fear enough to sail aboard *Brymsteda*.

The stone anchor was weighed and pulled over the side, dripping and draped with weed just as Drosten reached the ship. The same hands hauled the Pict over the side and he waved at us. With practised ease, the long oars were unshipped.

We had sat down on the harbour wall to wait and we could just make out Alf's voice as he gave the crew orders, then *Brymsteda* gracefully turned and slid across the water towards us.

"Whatever you might think about his watch-keeping," said Hereward, "you cannot deny Alf is an excellent seaman."

Runolf grunted in tacit agreement. "He can sail," he acknowledged and spat into the sea, as if it pained him to admit it.

We watched as the oars rose and fell in perfect time, bringing the sleek form of *Brymsteda* towards the harbour wall. At precisely the right moment, Alf called out to the crew and the ship veered off. The oars on the port side were raised and the longship slid close. Plaited hemp rope fenders were dropped over the side to protect the strakes and Mantat tossed a line to Runolf, who caught it effortlessly. Coiling the rope about one of the thick stone bollards on the wall, Runolf brought the vessel to a halt. At the stern, Gwawrddur took another line and secured it. The tide was not full, so we would need to clamber down to the ship, but the drop was not too far.

At a glance I saw that my initial fears about the ship and its crew had been unfounded. There was Gersine, Beorn, Eadstan and the others. I noticed Arcenbryht staring up at us, his eyes scanning the faces of those who had returned. He met my gaze and held it.

"Cumbra?" he said.

I did not wish to be the one to impart such dire tidings. I wanted to turn away, to help Revna and Hereward, who had started to pass down our meagre provisions into the ship. But I did not move. I owed it to Cumbra and to Arcenbryht. They had been friends for a long while and I alone had been with Cumbra at the end.

I gave a shake of the head. Arcenbryht's expression shifted, sagging under the weight of sudden loss. Feeling terrible to be the bearer of these bad tidings, I turned, meaning to pick up Drosten's discarded gear, but I saw that one of the beggars who had been huddled in a pool of shade now held the Pict's waterskin, clothes and scabbarded sword in his grimy hands. The pauper was swathed in threadbare rags that may once have been black, but were now the hue of the distant sandy mountains. His head was wrapped in a tattered scarf. The man's wrinkled face was nut brown, his dark beard thick and streaked with silver.

"That is not yours," I snapped at the beggar, stepping close and placing my hand menacingly on my sword pommel. I was tired and irritable and pleased to be reunited with my friends. I had no time for this vagabond.

"I meant no harm, master," the old man crooned, bowing and scraping, holding the items out to me.

"Begone," I said, snatching them away from him.

"You would turn me away without offering a scrap of food?"

"I have nothing for you." There was surely food aboard *Brymsteda*, but there was something in the man's demeanour that riled me.

"No alms to help alleviate my suffering?" he moaned, his tone pathetic.

"No," I snarled, turning away from him. "On your way."

"And I thought you were a man of Christ," the beggar said, halting me in my stride. "Is it not true you were once a monk?"

"How do you know this?" I growled, turning back to face the beggar. He cowered, keeping his eyes averted. I took a step forward. "Tell me, or I will beat the truth out of you."

"That is no way to greet an old friend," he said, looking up at me with a wide smile that showed strong white teeth. I recognised that grin at once, and the man's amused, yet emotionless eyes.

I let out a surprised gasp.

"Giso!"

"Who else?" he replied with a mocking bow. "Now, will you offer me some food, or am I to beg on the streets of Kyrenia?"

Nine

Giso leaned back and laughed. His humour rankled and I glanced at Drosten, who just shrugged and shook his head. Runolf though appeared to have had enough. With a growl he rose and stalked along the deck towards the stern. We were anchored once more in the harbour, so there was no need to steer, but perhaps Runolf thought it better to grip the tiller than wrap his hands around Giso's throat.

"Very ingenious," Giso said, wiping tears of mirth from his eyes. He had removed his tattered garb and was now dressed in a simple robe he had produced from a sack he'd carried tied to his back. He had combed his hair and beard too, taking a moment to ask for a bucket of sea water to clean his face. With his tanned skin, black hair and beard, he looked like a local merchant, and I wondered why he had not shaved his cheeks as he usually did. He chuckled again.

His amusement stemmed from learning of Theokleia and Artemis, and how they had duped us and stolen the Spear.

"That you should be bested by women! I had not anticipated such a thing. Which I suppose makes me as much of a fool as you men. For is not the ruler of Roma Nova herself a woman?" He shook his head and reached for a cup of the wine Gersine and Nicetos had procured. It was sweet and smooth, and we had all welcomed its taste after the previous days of thirst and drinking water soured by the leather of our waterskins.

"You would do well not to underestimate women, Frank," said Revna, fingering the hilt of the sword that rested on the deck beside her. She also had washed and combed her hair, which was now pulled back from her suntanned face. The sun, blazing low above the horizon, caught the gold of her locks and the piercing blue of her eyes. She did not blink as she stared at Giso.

He held up his hands. I noticed his palms were callused and I wondered what he had been doing since we had last seen him in Frankia.

"Indeed you are right, fair Revna," he said. "I stand rebuked and I beg you to accept my apology. You have no need to stab me with that blade."

Revna said nothing, but held his gaze. As so often happened when she was angry, I recognised her father in her glowering stare.

"We have told you our tale, Giso," I said, hoping to divert the conversation away from threats and reproach. "Now tell us how you come to be here."

"How I travelled to this island is a long tale that can wait for another time." He sipped his wine and reached for a piece of flat bread. He dipped the edge of it in the stew Gamal had served up and ate a bite. "This is good," he said to Gamal, who remained stern-faced, rather than pleased with the strange Frank's compliment. "All that matters now," continued Giso, paying no further heed to Gamal, "is that I am here, with my old friends aboard the mighty *Brymsteda*."

"Friends, you say?" rumbled Runolf from the stern. "You are no friend of ours, little man."

Giso sighed. "That is harsh," he said, "and I am hurt you should think so. But we are all servants of the same master, are we not? Therefore we are at the very least allies."

Runolf grunted, but said nothing more.

"And," said Giso, "as we are allies and servants of Alhwin and King Carolus, we are all in the same predicament. It matters not who it was who lost the Spear, only that it was lost."

Hereward drained his cup of wine and set it aside. The set of his jaw gave away his simmering rage. "It is as you say," he said, "the object of our search is lost. There is nothing left for us here but danger and..." he wiped his hand across his sweat-dewed brow "...more of this accursed heat. The time has come to go home."

"There is nothing for me in my homeland," said Drosten, watching Hereward carefully.

"And I feel," added Gwawrddur, "that there is more to see of the world, heat and all, before we head homeward. Would you really have us return empty-handed?"

"Better with empty hands than dead," snapped Hereward. "We could yet buy some of that famous purple dye. Nicetos says they make it from sea snails. That would fetch a good price in Britain and Frankia, I'd wager. We would not be poor."

"But would we be rich?" said Runolf, striding back from where he had listened by the steerboard. "I did not bring us all the way across middle earth for us not to return as wealthy men." He glanced at Revna. "And one wealthy woman. Alhwin promised us silver if we brought him the Spear. We know who has the relic. Those treacherous bitches are only a day or two ahead of us. I say we ask in the port and find what ship they took and where they were bound. With my hand on the steerboard and Nicetos to guide us, *Brymsteda* can catch any of these Greek tubs." He swept his arm about him to encompass all the vessels moored and anchored in the harbour.

Nicetos remained silent, but when Runolf looked to him for confirmation of his boast, he nodded in agreement. Nicetos was the shortest member of the crew, barely reaching Runolf's chest. His arms and legs gave the impression of being too long for his squat body and he walked with a rolling gait, even when on dry land. His hair was black, his skin the hue of the ship's timbers, and there seemed to be no part of the Middle Sea he did not know intimately. Runolf and Nicetos were as dissimilar as any two men could be, and yet they had formed a close bond on our voyage, united by their love of the sea and their boundless knowledge of the craft of sailing. I am not proud of it, but I was somewhat jealous of their closeness, for where Runolf would once have spent time explaining the intricacies of the running of the ship to me, now he was more likely to be found discussing the tides, currents and winds with Nicetos.

Giso clapped slowly in response to Runolf's words; his expression one of sincere, sombre understanding.

"I hear you all," he said. "Each of you make good points, but alas none of them is of consequence." He held up his hand to calm the protests at his words. "It matters not what each of you wishes for. I bring fresh orders from Alhwin."

"How could you have heard from Alhwin?" I asked. "*Brymsteda* is as fast as any ship. No message from Frankia could have beaten us here."

Giso smiled. "My dear Hunlaf. You would surely be speaking the truth of the matter if the message had followed in your wake across the sea. However, there are other ways to bear a missive." He waved his hand airily. "But none of that is important. What is, my angry friends, is that I have orders for us."

"Orders or no orders," said Hereward, "why should we follow you or Alhwin further? All the paths he has set us on have led to death."

Giso raised his eyebrows. "Have you not been rewarded well, brave Hereward? Did not Alhwin fill your sea chests with treasure? Has not Alhwin been generous? Did he not provide you with silver and provisions for this expedition without knowing whether you would succeed or not? And," he said with a frown of feigned perplexity, "since when are the Heroes of Werceworthe frightened of danger and the risk of death? It seems to me that your brothers wish to continue in the employ of the Teacher and to further the cause of my king, Carolus. Is that not so?" He swept his gaze across the ship, taking each of us in. None of us answered, not wishing to side with Giso over Hereward, even if the mysterious envoy was correct in this.

"It would be sad indeed," Giso continued, as if he had not expected an answer to his question, "for the fellowship to be sundered here, so far from your homeland. It would be a long and arduous journey back from Kýpros. Especially for one alone who cannot speak the tongues of the Romans." He paused, holding his hands palm up as if in apology, though his eyes showed no remorse. Hereward glared at him.

"Before you make any rash decisions," Giso said, "perhaps I should tell you of Alhwin's orders."

Hereward grunted.

"Speak, little man," Runolf said.

"We are to travel to a place where we might find many more relics. A land…" he looked me in the eye as he spoke "…where we can tread in the very footsteps of Christ Himself."

I drew in a sharp breath, knowing this could mean only one thing.

"We are commanded to travel to the heart of the Holy Land," Giso said. "We are to go to Ierusalem."

"What is it that Alhwin wants of us in Ierusalem?" I asked, my mouth dry. Even as I said the words I knew the answer was not important to me. To touch the Spear of Longinus had filled me with a holy fervour. I had been blessed to have held such a sacred relic. But now, with the prospect of travelling to the Holy Land, all I could think of was that soon I would be able to walk on the Mount of Olives, to tread upon the hill of Calvary where the Son of God was crucified. I would be able to kneel and pray before the altar of the church of the Holy Sepulchre. The loss of the Spear was terrible and I had wanted nothing more than to recover it and to avenge Cumbra's death. But now, with the suddenness of a shutter being thrown open to let sunlight into a darkened room, I knew that nothing could be more important to me than to visit the Holy Land. And I understood with certainty that no matter what Hereward decided, I would follow Giso on whatever quest Alhwin wished to send us on.

"One of King Carolus' most trusted envoys, a Iudeisc man by the name of Isaac, has been at the court of the Caliph Harun Al-Rashid in Madīnat as-Salām. Word has reached us that he has set out on the long journey back towards Frankia and he brings with him an emissary from the caliph. As you know, King Carolus has many foes and he does not wish to make an enemy of Harun Al-Rashid. The trade from the caliphate will fill the coffers to pay for Carolus' wars. It is of the utmost importance that Isaac and the emissary, Abul-Abbas, reach Frankia safely."

Runolf scratched at his thick thatch of beard. "Does Alhwin have no other servants who could accompany this Iudeisc and the emissary of the caliph?"

Giso chuckled.

"The Teacher is powerful and he has friends all over the world," he said, "but even his reach has limits. We are close to what used to be called Palaestina Prima, with a ship full of strong warriors. We are perfectly situated to carry out this task. And do not worry about your reward, Runolf Ragnarsson. Alhwin has given me permission to offer you double what he planned to pay for the Spear."

"Double?" asked Runolf, licking his lips.

Giso smiled and nodded, knowing he had snared the Norseman with his greed. And also understanding that what Runolf decided would dictate where *Brymsteda* went. And where the wave-steed travelled, the crew would certainly travel too.

Runolf turned to Hereward.

"What say you?" he asked. "Ready to risk your life for silver once more?"

Hereward bit his lip. After several heartbeats, he nodded, then stomped angrily to the prow where he leaned over the side and peered into the dark waters of the harbour. His anger was clear, but whether it was aimed at those who he felt had manipulated him, or at himself for so readily changing his stance, I could not tell.

I felt no ire. Gone was my annoyance at Giso and his smirking smugness. His bearing was sure to rankle me soon enough, once we set sail and I was forced to share the confines of the ship with him. But for now, my heart soared with a new excitement.

For we were going to Ierusalem.

Ten

Runolf picked up a stone from the beach and threw it out into the surf.

"Where has that worm gone?" he said. "I should not have allowed him to seduce me with his talk of more silver."

"No doubt he was lying," said Hereward, waving to the group of boys who stood some way along the sand. The youths were tending to three camels, the strange hump-backed beasts that seemed common in Yafah. I had heard of such creatures before in the Scriptures, but I had never laid eyes upon them and I found my gaze drawn to them, just as it was to the tall fronded date palms, the whitewashed walls of the houses, and the tower atop the hill.

This was Palaestina, the Holy Land!

Here, in Yafah, was where Peter had the vision telling him that the teachings of Jesus were not for the Iudeisc alone, but also for gentiles like me. One of the local fishermen mending his nets on the harbour wall told me he knew the exact location of Simon the Tanner's house, on the roof of which Peter had been praying when he heard the voice of God. The house, the man said, was just up that steep rise, overlooking the great expanse of the flat sea. I vowed I would see it before we left the town.

The boys with the camels watched us as intently as I stared about me, and I marvelled that for those who had been born here, *Brymsteda* and its crew of foreigners held more interest than places that Jesus and his apostles would have seen with their own eyes, walked upon or even touched. Still, I could understand that certain of our number would draw their attention. Drosten with his whorls of tattoos was strange indeed, as was Runolf, towering over the rest of us, with his flame-red hair. And of course, there was Revna, with her long golden hair. She was a beauty, no doubt, but I had not anticipated that her pale skin and lustrous hair would mark her out so distinctively. However, the further from her homeland we travelled, so Revna drew an increasing number of admiring glances. It made me nervous, but she did not seem to mind the lingering looks.

Gersine, Hereward, Gwawrddur, me and the rest of the crew were less exciting, causing more interest for the weapons we carried than for any especially imposing or attractive traits.

"If that weasel lied to me," said Runolf, "he will regret it." He flung another pebble far out to sea where it vanished with scarcely a splash.

Hereward did not comment, but his scowl made his feelings clear. He had agreed to join us, following Giso to the Holy Land, but he did not like it.

Before we had set sail from Kyrenia, Giso had questioned Nicetos about the distance to Ierusalem.

"We can be in the port of Yafah in four days," he'd said, after a moment's thought.

Giso had clapped his hands at that. "From there, it is only a two-day journey to Ierusalem."

That we would be able to reach our destination in under a week had gone a long way to swaying Hereward's opinion. That Giso had vanished as soon as we had moored at Yafah had darkened his mood and done nothing to alleviate his suspicion of the Frank.

"He'll be back soon," I said. "I am sure of it."

To my surprise, both men chuckled at that.

"What?" I asked, sensing I was the object of a jest.

Runolf shook his head and slapped me on the shoulder. "Hunlaf," he said, "Giso could piss in your ale and shit in your pottage and you would yet forgive the man."

"He's right," Hereward said. "You haven't ceased grinning since we first spied the walls of Yafah. You care nought for what Giso promised us, you are just happy to be in the Holy Land."

I bit my lip, embarrassed. "I suppose it is true," I admitted. "But can't you feel the power of the place? Look about us. The Son of God walked in this land, felt the same warm wind on his face, smelt the same—"

"Camel dung?" jibed Runolf. "I care nothing for your god, Hunlaf. But I do care about silver."

I frowned. He was goading me. He knew I hated it when he referred to Christ as 'my god', making a mockery of his own baptism. But I refused to allow myself to be drawn into an argument.

Taking a deep breath, I noticed for the first time that the breeze blowing down the beach was indeed tainted with the stench of manure. I scooped up a pebble from the sand and threw it out into the breaking waves. I rolled my left shoulder, testing it. There was still a ghost of pain there, but I had exercised it daily under Gwawrddur's expert supervision on the four-day voyage from Kyrenia and it was almost fully healed.

"You will get your silver, Runolf," I said. "Giso's ways are strange, it is true, but I am sure he will return soon and set us on our course once more. Why else bring us here only to abandon us? We are to go to Ierusalem and meet this Isaac and the caliph's envoy there."

"I pray you are right to place your faith in the Frank," said Hereward. "But the man lies as easily as others breathe. Who is to say he did not lie to us about the command from Alhwin and merely used us to transport him here?"

"Nonsense," I said, but a sliver of doubt scratched at my mind. Could Hereward be right? I dismissed the thought, pushing it away, turning my attention back to the boys with the camels.

Hereward was beckoning to them now, and one of their number, evidently braver than the others, was approaching. He was a lanky youth who looked as if he had been wrapped in discarded rags. Spindly legs jutted from a tattered tunic, his bare feet leaving perfect prints in the damp sand. His head was crowned with a scarf and his teeth were surprisingly white in his sun-baked face, as he offered us a broad smile.

"Peace be upon you," he said in Al-Arabiyyah, touching first his chest then forehead and bowing.

I returned his greeting with a smile of my own, amused at his formality. His eyes flicked to Drosten. The Pict was accustomed to the attention his tattoos brought. He disliked it when men stared or asked to see the paintings on his skin more closely, but he never seemed to tire of children, understanding and accepting their curiosity graciously. Drosten fixed the boy with a stare, then – without warning – he gave a growl like a wolf, holding up his hands as if they were claws and making a lunge in the boy's direction. The boy let out a shriek and staggered backwards. He would have fallen if Runolf had not caught him and set him upright.

"Drosten!" Revna admonished. "You are frightening enough without pretending to be a monster."

Drosten laughed. "I meant nothing by it," he said.

"The painted one is not as scary as his ugliness would make you believe," I said to the boy. He laughed.

"If he was as frightening as he is ugly," the boy said, "I would surely be dead. Where is he from? There are tales of blue-faced *jinn* in the desert."

"What is he saying?" asked Drosten.

"He wonders if you are a *jinni*, a devil."

Drosten repeated his earlier growl, but this time softly, with a twinkle in his eye. "Tell him I am just a man, but a thirsty one."

"Aye, my mouth is dry too," said Hereward. "Ask the lad if there is anyone up there who can give us a drink." He pointed to the cluster of tents that dotted the hill beyond the strand.

The boy waited for me to interpret Hereward's words. He smiled sheepishly, his eyes flicking from Drosten, to linger on Revna. She had brushed and braided her long hair and the golden rope of it draped down the length of her back.

"The *Badw* have water," he answered absently. "They will give you *marmaraya* tea, and even milk for a price."

We had gone some way from *Brymsteda*, wishing to walk on solid ground again after the days of sailing. We could yet see Yafah to the south, but it would take us some time to get back and the afternoon was hot indeed. The breeze was deceptive, cooling our skin, but a drink would do us all good.

"Lead the way then," I said, taking hold of the boy's shoulders, turning him around and pushing him back towards his friends, the camels and the tents beyond.

The other boys called out to him as we drew close, whistling and chattering. They stared open-mouthed at Drosten, with the tattooed patterns on his face, Runolf, with his fiery hair and beard, and at Revna, with her blue eyes, golden hair and freckled cheeks.

The first boy ignored the others and shouted a command at the nearest camel, cajoling and pulling on its bridle until it was kneeling on the sand.

"Would the lady care to ride?" he asked, touching his chest and bowing low before Revna.

"She'll walk," I replied gruffly without translating his words, jealousy making my tone sharp.

Revna had her own mind though. I suppose she might have understood his words, or perhaps the meaning was clear enough. Whatever the case, Revna pushed past me and, thanking the boy in his native tongue, she allowed him to take her hand and help her up onto the saddle on the camel's single hump.

With another command and a tug of its lead rope, the camel rose up. Revna swayed precariously as the beast stood, but she laughed all the while, the sound musical and lovely.

The boy proudly led the camel with its passenger up the beach towards the scattered tents. The other boys fell into step with them, each leading an animal. We trudged along behind them. I watched Revna's braid swish across her back as she rode.

The tents were pitched on a slight rise, and as we climbed the slope leaving the beach behind, a large herd of sheep and goats came into view. Amongst the tents several other camels and a few donkeys were tethered.

Before we reached the settlement, several figures stepped out from the shade of one of the larger tents and sauntered out to greet us. Even though their dark robes covered their bodies and heads, I could see from their swaggering walk that they were all young men, straight-backed and proud. They wore silver-decorated daggers on their belts and a couple of them bore curved swords in finely tooled scabbards.

The leader of the group was one of those who carried a sword, and when he was still a dozen paces from us, he halted, placing one hand on his hip, the other on the hilt of his blade.

"What is the meaning of this?" he snapped at the boy who had spoken to us. "Who gave you the right to offer my camel to a stranger?"

The other men fanned out behind him, staring at us with a mixture of curiosity and open dislike.

"I am sorry, Bachir," stammered the boy, pulling the camel to a halt.

"You *will* be sorry," snarled Bachir, taking a step forward.

Not liking the newcomer's demeanour, I moved to intercept him.

"Easy, Hunlaf," said Gersine, taking hold of my arm. "Best we don't get involved."

Barking a command at the camel, the terrified boy tugged the rope and the beast knelt once more, laboriously shifting its weight and forcing its rider to cling on or risk being thrown to the sand.

Seemingly only then seeing clearly the camel's passenger, Bachir sprang forward and offered his tanned hand to Revna. After the briefest of hesitations, she took it, and climbed down from the camel. Silent now, the boy lowered his gaze and did not look at either of them.

"What have we here?" said Bachir, hungrily taking in Revna's gleaming hair and fine features. I had seen several of the local women and their faces and heads were covered by thick veils. The sight of Revna's hair appeared to have bewitched the young man. Still holding her hand, he bowed deeply. "Peace be upon you. I am Bachir, son of Shaikh Rabab ibn Umari. What is your name?"

Revna turned to me. "Hunlaf," she said, "please tell me what he is saying."

I did not like the look of this Bachir, nor the way that Revna's eyes had widened as he took her hand in his. For a moment longer I held my tongue, then – realising how petty my silence would make me look – I translated Bachir's words.

"My name is Revna Runolfsdottir," she said, touching her left hand to her chest. "Peace be upon you," she continued in faulting Al-Arabiyyah.

Bachir beamed. "And from what realm do you hail? You must be a princess," he said. "Are these men your slaves?"

I did not wish to act as interpreter for the young man, but I could see no way to avoid it. Revna laughed as I translated Bachir's words.

"These are my friends," she said. "And this is my father, Runolf Ragnarsson."

At the mention of her father, Bachir took in Runolf's great size, the broad expanse of his shoulders and chest, and the great axe he carried lightly over his shoulder. Runolf glared at him. Bachir let go of Revna's hand, momentarily flustered.

"Peace be upon you," he said with a bow, quickly regaining his composure.

Runolf grunted in return.

Unperturbed, Bachir addressed the red-headed giant.

"Is your daughter spoken for?" he asked.

Runolf glanced at me. Sighing, I interpreted.

"She is not," Runolf rumbled.

Bachir's face lit up. "Then may I offer you five camels and twenty sheep?"

I could barely believe what I was hearing.

"What does he say?" asked Runolf. I was unsure of the Norseman's reaction to Bachir's offer. And if I am being truly honest, part of me hoped that Runolf would beat the man senseless for such an affront. I looked from Bachir to the other young men and wondered if the sand might soon be stained with blood.

"Well?" Runolf said. I could see no way out of translating Bachir's words, so spoke them in a quiet, clipped tone. To my surprise, Runolf leaned back and laughed.

"Tell him my daughter is not for sale, but if she were, I would demand more camels than Bachir could ever hope to own."

I translated Runolf's words, smiling to see Bachir's face darken at the insult.

"I am the son of the shaikh of this tribe," Bachir spat. "Tell that fat-headed kafir that if I wanted, I could take his daughter and leave his bones to be picked over by the jackals and vultures of the desert."

"Careful how you go now," said Gwawrddur. He comprehended more of Al-Arabiyyah than the others, having picked it up with ease in al-Andalus. I wasn't sure how much he had understood of Bachir's words, but evidently enough to know that to translate them would be bad.

Despite my previous desire to see Bachir taught a lesson, a chill ran through me.

"You do not wish me to speak those words to Runolf," I warned. "The moment I utter them, he will kill you."

Bachir looked at the men who stood behind him, then turned back to Runolf. He took in his bear-like size, the scars on his face and arms, the massive axe he carried. I saw fear in his eyes then, but a stubborn arrogance too. He dared not lose face in front of his men.

"Say my words," he said, his voice sharp and brittle as glass. "And we shall see who does the killing here."

"I don't like the sound of this," said Gwawrddur, stepping up close beside me and Gersine. "The man is a fool if he wishes to cross Runolf."

"No doubt he is a fool," I said in a hushed voice. "For that is what he seeks."

"Revna," growled Runolf. "Step away from that greasy cockscomb. I wouldn't like to splash you with his blood."

Revna made to back away. Bachir might not have understood Runolf's words, but his tone was clear. Lashing out, he grasped Revna's wrist. I tensed, dropping my hand to the hilt of my sword.

But before anyone could react, without hesitation, Revna drew the seax she wore on her belt. Without appearing to move, she pressed the blade to Bachir's groin.

"Tell him to release me," she hissed, "or whatever sorry woman he does buy in the future will have him without his manhood."

Nobody moved as I translated. For several heartbeats, Bachir glowered at Revna. Perhaps he did not believe she would use the knife, but when she applied some added pressure, he seemed convinced of her serious intent. At last he let go of her arm.

Revna stepped back quickly to join us. All of the men with Bachir had their hands on their weapons now. A couple had drawn their daggers. Runolf had swung his axe down from his shoulder and now held it easily before him in both his meaty fists. The rest of us were as taut as bow strings, ready to unsheathe our blades and fight.

For what seemed a long while we stood like that, each group staring hard at the other, willing them to put up their weapons, but each refusing to be the first to show any weakness.

Then a voice cut through the tension. It came from the direction of the tents and the sound of it made Bachir and his followers start. Two men came from the camp. The taller of the two strode towards us. He was dressed in similar robes to the young men before us, and his head was also covered. He did not carry a sword, but he walked with a casual acceptance of his power that Bachir lacked and had tried to make up for with bluff, charm and barely controlled anger. A shorter man, also garbed in the dark robes of the tribesmen, head shrouded in a scarf, followed closely behind.

"Bachir," said the tall man, "is this how you welcome guests to our tent?"

"Father, I—" Bachir began to protest, but the older man cut him off.

"I do not wish to hear your excuses," he said, his tone brooking no dissent. "Go and tell your mother to prepare more food for our visitors."

Bachir glowered at the man, then at Runolf and finally at Revna.

"Do not make me repeat myself," said the tall man.

Without another word, Bachir turned and stalked away, his robes flapping about him. The other young men sheathed their knives and followed him, not meeting his gaze or that of his father.

The boys with the camels stood nervously to the side. The

boy we had spoken to did not look up, but fidgeted, stepping from one foot to the other.

"Don't remain there as if you need to relieve yourself, boy," said the tall man. "Take the camels and get them ready to travel."

"We are leaving?" the boy asked, his tone surprised.

The man sighed. "Do as I say and you will learn what is happening when the time is right for you to know."

Without another word, the boys scampered off, the camels trailing behind them.

"I apologise for my son," said the tall man. "He has never wanted for anything. My success has made him weak and now he seeks to prove his strength in foolish ways."

I translated his words for the others.

Runolf nodded. "It is every father's bane to feel the weight of his offspring's foolishness," he said. "Just as it is his joy to revel in their every success."

The man listened patiently as I interpreted, then smiled, his teeth showing in his thick grey-streaked beard.

"My name is Rabab ibn Umari," he said, touching his chest. "Peace be upon you."

"And upon you," I replied automatically.

"Welcome to my camp. I have already heard some tales of your band, but I had hoped to meet you and to hear more of your travels before you left Yafah. You will stay to eat?"

His words confused me. I was not certain I had understood them correctly as I translated for my friends.

"What does he know of us?" asked Hereward.

Before I could translate, the short man who had come with Rabab stepped out from behind him.

"Only what I have told him," he said in Englisc. "Which is more than enough, but the *Badw* tribesmen are always so thirsty for tales." I recognised the voice then and peered at the features partially hidden in the shadows beneath the scarf that was tightly wound around his head. I knew that face.

Hereward clearly recognised him too.

"Good of you to show yourself, Giso," he said, scowling.

Giso acted as if he had not heard him.

"But what the *Badw* take," he continued, "they repay tenfold. For if they love one thing more than hearing stories, it is telling them. I have learnt much from Rabab here, and he is a most generous host."

"I had thought perhaps you had abandoned us," said Hereward.

"Why would I do such a thing," Giso said, "when I still have use for you?" He glanced at the backs of Bachir and the other young men. "Perhaps I need to keep a closer eye on you, for you seem to find trouble wherever you go. Now, let's not keep our host waiting. He is generous, but not the most patient of men. His son has inherited his impetuous nature from his father, no doubt, and I imagine Rabab had his share of fights as a young man."

I looked at the tall *Badawi* leader. There was a pale scar running from his forehead to his chin. His eyes flicked from one of us to the other, missing nothing. He had remained silent while we spoke, but I detected a tension behind his dark eyes. This was not a man accustomed to being ignored. I bowed low.

"Apologies, Shaikh Rabab," I said. "We were surprised to see our friend here with you. We would be delighted to accept your hospitality."

"Good, good," Rabab said. "You can tell me what you have seen of the world, for I hear from Shabah here that you have travelled far."

"Shabah?" I whispered to Giso, raising an eyebrow.

"It translates to 'ghost'. It is the name by which the *Badw* tribes know me," he said with a shrug. "But that is of no importance. The women of the tribe are roasting mutton and I am hungry. You may have spent the afternoon wandering along the beach and picking fights, but some of us have been busy."

Eleven

Giso had been busy indeed. After we reached the camp and were settled in the largest of the tents, we heard what had occupied his time since disappearing from *Brymsteda*.

"I have purchased donkeys for the journey to Ierusalem," he whispered to me as we were ushered to sit on cushions and mats within the shade of the tent. "Rabab likes me and has offered me a good price. All we need to do is to tell him tales and eat and drink with him. The women of the tribe are good cooks, so that will be no hardship. I have learnt more of interest, but that will have to wait till later, for I can see our host grows restless at our chatter."

I wondered what else he had discovered, but saw from Rabab's hooded expression that Giso was right. I relayed the information about the purchase of the mounts to the others, then turned my attention fully to the tribal leader.

The tent's walls were made of thick, woven goat hair and kept out the sun's rays. One side of the dwelling was open and faced a large area surrounded by the tribe's homes. The shade inside the tent was welcome after the heat of the afternoon. Flies buzzed lazily around the central pole. Dogs lay in the dusty shade between the tents where ropes criss-crossed. In the middle of the area encircled by the tents, a cooking fire smouldered and smoked. Women, dark-robed and covered so entirely that only their eyes and hands could be seen, busied themselves preparing food. The smells of cooking made me realise how hungry I was.

While we waited for the food to be served, some of the women brought a hot drink that they served to us in small silver beakers. Infused from the leaves of a desert plant they called *marmaraya*, it was bitter, but refreshing.

One of the women also brought a long plain headscarf. Without a word, she covered Revna's golden hair, tying the scarf expertly about her head. She did not add the full veil, so Revna's pretty face was still visible.

"They are not used to such fair hair," Giso said. "Best to cover your head to avoid more trouble."

Revna's discomfort was evident, but she smiled at the woman and did not complain.

We sipped the hot *marmaraya* tea and answered Rabab's many questions. Where did we come from? What brought us to these lands? What meat was most prized in our homelands? How did our people live? What tidings of the men of al-Andalus? What news of the Romans of Byzantion?

Other men came to the tent, and sat cross-legged, drinking *marmaraya* and listening to our replies intently. It was tiring for me, as I found myself in the role of interpreter, and I soon learnt there were certain topics Giso did not wish me to speak about. When asked who we served, he interrupted me, answering smoothly that our master lived in a far-off land to the west, but he mentioned no name.

Rabab was as intrigued by Drosten's tattoos as the boy we had spoken to on the beach had been. He asked about their significance and Drosten told him of the Pictish people and how their warriors marked their skin. Rabab was too polite to ask him to remove his robes, but I could tell he would have liked to see how much of the man's body was covered with the painted lines.

When the food arrived, it was sumptuous, rich and

flavoursome. The sun had dropped into the sea and darkness was beginning to shroud the land, but it was worth the wait. There was spicy meat and vegetables that had been roasted slowly in a hole in the sand. Alongside this, a bowl of a wonderful stewed lamb was brought in. It bubbled and glistened and was garnished with a sauce of fermented curds and pine nuts. All of this was served with thick flat loaves of bread that I discovered had also been baked in an underground oven.

A grizzled old man with a thick flowing beard of white produced a gourd flask and poured us all a drink from it into small earthenware cups. It was a potent, sweet brew called *Nabidh*, and was made from the fermentation of dates. It burnt the throat somewhat, but as with the *marmaraya*, it was not unpleasant.

After darkness had fallen and the sheep had been penned for the night, their bleating reaching us over the chatter and the distant murmur of the surf, the young men – led by Bachir – made their way into the tent in search of food and drink. At the sight of his son, Rabab held up a hand, halting him.

"Before you sit and eat, you will apologise to our guests," he said.

Bachir glowered at us for a few heartbeats, then through tight lips he muttered words of pardon.

Runolf, relaxed by the food and drink, nodded. "Tell him there is nothing to forgive," he said. "I was young once too."

His reply made Rabab grin and the old men bob their heads. Bachir seemed less impressed with the response, but he nodded curtly and settled himself in a corner of the tent with his friends, where they finished off what food remained on the platters and trays.

The feasting and conversation went on for a long time. When at last we rose and stepped out into the night, the new moon was high in the sky, almost invisible save for a cool ring of silver.

"We thank you again for the generosity of your tent," Giso said to Rabab.

"And I thank you for your tidings, and your silver," said Rabab with a chuckle. "Those animals are strong and will serve you well. Should you return here before we are on our way again, I would be happy to take them back."

Without warning, first one, then another of the dogs began to growl and bark. By the flickering light of a torch and the glow of the stars I saw they were all staring into the darkness, hackles raised, bodies stiff and tails up.

Rabab called for Bachir and sent him and the other young men out into the dark. Each of them carried a burning brand and I could see the lights bobbing out there on the edge of the sandy land that sloped away to the east.

We stood still for a time, listening to the night. The dogs slowly calmed down, sensing that the threat to the livestock was gone.

"Lions," said Rabab, his expression sombre.

"Lions?" I said, wondering if the creatures were as fierce as they were described in the Scriptures.

"Dangerous for the sheep," he said. "But they are scared of fire. They will seek easier prey than my animals now."

It seemed he was right. The dogs were silent again and one by one they stretched out in the dust and slept.

"Easier prey?" I asked, my fear embarrassingly clear in my voice.

"A solitary child, or young animal," he replied, smiling. "You carry sharp steel and would fight. You are no easy prey, Hunlaf."

Rabab did not call back his son and the other men, and I was not sorry to be leaving without seeing Bachir again. We each thanked Rabab before we set out along the beach. Even Hereward, mood lightened by the *Nabidh*, grinned at the old *Badawi* and had me say to him that if he should ever travel to Northumbria, he would see that he was treated like a king.

"Can a camel walk to Northumbria?" asked Rabab with a wink.

Hereward laughed. "Alas no," he said, "unless the beasts can swim further than any fish."

"Ah, then I think I will not see you there," replied Rabab. "This is as close to the ocean as I go. I am born of the desert and have no desire to leave it for the rain and cold of your land, even if the people are as warm-hearted as you."

We trudged back along the beach, the stars gleaming on the waves that whispered in from the dark sea. The night breeze cooled our faces. Our stomachs were full and I was not the only one of us who was light-headed after drinking too much of the *Nabidh*. Gersine, Gwawrddur and Revna led the animals that Giso had bought.

"You said you had learnt more from Rabab," I said, remembering Giso's whispered words to me in the tent.

"Indeed I did," he replied. His eyes glimmered in the starlight. "Theokleia is here."

"In Yafah?" I asked, my voice loud with surprise.

"She was," he replied. "At least I believe so. Two women matching the description you gave of this Theokleia and Artemis arrived here by ship two days before us."

"But why would they come here?" I said. "They have the Spear. I thought they would take it to Byzantion and Eirene."

"I too believed they would head back to Constantinopolis with their prize," Giso said, "but it seems this Theokleia has the scent of the same quarry as us."

"Isaac and Abul-Abbas?" Hereward asked. "What interest would that whore have in a Iudeisc envoy and an emissary from the Caliph of Madīnat as-Salām?"

Giso's teeth glinted in the gloom as he grinned. "Ah," he said, "did you truly think that was all that brought us to the Holy Land? I thought you knew me better than that, Hereward."

Hereward growled in the darkness. "I know you are a

weasel and a liar," he said. "Tell us the truth of it then. Why did you bring us here?"

Giso seemed not to notice Hereward's anger or his insults.

"I did not lie," he said. "We have truly been given instructions to meet Isaac and Abul-Abbas. But there is more that we seek here. A relic of such divine potency that its bearer will be invincible. It is spoken of along with such artefacts as the Holy Prepuce, the flesh of Christ the babe Himself, but this is more powerful than any other relic."

My head swam, whether from the *Nabidh* or from Giso's sudden talk of relics, I was not certain. My shoulder ached, a painful reminder of the last relic we had searched for and how we had lost it.

"What relic do you speak of?" I asked, my mouth dry.

"I am referring to the very Blood of Christ Himself," said Giso. "Soaked into a cloth by Maria Magdalena during his Passion upon the rood."

Twelve

Before the dawn, I watched Giso slip over the side of the ship and disappear into the shadowed streets of Yafah. He was dressed, as ever, in simple attire, a plain leather bag slung over his shoulder. I was already wide awake, dressed and ready to travel, eager to set off. I was not the only one keen to be on our way it seemed, for the ship was bustling with life.

Nobody else appeared to have noticed Giso.

Intrigued, I jumped over *Brymsteda*'s side, hurrying after the mysterious Frank.

"Where are you going?" called Gersine, looking up from where he was packing clothes into a sack.

"I want to see the roof of Simon the Tanner's house," I called over my shoulder. "I'll be back before you're ready to leave." I had told him before of my desire to see the house mentioned in the Scriptures. Gersine did not share my interest. He nodded and went back to his packing.

I hurried after Giso, but when I reached the end of the street he had taken, there was no sign of him. Listening, I heard nothing to suggest which direction he had taken. Choosing between the two available paths, I set off on the one that sloped upwards.

A cat eyed me suspiciously from the top of a crumbling wall, but there was no movement when I reached another junction. I carried on up the hill, winding through the alleys and narrow lanes, but I saw nothing of Giso.

Even though the dawn was still some way off, it was warm, heat seeping from the stones of the buildings. Sweat prickled my forehead and I swiped at it as I looked about me for a clue as to where Giso might have gone. There was nothing.

A dog barked, and faintly I heard the men down at the harbour calling to one another. A donkey brayed, its cry strident in the quiet of the pre-dawn gloom. From time to time I had passed middens, their acrid stench hitting my throat like an assault. Here, another altogether more pleasant smell filled the air. A door opened nearby and a man stepped out, a warm glow illuminating him from behind. The aroma of baking bread filled the street like a fog and I saw from the pale light that he carried a large tray piled high with loaves.

"Do you know the way to Simon the Tanner's house?" I asked him.

He paused momentarily, looking at me as if I were mad, or stupid.

"I know no Simon," he said, before scurrying away down the hill.

I stood motionless, lost and wondering. Slowly, I was coming to the conclusion that I would need to return to the harbour, when a sound startled me. Spinning around, I dropped my hand to the hilt of my sword.

"You'll not be needing that, Killer," Giso said. There were no doors or openings there and I could not see where he had come from.

"Don't call me that," I said.

He gave me a thin smile and inclined his head. "Looking for Simon the Tanner's house, are you?"

"I would see the roof before we leave," I said. "Pray there, if possible."

"I know the way," he said with a curt nod. "It is not far. Though I have to say, I cannot vouch for it being the same building where Peter fell asleep and had his dream. It is owned by a potter now, I believe. He says it is the same house, but I'm not so sure he is trustworthy."

Did I detect a smile in his voice? He knew that none of us trusted him, and it always seemed to amuse him. I watched his back as he led me up a steep alleyway. A grapevine grew thick along one wall, wide leaves draping over the top.

"Where have you been?" I asked, knowing that he would take a perverse pleasure in my interest, but unable to curb my curiosity.

"A simple errand," he said, that same smirking tone in his voice. "One that will benefit us all." When I did not ask for more information, he sniffed and continued. "I went to the house of the harbour master to see that *Brymsteda* would have permission to remain here in our absence."

"I take it you succeeded in your mission," I said. I wanted to ask more, but bit my tongue, refusing to give him that satisfaction.

"Indeed. The ship has permission to remain moored for the next fortnight."

"And if we take longer than that to return?" I asked.

"I don't foresee a problem," he said with a grin, as if at some secret jest. "I think the harbour master will be accommodating."

We had reached a small door set into the wall of a solidly built stone building. A twisted fig tree grew beside it. Without hesitation, Giso rapped upon the door. When there was no immediate response, he thumped on the dark timber again. We waited and I eyed him in the gloom. Giso stood perfectly still, head cocked to one side, apparently listening for signs of movement within. I heard nothing, but without warning Giso stiffened and stepped back. A moment later a bolt squealed and the door opened a crack.

A stocky man peered out. His hair was thinning, his cheeks plump, yet somehow sickly-looking, his beard grey-streaked and wispy.

"What do you want?" he said, his voice thick with sleep.

"My friend and I wish to see your roof," said Giso.

The man's demeanour instantly changed. Bowing, he forced a smile onto his fleshy features. "You wish to stand in the footsteps of Peter? Of course, of course." He did not move, or open the door more fully. Instead, he held out his hand. "The house of Simon the Tanner costs me much to keep up, what with so many Christ followers traipsing through it day and night."

Giso looked down at the man's sweaty outstretched palm as if it were an insect.

"It will be dawn soon," added the man, "when the view from the roof is best."

"Pay him," Giso said.

I rummaged in my pouch and found half a silver coin. I placed it in the man's sweaty palm and he dragged the door open wide, ushering us inside. A woman and three children stared at us from the shadows as the man showed us to a ladder leading up to the roof. I followed Giso up the rungs and out into the dawn light.

"Half a *denarius* is more than that rogue deserves," I said.

Giso shrugged. "He has mouths to feed. He just seeks to profit from what he has."

I looked about at the area on which we found ourselves. The roof was small, flat and covered in white and blue patterned tiles.

"You know," I said, stooping to touch the tiles, "I think you are right and this is not the house of Simon the Tanner. There are no tanning pits nearby and these tiles look new to me."

Giso made his way to the edge of the square roof and looked out over the vast expanse of the sea.

"What matter if it is or not?" he asked. "Even if Peter prayed upon a different roof in Yafah, this view will be the same as the one he witnessed. Does it matter if the tiles under our feet are the ones the apostle stood upon, if our faith is strong?"

From here we could see down into the harbour and the animals and men that gathered there. I fancied I saw a flash of gold from Revna's hair.

"Perhaps you are right," I said. "Still, now we are here, I would pray." I didn't like Giso, but felt indebted to him for leading me here. "Will you join me?"

Giso knelt beside me and seemed genuinely pleased that I had asked him. Quickly, I led us through the liturgy of Prime, easily recalling the words from my years in the minster at Werceworthe.

We hurried through the rite and I added a prayer for our journey and the search for the Blood of Christ.

When we had finished, we rushed back through the awakening streets of the town. At the harbour Runolf, Hereward, Gwawrddur, Drosten, Revna and the warriors from the ship were waiting impatiently by the laden pack animals. A good portion of the crew, those men who had once been fishermen or thralls, would remain aboard, once more under Alf's command.

"Where have you been?" snapped Hereward.

"To see that the harbour master would allow *Brymsteda* to remain moored here while we are gone," I said, "and to pray for our safe journey."

Hereward grunted. "We've been waiting," he said, clearly angry but finding little to justify his fury.

"Well, we are here now," I said, "so let us be on our way."

Thirteen

The sun rose over the dusty scrubland before us. The horizon was hazed by distance, but Giso had told me that hills rose there, and in those hills lay the jewel of the Holy Land, the place where Christ sacrificed himself for all mankind. The city where the son of God was entombed and from which he ascended unto Heaven.

Ierusalem.

"How long will it take us to reach the city?" I asked.

Giso shrugged and glanced back at the line of people and animals on the road. "At this pace, three days. We could perhaps make it in two, but the ground grows steeper and one day won't make a difference."

I thought of all that lay before us and of the revelation that we were in search of a new relic. I imagined Theokleia and Artemis hurrying ahead of us and thought a day could make a big difference. But Giso seemed quietly assured, so I accepted his words, praying that he was right and that my faith was not misplaced.

I followed his gaze, looking back towards Yafah and the sea beyond. The sun glinted on rippling waves and picked out the sails of several fishing craft and larger ships transporting goods across the Middle Sea and along the coast. *Brymsteda* was back there, moored at the harbour of Yafah.

We didn't have enough animals for us all to ride and as the morning wore on and the day grew hotter, it became evident we would not cover a great distance. Still, the road was straight and we had learnt our lesson on Kýpros so we now carried ample waterskins, despite both Giso and Rabab assuring us there were many settlements and farms on the way where we could replenish our water supplies.

Despite the heat and the constant swarm of flies that clouded around the pack animals, there was a lightness of spirit in our band. Hereward remained sombre and tight-lipped, but the rest of our party were in a more buoyant mood. Beorn, Eadstan and the other warriors who had joined us were all pleased to be free of *Brymsteda* and striding along the dusty road.

Gamal and Oslaf chatted and jested, while Ida, Pendrad and Sygbald were more subdued, looking about them with wide eyes. All of them were moved to be walking on the very land upon which so many of the tales from the Scriptures took place. They had all listened to such stories from priests since childhood and now found themselves to be in the lands they had once perhaps scarcely believed in.

Arcenbryht alone appeared unmoved by his surroundings. He morosely walked apart from the others, his eyes lowered and his face twisted into a scowl. Cumbra's death weighed heavily upon him and he had made it clear he did not wish to talk to any of us.

The sun was low in the sky, casting our long shadows before us, when we saw a collection of buildings ahead. Several fig trees grew nearby and the welcome smell of cooking wafted to us on the hot breeze. As we drew closer we noticed beyond the trees a group of men were constructing a makeshift shelter using sticks and strips of cloth. A couple of donkeys were hobbled nearby. Four women were tending a fire and had a couple of pots hanging from tripods over the flames.

Seeing our approach, about a dozen children, ranging in age from perhaps three to ten years old, came running up to greet us. They trotted along beside us asking questions, laughing and chattering incessantly. Drosten soon became the focus of their attention and he snarled at them, making them shriek. Such was the joy of these children that even Hereward could not maintain his serious frown. He smiled along with the rest of us as we followed our welcoming party into the camp.

But before we reached the trees and the fire, a tall man strode out from the largest house that stood off to one side. He shooed the children away with a growled command. They fled back to the fire and the women.

The man's face was pinched and lined from age and exposure to the sun. The wrinkles on his forehead and around his downturned mouth indicated he frowned much more than he smiled. Today was no exception, it seemed, for he scowled at us as he held up a hand in what might have been a welcoming gesture or an indication for us to halt our progress.

"I am Uthman," he said, his tone terse.

"Peace be upon you," Giso said with a bow. "This is your land?"

"And my father's before me," Uthman said. "It has been in my family for more generations than I can count."

"We are travelling to Ierusalem," Giso said. "We seek somewhere to rest for the night."

Uthman took in the large group of us: the armed men, the donkeys laden with provisions.

"There's no room for you in my house," he said, his voice gruff. "You can camp where those other families are setting up for the night. They're pilgrims too. There is water in the well."

Giso bowed again. Taking the man's hand, Giso produced a coin from his leather bag and slipped it into Uthman's palm.

"You are most kind," Giso said. "May God bless you and your kin."

Uthman's scowl grew more pronounced, but he nodded curtly, and went back into his house. A dark-robed woman stared at us silently from the doorway.

We made our way towards the fire near the trees. The children had congregated around the women, quiet and nervous now, perhaps frightened of Uthman, or chastised by their mothers.

The men had finished erecting their shelter and now walked towards us. One of their number, a wide-shouldered man with a black beard and soft eyes, bowed his head.

"My name is Musa," he said. He indicated the other men. "These are Nur ad-Din, Umar and Qasim. These are our families."

I introduced myself and my companions.

"Uthman told us we could rest here for the night," I added.

"You are welcome," said Musa. "Our women are preparing food. Will you join us?" There were sixteen of us and it was clear there would not be enough food for us all, but Musa smiled and his offer appeared sincere.

"We have our own food," I replied, "but we would be honoured to share it with you."

We set about preparing our own camp for the night. We had no tents or the means of building shelters, so would need to sleep under the stars. And yet there was still much to do before night fell. Beorn and Eadstan fetched some wood, though there was little to be had on the ground in the thin copse of trees.

Pendrad offered to fell a tree, but Runolf shook his head.

"The night will be warm and we will have little need for fire," he said. "Uthman has few enough trees without us chopping them down."

Using two sticks, Gwawrddur lifted a large ember from the women's cooking fire and used it to light our own. We had bought a couple of sheep from Rabab. The animals had walked with us all day. Now Oslaf and Gamal slaughtered one of the beasts and set about butchering its carcass as the other animal gazed on in bemused ignorance.

Ida and Sygbald took our skins to fill at the well. There were a lot of skins and they struggled to carry them all. Seeing

Arcenbryht sitting on a stone, absently staring at the playing children, Ida called out to him for his help.

As if awakening from a dream, Arcenbryht pushed himself up and, without a word, gathered up some of the half-empty waterskins.

Runolf, Hereward, Drosten and Giso sat with Musa and the other men. They sipped cups of drink that the women brought them and talked in hushed voices. I longed to know what they spoke of, but I did not shirk my duties, not least because I found myself, along with Gersine, helping Revna to tend to the pack animals. She had a natural way with animals, and they responded well to her soft voice and gentle touch.

We removed the baggage and the pack saddles, then, using handfuls of the dry grass that grew plentifully on the thin soil, we rubbed the animals' backs.

"Arcenbryht regrets leaving home, I think," said Revna, tugging a sack free from one of the donkey's backs.

"He would never have come without Cumbra," said Gersine. "He's always complaining that his wife is a shrew. Says he has never been happier than when on the march with other warriors."

"He thought he missed adventure," I said, dragging the fistful of rough, dry grass along one of the donkey's flanks. "I think what he really missed was his youth."

"He misses his wife now," said Revna, "and his children."

Gersine shook his head. "He misses Cumbra too. His last words to Cumbra were in anger, and he regrets that now. But it is too late for remorse."

"True," I said. "There is nobody but Cumbra to blame for his own actions. We each must live with our decisions."

"With luck," said Revna, "we will find this relic Giso spoke of and King Carolus will reward us well. At least then Arcenbryht will return to his wife with silver in his pouch."

Gersine grinned. "Yes, I imagine a woman might be less of a shrew if her hands are filled with silver."

"And what do you know of a woman's ways?" Revna asked, her face stern and unsmiling.

Gersine's cheeks reddened in the ruddy light of the setting sun. "I... I never meant..." he stammered.

Revna stared at him unsmiling for several heartbeats until eventually she could no longer hold her serious expression and she burst into laughter.

That evening was a relaxing time of companionship and new friendship. Musa told us that the families were not pilgrims as Uthman had said. The four men were in fact brothers and they were taking their families to a place called Bab al-Wadi in the hope that their father's brother, a rich landowner, would be able to give them work and a place to live. Until recently they had worked the land with their father, but when he had died not two months before, the owner of the land had sent them away, finding new tenants for his fields. They were clearly poor, carrying with them all they owned, which did not amount to much. I marvelled at Musa's smiling good nature.

"Allah will provide," he said.

"If your uncle does not," replied Giso snidely.

Musa laughed at that, slapping Nur ad-Din on the back in case he might have missed Giso's words. Nur ad-Din and the other brothers did not seem to find Giso as humorous as Musa did. From time to time I saw them scowling as they looked at their brother. They watched us with barely concealed suspicion. Perhaps they imagined we would take advantage of their women, for they had nothing worth stealing.

I imagined how they must feel, recently bereaved and driven from the home they had always known, and now, surrounded and outnumbered by rough-looking warriors from distant lands. Taking their situation into consideration, it was no surprise that they would be nervous of us.

Their wives, perhaps also fearful of us, barely spoke and

kept their eyes downcast. Despite their nervousness, they were happy to partake of the mutton Gamal and Oslaf roasted. The meat was dripping with fat and filled with flavour. And it was a joy to see the grinning faces of the children as they chewed on the greasy meat.

If the adults were understandably cautious of us, the children shared none of their fears. They ran about the camp, laughing and playing as the sun set, turning the western sky the hue of steel freshly lifted from a forge. We all enjoyed watching the youngsters cavort around the campsite, but none more than Arcenbryht. For the first time since he'd learnt of Cumbra's death, I saw him smile.

One of the boys, a bright-eyed scamp by the name of Yakub, was chasing one of his cousins when he tripped, sprawling and tumbling. Such was the speed with which he had been running he would have tumbled into the fire's embers if Arcenbryht had not jumped up and caught the lad.

He set Yakub, wide-eyed and tearful, back on his feet and sent him on his way to continue playing with his siblings and cousins.

Umar was Yakub's father. Seeing what had happened, he rose and went to Arcenbryht.

"I thank you," he said, bowing low.

I translated his words.

"It's no matter," Arcenbryht said, embarrassed at the attention and the man's formality. "He reminds me of my own boy."

After that, the men's demeanour softened and they talked more openly with us as darkness settled over the land. Bats flitted around the trees and I listened to the insects chirruping in the grass. Eventually, the women took the children into the shelter. For a long time, we listened to the sounds of the boys and girls whispering and giggling, until one of the women, exasperated, shouted at them to be quiet.

Arcenbryht and Umar exchanged a look of understanding,

and for a while longer we sat about the fire talking of all manner of things with these strangers with whom we had shared food. It was as pleasant an evening as I can recollect in my long life, and when I lay down to sleep, staring up at the brilliant stars sprayed across the sky above me, I was contented. My stomach was full and I was surrounded by old friends and new.

The aroma of the fire's smoke and the mutton grease was comforting, reminding me of my childhood home far away on the banks of the Tuidi. The sounds of the camp and the drone of the night insects enveloped me, pulling me down towards slumber. And, as I welcomed the soft embrace of sleep, I had no idea I would be awoken all too soon by the heart-rending sound of a child's screams.

Fourteen

I was not certain what had awoken me at first. I had been deep in sleep, walking the hidden pathways of my dreams. Then came a sound that at once brought me fully awake and yet seemed to send my mind reeling into the past, to a dense forest beside a river in Rygjafylki. But even as my eyes flew open and I leapt up from my blanket, I knew I could not be there, for that was long ago and far away.

That dreadful sound came again, rending the night. A growling roar, louder and more terrifying than any human throat could produce. I had imagined this might belong to a bear, like the giant beast that had torn Bealdwulf apart, but this roar was different: deeper, louder and – though such a thing seemed impossible – even more frightening.

All around me the camp was in turmoil. The fires had died down to glowing embers, and offered no real illumination. The sky was clear. The crescent moon and stars gave off but a thin light, and it was difficult to make out what was happening. I cast about me, hand gripping my sword tightly, even though I did not recall picking it up or unsheathing it. I tried to make sense of the chaos, to determine the source of the danger.

The women and children were screaming and crying, and I heard their men shouting. Another rumbling growl turned into an ear-ripping roar and the hairs on my neck prickled as terror washed over me.

"Spears!" shouted Gwawrddur. "Take up spears. Your swords will not serve you against a lion."

A lion!

The thought of it was nebulous in my mind. I had no real idea what such a creature could be like. But it roared again in the darkness and I saw a shadowy shape crouched on the edge of the camp.

A sudden blaze of flames made me blink. Instantly, light shone on the scene before me. In that moment, I wished I still dreamed, for this was worse than any nightmare. The women and children huddled together beneath the shelter in a fearful clump of weeping and screams.

Before them, Musa, Umar and the other men waved their arms and shouted, trying to frighten off the beast that had entered the camp in search of prey. Umar scooped up a stone and flung it at the animal. The projectile hit its side, but the creature did not flee.

Instead it lowered its great head, bared its finger-long teeth and roared again. The flamelight gleamed from its eyes and the sight of the lion almost made my legs buckle. It was huge, muscled and lithe, the hair about its head darker and thicker than on its body. Its paws were as large across as my hand with fingers outstretched, and its claws as long and sharp as knives.

Another stone hit the creature, this time striking its shoulder, just behind the shaggy mane. The lion growled, a deep rumbling warning, but the men did not retreat. I marvelled at their bravery to stand before such a beast, but I also wondered at the lion's courage. Why not run in the face of such resistance? Surely there was easier prey out there in the dark: sheep, cattle or donkeys.

Flames flared nearby and I saw it was Arcenbryht who had kindled some cloth wrapped around the tip of a spear. He must have dipped the material in oil, perhaps grease from the remains of the roasted sheep, for the linen sputtered and hissed, but the flames burnt bright.

Arcenbryht added his bellow of fury to that of the men standing before the lion and, as he advanced, so I understood not only the men's determination and the lion's steadfast refusal to retreat, but also Arcenbryht's anger.

Beneath the lion's dagger-like claws lay the still form of one of the children we had watched play as the sun set. Perhaps five or six summers old, Safiyyah had made us laugh with her cavorting and cheeky giggle. As the light from Arcenbryht's torch flickered on her motionless form, I saw this would be her last summer. Safiyyah's eyes were open and staring, the torchlight gleaming in the child's lifeless gaze.

Near the girl's corpse, almost close enough for the lion to swipe with its deadly claws, Yakub lay sprawled in the dust. He had his back to us, but he appeared to be unscathed. He lay transfixed with fear, unable to move.

"Arcenbryht, wait," shouted Hereward.

He had found a spear and was hurrying to join Arcenbryht. The rest of the warriors were following his lead, taking up spears and other weapons and rushing to form up around Hereward with Arcenbryht's burning spear as a beacon in the centre, drawing them together.

But Arcenbryht did not wait. With a roar almost as loud as the lion's he sped forward, holding the burning spear before him.

Hereward and the others were around me now and, even though I still held my sword in my hand and not a spear, I advanced with them. We moved with well-trained urgency, each step purposeful, our eyes intent on our enemy. But I saw in an instant we would never reach the lion in time to prevent it from slaying Yakub or Arcenbryht.

Snarling, the lion sprang, slashing with its claws, its teeth flashing in the flame flicker. Arcenbryht did not hesitate in his headlong rush. Grabbing Yakub by the collar, he flung the boy bodily behind him, out of the lion's reach. At the same moment his flaming spear struck the beast. There followed a frenzy of snarling, growling and spitting, while Arcenbryht thrust the spear hard, over and again.

A heartbeat later, as if it had never been, the lion spun about and vanished like a ghost into the darkness.

For a moment nobody moved, and then – in a torrent of movement – everybody ran forward. Umar rushed to Yakub, lifting him into his arms. Musa stumbled to Safiyyah's fragile form. He fell to his knees, his shoulders heaving as his body was racked with sobs. His wife was at his side a moment later and her wailing cries of grief filled the night as wholly as the roars of the lion had moments earlier.

Yakub's mother fussed over the boy, her face streaked with tears, her expression alternating between anguish and joy as she discovered her son to be whole and unhurt.

The other women clung to the children, trying in vain to soothe their fears and horror at what they had witnessed.

I scabbarded my sword and dropped down beside Arcenbryht. He was sitting on the earth, his head lowered. He was so still that I thought he might be dead. Then I noticed he was drawing in great gulps of air. His clothes were ripped and I saw a great gash on his left arm. His lips were moving. I leaned close to him, wondering what he was saying. With a start, I heard he was whispering the Lord's Prayer.

"I told you to wait," said Hereward, looking down at him.

Drosten had found some more material for a torch and now carried the burning brand over to us. The light clearly showed the blood soaking Arcenbryht's kirtle. His face had an unhealthy pallor I did not like.

"Saving the boy seemed more important," said Arcenbryht, with a pained grin. "Is he well?"

"He is just fine," said Gwawrddur. "I suppose we'll need to call you Lion Killer from now on."

"I don't think I killed it," said Arcenbryht, with a thin smile.

I tore away the cloth of his sleeve to get a better look at his wound. It was dark with blood, deep and bleeding heavily. Arcenbryht stared at the gash with a grimace.

"But perhaps it killed me," he said, and collapsed senseless into my arms.

Fifteen

None of us slept for the rest of that night. The children eventually settled and dozed, but their mothers and fathers sat in shock and grief, faces haggard with sorrow in the light of the fire that we had stoked up into a blaze.

Following the attack, our concern for Uthman's trees had vanished, so Runolf went into the copse of fig trees and expertly felled one. The thudding blows of his axe resonated around the encampment. Musa flinched with each strike of the blade.

We threw the logs onto the embers of the fire nearest to the family's shelter until the flames danced high, bathing us in their ruddy glow and casting light out into the night.

We sat staring nervously out into the darkness. Every now and then, one of us would call out, convinced we had seen the lion, but it always turned out to be one of our own shadows, gliding across the long grass, moving with the flicker of the fire.

"Will he live?" asked Hereward, laying his spear onto the ground and lowering himself down beside me.

Arcenbryht slept fitfully. I had boiled water on the fire and cleaned his wound before binding it with some clean cloths one of the women had handed to Revna.

"He has lost a lot of blood," I said, "and I fear that beast's claws might have infected the wound. But all I can do for him now is pray."

Revna sat close to Arcenbryht. On hearing my words, she reached out and touched my arm.

"You have done all you can," she said.

I hoped she was right. My mind was full of prayers that tumbled over themselves in a confusion of anxiety.

Gwawrddur did not sit, preferring to pace around the perimeter of the camp. Drosten went with him. Each of them carried spears, ready for the lion, if it should choose to return.

"We all pray he will live," said the Welshman from the shadows. "But if the Lord should take Arcenbryht, there can be no doubt of his bravery. That boy breathes because of him."

"But not that poor girl," said Runolf, his voice low.

I looked over to where Musa and his wife sat cradling the swaddled body of their daughter.

"Umar says lions do not attack people like this," I said, my voice not much more than a whisper.

"Arcenbryht and that poor lass would say differently," said Drosten.

"Umar said perhaps the creature's spirit had been taken over by one of the desert devils." The thought made me shudder. "A *jinni*."

"Who can say what made the beast attack?" said Giso. He had been sitting so quietly, wrapped in a dark cloak, that his voice startled me. "But if the lion was sent by some evil spirit to prevent us from completing our quest, it has failed."

I shivered, recalling the lion's powerful bulk, the impossibly long teeth, sharp claws and horrifying roar. And, as it had crouched over its prey, how the firelight had reflected from its dark, hate-filled eyes.

When the sun slid into the sky over the hills, we rose from the fire, stretching and blearily rubbing the night from our eyes.

There was no sign of the lion in the scrub, grass and trees that surrounded us. Nor in Uthman's fields of wheat.

Giso, looking as fresh and alert as if he had slept soundly all night, walked away from the fire. Perhaps two dozen paces away, he stooped, examining the dusty earth closely.

"It bleeds like any other animal," he said. "Arcenbryht's blows were well struck, it seems."

Along with the others, I made my way to where Giso knelt. There, clearly picked out in the dry soil by the shadows cast from the rising sun, were two paw prints. They were as large as shield bosses, the claw marks deep, showing that the creature had been running away. Between the tracks was a splash of dark blood. Flies hovered over the stain on the earth. Giso pointed to more blood on the dry blades of grass further from the camp.

"If we follow that trail," he said, "we might well find the animal dead. Losing so much blood it won't get far."

"I will go after it," said Drosten. His tone was hard.

"I will join you," said Beorn.

Eadstan, never far from Beorn's side, nodded in agreement.

Soon all the warriors had vowed to track the beast and bring its body back to the family whose daughter it had killed. The thought of facing the creature frightened me, but I offered to go too. I would rather hunt it down, than imagine it out there when night fell again.

"We cannot all go," said Hereward. "We need to guard our animals. And these people are travelling in the same direction as us. We will protect them too. I would not wish to see any more misfortune befall them on the road."

"Hereward is right," said Giso. "We must not forget our mission. And yet," he went on, surprising me, "it would give these people some solace to see the body of the creature that took Safiyyah's life. I have some skill at tracking animal sign. One as large as this and bleeding too should be a simple task."

Hereward chewed his moustache as he pondered the

options. "Very well," he said at last. "Take Drosten, Beorn, Eadstan, Gwawrddur, Pendrad and Sygbald and go after the beast. The rest of us will continue on the road to Ierusalem. And if you have not found the lion by the time the sun passes its high point, turn back and find us on the road."

"What if we are on its trail when the sun begins to go down?" asked Drosten.

"Then turn back. We are not here to hunt lions, and there is nothing to be gained from you being out there after dark if that monster is still on the prowl for man flesh."

Giso, Drosten and the others packed quickly. They would travel light. Each took weapons, water and a small amount of food, but little else. Before leaving, Drosten came over to where Arcenbryht lay.

"Do your best for him," he said to me. "It was a brave thing he did."

"Don't worry about me," said Arcenbryht, stirring and surprising both of us. Opening his eyes, he sat up, grimacing at the pain in his arm. "It will take more than a big cat to kill me."

I noted his eyes were clear and when I touched his forehead, there was no fever.

"You are going after it?" he asked.

Drosten nodded. "If it yet lives, we'll finish what you started."

"Be careful."

Drosten grinned. "Always."

I removed the bandage from Arcenbryht's arm. The wound was swollen, the edges bruised, but there was none of the tell-tale reddening of the skin that presaged the wound rot. I sniffed the cut, before replacing the bandage with a clean one. It smelt free of elf-shot.

"It hurts," Arcenbryht said.

"Pain is better than death," I said, winding the clean bandage tightly about his forearm.

He looked over at Safiyyah's small, shrouded form. Her mother sat beside her, eyes red and swollen.

Arcenbryht let out a long breath.

"You did all you could," I said, patting him on the shoulder.

Gamal and Oslaf helped the women prepare food for everyone. The children did not play now, but sat in hushed silence, hollow-eyed and fearful. The happy memories from the previous evening had been seared away and we were all keen to move on from this place.

Musa came over to us as we were tying the last of our packs onto the donkeys.

"We will bury Safiyyah on my uncle's land," he said. "We should be there by the end of the day. It is on the road to Ierusalem."

"We would be happy to travel with you," I said, and he nodded his thanks.

The men had packed away their sparse shelter and we were ready to leave when Uthman came striding out of his house.

"What is this?" he shouted, waving his arms angrily. "Who has cut down my fig tree?"

"What does he say?" asked Runolf. I told him.

"Tell him I did," he said, raising himself up to his full height and walking forward to meet the man. "Say we needed the fire to keep a lion at bay."

I conveyed the message to Uthman. He paid no heed, but continued to rave.

"That tree has been there since my father planted it! It is older than me. I loved that tree." He sounded as if he might cry, such was his fury and outrage. "It has the best shade in the afternoon. Where in the name of *Allah* will I sit now?"

"A girl died in the night," I said, anger giving my voice a sharp edge. "Her life was more precious than your tree."

"What do I care about one of these brats?" yelled Uthman. "One less mouth to feed for her poor parents, I say. But this tree—"

I cut off his words with a straight punch to his face. I had not planned to strike him, but as he spoke, my anger boiled up within me. It bubbled into my chest and I made no effort to slow its progress into my arm and fist. I hit him hard.

I felt Uthman's nose break beneath my knuckles. He stumbled back, falling against the stump of the tree. Blood streamed from his nose. He spat, struggling to get his feet under him. Finally, he pushed himself up.

"Why you—"

I punched him again, even harder than before. He fell against the tree, sliding to sit stunned and dazed on its exposed roots.

"Stay there," I snarled, "beside what is left of your beloved tree. If you rise again, I will gut you." I placed my hand on the pommel of my sword. The battle fury was upon me then and I would have been glad to have killed him, may God have mercy on my soul. Cuffing at the blood on his face, he looked set to say something, but taking in my glower and the grim faces of the men around him, he blanched. Shaking his head, he remained silent.

As we walked away, leading the donkeys and following behind Musa and his kin, I looked back to see Uthman pushing himself up. I turned and half drew my sword. Seeing me, he promptly sat once more and did not move again until we were out of sight.

"I wish I'd cut down all his trees," said Runolf. "We might have need of more timber tonight."

We walked until midday when we rested beneath a small stand of cypress trees growing beside a dry stream bed. Arcenbryht slumped down in the scant shade. He had tried walking at first, but after a short time it had become clear he would not be able to keep up with our pace. Even the children were faster. He had not wished to ride, but he didn't need much convincing to see that it was for the best.

Arcenbryht was pallid and feeble from blood loss, but

despite his weakness and sorrow at the death of Safiyyah, his demeanour was noticeably improved from previous days.

Hereward and Runolf walked some way from the others and stared out over the hazy land to the north. There was no movement there apart from a single bird of prey, perhaps a buzzard, circling languorously in the pale sky.

After checking on Arcenbryht's bandage, I joined them.

"No sign of them?" I asked.

Hereward shook his head. "I should not have allowed them to go."

"How fares Arcenbryht?" asked Runolf.

"Weak," I said, "but the wound is clean. He'll live."

Runolf scratched at his beard and took a pull from his waterskin.

"It seems to me he did more than save that boy last night," he said.

"Aye," agreed Hereward, taking the proffered skin from Runolf. "He reminded himself of what it is to be a warrior."

"Good," said Runolf. "For I am not sure I could have endured much more of his moaning."

Hereward chuckled, then took a swig of water. "Do you think you will be able to endure more of mine, big man?"

"Anything is possible," Runolf said, clapping him on the shoulder so that he spilt the water he was drinking. "But I would not test my patience."

It was dusk by the time we reached Bab al-Wadi. The sun, low at our backs, streamed our shadows long and dark before us, as if leading the way to the farmstead. As we walked through the gates of the walled enclosure, Hereward paused, looking back towards the setting sun.

I shaded my eyes with my hand, grunting at the tightness in my shoulder, and stared westward. The scrubby land we had passed through was hazed and golden in the evening light. The sun was a blazing orb, dipping towards the horizon. There was no sign of Drosten, Giso and the rest of the hunters.

Hereward frowned, turning away and following the others into the yard, which was abuzz with welcoming relatives greeting the newly arrived families with embraces and kisses.

I scanned the distance a while longer, searching clumps of trees and dips in the ground, looking for anything that might indicate our friends' location. I saw no movement. At last I joined the others, moving to help them unload the donkeys.

The farm was clearly prosperous. We had passed through fields of wheat, peas and lentils and slopes dotted with olive trees and grapevines. A high stone wall encircled several solid-looking buildings, the largest of which was the size of the hall of Ubbanford. The buildings were smooth-walled and daubed with white paint that reflected the setting sun's rays.

The joyful chatter of reunited kin filled the yard as I pulled the sacks from the nearest donkey's back.

"Their journey is over," Revna said, watching as one of the women knelt beside two of the smallest children, cooing to them and pinching their cheeks.

"Are you saddened that we must travel further?" I asked.

Revna hesitated, then shook her head, the sun making her hair gleam. "I have inherited my father's joy for the voyage," she said. "I cannot look at the waves on the Whale Road without wishing to set sail for the far-off horizon. When I spy a distant mountain, I must strive towards it." She watched as the woman who had been warmly greeting the children now spoke with their mother. The women grew sombre. No doubt they were speaking of Safiyyah's death, for both women began to weep. Sobbing, they clung to each other.

Revna tugged a bag free of the pack saddle, dropping it on the dust. "And yet," she said, her voice growing wistful, "I sometimes wonder what it would be like if I had been able to remain on the farm where I was born. If my mother had not—"

Her words were cut off by the sudden clang of a large timber locking bar being dropped into place. Two young men had closed the gates for the night. I thought of Giso, Gwawrddur,

Drosten and the others, out there with the darkness drawing its cloak about them.

"You think they've found it?" I asked. The image of the lion was seared into my mind. The thought of the beast terrified me.

For a moment, I thought Revna had not heard me, for she did not reply immediately.

"Who can say?" she said after a time. Her words were clipped, her tone tight. "But they are seven armed men against one injured lion. If they find it, they'll slay the creature."

"You truly think it will be so easy?"

When she did not reply, I turned to her, wanting to say more, but she was already striding away, carrying two heavy sacks towards the house.

Sixteen

"You have had no trouble with lions then?" I said, translating Hereward's question for Musa's uncle. Nu'man was a large man, his prosperity evinced by the size of his girth rather than fine clothes or expensive baubles. His garb was simple. A dark robe cinched beneath his barrel-like belly with a plain leather belt.

Reaching for a napkin, he delicately dabbed at his lips before answering. "At times lambs are taken, but it has been years since we have been worried by lions. Thanks be to Allah we have been spared." He turned his gaze on Umar. "Lions are dangerous beasts, but do not usually trouble the people who live here. There is prey enough for them, antelope and deer, without the risk of taking the life of a person." He picked up a cup of watered wine and drank, licking a drop from his full lips. "Once a lion has tasted the flesh of man, it will return for more. I pray your friends will bring the head of the beast who took the life of my great-niece. We cannot allow such a monster to continue to hunt these lands."

I interpreted Nu'man's words. Hereward nodded gravely.

"I pray that too," he said.

The mood in the large room had grown sombre with the talk of lions and death, but Nu'man now clapped his hands. "Enough of sadness," he said. "Eat and drink."

The long table was heaped with food and we did not need to be urged twice to partake of the wheat and herb-stuffed vine leaves, roast chicken with onions and olive oil, and the fresh, crisp flat loaves that were so popular in these eastern lands. The journey had been long and tiring. We were all hungry and thirsty.

Musa's plate was empty. He had eaten but sparingly. His sorrow wrapped about him like a cloak. All that day he had trudged along the dusty path beside his wife, both hollow-eyed and pale. The other women had seen to their surviving children, allowing the pair to travel in the quiet shelter of their grief.

Now that the women had gone to a separate room with the children, leaving the men to eat alone, Musa seemed more lost than ever. Umar had tried talking to him for a time, but after a while, his words had dried up and he had turned to the rest of us, leaving his brother to brood darkly.

For my part, I wished Revna had not gone away with the womenfolk and children. She had not spoken to me since we had come in from the courtyard, but though I could sense she was angry, I did not know what had upset her so.

I had asked Gersine about it, recounting what we had been speaking about. He had rolled his eyes. "For a clever man," he said, "you can be a real fool."

I had wanted to ask him to explain what he meant, but Nu'man had come out and greeted us and my services as interpreter had been needed.

"What did you say the man's name was again?" asked Nu'man now, pulling my attention back to where he sat at the head of the table. On seeing my blank expression, he went on: "The one who drove off the lion. His name?"

"Arcenbryht," I said, nodding at where Arcenbryht sat. I had cleaned and replaced his bandage earlier and I was happy with his progress. The wound remained clear of rot. His colour and strength were returning. The wholesome food served by

Nu'man's servants would do him good, as would the rest beneath a roof without the fear of attack.

"*Arcen-bruuct*," said Nu'man, struggling to pronounce the strange name. "I thank you all for driving off the lion, but my nephews tell me it was you who saved young Yakub from the beast."

As I translated Nu'man's words, Arcenbryht blushed.

"I did what any man would do," he muttered.

On hearing those words from me, Nu'man shook his head.

"No, no!" he said. "You are wrong. Not all men are so brave, and I would reward you for your courage." He beckoned to one of his servants, who handed him a long knife, sheathed in dark leather. "This knife was given to me by a great warrior. I have cherished it all these years, but alas…" he patted his bulging stomach "…I am no warrior. I want you to have this blade as a token of my thanks."

Arcenbryht fidgeted nervously. He looked at the rest of us. "My friends stood before the lion too," he said. "And your nephews as well."

Nu'man waved his protests away. "And they are all welcome at my table, but you saved Yakub's life. You have the wound to show it. The knife is yours."

Arcenbryht accepted the weapon reluctantly, but he could not hide his beaming smile as he pulled the blade from the sheath, admiring the steel.

"You honour me with this gift," he said. "I will carry it with pride."

Nu'man clapped him on the back and called for more food and drink.

It was close to midnight when Drosten and the others arrived. I had stepped outside the hall looking for somewhere to relieve myself when I heard a shout from outside the walls.

"Open the gates," came the cry.

I recognised the voice as belonging to Giso.

"Are you well?" I called back, hurrying over to the stout doors.

"Tired and thirsty," Giso replied, "but well enough."

I heaved the locking bar up, lifting it from the brackets. It was normally a job for two men and my shoulder screamed at the strain on already damaged muscles and tendons. Setting the locking bar aside, I hauled open one of the doors.

Giso slid into the courtyard, followed by Beorn, Eadstan, Sygbald and Pendrad. For a terrible moment I thought Gwawrddur and Drosten were not with them, but then the Welshman and Pict slipped out of the gloom and made their way inside.

None of them carried anything but the weapons, waterskins and packs they had set out with that morning.

"You did not find the beast?" I asked, pushing the door closed behind them.

"We tracked it until the sun was setting," said Giso, scratching beneath the strap of his bag. "But it was ever ahead of us."

I glanced at their grim, dust-smeared faces.

"It was injured," I said, bending to lift the locking bar. "Bleeding." Pendrad stepped forward and helped me with the heavy timber. "Did its wound not weaken it?"

"If it did," Pendrad said, his tone bleak, "it was not enough."

"That creature is a devil," hissed Giso. "I swear it was taunting us."

"Surely it is just an animal," I said, a shiver of fear scratching down my spine.

Without warning, a loud sound ripped asunder the hush of the night. It was a dreadful, primeval noise, resonant and booming, part growl, part roar. I grew cold. The lion was out there in the darkness.

And it was close.

Fear filled me and I wondered whether the men had been hunting the beast, or if it had been stalking them.

With a grunt Pendrad and I hurriedly dropped the locking bar into place, shutting out the night. The roar of the beast filled the gloom again and I looked up at the walls, suddenly sure they would be no deterrent for the massive lion I had witnessed the previous night.

Seventeen

We set guards that night.

Nu'man told us we had nothing to fear. No lion had ever scaled his walls and entered his home. But when he had come out into the courtyard and heard the booming roar of the beast echoing from the hills, seeming to come from all sides at once, his demeanour had changed. He ordered torches to be kept lit and had his own men spend time keeping watch until dawn.

I slept fitfully and my dreams roiled with visions of teeth and claws, punctuated by growling roars. I was almost glad to be called to take my turn as sentry outside the stables. Two men were stationed before the door of the house, but the donkeys were tethered beneath a timber lean-to built against the perimeter wall. If the lion were to leap over the wall, the pack animals would be the easiest target.

Gersine and I stood guard there, listening to the night. The scent of the donkeys was strong in the cool darkness. I imagined the lion, open-mouthed, great fangs glistening, as it breathed in the scent of our animals and stealthily prepared itself to spring over the wall.

The beast's roars had stopped by then and the only sounds were the insects in the vines and olive trees outside the wall, and the murmured conversations from the men guarding the house.

"You think it is still out there?" asked Gersine.

"Better than in here," I replied.

"Perhaps it's died. Arcenbryht stabbed it well."

"Perhaps," I said, not truly believing it. I had thought the animal would succumb to its wounds quickly, but Arcenbryht's spear must not have dealt as deep a blow as I had imagined.

We stood in silence for some time, listening to the cicadas chirring in the dark. One of the men near the house coughed. The loud sound startled us both.

"What did you mean before?" I said. "About me being a fool."

Gersine chuckled quietly. "Do you really not see it?" he asked.

"See what? That Revna is annoyed with me? I see that well enough, but why?"

Gersine shook his head. "By God. It's worse than I thought. All she wants is for you to listen to her. To see her."

"I see her." The truth was that oftentimes I could not avoid staring at Revna. Her curves, the sheen of her hair, her smooth, freckled cheeks. "I see her," I repeated, shuffling awkwardly. "The sight of her is... distracting."

"I know you are not blind, Hunlaf," he said. "Any man who has eyes for women sees Revna. She is beautiful – of that there is no doubt."

His words annoyed me and I stiffened. I had no right to be jealous, but the thought of other men watching Revna as I did filled me with rage.

"Then what are you speaking about?" I asked. "Talk plainly."

"You have been with more women than I," he said. "Perhaps you know best..." His voice trailed off.

"Tell me what you think and be done with it," I hissed.

"All I am saying is that perhaps you would do well to show Revna you are her friend..." He hesitated. "If you ever hope to be more than that."

"Of course I am her friend." I struggled to keep the irritation from my voice. "I would die for her. She knows that."

"Maybe," Gersine said. "But do you listen to her as a friend should? Do you truly see her when she speaks?"

I brooded on this for a long while. "Do you think we could ever be more than just friends?" I asked at last.

Gersine grinned, his teeth bright in the torchlight. "Anything is possible, Hunlaf," he said.

The attack never came. We heard no more of the lion and, as the sun tinted the eastern sky, we surmised the beast must have either gone in search of easier prey, or sought a place to recover from its wounds. I hoped it had merely crawled away, too weak from loss of blood to trouble us further, but the roars we had heard in the night had not sounded like those of a dying animal.

Nu'man seemed unconcerned, shrugging as if he had never expected the lion to appear.

"You'll reach the Holy City by nightfall," he said. "They close the Yafah gate at dusk, so do not tarry unless you wish to sleep outside the walls."

We thanked him for his hospitality and again he thanked us for guarding his kin. Musa embraced Arcenbryht then bade us all farewell. The other men muttered their own goodbyes. The women and children watched us as we led our pack animals out of the farm gates and down towards the road to Ierusalem.

"Perhaps those roars were the lion's death song," said Gwawrddur, as we trudged down to the road.

"It sounded strong enough to my ears," I said.

I could not shake the feeling that we were being watched. I scanned the scrubby patches of long grass that grew on the hill slopes, searching for any sign of stealthy movement, for the sleek shape of the massive predator stalking us.

I saw none, and as the day wore on, I finally began to relax.

I had thought much about what Gersine had said and I slowed my step to walk beside Revna as the sun rose to its zenith. It was another hot day and I squinted at her sidelong.

"Water?" I said, holding out my skin.

"I have my own," she replied, keeping her eyes ahead on where the road curved up into the hills.

I glanced at Gersine and was glad to see he was conversing with Sygbald and seemingly oblivious of my interaction with Revna.

We walked on in silence for a while.

"I sometimes think of home too," I said, keeping my voice light.

At last she looked in my direction. "You do not need to feign interest in what I have to say, Hunlaf."

My cheeks burnt. "Revna," I said, "please forgive me. I *do* care for what you say. I hear you." I thought of what Gersine had said. "I *see* you."

She laughed then, and in an instant I was lighter of spirit.

"Where is home for you then?" she asked. "Uuiremutha? Werceworthe?"

I scratched at my beard. The heat made it itch. My neck was slick with sweat. I wondered if I should perhaps shave my cheeks as Giso often did.

"Both of those places, I suppose," I said. "Lindisfarnae too, perhaps."

"Those are all minsters. What of your birthplace, your home?"

I thought of where I had been born and grown before being sent to join the brethren at Werceworthe. "You have not visited Ubbanford, have you?" I said. "You would like it, I think. There is a hall on the hill overlooking the river. The land is fertile and the sheep are fat." I smiled at the memories that flooded my mind. Looking about us at the barren slopes, the dry, rocky earth dotted with shrubs and the occasional spindly tree, it was hard to believe the lush valley of the Tuidi truly existed. It was like a different world. "The river is wide and full of salmon so large each one can feed a family for a week."

"It sounds perfect," Revna said. "And yet I don't think I have heard you speak of it before."

I thought of my father's stern face, his sharp words. It had been years since I had seen him, and I rarely thought of him. Now, I wondered if he might have mellowed. Perhaps if I should return now with a sword at my side, silver in my pouch and a beautiful fair-haired maiden on my arm, he would be proud of me and welcome me into his hall.

"Ubbanford is a fine place," I said simply.

Her face clouded, and I wondered if she was thinking of her own home and the last time she had seen it, full of flame and death.

"Will you take me there one day?" she asked.

Before I could answer, Giso shouted out. He was kneeling in the grass off to one side of the road.

"The beast yet lives," he said, his voice uncharacteristically strident. "See its sign here."

I hurried over and joined Gwawrddur, Drosten and the others gathered around the small Frank. Giso showed us where there were fresh prints of a large lion in a patch of soft sand.

"Could it be a different animal?" asked Drosten.

"Possible," replied Giso. "But I would wager it is one and the same as the monster we tracked yesterday."

"Not dead then?" Runolf said.

"These tracks were made during the night," Giso said. "This lion is very much alive."

"And ahead of us," said Hereward.

We all peered into the distance, as if the great cat would leap out at any moment.

"Let us press on to Ierusalem then," said Gwawrddur. "However strong the beast is, I do not believe it will enter the city's walls."

I looked back the way we had come. We had been walking

for some time and Nu'man's farm was far behind us, out of sight and lost in the hills.

We set off again and I sensed a renewed urgency in the party. These were all brave warriors, but none of them much liked the idea of facing that lion again, especially not in the dark.

When I joined Revna once more on the road I cursed myself. Gersine was right. I was a fool. I had allowed myself to be distracted and now she was once again angry with me, and I could not blame her.

I tried to engage in conversation, but Revna studiously ignored me. I trudged along silently in her wake. In that moment, I might have welcomed an attack from a savage beast. It would have been a distraction from Revna's cool ire and my own stupidity.

Eighteen

It was getting late when we finally reached Ierusalem. For a long while we could see the city ahead of us, the lowering sun picking out stark details of the huge stone walls, and some of the buildings that rose behind them. The sun glinted on a great burnished dome and several towers jutted up into the blue sky. Revna had not spoken to me since midday, and I had felt no inclination to talk to anyone else. I had walked in dejected silence, wallowing in self-pity and rebuffing all attempts at conversation.

The sight of the City of David drove away all my thoughts of sadness and foolishness.

This was the holy city of Ierusalem. Solomon had reigned here and David after him. This was the city of Herod, where Jesus had been welcomed on its streets by cheering crowds waving palm leaves. A week later He had been killed there, broken and in agony, hanging on a cross of wood. His sacrifice was absolute, his suffering unimaginable. Jesus had died for the sins of all mankind, risen from the dead, and ascended into heaven from the Mount of Olives. All of these things had transpired within the city that spread out before me in the hot, golden sunshine. My petty squabbles with Revna and my own feelings of inadequacy were of no import when placed against the grandeur, history and sacred power of Ierusalem.

"See there? That is the dome of the Holy Sepulchre. The tomb of Jesus Christ Himself."

I had been lost in my thoughts, in awe of the enormity of what my eyes beheld. Giso's voice, so close, startled me. He moved as silently as thought, and I wondered if I would ever grow accustomed to the man's uncanny stealth and his sudden, unannounced appearances.

"I can scarcely believe I am seeing this with my own eyes," I whispered.

"There are many wonders to behold beyond the Yafah Gate, Hunlaf. So much more will your eyes see. But if you would witness the streets and buildings of the city this night and do not wish to be sleeping outside the gates with that rabble, you had best hurry."

I saw immediately that he was right. The valley to the west of the city was already in shadow, though it was yet some time until night would fall. The road tracked along the north-eastern side of the valley, ending at an open area before a great gatehouse. Beyond that loomed a huge citadel built into the very walls of the city. White-cloaked warriors dotted the ramparts. The lowering sun flashed on their polished helms. On the ground before the gate thronged dozens of people and countless animals. *Badw* tribesmen sat crook-legged and aloof atop their camels, while men and women jostled for position with their carts, waggons, mules, donkeys and oxen. Many armed guards stood atop the city walls, and yet more manned the gates.

We picked up our pace, hurrying along the road, adding the dust of our passing to that of the other travellers who had gone before. It was as if a mist hung in the sultry afternoon air. It was stifling and dry, and the dust clogged our throats.

We were forced to halt before the road widened out, such was the density of pilgrims and travellers before the gates.

"Where is he going?" Runolf asked.

I followed his gaze and saw Giso threading his way between

the amassed people, heading towards the city and the Yafah Gate. He was quickly swallowed by the crowd and I marvelled that he had vanished as effortlessly as he had appeared at my side.

"I'll wager you a *solidus* we'll not see him again before nightfall," said Gwawrddur.

"I'll not take that bet," said Hereward. "This place is busier than Eoforwic on a feast day. We'll not be getting through those gates today. If Nu'man spoke true and they close the gates at dark, we'd best make ourselves comfortable for the night."

I glanced back the way we had come. In the distance, a small handcart crested the hill. Half a dozen figures walked along with it.

"If that lion is following us," said Drosten, "he'll have his fill of meat tonight."

I shivered, dropping my left hand to the hilt of my sword and making the sign of the cross with my right.

"There are too many people here," said Beorn. "No lion would be so bold."

I was not so sure. I recalled how the beast had stood before us, holding its ground in the face of many armed men.

"Perhaps," I said, "Giso goes to arrange for us to access the city more quickly than these other travellers."

Runolf whistled. "And maybe those camels can leap over that wall," he said. "That Frank may well find his way to a warm bed this night, but I do not see him helping us."

We slumped down beside the road, dropping our packs, and washing the dust from our mouths with water from our skins. The ground was hard. Large, sharp rocks were piled on either side. The drop down to the valley floor was steep.

"We will not get much sleep here," Gwawrddur said.

The men set about grumbling at our lot, cursing Giso and looking out nervously at the shaded valley. We had all heard the lion's roars the night before. The idea of being out here, exposed and in the open, filled us with dread. Revna did not comment, but I could see from the tension in her shoulders and the way her eyes furtively flicked over the horizon and down the scrub-strewn rocky slopes that she was scared too.

"Look there," said Arcenbryht, pointing towards the gates. He had ridden again for much of the day, but his colour was better and his wound was healing well.

The densely packed people outside the gates began to ripple and shift. At first I could not see what was causing them to make way, but the sound of their angry voices drifted to us. Slowly, they parted, opening up a path along which a score of armed men walked. These warriors wore the same gleaming helms and white cloaks as the sentries on the walls. They pushed back the congregated travellers with their spears, moving inexorably towards us.

We rose to our feet.

"You see?" I said. "Giso must have spoken to the guards."

"I am not sure about this," said Hereward, scanning the warriors' stern faces as they approached.

"If this is Giso's doing," said Gwawrddur, "where is he?"

"That man is as slippery as a rat in a midden," said Drosten. "I wouldn't put it past him to have turned the guards on us."

"To what end?" I said. "He is our companion and comrade. We must have faith in him." But despite my words, like the others, I could not bring myself to fully trust the small Frank. Now, as the guards halted before us, grim-faced and menacing, I could not shake the feeling that perhaps my friends were right and Giso had done this for some unknown reason all of his own.

One of the guards, a wiry man with a forked black beard and the tanned skin of someone who spends much of his life outdoors, stepped forward. He did not bear a spear, but an ornately hilted sword hung from a baldric slung over his shoulder.

"My name is Aziz ibn Fawaz," he said. "Who is your leader?"

"This is Hereward of Bebbanburg," I said. "He is our leader, but he does not speak your tongue. I interpret for him."

Aziz ibn Fawaz scowled, but appeared unconcerned.

"He says his name is Aziz ibn Fawaz," I said to Hereward in Englisc. "I have told him you are our leader."

Hereward bowed and touched his chest and face as he had seen others do in greeting. "Offer him my greetings," he said, "and ask him if Giso sent him."

"Giso?" said Aziz, frowning when he heard my words. "What is this Giso?"

"A Frank," I said. "A small man with dark features."

"Look about you," he said, raising his eyebrows. "We have many small dark men in Ierusalem, but I know nothing of this Giso. Franks come here from time to time. But you are the first Frankish men I have seen in many weeks."

"We are not Franks," I said.

Aziz scowled at this. "You are not envoys sent from Carolus, the great ruler of the Franks?"

I translated his words. Hereward shrugged. "Why should it surprise us that the ruler of Ierusalem should know of our coming?" he said. "Alhwin and Eirene are unlikely to be the only people to employ spies. There seems no point in denying it now. Tell him we do serve Carolus and enquire as to the name of his master."

Aziz remained still as Hereward spoke and I translated his words.

"My master is Kawthar ibn Barmaki al-Yahya, wali of the city of Ierusalem, most humble servant of the great Caliph Abu Ja'far Harun ibn Muhammad al-Mahdi. I am ordered to welcome you to the city and escort you to my master's palace."

Hereward bowed. "Thank him again, Hunlaf," he said with a thin smile. "Truth is I would rather sleep in a palace than on this stony road."

Aziz returned Hereward's bow. He seemed poised to lead us towards the city gate when he halted. "If you are envoys of Carolus, why did you profess not to be?"

"I did not deny we were the king's envoys," I answered without hesitation, "merely that we are not Franks, and that is true. We hail from different kingdoms outside of the Frankish realms."

"And yet you serve the king of the Franks?" Aziz seemed puzzled by the idea.

"We do," I said, adding no further explanation.

He thought on that for a moment, then – seemingly satisfied – he spun about and snapped an order at his men. The warriors formed up around us and our pack animals. Acting as our escort, they pushed men and women roughly away with their spears.

The people on the flat ground outside the gate glowered at us with undisguised anger. Someone shouted a curse. Others grumbled. One brave man spat towards the guards, his spittle spattering Aziz's cheek. The captain of the guards halted and held up his hand. His men stopped instantly. Aziz touched the fleck of spit on his face. The crowd grew hushed and the man who had spat tried to push his way into the throng. He was pale now, his brash courage vanished.

"I would not like to be him," muttered Gersine.

Aziz clicked his fingers. Four guards hurried to the foolhardy man and dragged him away from the gathered onlookers. A few shouted for the man to be left alone, but their voices were quiet and from the rear of the crowd, where they were safe from reprisals.

The man was begging now, but the guards cuffed him and kicked the back of his leg until he was kneeling before Aziz. The captain looked down impassively for a time.

"Spit at me, would you?" he said at last, his tone light.

The man sputtered a response that might have been an attempt at an apology, but Aziz silenced him with a raised hand. Snapping his fingers again, he ordered the nearest guard to hand him his dagger. Without a word, the guard unsheathed his blade and handed it, grip first, to his leader.

"I wonder if you will be able to spit without a tongue," Aziz mused, fingering the blade. The kneeling man began to blubber. Aziz ignored his pleas for clemency. "We shall see," he said. "Hold him tightly."

A groaning grumble ran through the crowd. The guards who were not restraining the man formed up protectively around us, holding their spears towards the gathered people.

"I have a bad feeling about this," said Runolf.

"Not as bad as him," said Drosten grimly.

"We should do something," I said, as the guards grasped the poor man's face.

"What can we do?" asked Hereward, looking at the guards around us, the ranks of guardsmen at the gate and the sentries on the walls above.

He was right. There were few of us and scores of them. We could do nothing to save the man from his fate. My stomach roiled. I wanted to look away, but I did not. For a moment more, he struggled, still defiant. Aziz punched him savagely in the mouth with the pommel of the dagger, splitting his lips and breaking his teeth. The man's defiance crumbled and he sagged between the guards who held him.

My gorge rose as Aziz went to work with the blade. The man's wailing screams were soon replaced by gurgling, sobbing whimpers. A few heartbeats later, Aziz stepped back, holding a bloody chunk of flesh up for all to see. His fingers were crimson.

"Anyone who spits at me, spits at the wali himself," Aziz said, raking his gaze over the crowd. Throwing the severed tongue into the dust before the quivering man, Aziz handed the blood-smeared dagger back to the guard. Stooping, he wiped his fingers on the man's robe. Without another word, Aziz strode through the shocked onlookers. They parted before him, eager to show him deference. Nobody else made a sound, as we followed him past the lines of guards before the open gates.

"Not a man to cross," whispered Gersine.

"Yes," murmured Hereward, his expression sombre. "Even without speaking the language of these people, that message was clear enough."

It was cooler under the walls as we walked through the stone portal, the solid weight of the towers at either side, the sound of our feet loud on the cobbles. Behind us, the man's shuddering cries were smothered by the seething anger of the crowd.

Spearmen stared down at us, eyes dark, faces stern. I could not help but feel we were being swallowed into the mouth of a giant beast. It reminded me of stepping down into the Maw of the Serpent. With a shudder, I wondered if there might be worse dangers than Aziz within the walls; and whether, like in the cave on Kýpros, there would be venomous vipers lurking within the relics of this holy city.

Nineteen

Aziz ibn Fawaz led us through the shaded streets. People stepped quickly out of our way, clearing our path so we did not need to slow our pace.

I was still shaken by what we had witnessed outside the gate and I had not lost my sense that we were stepping into the lair of a beast. And yet my concerns receded as I gazed about me, trying to take in everything. Passing through the courtyard of the imposing citadel and leaving the high city walls behind us, Aziz marched us along a straight road.

A *souk*, thick with the aroma of spices and the clamour of tradesmen hawking their wares, lay to our right. I peered into the narrow alleys, snatching a glimpse of shining metal hanging outside a stall, the bright flash of bolts of cloth, heaps of za'atar, cumin and cardamom pods.

To our left, surrounded by stone buildings, the reddening sky was reflected in a large expanse of water. Beyond, the sun gleamed on the dome of the Church of the Holy Sepulchre. I longed to hurry in that direction. To be this close to the holiest of holy places made my nerves thrum.

"Never fear," Gwawrddur said as if hearing my thoughts, "I am sure you'll be able to visit the holy places tomorrow."

"If we are not walking into a trap," growled Runolf, voicing the fear I had not spoken aloud.

"What alternative do we have but to follow?" asked Hereward.

Runolf sighed. He was taller than all of us and towered above our guard escort, and yet as we walked further into the city with its crowds of people and animals, stone buildings, narrow, noisome alleys and cobbled streets, so Runolf appeared to become smaller, less imposing. His place was the open sea and the windswept mountainside, not this jumbled warren of ancient stone, filled with the sounds, sights and smells of humanity.

"By Óðinn," he said, "that little Frank had better have a plan. If he has vanished to leave us prisoners here, I will rip his hide from his flesh."

"Nobody is a prisoner," said Gwawrddur softly, "but perhaps best not to mention our Frankish friend again. He may well have a plan, and you can be sure he has his reasons for disappearing. And where we are heading, I think knowledge and secrets might be all we possess of value."

Ahead of us rose a gleaming golden dome, much larger and taller than that built over the Holy Sepulchre. It was part of a massive structure within a huge walled complex. Tall trees grew behind those walls, and for a time I thought that must be our destination. But Aziz turned to the right and led us down a long sloping street.

"That is not the wali's palace?" I asked, hurrying to keep pace with the leader of the guards.

Aziz looked surprised at my question, but smiled. I imagined it was a rare expression on his severe features.

"No, no, young Frank," he said, "that is the *al-Masjid al-Aqsa* and the *Qubbat as-Sakra*. It is the holiest place in the city for Al-Muslimun and Al-Yahud too. This is the palace."

I chose not to repeat my assertion that I was no Frank. The distinction seemed insignificant in this strange land.

Aziz had led us down an incline and we now stood before a gateway through yet another high wall. At a word from Aziz the tall double doors, decorated and strengthened with iron strips, opened soundlessly before us. Without hesitation Aziz strode through the archway. We followed and entered a garden the like of which we had not seen since our stay in Qurtuba. The palace and grounds here were not as vast as those of the capital of al-Andalus, but they were every bit as sumptuous. There were violets and peonies, mastic bushes in earthenware pots, and roses lining stone-covered paths. Bees droned and buzzed, and the air was heavy with the scent of flowers.

Servants had been awaiting our arrival and now stepped up quickly to take command of our donkeys.

"Do not fear for your possessions," said Aziz. "You are here as the wali's guests. Your animals will be cared for, and your belongings will be unpacked and taken to your quarters."

I translated his words.

Reminding us that we were confined here, the great doors clanged closed, shutting out the hubbub of the city.

"Thank you," Hereward said as graciously as he was able. I could see from the stiffness of his shoulders that he too did not like the feeling of being trapped.

A servant held out a hand for Runolf's axe. The Norseman shoved him away, sending the slight man stumbling. Runolf was not alone in his reluctance to give up his weapon. Beorn, Eadstan and Pendrad had drawn close together and looked ready to fight the servants who had reached for their blades.

"You will not need your weapons here," said Aziz. "They will be kept safe in the gatehouse."

Gwawrddur quickly pulled his baldric over his shoulder and handed his sword to the nearest servant.

"We won't be fighting our way out of here, lads," he said, looking about him. "We'd best just hope this wali is as friendly as Aziz says he is."

"Of that you can be certain," said a voice in heavily accented Englisc. "A man can never have too many friends. Welcome to my humble home."

A man stepped from the shade of a path that was lined with cunningly trimmed box trees. The plants were cut into the shapes of animals. A leafy deer sprang over the path, chased by a shrubbery lion, crouched, muscles bunched and ready to leap after its prey. The detail in the living sculptures was magnificent.

Aziz bowed low, as did the other guards. The servants averted their gaze and remained motionless until the newcomer waved his hand, indicating that they could continue with their tasks.

Aziz regained his composure quickly.

"This is Kawthar ibn Barmaki al-Yahya, wali of Ierusalem," he said.

I handed my sword to the nearest servant and bowed to the wali. He was a man of perhaps thirty summers. Slender of hip, with broad shoulders, he wore fine silks and linen, and his head was covered with a tightly wrapped scarf of white. His eyes were dark and clever, his skin unblemished. The wali's cheeks were shaved smooth, but a close-cropped beard adorned his chiselled chin. He was very handsome.

I introduced my companions in Al-Arabiyyah. Kawthar nodded to each in turn.

"And your name is?" he enquired, when I had finished.

"I am Hunlaf, lord," I said.

"Well, Hunlaf," Kawthar said, "your grasp of Al-Arabiyyah is far better than my understanding of Englisc. I think I will have need of your skills if I am to communicate with your fellows."

"We are very far from my home, lord," I said. "That you speak any words of the tongue of Britain's people amazes me. You are a scholar of languages?"

"A man must exercise his mind as well as his body if he is to find paradise. I find learning the tongues of others brings much wisdom. And what of you, Hunlaf? I have rarely met a stranger to these lands with a better command of our language."

He stared at me in open admiration and despite myself, I felt my cheeks redden beneath his gaze. I inclined my head.

"I too enjoy the study of language. I was a monk once."

"A scholar!" Kawthar clapped his hands together. "We will have much to talk about, I think."

"I am simply a warrior now," I said, embarrassed.

Kawthar stared at me for several heartbeats. "There is nothing simple about you, I think, my friend," he said. "But there will be time enough to talk later. You asked about my understanding of Englisc. A pilgrim from the kingdom of Mercia stayed here a couple of years back." He grew quiet again, wistful.

"What happened to him?" I asked.

His attention snapped back to the present and for an instant, the red sun gleaming in his pupils, I recalled the eyes of the lion in the night.

"He died," Kawthar said. "A fine man. Devoted to his wife. Sad that he should die and leave her behind so far from home. Fair as a rose, she was." His attention slid away from me and he fixed his penetrating gaze on Revna. "Speaking of lovely wives, who is this beauty married to?"

I did not like the hunger in Kawthar's eyes. Runolf did not understand the wali's words, but the sentiment behind them was clear to all.

"What does he say?" Runolf asked, his deep voice threatening.

"He asks which of us is Revna's husband."

"She is my daughter," said Runolf, "and she has no wish to be wed." The Norseman had finally relinquished his axe to the servant. Seeing the furrow in his brow as he looked down at Kawthar, I was glad of that.

"Your daughter," Kawthar said. "Master... Runolf, wasn't it?" His eyes glimmered with mirth as he looked from father to daughter. Revna was tired from travel, her plain clothes stained, her face smeared with dust and sweat, yet still she was radiant. Her hair glowed in the setting sunlight as if gilded. "We must all be thankful that she took her looks from her mother." Kawthar grinned. Runolf's scowl deepened and I thought Revna might say something insulting in response to Kawthar. The Almighty knew she was quick to judge, slow to forgive and did not suffer fools. But to my great surprise, Revna said nothing. Instead she lowered her eyes, looking up at the wali of Ierusalem through her lashes, and giggled.

Her cheeks were flushed and they grew redder as Kawthar held her gaze, unblinking. He licked his lips slowly and suggestively, then bowed low before her with as much pomp as if she were a princess or a queen.

"Revna's mother is dead," growled Runolf savagely, stepping close and placing his arm about his daughter's shoulders.

"Please accept my sincerest condolences for your loss, Runolf," said Kawthar.

Turning to one of the plants that grew beside the path, he plucked a white and yellow flower and handed it to Revna. "And to you, Revna. Please accept this flower, though it cannot compare to your beauty." He drew in a long breath and stared off into the distance, once again lost in thought. "It always saddens me to think that even the sweetest rose must die." As quickly as it had come, so his reverie evaporated, and he was of a sudden brimming with energy. "Now come," he said, clapping his hands together again. "Enough of this chatter. I have had clean clothes prepared for you. And warm baths await. My servants will show you to your quarters."

Before any of us could reply, a wailing went up from the nearby temple, the *masjid*. It was the *muezzin* calling the faithful to evening prayers, and the doleful sound would be heard all over the city.

"I must pray," said Kawthar. "Later you will meet me for a feast held in your honour. And you will tell me all about how it is you come to be here, and yet you are not Franks. I was certain you would be Franks."

Without waiting for a response, Kawthar bowed to Revna once more, then swirled away in a flurry of linen and silk.

"We will have to be careful of that one," snarled Runolf.

I nodded, still dazed and somewhat bemused at the wali's sudden appearance and the force of his character. He seemed more akin to the power and chaos of a desert wind than a man.

As we followed the servants across the gardens to our rooms, I tried to make sense of the wali. His wealth and power were on display all around us, and yet there was something else about Kawthar that made me uneasy.

I have met many powerful men in my long life: kings, emperors, emirs, caliphs and khans. Most such men like to make their visitors wait. It shows the power they hold over you. They control everything and want to make sure that you are aware of that.

Kawthar ibn Barmaki al-Yahya was the opposite in that regard. He had sent Aziz and his guards to meet us at the gates of the city and then, as if unable to wait to greet us, he had come to us in the gardens, unannounced and excited to make our acquaintance.

Thinking back to our conversation, he had said nothing to alarm me. Perhaps my prickle of concern was mere jealousy, for as Kawthar had stalked away, his cloak billowing, I had seen Revna staring after him. And I had never before seen her looking at someone with such an expression of longing on her face.

Twenty

"And that," said Kawthar, pointing to the shadowed hill to the east, "is the Mount of Olives, from which the Christians say Jesus ascended to heaven." He turned to me, the smile playing on his handsome face, illuminated by the countless torches that burnt around the garden. "I have seen that look on your face many times before, Hunlaf. The awe of the true believer. The pilgrim amazed to be here, walking in the steps of Jesus himself."

"I cannot deny it," I said, my mouth dry despite the sweet *Qamar al-Din*, an apricot beverage I had been drinking. "Since we moored in Yafah, I have walked as if in a dream. I very much hope I am able to find time to visit the sites. The Church of the Holy Sepulchre, the Garden of Gethsemane, the Mount of Olives." I waved my hand to encompass all the land I could see from the garden wall. "I would see everything."

Kawthar laughed. "For that you will need to have a different guide, I fear. When day breaks my duties as governor of the city are many."

"Of course," I said. "I am sure I will find my way about the city well enough."

"Nonsense. You shall have a guide and I know just the man for the job." Kawthar clapped his hands and a servant ran out of the shadows. "Have Aharon attend us."

The servant bowed and scurried away.

It was dark now, the sky purple and studded with stars behind the bulk of the Mount of Olives. It was pleasantly warm and here, overlooking the valley, a light breeze stirred the leaves of the trees in the garden, making the torches and lamps flicker and dance. The wind shifted into the west momentarily and Kawthar wrinkled his nose.

"I do so like to dine under the stars, but I always forget that the tanners are nearby. Why my forebears built the palace here, I will never understand."

"The view, I imagine," I said. The stench of the tanning pits, acrid with the shit and piss used to cure hides, reached my nostrils and I coughed. "Not the smell."

"Perhaps I should have the tanners moved," Kawthar mused. "But to where? Come, the air is sweeter in the shelter of the wall there, and see, the meal is served."

Servants were carrying out platters and serving bowls heaped with food. Others carried fresh pitchers of *Qamar al-Din* and cool hibiscus tea. The dining area, with long tables and low, comfortable seats of polished olive wood with silk cushions, was lower than the raised garden from where we had been looking at the vista outside of the city. Turning, I followed Kawthar down the half a dozen steps. My toe caught in the hem of the robe I wore and I stumbled. Only the wali's quick reflexes halted me from tumbling down. His grip was firm as he pulled me upright. Guards were posted all around the garden and three took several quick steps towards us, hands already drawing their blades, before Kawthar waved them away.

"Perhaps the robe is too long?" he said, graciously excusing my clumsiness. The robe had been laid out on my bed when I returned from my bath. The experience of that bath had been awkward and embarrassing. All of us, except for Revna, had been shown to a large bath house within which we submerged into a huge pool of warmed water. After that, several burly slaves bade us lie down on the wet tiled floor where they wiped us with oil and sticks, massaging our muscles and kneading our skin.

Drosten had slapped their hands away. "He'll not be touching me, the heathen," he said, covering himself with a cloth.

The rest of us laughed.

"You scared he'll wash the paintings off your body?" asked Beorn.

"Perhaps that's Drosten's secret," Eadstan said with a chuckle. "He can never wash in case we see he is no true Pict."

Drosten spat and stalked away, while the rest of us followed the servants' signalled commands and succumbed to the strange cleaning ritual.

My shoulder was stiff and painful, and while the servant made me gasp with pain as he pushed and prodded, after I stepped from the bath house wrapped in a towel, my skin tingled and my arm felt better and looser than it had for a long time. The robe was simple and wearing it and the sandals provided for me, I felt much cooler than in my own clothes.

"No, no," I said to Kawthar. "The robe is fine. But I am not used to this garb."

"So much time has passed then since you were a monk?"

"Not so long," I admitted. "Barely four years." It was hard to believe. I thought of all that had happened since that mist-shrouded morning on Lindisfarnae. "It seems like a lifetime."

"Let us hope your life will prove long and fruitful," Kawthar said. "You are still young, with much to live for."

Servants handed us fresh cups. I sniffed the contents. It was light and fragrant. Kawthar sipped his drink and sighed appreciatively. "Of course," he went on, eyeing me over the rim of his cup, "no man knows when death will come for him."

I looked at Kawthar sharply. Was there a threat in those words? But he was smiling and explaining now with relish the ingredients of one of the other delicacies on the table. This was a kind of small baked roll.

"You really must try it," he said. "You will find no finer south of Dimashq."

I took one of the small rolls. Biting into it, I was surprised to find it filled with a thick paste. It was very sweet and subtly flavoured with almonds, sugar and rose water. It was delicious.

Kawthar grinned.

"You see? Is it not a marvel? They are called *ka'b al-ghazāl*."

"Ankles? Of what?" I asked, my mouth full of the delicacy.

"Ankles of an animal. An antelope, I think you would say."

"They are good," I said, chewing the morsel.

"What's that you are eating?" asked Runolf.

"They are like bread, stuffed with sweet filling," I said.

Runolf popped one of them into his mouth, chewed and swallowed. He shrugged.

"Too rich for my liking, but this is not bad." He dipped some flat bread into a thick paste similar to one we had tried before in al-Andalus.

"You may sit, my friend," Kawthar said to Runolf, smiling. "My people will serve you."

Runolf, Drosten, Gwawrddur, Hereward and Gersine had surrounded the table and were busy shovelling food into their mouths as if they had not eaten in a month. The servants fussed about them, proffering platters and refilling their cups.

Kawthar seated himself on one of the cushioned seats. I copied him.

"You are hungry, I see," he said, grinning as he watched my comrades devouring the food provided. "But never fear, there is more than enough to fill your bellies."

Abashed, Runolf and the others found chairs and sat down, awkwardly accepting the food offered to them by the servants. We ate in silence for a time. The food was sumptuous and flavoursome, but none of the men from *Brymsteda* were at ease. They looked about them at the ornamental gardens, surrounded by high walls. The flickering torches shimmered on the armour and weapons of the guards in the shadows, and I could imagine my friends' thoughts. The walls and guards might be there to protect the wali and his household, but they served to keep us prisoner just as well.

The rich scents of the food hung heavy in the air, but a sudden warm gust of wind brought again a whiff of the tanneries, turning my stomach.

"Where is Revna?" Runolf asked without warning.

When we had been escorted to this garden, we had been informed that the wali wished to converse with the leaders of our band. The remainder of the men would have food sent to them in a communal room of the quarters we had been given. By common consent, those of us who had defended the minster four years earlier, the so-called Heroes of Werceworthe, had been deemed the leaders. Gersine was the only exception to this. But as the son of a lord, and the lord who had enabled the building of our ship, it seemed just that he should join us too.

While I had fought at Werceworthe, I did not feel like a hero. It was true, though, that without me, there would have been no defence of Werceworthe and therefore no *Brymsteda*. I was also the only one of our number who could understand the tongue of Al-Arabiyyah.

Runolf had enquired as to Revna's whereabouts when we had left our quarters, but the servants and guards who guided us to the walled garden merely nodded their heads and said the Norseman's daughter was being well cared for.

"That is what I am afraid of," Runolf had growled. "I do not like this."

I understood his concern. I had hoped Revna would be awaiting us when we reached the torchlit garden, but there had been no sign of her and I had not found a suitable moment to ask the wali of her whereabouts.

"My daughter," snapped Runolf now, clearly out of patience, "where is she?"

Kawthar reached out a hand and a servant instantly placed a white linen cloth in it. The wali dabbed at his lips, taking his time and seeming to enjoy Runolf's building anger. Tossing the cloth back to the servant, Kawthar took a sip from his silver cup.

"A lady takes longer to prepare herself than us rough men," he said. "Do not fear for your daughter, brave Runolf. She is being bathed and tended to and will join us soon enough."

I looked about the garden at the seated men, the anxiously attentive servants and the watchful guards. Seeing there were no women, I asked, "Do the womenfolk not dine separately?"

"That is the way of our people," Kawthar said, "and Revna should in truth dine with the ladies of my household, but she is not Muslim, so I have made an exception in this case. Besides," he went on, a mischievous glint in his eye, as he stared at Runolf, "how could I miss seeing her after she has been bathed and perfumed and dressed in the finest silks? She was a vision when dusty and weary from travel, I am excited to see what she looks like after the women have readied her in more appropriate clothing."

Runolf's scowl deepened. Kawthar could not be oblivious to the effect his words were having on the huge Norseman, but he seemed to be openly goading Runolf now. Gwawrddur placed a calming hand on Runolf's arm. He whispered something too quiet for me to hear.

The sound of steps at the entrance to the garden broke the tension. The servant that Kawthar had sent in search of a guide stepped into the torchlight and offered a small bow.

"Aharon," he said.

Beside him stood a small man with thinning grey hair and a full, silvery beard. His head was covered with a black hat, and his clothes were simple and of the same hue. Kawthar beckoned him over.

"Do not just stand there," he said in Al-Arabiyyah, "come closer so that everyone can see you."

Aharon strode forward with surprising alacrity and purpose. He might have been elderly, but this man was proud; he held his head high.

"Lord?" he said. "You summoned me?"

"Indeed," said Kawthar. "I have need of your knowledge. You have forgotten more about this city than most men will ever know."

"You flatter me, lord," Aharon replied.

Kawthar laughed at that. "If I were to flatter someone, you think it would be a shrivelled old *Yahudi*?"

"When you phrase it like that," said Aharon, with a raised eyebrow, "it seems unlikely."

"He's a sharp one, Hunlaf," Kawthar said. "Make no mistake. Aharon was born and raised in Ierusalem and knows everything you could hope to find within its walls. And without. Isn't that so, Aharon?"

The grey-bearded man inclined his head. "It is true I was born here," he said. He looked at me, then at the rest of our band seated on the cushioned chairs. "You would have me guide your guests around the city?"

"Just so," said Kawthar. "On the morrow, you will take Hunlaf here and his friends to any of the sacred places they wish to see. Then you will see that they return to the palace before sundown."

They were speaking in Al-Arabiyyah so none of the others were following the conversation. But the implications of what the wali had said were not lost on me.

"I thank you, lord," I said, "on behalf of my companions and myself for your generous hospitality, but I am not certain that our plans will allow us to stay another night."

"Your plans?" he said, fixing me with his hawk-like gaze. He was serious now, all sign of humour vanished. "You mean meeting the Frankish envoy, the *Yahudi* called Isaac?"

I swallowed against the sudden dryness in my mouth. How much did Kawthar know? Gwawrddur had said secrets and knowledge were our only commodities of value here, but it seemed we had little enough of those. Raising my cup, I found it empty.

Kawthar chuckled, his sombre expression dispelled in an instant. He snapped his fingers and a servant stepped forward with a pitcher, filling my cup without a word.

"Do not look so shocked, Hunlaf," Kawthar said. "Did you not think that as the caliph's governor I would know of official emissaries from the courts of other kingdoms?"

I drank deeply in an effort to disguise my surprise. "As you say," I replied, "only a fool could think you would not know of our reason for travelling through your lands."

"And you are no fool, eh, warrior monk?"

I smiled, but said nothing. I was not so certain of that. And yet it was possible Kawthar did not know everything about our journey. I vowed I would give up none of our secrets.

"As you know of our mission," I said, "you know we cannot tarry. We must find this Isaac and the man he travels with?"

Kawthar's brows furrowed. "What man?"

Anew I felt foolish. So much for not giving anything away. But was it truly possible that the wali had not known that Isaac was accompanied by an emissary from Madīnat as-Salām? Even if that were the case, he would learn of that soon enough. Despite my vow moments before, I could see no reason to withhold this snippet of information.

"He travels with one named Abul-Abbas," I said. "An envoy sent from the caliph himself."

For several heartbeats Kawthar stared at me, then – slowly – his features split into a broad grin. He chuckled deep in his throat.

"Of course," he said. "I had forgotten he was travelling with Abul-Abbas. Allah only knows how I could forget an envoy of such stature!" He laughed some more, before holding out his hand for the linen cloth again. This time, he wiped the tears of mirth from his eyes.

"What are you speaking of?" hissed Hereward. "What is so funny?"

"Forgive me, Hereward," said Kawthar, dabbing at his eyes and handing the cloth to a servant. "I was merely amused at my own forgetfulness. I already knew you were to meet the *Yahudi*, Isaac, but Hunlaf reminded me that he travels with one Abul-Abbas, sent by our beloved caliph."

Hereward frowned. Like me, he did not appear to see why this had caused the wali such humour.

"But these are all good tidings," Kawthar continued. "Riders arrived yesterday saying that Isaac and Abul-Abbas are still several days from Ierusalem. They are well guarded and need fear no attack on the road. You can rest here as my guests until they arrive. Then you can escort them onwards on their journey to Frankia. That reminds me," he said, clapping his hands so loudly that a pigeon flashed out of a cypress tree in alarm. I watched as it flapped through the torchlight, to be lost in the dark sky. "You must tell me how it is that you are sent by Carolus, the king of the Franks, and yet not one of you is a Frank."

I was about to attempt an answer, when Kawthar spoke again.

"Be off with you," he said to Aharon, who was still standing before us. "See that you tend to Hunlaf and his friends first thing in the morning. Take a contingent of the guard with you too. The streets can be dangerous for strangers."

"There is no need for that," I said.

"Nonsense," he said. "I will hear no more about it. Aharon will be your guide and my men will protect you."

Aharon bowed his head and retreated.

"Till the morning then," he said to me in a tone that said he could think of nothing worse. Without waiting for a reply, he turned and stomped out of the garden.

Kawthar chuckled again. "Aharon is as sour as a tamarind," he said, "but he's a good man, for a *Yahudi*." His eyes flicked past me and opened wide. "Ah, now here is something sweet to wash away the bitter taste left by that old *Yahudi* goat."

We all turned to look. My breath caught in my throat. At the entrance to the garden, flanked by two stern-faced, stone-still warriors, stood Revna.

But this was Revna as I had never seen her before.

I knew her shape better than I knew the form of my own hand. I had watched her more often than I cared to admit, even to myself. I loved snatching glimpses of her as she brushed and braided her hair in the morning. I would pretend I was busy at some menial task, all the while flicking glances in her direction. Gersine would jest with me, saying that love had made me moonstruck. I had not been sure if I loved Revna, but I could not deny that I enjoyed her company and I could not keep myself from looking at her whenever she was near.

In that moment, watching Revna standing nervously atop the steps that led down into the sunken garden, it was all I could do not to gasp. She was more beautiful than ever. Her body was draped in silk the colour of the sun. While she often wore breeches and a kirtle that showed off the curve of her hips and the shape of her long legs, the dress she now wore hid her form more thoroughly, and yet somehow the fall of the fabric suggested the smooth pale skin beneath the silk. Her long hair was covered by a scarf in the way of Al-Muslimun women. Strangest of all, and yet still more alluring than I would have thought possible, Revna's face was hidden behind a veil. The translucent material was dotted with tiny discs of silver that caught the torchlight. Her eyes gleamed, the golden silk of her scarf and veil making them bluer than ever.

"You are most welcome," Kawthar said, stepping forward, holding out a hand. "Please, come and be seated."

Timidly, seemingly as shy as a fawn, Revna descended the steps. I barely recognised her as the brisk, ruthless fighter I had so often sparred with. Kawthar moved back and, though he extended his hand as if in support, I noted he did not touch her.

I was dumbstruck by Revna's appearance and conflicting emotions boiled within me. I must have looked foolish indeed, for Gersine elbowed me in the ribs and hissed, "Close your mouth. You will catch all the flies in the Holy Land."

Feeling my face redden, I snapped my gaping mouth shut, but could not look away from Revna.

Her feet were covered in silken slippers of exquisite craftsmanship. Upon her ankles were thin chains of silver adorned with more discs that made a tinkling sound as she moved. Bangles and bracelets encircled her wrists.

"I trust my ladies treated you kindly," Kawthar said, bowing low.

"They bathed me and dressed me in this finery," Revna said. "They gave me food and drink too."

Her voice was strange. I wondered what might have happened since I last saw her. Perhaps Kawthar sensed it too, for his eyes narrowed.

"They can be..." He hesitated, unsure of the word in Englisc. Lifting his hands like claws, he hissed like a cat. "One as beautiful as you can make other women angry, like cats splashed with hot oil."

Revna lowered her eyes demurely. I had never seen her so poised and cool. Wherever we went, when Runolf was not near to scare men off, she frequently received compliments and offers of marriage. She rebuffed all such approaches quickly and sometimes, when necessary, with a drawn blade. She was no stranger to men's gazes, but never before had I seen her content to accept such open flattery.

"You look like a princess," I blurted out, envious of the attention Revna was giving Kawthar. "Or a queen."

"Do I?" she said, barely glancing in my direction. I smelt her perfume as she swished past me to take the seat nearest Kawthar.

Beside me, Gersine let out a barking laugh and slapped me on the back. Runolf growled deep in his throat. The sound reminded me of the lion before it attacked.

"The monk speaks true," Kawthar said. "You wear those silks as if born to them. You are as at home in this palace as a gem in a piece of fine jewellery."

Kawthar clicked his fingers and one of the servants stepped forward bearing a velvet cushion, upon which rested a glittering necklace. With a flourish, the wali took the necklace and moved to stand behind Revna.

"Allow me," he said, holding out the circle of gold and gemstones.

After the briefest of hesitations, Revna raised her chin, permitting Kawthar to stoop and place the necklace about her neck. I fancied he murmured something in her ear as he did so, but I could not make out his words.

The necklace rested in the cleft between Revna's breasts, further accentuating the shape of her. It was studded with white stones, and at its centre nestled a sapphire that flashed in the torchlight. It was the blue of Revna's eyes.

Runolf had risen from his chair. "Easy, child," he said in his native Norse. "This man seeks to buy you with trinkets."

Revna flicked a look at me, then turned to stare at her father. Her eyes were cold.

"I am no child," she said simply. "And I cannot be bought so easily."

Kawthar may not have understood the words, though they were similar enough to Englisc that he might well have garnered the gist of them. Words or not, the frostiness between father and daughter was all too apparent. I wondered at this change in Revna. My cheeks were hot with jealousy, but I had no claim to her beyond friendship.

"Be wary," Runolf said. "Take care, daughter."

"Do not worry about me, Father," she said. "I do not need your protection."

An awkward silence fell over us. Kawthar hurried forward and lifted a tray of what looked like small golden apples.

"You must try one of these," he said, offering the platter to Revna.

Taking one between her long fingers, she lifted her veil with her other hand and popped the morsel into her mouth.

"Oh, it is meat," she said, surprised. "It is good."

"Meat covered in pastry. They are my favourite," Kawthar said. "Hunlaf here has been telling me of your journey all the way from Frankia. You must tell me how one so lovely as yourself has survived the hardships of such a voyage. You must be as strong and resourceful as you are beautiful."

Revna flashed me an icy glare, then turned back to Kawthar, the smile for him clear in her eyes. Without paying us further heed, she set about recounting the tale of our travels. Kawthar stared at her in open and rapt admiration.

"This is going to be trouble," whispered Gwawrddur, beckoning to a servant to refill his cup.

Runolf came to where we were sitting, glowering at Kawthar and Revna all the while. The wali was leaning forward attentively, nodding as he listened to each word that Revna uttered.

"Do not take it so hard, Runolf," said Drosten. "You are no fool. You knew this day would come."

Runolf picked up a piece of fried chicken from a tray and took a bite. "I did not think she would become besotted with one such as this wali," he hissed, chicken grease spattering his beard. He made some effort to keep his voice low, but for Runolf, that was like telling thunder not to roar. His words must have been clear to Kawthar, but if he heard, the wali gave no sign.

"You mean a wealthy and powerful man?" said Drosten. "Governor of a city and owner of a palace? Most men would be content with such a match for their daughter."

Kawthar laughed loudly at something Revna said. At no

point did he look away from her. In turn, she remained focused on his handsome face. I bunched my fists at my sides, fighting to master my anger.

Runolf rubbed his hand over his beard, dislodging the remnants of food that had settled there. "I know Revna is a woman," he admitted. "And one day she will be wed. But not here in this place, where the days are hotter than a furnace and lions stalk the night."

Hereward rose and joined us where we had huddled together. "You gossip like goodwives," he said, allowing a servant to pour more *Qamar al-Din* into his cup. "Anyone would think they had become betrothed, the way you whisper and gripe."

"We all know," whispered Runolf, "that a man such as Kawthar does not seek to plight his troth with the likes of Revna."

Hereward took a swig of the sweet apricot drink, licking his lips. "Do not fret," he said. "Do you not see that the man does not even touch her? Such is the way of these people, isn't that so, Hunlaf?"

"I believe it is forbidden for a devout Muslim man to touch a woman who is not his wife—"

"There you are," Hereward said, cutting me off before I could add, "or concubine". Judging from Runolf's face, it was just as well not to sow the seed of the thought in his imagination. It had already taken root in mine and my mind was clogged with dark thoughts of what might be. "There is nothing to worry about," Hereward continued. "You forget perhaps that Revna is a warrior, but she is also a woman. She has been surrounded by us for too long. Women like to be listened to. They like to be heard."

Gersine looked at me knowingly. I bit my lip. I recalled my recent conversations with Revna and knew I was to blame for her coolness towards me. Perhaps it was my doing that now she sat talking with Kawthar as if they were old friends.

"Be thankful of one thing, Runolf," Gersine said, winking at me, a smirk tugging at his lips.

"What?" snarled the Norseman.

"Revna could do much worse for herself than this wali. She could end up hand-fasted to someone with few prospects and less sense. A lowly monk turned warrior such as Hunlaf."

The men laughed and the tension eased from the gathering.

Runolf did not find it amusing. He used a piece of flatbread to scoop up a huge mouthful of spiced stew and chewed in taciturn silence, all the while glowering at where his daughter sat with the wali of Ierusalem.

For my part, I could feel my face grow hotter than ever as the men's laughter washed over me. I cursed Gersine, but deep down knew my feelings for Revna must have been clear to them all. Now, in the way of shield-brothers, they were having fun at my expense.

And yet, despite my flushed face and embarrassment, the truth was I did not care what they thought. All that mattered to me in that moment was that I had not listened to Revna when I'd had the chance.

I had not *seen* her, and now she was lost to me.

Twenty-One

When I look back over the vast distance of more than fifty years and recall the emotions that raged through me on that warm night in the palace gardens, I marvel at the certainty and ignorance of youth. I was no innocent child; I had killed many men, performed questionable acts to protect myself and others, and I had bedded several women. And yet I was still so unutterably young.

Sitting here in my cell, back aching and vision blurring from writing, my gnarled fingers stiff from holding the quill since shortly after dawn, it is hard to remember I was ever thus. I am still frequently foolish, and God knows I am a sinner, but to imagine I was ever so sure of my thoughts and feelings and those of others, amazes me.

Now, I am uncertain whether I will awaken each morning. It is a surprise to me, as I rise each new day, groaning and aching from my pallet, that the Lord has spared me once more. And yet with every daybreak I find myself in the land of the living. Outside my cell I can hear the brethren going about the daily routines of the minster. My day is punctuated by the stillness of the offices, when the remainder of the monks congregate in the chapel. When I am not lost in the world of my memories, I pause in my writing and pray with them, whispering the familiar words of the liturgies.

Each morning, it is the singing of the psalms at Prime drifting to me through the small window of my room that marks the moment I must sit down to continue the task that Godstan and the Almighty have set before me.

The abbot in his wisdom still allows me a small dose of the cunning woman's brew each night before Compline, and my sleep is mercifully deep, devoid of the nightmares that have so frequently plagued my slumber.

My mind is clearer now, though it took me some effort to rekindle the flame of fervour I had felt for writing my life's tale. In those first days, after picking up my pen once more, my head was fuzzy, as if filled with the wool that catches in clumps upon the teasels that grow on the edge of the lower meadow. But as the days wore on, so the wool clinging to my memories fell away and I could see the past clearly once more.

With that clarity, the pain at the losses I had suffered returned. And yet, although it hurts to recall some of what transpired, I do not begrudge spending these days once again with friends who have long since departed this life. My memories are oft a bitter draught to swallow, but there is joy in them too, as I think of the family I had found for myself aboard *Brymsteda*. Of course, I cannot ignore the torments that will come. I know what sorrows lie ahead. I can feel the pressure of them in my mind. Soon enough I must again write of dark events, of death and heartache, but I will not gallop ahead and spoil the telling of the tale.

Each day, Godstan sends one of the brothers to bring me food and drink, and *encaustum* and fresh goose feathers when I need them. It is never the same monk two days running. They do not wish to see me, and I am sure the abbot must need to order them to fulfil the onerous task of bringing sustenance and supplies to this cantankerous old man who now scratches out his life's story while they pray, tend to the sick, till the fields and welcome pilgrims to the minster. I do not blame them. If

I were in their shoes, I would resent the wizened old fool they must surely take me to be.

Godstan allows me to remain within my cell and for this I am grateful. Judging from the terse grunts from some of the brethren when they bring me a tray of food and a fresh jug of ale, the monks are content enough not to have to spend more time with me also.

My daily visitors are taciturn, but on the whole pleasant enough. They perhaps see tending to my needs as Christian charity.

It is only Ordric, a fat, spiteful man, who has been openly hostile to me. He insults me and mocks Coenric for a fool.

"You filled the boy's head with nonsense, and now he's dead. You're a sinner and a fool, Hunlaf. It would have been better if it had been you those Norse raiders had slain."

I could not disagree with him.

Twice he has spilt ink on perfectly good pages of vellum, sneering as he did so, despite his hollow apologies. He hates me, as the previous abbot, Criba, had. Ordric had long curried favour with Criba, an ill-tempered and choleric man, and he must have been sorely disappointed when he discovered he had not been given the position of abbot after Criba's sudden death, may the Lord rest his eternal soul.

When I was a younger man, when I still bore my sword in a baldric slung over my shoulder, I would have knocked Ordric senseless for his slights. But I am old now, and Ordric is younger and stronger than me.

It amuses me to imagine him reading these pages after my own demise. If he should do so, I must tell him that I would sometimes leave my quarters to repay his sharp words with an insult of my own. Was perchance the water in his ewer not as sweet as it should have been at times? I hope he did not blame whoever had drawn it from the well. The walk to the midden was sometimes too far for these old legs to trudge with a full bladder.

I miss Coenric. He would have laughed at that. He would have told me to confess my sins too, but still he would have laughed. I manage well enough without him now. And yet I have come to understand that his presence had made it easier for me to recollect the young man I had once been. We were different in countless ways, Coenric and I, but he was young, and there was no disguising the energy that came with youth.

Or the power of one's emotions. The strength with which anything could grab hold of one's thoughts, driving out all sense. Coenric's youthful exuberance and misplaced belief in his own abilities had led to his death. My youthful passion for Revna blinded me to all else that took place in that torchlit garden in Ierusalem.

Revna studiously ignored me just as Kawthar gave her all of his attention. The closeness between them enraged me and consumed my thoughts.

Now, thinking back with the eyes of an older and, I must hope, wiser man, I realise that Revna too was young. She was a strong warrior, able to defend herself with shield and sword, but in truth, she was little more than a girl; a young woman whose life had been sundered when her mother was slain and she was taken by Ljósberari. She had lost her innocence then; had done what she needed to survive. Her assurance in her abilities gave her an air of strength and control, but she was younger even than I, and for her part, she too felt her emotions with the force of youth, and she was certain that she would be able to make me jealous by feigning to feel affection for the impressive wali of Ierusalem.

I was too young and stupid to see this, and perhaps would never have understood her motives if she had not confessed to me later. But that night, as she laughed at Kawthar's words, fluttering her blue eyes and staring into Kawthar's dark ones, jealousy seethed within me. I had left it too late to express my feelings to Revna, and I had thrown away whatever chance at happiness I might ever have.

Her plan worked perfectly. I boiled with passionate fury, desperate for her attention and to tell her how much she meant to me. What Revna had failed to comprehend was that although her scheme was directed at me, there was another who believed he was the object of her favour. And while she tittered and smiled at whatever Kawthar said, so the wali's desire for her increased.

She had set out to ensnare me with my jealousy, but in doing so she had inflamed Kawthar's passions. Unwittingly, with her youthful naivety, Revna had set herself as the wali's prey, and just as with a lion that scents a hunk of bloody meat, she would have no hope of controlling Kawthar now that he was on the prowl.

Twenty-Two

The evening in the garden dragged on interminably for me. Moths and tiny insects flitted around the torches and, every now and then, the stink of the tanneries wafted to me, cutting through the warm sweet scents of food and flowers, and the delicate aroma of Revna's perfume. The rest of the men chattered, ate and drank, content to ignore me.

Absently I was aware of Gwawrddur and Hereward discussing what we should do on the morrow. Gwawrddur did not feel comfortable remaining within the palace and would rather continue on our journey. Hereward pointed out that without Giso to guide us, we did not know where we should go. Besides, he reminded Gwawrddur, Kawthar had already agreed that the old Iudeisc man, Aharon, would accompany us around the city come first light.

All the while I sat in dejected silence, watching as Kawthar charmed Revna. I could sense her drifting further from me each moment, like a man adrift at sea watching a sail glide away towards the horizon. My sudden feeling of sorrow was as strong as grief.

"Come," said Gersine, smiling in an attempt to lighten my mood, "sit with us and try some of these. They are sweeter than honey cakes." He held up a small baked treat, glistening with butter.

"I'm not hungry," I replied petulantly.

After a time, Gersine gave up trying to converse with me and returned to the others.

Like me, Runolf was sombre and serious, but after glowering at Kawthar and Revna for a while, he turned his back on them, joining in the talk with Hereward, Gwawrddur, Drosten and Gersine. The only indications that he was not content were the tension in his shoulders and the copious amounts of food he consumed. He might well have preferred wine, or ale, to take his mind off his daughter's behaviour. God knew I would have. But there was no intoxicating drink served at the wali's table, so instead the Norseman chewed continuously on one rich delicacy after another until he belched as loud as thunder, drawing a sharp look from Revna and a raised eyebrow from Kawthar.

It was late and the city that surrounded the palace was hushed when at last we retired for the night. Kawthar rose, ostentatiously stifling a yawn.

"Forgive me, my friends," he said. "I have been a poor host, but just as the moths are blinded by the flames of the torches, so my eyes have been blinded by Revna's beauty. Still, I trust you have enjoyed the provender." He smiled broadly at Runolf, who merely grunted in response. "And I am sure you will find your beds comfortable. I fear I will not see you in the morning, as there are many pressing matters I must attend to. But Aharon will take you where you wish to go, and tomorrow evening, I look forward to hearing of your day in my city. Until then, I bid you farewell."

He bowed deeply to Revna, and I thought for a stomach-twisting moment he was going to take her hand and lead her to his bedchamber. Instead, his eyes lingered on hers, and then, turning on his heel, the wali strode from the garden.

At once, two dark-garbed female servants stepped from the shadows. All that could be seen of them were their eyes above their veils.

"We have come to take the lady to her quarters," the shorter of the women said.

"They are here to lead you to your chamber," I said, my tone awkward and hollow as I stared with barely disguised longing at Revna.

"Whatever you think of me, Hunlaf," Revna replied, "I am no fool."

"I do not think you are," I said, but already she was following the servants up the steps and out of the garden, and I doubt she heard me. "*You* are no fool," I whispered to her back, so quietly none of my comrades would hear, "I am."

Looking back, I see that the two of us were fools, in our own way. Both so young and yearning for the other.

Gwawrddur slapped me on the back. "Don't look so glum, Kill—"

I cut him off, my voice hard. "You gave me your word."

"I did at that," he said, nodding. "And I give you my word on something else. Nothing is as bad in the light of day as it is in the dark of night. Things will seem less dire come the morning."

Sullenly I trudged back to our quarters, following the silent guards across the gardens, through arched gateways and along corridors lit by the flickering flames of small oil lamps.

I didn't speak further. I lay down, dejected and brooding, on one of the beds provided for us. Whatever else I thought of the wali, he was a generous host and the bed was indeed soft and comfortable.

I lay there in the darkness looking up at a pale line of moonlight on the ceiling, and listening while the others murmured and banged about the large room. When I closed my eyes, all I could see was Kawthar and Revna, leaning close as lovers. I wondered what madness this was that had gripped me. We were in Ierusalem, the holiest of all cities, and tomorrow I would see the church of the Holy Sepulchre, the Mount of

Olives and the Lord alone knew what other wonders. And yet my mind was filled with images of Revna and the wali.

I offered up a prayer that Gwawrddur would be proven right as he so often was, and that, with the fresh light of a new day, my concerns would be lessened.

When I awoke with a start in the darkest part of the night, tugged to wakefulness by a light touch on my arm and Revna's muffled sob, I knew with a sinking feeling in my stomach that the Welshman's optimism had been unfounded.

Twenty-Three

I sat up quickly, rubbing my eyes to clear them of sleep. It was very dark in the room. And hot. I had lain down without removing the robe I had been given and now it was plastered to my body, sodden with sweat.

Revna's face was a pale smudge in the gloom, illuminated by the thin light oozing through the window.

"Revna?" I was confused. "What—? How—?" For a heartbeat I wondered if I might be dreaming, but her hand gripped my arm tightly, digging her fingers painfully into my skin and snapping me fully alert.

"Help me," she whispered, a sob catching in her throat. "I don't know what to do."

I glanced about the room that I shared with Drosten, Gwawrddur, Hereward, Runolf and Gersine. Amazingly, none of them had awoken. Revna shifted her position and a shaft of silver moonlight fell on her face. A dark smudge stained her cheek. A sudden coolness washed over me.

"Is that blood?" I asked, brushing my fingertips over her smooth skin. She flinched at my touch. My heart clenched. "Is it?" I asked again, my voice hard and sharp as flint.

She wiped at her cheek and seemed surprised to find her fingers smeared with the dark substance. It looked black in the darkness.

"It's not mine," she said. She let out a trembling sigh in an effort to master her emotions. "It is Kawthar's."

"What happened?" I asked, pushing myself to my feet. "If he hurt you—"

"Hush," she hissed, some of her usual controlled demeanour returning. "Kawthar is tied up in my chamber—"

"Tied?" My thoughts whirled around my head like autumn leaves in a gale. I could not seem to grasp one long enough to comprehend what was happening.

The loud clatter of a stool startled us both. Revna let out a small cry of alarm.

"What has that whoreson done?" came Runolf's rumbling growl from the darkness. "I told you to be wary of him, girl."

For an instant I thought perhaps Revna would correct her father, as she had the previous evening, but after the briefest of hesitations, she flew across the room and into his muscular arms.

"Sorry," she said, burying her face against his chest. "I'm sorry."

Runolf stroked her hair and patted her back awkwardly.

The others were awake now. A light flared in the doorway and I tensed, thinking perhaps Kawthar had sent guards to find Revna. Whatever had occurred, if it had resulted in the shedding of the wali's blood and Revna's tearful state, I could see no way this could end well for us. The door closed as quickly as it had opened and the room was bathed in a warm glow of an oil lamp. The light from its flame showed the consternation and worry on Gwawrddur's features. He had reached outside the door and taken the small lamp from the corridor outside our room.

I blinked against the sudden brightness. In the lamp's glow I could see that Revna was no longer dressed in the fine silks Kawthar had given her. She was clad once more in breeches and kirtle though I noted her golden hair was covered by a dark scarf bound about her head. The lamplight showed clearly the blood on her face, crimson against the pale, freckled skin.

Holding her at arm's length, Runolf saw the blood for the first time. His face clouded, his lips pulling back in a snarl of fury.

"What did that nithing do?" he spat through clenched teeth. "I will kill him." His voice was rising along with his anger. I felt that same fury burning within me. Sleep had fled completely now, and I wanted nothing more than to have a sword in my hand and Kawthar standing before me.

Drosten and Hereward too sprang to their feet on seeing Revna's bloodied face. From their scowls, I judged them to have the same thoughts as Runolf and I.

"Hush, Father," Revna said, wiping away her tears and gaining control of her emotions. "I am not harmed. This is not my blood."

"Did he..." Runolf's voice choked off. He could not bring himself to utter the words.

Revna gave a curt shake of her head. "He tried." She bit her lip. Tears welled in her eyes, but she swiped them away. "I do not think he enjoyed the experience of coming to my bed uninvited."

"Did you kill him, lass?" asked Drosten. His hands were bunched into fists and the flickering lamplight made his tattoos appear to writhe along his bulging, powerful arms.

Another shake of her head. "Broke his nose and blackened his eye." She took a deep breath. "He might not drink wine or ale, but his head will feel as though he has drunk a pigskin full of the stuff come morning. I cracked a stool over his head. And I gave his balls a good stamping when I had bound him."

Runolf chuckled, proud of his daughter. "We should kill him," he said. "No man forces himself on my daughter and lives."

"He did not succeed," Revna said.

"Our weapons are in the gatehouse," I reminded Runolf.

"I need no weapon to kill the likes of that perfumed peacock," he said.

"Wait," said Gwawrddur. We all turned to where he stood by the door. Placing the lamp on a small table, he stepped closer, keeping his voice low.

"Much as I too would like to see the man pay for what he has done, it seems perhaps Revna has already punished him enough. There is little to be gained by slaying him."

"He wouldn't be able to touch any other man's daughter," said Runolf. "There is that."

"True," conceded Gwawrddur, "but what would happen to us? To Revna, if we killed the wali of Ierusalem? Would you see your daughter executed?"

"The Welshman speaks sense," said Hereward.

"I try," said Gwawrddur. "Now, keep your voices down. The dawn is still some way off and from the stillness of the palace, I would say Kawthar has not yet been discovered."

Revna was nodding. "He placed guards on my door and told me he had given them orders not to disturb him until morning."

"How did you leave the room?" asked Gwawrddur. "Were you seen?"

"I don't think so," Revna said. "I climbed from the window and came across the garden. When I'd found the window to your sleeping quarters, I climbed through."

"How did you know this was the correct window?" asked Hereward.

Revna gave a sheepish smile. "Nobody else in all the world snores like my father," she said.

Gwawrddur chuckled. "We can all attest to that. You did well, girl."

She lowered her gaze, making no comment that he had called her 'girl'. "Do you truly believe we can escape from the palace?" she asked, her voice small and fearful.

"Until Kawthar is discovered," he said, "anything is possible."

"I do not see how," Hereward said.

"By Óðinn," Runolf grumbled, "I say we slay the bastard and be done with it."

"Perhaps there is a way," I said tentatively. All eyes turned to me and I swallowed back my nervousness. "First, one of us should rouse the others."

Arcenbryht, Beorn, Eadstan and the rest of the warriors from *Brymsteda* were billeted in a nearby room.

"How do we do that without rousing suspicion?" asked Hereward. "There are guards in every passageway of the palace."

"The same way Revna came here," I said, pointing to the window. The arch in the stone wall was divided by a slender column, making two narrow openings. The shutters were open, letting in the grey light of the pre-dawn. Outside, I could just make out the looming forms of the animal-shaped hedges that dotted the grounds.

"There is no way any of us will fit through there," scoffed Hereward.

He was right, but the answer to that problem was obvious to us all.

"I'll do it," Revna said.

"Are you sure?" I asked.

"You said so yourself – the others must be warned and none of you can squeeze through there. It is tight enough for me. But what do I tell them when I reach their room? What plan do you have for getting us out of here."

"I would not call it a plan," I said, my mind spinning as I tried to think of every possible eventuality. "I urge you all to pray, for there are many more ways this can go wrong than right."

"Well," said Drosten in his Pictish burr, "if there is any

place in the world where God might be inclined to listen to our prayers, I'd say Ierusalem must be it."

"Very well," said Runolf with a sigh, "I can save my vengeance for another day. But I hope you know what you are doing, Hunlaf."

I hoped so too. The sweat had dried on my skin and I shivered. Through the window I could see the sky was paler than it had been a few heartbeats before, turning slowly with each passing moment from the purple darkness of night to the cool steel grey of dawn.

"Well, Killer?" Gwawrddur asked, breaking his promise again. "What do you have in mind?"

It would be day soon and the palace would awaken. Once that happened, Kawthar would be found and all would be lost. As it was I had little faith in the idea that had come to me, but I offered up a silent prayer to the Almighty that He might smile on us and deliver us from this house of an infidel, one of the Al-Muslimun who had taken command of God's holy city.

There was no time to ponder what would happen if the Lord did not aid us. So, taking a calming breath, as quickly and simply as I was able, I told my friends how we might escape the palace.

Twenty-Four

Sweat trickled down my neck as the commander of the gatehouse guards inspected our party. He was a thickset man, with a thick black beard and skin the colour of seasoned oak. The sky above the gates was lightening with the dawn, but the area before the gates was still in shadow. At my back stood all the men from *Brymsteda* who had come inland from Yafah. They were crowded in a tight group. Revna was in the midst of them, her head bowed, her gold-bright hair covered. The commander's expression was one of incredulity. I did not look behind me. I knew well enough my companions and knew we made for a strange sight.

Some of them had chosen to don their travelling garb, while others, like me, still wore the robes they had been given after the bath the previous day. Outside the walls, I could hear the calls of traders and the clatter of carts on the cobbled streets of the city. Ierusalem was awakening and, behind us, the servants and slaves of the palace were readying the wali's residence for the day.

"You call this a plan?" whispered Drosten. I ignored him, but the Pict was not wrong. There was precious little guile to what we were attempting. But with each passing moment, the time grew closer when the master of the palace would be discovered, bloody, bound and gagged. I could feel the pressure of time like a physical thing. But there was nothing for it now. We were committed and all we could do was forge ahead and pray to the Blessed Virgin, her son, the Almighty, and all His saints that we would be outside the palace walls when the alarm was raised.

"It is early indeed," said the commander of the guard, frowning. "I have barely finished prayers."

The chanting cry of the *muezzin* had resonated from the nearby *masjid* shortly before, and when we had arrived at the gatehouse, the guards were just rising from their mats.

I shifted closer to Aharon, reminding him with my closeness of the threat we had made to him, though I doubt it was necessary. After we had sent one of the guards to fetch Aharon to our quarters, Runolf had taken the old man's neck in his massive hands and lifted him from his feet. I had hissed that the huge Norseman would rip Aharon's head off if he betrayed us.

I could still see the red marks about the old man's scrawny throat. But to his credit, Aharon had regained his composure quickly. He was nodding at the guard now.

"We wanted to leave sooner," he said, "but we were respectful of your faith."

The guard grunted. "I would have thought the visitors would wish to break their fast before leaving," the commander said, a scowl on his tanned features.

Aharon shrugged. "They are not from these parts. Who can understand the ways of strangers, and Christians at that? They say they wish to pray at the tomb of Jesus before they eat."

"All of them?" The guard looked sceptical.

"They have travelled for many weeks to come here and they are devout. I would not stand before them and their prayers. We are all *Ahl al-kitab*, after all."

A cockerel crowed somewhere in the city. Several dogs started barking, quickly followed by the shouts of an angry woman, her shrill voice thinned by distance. The rays of the rising sun were bright on the walls of the palace buildings, the scent of the flowers and earth of the garden thick in the cool air. Our time was running out, I could feel it like a hand pressing between my shoulder blades, pushing me forwards. There was no time to waste.

"We must leave at once," I said, using my sternest tone. "You would not wish for the wali to hear how you impeded his guests from attending mass, would you?"

The guard sneered, fixing me with a disdainful glare. For a moment I worried I had gone too far, that he would push back against my command, but one of the guards under his command, clearly deciding this was not worth the trouble, was already moving to the gate. The young guard looked expectantly at his commander. My heart thumped in my chest, but I raised my head, meeting the guard commander's stare; feigning righteous indignation at having our progress blocked.

At last, the commander relented. Waving his hand at the two guards who were now poised by the iron-bound timber doors, he gave the command to raise the locking bar. Done with us, he turned and stalked away back to the gatehouse.

I let out my breath as the guards moved to lift the solid wooden bar from the gate. I could scarcely believe we had done it. We would be out of the palace in moments. Of course, it was only a matter of time before the wali would be found and then men would be sent after us, but our first obstacle had been these gates. What happened after that would once again be in the Lord's hands.

I looked back at my friends. Gwawrddur raised his eyebrows. Runolf gave me a curt nod. Drosten grinned at me, the marks on his face stark in the dawn sunlight that now crested the wall and lit the tops of the plants in the garden.

"Your plan was never in doubt," Drosten said, shaking his head in disbelief.

In that exact same instant, shouts of alarm went up from the wali's quarters. The guards at the gate faltered. The locking bar was still in place. The smirk on Drosten's face evaporated as the shouts grew in intensity within the palace compound.

For the briefest of moments the guards did not move. The commander halted in the gatehouse doorway, half turning and cocking his head to listen. They were unsure what was the cause of the disturbance.

I had no such uncertainty. Seizing the sliver of opportunity for surprise that yet remained, I shoved Aharon towards Beorn and sprinted in the direction of the gatehouse.

"Open the gates," I shouted, abandoning all caution.

I did not turn to see how my companions reacted. I dared not take my eyes from the commander who had turned to face me and had lowered himself into a defensive stance. Already suspicious, his surprise had lasted only an instant. Now he waited for me, crouched and prepared for my charge, teeth bared and sword drawn.

I was on him in a heartbeat. He lunged and I twisted my body, the wicked blade of his sword tearing through my robe and narrowly missing my chest. Grabbing his sword arm, I twisted his wrist and punched him hard in the face. He staggered back, dropping his sword and spitting blood. I snatched up the blade, but before I could use it, he threw himself back through the doorway and slammed the door shut.

I could hear him cursing and fumbling with a bolt. There was no time to think now. Without hesitating, I barged my shoulder into the timber. The commander had not yet locked the door, and it slammed open, hitting him and tumbling him to the floor.

Behind me, Gwawrddur called my name. Flicking a glance in his direction, I saw that the guards at the gate already lay motionless. Pendrad and Sygbald were lifting the locking bar.

"Come on, Hunlaf," Gwawrddur shouted. "We have to go."

Across the gardens, dozens of guards were streaming from the palace buildings. The early morning sun glinted from spear points and helms.

"Our weapons are in here!" I yelled, turning back to the commander of the guard. He had scrambled away and taken another blade from a table. Rising to his feet, he hawked and spat a wad of bloody spittle onto the stone floor.

"You die now, Christian," he said.

"We shall see about that, you heathen dog," I snarled, consumed by rage. All of my frustration and anger at the events of the previous evening, my hatred for Kawthar and what he had done to Revna, my fear at being caught and killed here, coalesced into a white-hot flame of fury. Stamping forward I slashed at his face. He feinted, then flicked out a riposte. He was skilled and fast, and his blade cut a shallow slash along my forearm.

Cursing, I drew back. I could not allow my ire and dismay to control me. Recalling all Gwawrddur had taught me over the years, and drawing from my experience in combat, I ignored the sounds of shouts and fighting behind me. Forcing distractions from my mind, I focused on my adversary's eyes and his movements.

He spat again and licked blood from his lips, then, seemingly without warning, he lunged. But I had noticed the tiniest shift in his shoulders, the merest hint of his intention as his eyes narrowed, and I was ready for his attack. Parrying his blade, I pushed it out of line. I stepped inside his guard and drove his own sword's blade into his throat. Blinking stupidly, he tried to pull back the blade he held; to deal me a killing blow even as he died, choking on his own lifeblood. I slapped his arm away with my palm and savagely twisted the blade in his neck. With a shudder, he died, the sword falling from his lifeless fingers with a clang to the stone floor.

I tugged the sword from his throat, sending a freshet of blood spraying up the whitewashed wall and across the flagstones. Movement behind me made me spin around. It was Gwawrddur and at his back were Gersine and Gamal.

"There is no time," Gwawrddur said, breathless.

"Then speak less and help more," I snapped.

Rushing to the large chest that rested along one wall, I flung it open. I had been worried that our weapons would no longer be there, and I would have placed us in more danger for nothing, but I recognised at once Runolf's great axe and the swords, seaxes and knives of the others.

"Take what you can," I said, offering up thanks to God. "But be quick about it."

We had hoped to slip out under the guise of pilgrims heading to mass at the Church of the Holy Sepulchre, and as such we had reconciled ourselves to forsaking our byrnies, helms and shields, our pack animals and supplies too. I had no idea how we might escape the city now with so many of the wali's guards alerted to our presence, but if we were to stand any chance at all, we would surely need our weapons.

Clumsily taking Runolf's axe and an armful of scabbarded swords, I moved to the door. Hereward and Drosten had taken up the spears from the fallen doorwards and were holding off the guards that flowed from the palace. As I watched, Runolf took up the great timber locking beam and charged with it towards the mass of warriors congregating in the gardens. Before he reached them, he released the heavy plank, sending it hurtling into their ranks and scattering them.

"Swords!" I cried, running towards the gates.

Gwawrddur, Gersine and Gamal were close behind, each struggling under the weight of several blades and a tangle of belts. I flung the swords I carried onto the ground before my friends. "Arm yourselves."

Runolf was roaring at the guards, screaming his defiance, and I thought he might be lost to the battle fury that sometimes gripped warriors. But he turned and sprinted back. One of the guards threw a spear after him, but it missed by a hand's breadth, landing at Eadstan's feet. Without pause, Eadstan scooped it up and, taking three short running steps, he let fly the spear at the amassed guards. It flew true, punching into one unfortunate man's stomach, sending him flailing backwards to lie panting and moaning on the earth.

I tossed Runolf his axe as he approached. "Thought you might need this," I said.

Deftly, he caught it without slowing his pace. "Anything is possible," he replied with a wolfish grin.

I hoped he was right, and – turning away from the palace – I rushed out of the open gates, Revna and my shield-brothers following close in my wake.

Behind us, the angry yells of the guards were clear in the bright morning air. And the sound of their boots crunching on the garden's paths as they rushed after us was as loud as thunder.

Twenty-Five

We streamed out of the gates and sprinted up the sloping road. It was just after dawn and the city had not yet completely thrown off the blanket of night. The street was almost deserted, the buildings casting deep shadows, the roofs above bright where they caught the rising sun.

"Ask him where we should go," yelled Beorn over the slapping of our footfalls on the cobbles and the shouts of our pursuers.

I glanced at the broad-shouldered warrior and was shocked to see he was dragging Aharon along by the collar. The old man's eyes were wide, his face wan with terror. I had not realised Beorn still had hold of him, and judging from his heavy breathing, Aharon would not be able to keep up this pace for much longer. Beorn was right though. We had no idea where to go, so I yelled at Aharon as we ran.

"Guide us!"

Aharon was aghast. "There is nowhere," he panted, looking over his shoulder to where a mass of guards filled the road behind us, no more than a spear's throw distant.

"Think!" I urged him. "Anywhere we might evade them. Or take a stand."

"You are doomed," he said. "They will crucify you all."

"Help us, and we will let you go." My own voice was ragged, breathless from the fight and the uphill run.

"If I help you," Aharon wheezed, "Kawthar will have me killed."

"If you don't," I said savagely, "you'll not live to face him. I will kill you myself."

His horror was plain on his face, but still he did not respond. Already I could sense he was slowing us down, forcing Beorn to pull him along bodily every few steps. If we had any hope of escape, we would need to release the old man.

"Where is the nearest city gate?" I demanded, changing the tack of my questioning.

Aharon stumbled, and Beorn hauled him roughly up and onwards. The guards were closer now. They would be on us in moments.

"Which way?" I bellowed in Aharon's face. I clenched my fist, ready to strike him, but it was not necessary.

"Turn right when you reach the second road," he panted. "Lions' Gate is that way."

I could do nothing but trust he spoke the truth. He was flagging and there was no time for more conversation.

"Release him," I said to Beorn. "He cannot keep up with us."

Beorn immediately relinquished his hold on Aharon and shoved him away. The old man staggered and fell to his knees.

Ahead I could see the first road he had spoken of. At the junction, three men dressed in the garb of the *Badw* were leading heavily laden camels. They had heard our approach and were busy trying to pull their animals out of our way.

"Those beasts," I shouted, renewing my speed, "we can send them into the guards." I sprinted directly at the merchants and their camels. Gersine ran with me and Gwawrddur was close too. The sight of us closing on them at a run, swords drawn and blood on the blade of my weapon, gave the *Badw* pause.

They shouted at us, warding us off with outstretched hands. The camels bellowed and spat. One of the men, young and tall, drew a long curved blade.

We did not slow our run.

"Out of our way!" I screamed. "Leave the camels." I did not wish to harm these men, but I would if I had to. They must have seen that in my eyes, for at the last moment, the two older, unarmed men, let go of their camels' harness and backed away, dragging their protesting younger companion with them. He waved his sword at us ineffectually. These men had done nothing to me, and I was glad I had not needed to shed innocent blood.

"Run! Run!" I cried, waving the rest of our party past, and dragging on the rope of the nearest camel, pulling its head around to face the oncoming guards. Gwawrddur and Gersine each grabbed the bridle of a beast and did their best to turn them.

The guards were not shouting now. They ran on determinedly. A few had slowed their pace, evidently winded by the slope. But several more were only a few paces behind us.

The instant Runolf and fat Oslaf, the slowest of our number, were past, I slapped the rump of the camel. It bellowed in annoyance and rolled its eyes, but it did not budge. The guards were closer now. In a few heartbeats we would be forced to stand and fight. Desperately, I hit the camel again, harder this time, but to no avail.

The young *Badawi* yelled at me, fighting himself free of his companions. I brandished my bloody sword at him. He hesitated.

"Give it the blade," Gwawrddur shouted. In that same moment he jabbed his sword into his camel's haunch, sending the animal leaping forward with a howl of pain.

Gersine and I copied the Welshman, stabbing our swords into the camels' hindquarters. I did not stab deeply, but enough to draw blood and propel the animal careening in fear down the slope and into the guards. The warriors were dispersed, throwing themselves out of the path of the terrified animals.

The *Badawi* swordsman shouted in anger at our treatment of the valuable creatures. He rushed forward, sword raised high. There was no time now to become embroiled in a fight. Taking two quick steps to close the gap, I caught his blade on my sword. Without slowing, I grasped a handful of his robe, pulling him forwards. Twisting my hips, I pulled him over my outstretched left leg. He sprawled on the muck-spattered cobbles. He still gripped his sword, so I stamped on the blade and, stooping, delivered a savage punch to his face with my sword hand. The sword guard split his lip and he spat blood. He was open for a killing thrust then, but I did not wish to slay him. He had done me no wrong. Kicking his sword away, I turned and fled after my friends.

"I should turn and fight," said Runolf through gritted teeth. Never a fast runner, the giant Norseman was labouring up the hill, his face slick with sweat. "Oslaf and I could hold them off while the rest of you escape."

"No," I said, unwilling to contemplate such a drastic course of action. "Turn right at the next road."

Oslaf too was blowing hard and crimson of face, but he nodded his thanks.

"I'm no craven," he panted, "but I would rather not meet my maker this day, if it can be avoided."

"Pray it can be so," I said. In truth, I could see no way out of this predicament.

We kept running, speeding past men and women who jumped out of our path. A small girl ran out of a doorway, then halted. Shocked and frightened, she cried out and fell to the ground in the middle of the road. The child's mother screamed.

The men barrelled past the terrified girl, avoiding her as they ran. When Runolf reached her, he scooped her up, dashing to the side of the road, where he handed her to her screaming mother, before running on.

We had reached the corner that Aharon had indicated now and as we rounded it, I cast a glance down the hill. The camels had ceased their running and were standing, shaking and lowing pitifully. Their owners had pulled the young swordsman to his feet and together they were making their way tentatively towards the camels.

The guards had recovered and were once again running after us. With a start, I recognised Aziz ibn Fawaz leading them, his face contorted with rage. Two of the guardsmen remained behind, leaning on each other for support, evidently injured by the stampeding camels. A small victory, but a triumph all the same. I turned my attention to the road ahead.

This thoroughfare was busier, with groups of traders setting up their stalls. The air was dense with the aroma of cooking meat, baking bread, the pungent tang of spices, and the acrid bite of ordure from the donkeys, camels and horses that dotted the street.

I was at the rear of the group now, and I goaded Runolf and Oslaf on. We clattered past a stall where a black-clad man was opening the shutters and setting out a table for his wares. The sun, bright in my eyes, glittered off the trinkets and jewellery on display. Without thinking, I grabbed the edge of the board and heaved it over. Silver baubles flashed, to land in the muck, strewn across the cobbles. The jeweller yelled furiously, but I was already past. People moved into the street behind me to help him recover his wares, or perhaps to pocket them for themselves.

The guards reached the crowd a few heartbeats later, pushing and shouting for them to clear the path. I recalled what Aziz had done to that poor man before the Yafah Gate and prayed that God would forgive me for placing these innocents in that brute's path. Gwawrddur ran alongside me, looking back over his shoulder.

"They are slowed again," he said, "but we cannot run like this for much longer. Soon enough, there will be guards ahead of us as well as behind. What do you propose when we reach the gate?"

"I've not thought that far ahead," I admitted.

"That's what I had feared," he replied.

As it was, I did not need to concern myself with that eventuality. We did not make it to the Lions' Gate. Even as Gwawrddur and I conversed in gasping breaths, so Hereward, Drosten and the others at the head of our band came to a skidding halt. A waggon, drawn behind a team of mules, had come from a narrow side street. The muleteer was attempting to turn the team, but the waggon was cumbersome and heavily laden with barrels and it had become stuck. The turn was impeded by a great heap of rubble where a building was being repaired. This prevented the mules' movement, with the outcome that the waggon, the mules and the pile of rocks blocked our path as effectively as a wall.

Instantly, it was clear we would not be able to move the waggon before the guards were upon us. Seeing this at the same time as me, Runolf growled and turned to face our enemies.

"We stand and fight after all," he said, wiping sweat from his face and spitting. He sounded almost happy at the prospect. My guts churned. I was always exhilarated by combat, but this would end in death or capture for us all, and I was certain that Aharon had been right about what the wali would do to us should we be seized. I did not wish to remain in the Holy Land to discover what Christ's Passion had felt like by reliving his fate.

"Shieldwall," Hereward roared, and even though we carried no shields, we quickly fell into position on either side of the Northumbrian. As ever, Runolf took a central place, where his bulk and great axe could punch a hole in an enemy line, whilst Drosten and Gwawrddur positioned themselves at the flanks.

The ends of the wall were often the most dangerous and, as such, we put the bravest and best of the warriors there.

We were quickly formed up. Numbering fifteen we were able to stand two deep across the road. The guardsmen, seeing we were trapped, slowed their frantic pursuit. Aziz began barking orders. Stragglers were still joining them as they dressed the line. Like us, they were all panting and appeared content with this pause and a chance to catch their breath.

The traders and townsfolk, who moments before had been going about their early morning business, had fled, vanishing into doorways and down alleyways. The muleteer dropped down from his waggon and ran off. I saw faces at windows, but the street was empty now apart from us and the wali's guardsmen. Nobody wanted to be caught between the two groups.

"No time for resting," snarled Hereward. "Our only chance is to break their line now, before they are set and ready for us. The longer we tarry, the more their number will grow."

Runolf hefted his axe. His flushed face was almost the same hue as his hair and beard. Sweat drenched the robes he wore and his chest heaved, but I knew there was plenty more energy in the huge Norseman yet.

"By Óðinn's wounds," he said, "enough talking. Let's kill the bastards!"

"Bebbanburg!" bellowed Hereward, taking up his old battle cry and rushing forward. Those men who had come from that great northern fortress took up the cry and ran with him, weapons held high.

"Óðinn!" roared Runolf, and I fancied I heard Revna's voice, echoing her father's shout to their old pagan god.

Every one of us was screaming, each warrior calling out their own particular cry. The street reverberated with the cacophony of our voices and the thunder of our footfalls as we ran.

I yelled my own rallying call: "*Pro Christo!*" my hoarse

voice tearing at my throat. My mouth was sour with the fear of what we were doing; the danger it put us all in. Had we rescued Revna only to see her cut down in the street?

It was madness, that headlong charge into armed and armoured men, and yet I never considered running from the fray. These were my shield-kin. I would stand and fight with them; die with them too, if that was what the Lord had in store for me. I screamed for God's protection, hoping beyond all reason that He would spare Revna.

Then we were on them.

They had raised their shields, bracing themselves for the impact of our charge, but still they could not halt Runolf's barrelling bulk. He crashed into the centre of their line, pushing a shield aside and bringing his axe down on a man's head, cleaving helm and skull in a spray of blood.

A racing heartbeat later, we were all there, shieldwall of the wali's guardsmen against our ragged, frantic line of savage warriors. There was no time for thought now and my heart soared with the wanton joy of the killing.

A blade flickered at my face. Without thought I caught it on my sword, deflecting it so it hissed harmlessly past my eyes with a glinting flicker. Bringing my sword down, I sliced into my enemy's neck. A young man, he fell away, bleeding in great sheets from a severed artery, the knowledge that he would never grow old graven on his shocked features.

Instantly, I was faced by another guard. This man was older, with a face as dark as a chestnut and grey streaking his black beard. He held his shield high, his sword ready at his side. I saw immediately he was a skilled and experienced fighter.

All around me the two lines were battling ferociously. Men were screaming in agony. I thought I heard someone cry out in anguish in Englisc, but I could not look to see who had been injured, or worse.

The blood from the wound in my arm was soaking the sleeve of my robe, reminding me of the danger of complacency. I kept my eyes on the grizzled warrior before me, waiting for him to make the first move. He was a cagey one, though, and seemed content to stand his ground. We both knew that each moment that passed could only strengthen his position and that of his comrades. I needed to draw him out, or risk an assault on him.

He had an oval shield – that made striking him difficult. Ideally, I would tire him, relying on my youth to wear him down. But there was no time for that. I swung my sword in an awkward swipe at his right, knowing this would leave my own right side exposed. I prayed he would react.

He did. Raising his shield to take my sword blow, he lunged forward, aiming a strike at my undefended side. Leaping forward, I changed the direction of my blade, catching his sword with a clang of steel on steel. With my left hand, I grasped the rim of his shield and twisted it down and away.

Gritting his teeth against the pain in his wrist and arm, he struggled with me for control of the shield, momentarily ignoring his sword and my own blade. He had not anticipated this move, but I had planned it. With a gleeful rush of triumph, I thrust my sword in a vicious stab into his face. The blade pierced the flesh just beneath his nose. Howling in agony, he collapsed backwards. I sent another slicing cut at him, but it skittered across his byrnie.

The man's face was a bloody ruin, but he was not dead and he yet held his sword. He flailed it at me from where he lay in the muck, roaring in fury and pain. I skipped back out of his reach.

I looked about me, taking stock of how things went for us. My stomach twisted. It was not good. We had acquitted ourselves well. Several of the guardsmen lay bleeding or dead on the manure-clogged cobbles. But two of our own had also fallen. Oslaf was on his knees, blood soaking the voluminous robe he wore. Hereward, Beorn and Eadstan stood over him, fighting hard to keep the wali's men away.

Ida too had been wounded. As I looked I saw it was worse

than that. There was nothing anyone could do for Ida now. He lay on his back unmoving, skin white, vacant eyes staring up at the pale blue sky. The ground around him was pooled in the blood that still pumped in great gushes from his opened throat.

Gamal and Pendrad struggled to drag Oslaf away from the fighting. His face was as pallid as curds, his hands – clutching at his bulging stomach – were coated in blood.

Runolf joined Hereward and the others, closing ranks around Oslaf and those who were pulling him to safety. Seeing that no enemy had stepped into the gap before me, I moved closer to Runolf, snatching up a fallen shield as I went. We formed a tight knot about the wounded man and stared balefully at the line of guards before us.

I counted eight of the wali's men prostrate on the cobbles. One was crawling back towards his comrades, weeping as he went, leaving a trail of blood from a deep gash in his thigh. He looked little more than a child. Despite their losses, there were still more than a score left standing. More were running along the road to bolster their numbers.

"Has your god any magic that can help us?" growled Runolf.

"If it is the Lord's will," I said, panting, "He will see us safely from this."

Runolf laughed.

"I admire your faith, Hunlaf," he said. "I put my trust in this." He slapped the haft of his axe. Blood spattered from the gore-soaked iron head. He surveyed the guardsmen glowering at us from no more than two dozen paces away. They were all grim-faced. Aziz was shouting orders. Soon they would be ready to renew the fight. In truth, despite my words, I had no faith we would live to see the sunset.

"Well, Killer," Runolf said, "if this is to be the end, I am proud to have you at my side. Perhaps the All-Father will take a Christ follower like you into his Hall of the Slain."

"Anything is possible," I rasped, trying to force a smile. My words snagged in my dry mouth. I was not ready for death, and yet it seemed death was ready for us that day, ready to welcome me with open skeletal arms and grasping bony hands.

"You should have let Oslaf and me hold them off," Runolf said. "You might have lived then. Now Oslaf won't survive that wound, and I would gladly have given my life to save Revna and the rest of you."

His words filled me with dismay. It was true. If I had listened to him, things might have been very different.

"No time for that now," said Gwawrddur, his voice cutting like a blade. "The lad did nothing wrong. You hear me, Hunlaf?" he said. "Nobody can tell what will happen in battle. Only a fool thinks of what might have been. I know you and how you fret on things without your control. If we meet our maker today, you must not feel guilt for anything you have done. None of this is your doing."

His words did little to assuage the guilt I felt, and to hear Gwawrddur speak of dying made it all the more real. I shuddered.

"I am not shriven," I said weakly. "I have not given my confession for months." I had hoped a priest in the Church of the Holy Sepulchre would hear my confession, but now I would die without absolution. I glanced at Revna. She looked back at me, pale-faced, but chin raised, proud and defiant. The sword in her hand was smeared red. The blood was bright in the morning sunshine. I regretted terribly not having spoken to her of my feelings. Now I feared I would never have the chance.

"Ready, men," shouted Hereward. "The whoresons are coming again. If we are to die here today, make the blood price high!"

The wounded guards had been dragged behind the line of guardsmen. And now, once more cajoled into formation by Aziz, the wali's force began to march forward.

I drew in a deep breath. The air was warm and thick with the aroma of manure, sweat, spices, the metallic bite of fresh blood, and smoke from the city's cooking fires. With a last nod and pleading look at Revna, I turned to face our enemies. Sorrow filled me then, for everything that I would never know. But the guardsmen were already marching forward and there was mercifully little time to think. Whispering the paternoster, I hefted the shield I had picked up, preparing to fight.

And to die.

"Bebbanburg!" shouted Hereward, and – in a more orderly fashion this time – we stepped forward as one.

I stared at the men moving towards us, fixing my gaze on the eyes of a stocky warrior with a steel helm that partially covered his face. I would kill him when the lines met, I vowed. If I did nothing else before death, I would take that man with me. My mind cleared of all other concerns, the immediacy of battle washing away all worries, as I focused on the enemy I would slay.

Something flickered past my vision and thudded onto the blood-slick cobbles between the two groups of fighters. Both lines faltered.

It took me a moment to understand what had happened. A loosely tied bale of straw had landed between us. Just as I made this out, so another bale struck the ground beside it. This one was not tied at all and straw spilt out over the cobbles, clouding the air with dust and dry strands of hay.

Looking up, I saw a third object come hurtling down. For an instant, it was clear against the sky, caught in a flash of sunlight. An amphora, an earthenware jug, half as high as a man. A heartbeat later, it crashed into the cobbles, shattering and spilling its contents, a pale liquid, splashing over the stones and soaking into the straw.

The guardsmen were shouting now, pointing and gesturing upwards. There must be someone, or several people, up on the nearest rooftop throwing these things down.

Runolf was pointing with his bloody axe.

"I should know by now not to underestimate the strength of your god's magic," he said, bearing his teeth in a fierce grin.

I was still reeling, trying to make sense of everything. I did not at first understand Runolf's meaning, and then, as I saw the next item that soared from the roof to arc down towards the street, it became clear and I returned his smile.

A flaming torch, trailing a thin cloud of smoke, landed in the middle of the broken amphora and straw. An eye blink later the mess of oil and hay burst into flames with a whoosh. In moments, the heat was unbearable. Thick black smoke roiled and eddied in the street. The faces of the guardsmen were blurred through the fire, shimmering and diffuse. They were moving back from the blaze.

So were we.

"What now?" said Gwawrddur, raising his voice over the roar of the flames.

I looked back at the waggon that still blocked the road. I had no idea who had started that fire, but I did not plan on wasting the opportunity that had been given to us. I offered up a prayer of thanks for whoever disliked the wali and his guards enough to aid us, and broke into a run.

"Come on," I said. "We can scale that waggon and be free."

"Free, you think?" said a mocking voice beside me. "Beyond that waggon lies the Lions' Gate. Do you think the guards there will stand aside and let you walk out of the city?"

Spinning around, I gasped to see the small man garbed in the dark robes of a local. His head was covered and his skin appeared darker than it had been just two days before, but as close as he was to me there was no mistaking him.

"Giso," Runolf hissed. "Where have you been?"

Giso fixed Runolf with a sharp stare.

"A better question, my huge friend, would be, where am I going to take you so that those guards do not find you the instant those flames die down."

Runolf glowered at him, but stubbornly said nothing further.

"There is no time for this," snapped Revna. "Where are you taking us?"

"Ah," Giso said, "the beauty and the brains of the family. Follow me. And be quick about it. That fire won't keep them away for long."

Turning, he moved quickly to a doorway. I was certain it had been closed when we passed before, but now it stood ajar. Beyond it, all I could see was darkness. The fire crackled, its heat making me flinch. Seeing Pendrad and Sygbald hefting Ida's still form between them, he held up a hand.

"Where we are going, you will not be able to carry him."

Pendrad, face splattered with blood, his black hair plastered against his head with sweat, looked about to draw his sword and hack the small Frank down.

"Ida is our shield-brother," he snarled. "We will not leave him behind to be desecrated by these Moorish heathens."

"Then you shall die too, young Pendrad. You cannot travel fast enough carrying a corpse. Nor can we be slowed by one who will die before noon." He glanced at Oslaf's pallid face and his blood-drenched robes. The fat warrior sagged between Hereward and Gamal, who had half carried, half dragged him to the door. "Hereward," Giso went on quickly, "explain this to your men, or remain here with them and face the full force of the wali's retribution." He flicked a glance at the flames. They were already lessening in intensity. "We will all surely die if we tarry here."

Hereward's face clouded. For a moment, I thought he might strike Giso, but then he sighed.

"The Frank is right," he said. "Ida would not want us to die or be captured. Leave him. But Oslaf yet lives and we will not abandon one of our own while there is still hope."

Giso looked hard at Oslaf. "You know there is no hope for him," he said, coldly. "See that you keep up." He pushed the door open and, without a backward glance, he stepped into the gloom.

Pendrad's face was a mask of anguish and fury.

"Hereward speaks the truth of it," said Sygbald. "Let us escape this place and live to avenge Ida's death."

Pendrad let out a ragged breath. His shoulders slumped as he admitted defeat. Laying Ida's body down carefully on the cobbles, they moved to the door.

Hereward and Gamal pulled Oslaf through the small opening with difficulty. The rest of us followed into the cool darkness, leaving the blistering heat of the fire along with the stench of smoke and death behind us.

Twenty-Six

I closed my eyes for several heartbeats then opened them wide, so that I would better see in the darkness. By the thin light of the quarter moon, from my vantage point just below the summit of the crag, I could see the terrain rolling away in every direction, a vast expanse of barren undulating hills and hidden gulches. The rest of our number was in one such deep ravine behind me. There was a stream running out of the rock down there, forming a small pool. It was the perfect place for a campsite, deep enough in the earth that a fire could be lit at night with no fear that the light would be seen. I could smell the wood smoke on the light breeze. There must be dozens of such places in this broken landscape. Hundreds perhaps. And yet in this land that seemed devoid of vegetation, with the sun hammering down from the heavens, without a guide, I could well imagine a traveller could die of thirst and heat, unknowing that a spring and shade lay within a spear's throw of their position.

Without the aid of locals who knew this area, which was only a day's hard walk to the east of Ierusalem, we would never have found this place. And likely we would never have found each other after each of us had left the city.

Four days had passed since the street battle at dawn. The instant we were inside the building, Giso had led the way through a series of passageways, through small openings in walls, up ladders and onto the roofs of houses. There had been two dour, middle-aged men with him, dark-bearded, weathered and grim-faced. They had barely spoken, urging us to hurry with their movements.

Atop a tiled roof we had met another pair of men, younger versions of the first. These young men had jumped over from another building, seemingly oblivious of the danger. Behind them, in the distance, the plume of smoke from the fire smudged the sky. The older men welcomed them, slapping them on the back. The young men were excited, filled with the thrill of battle. I could picture them tossing down the hay and oil and delighting in the chaos that ensued when they had flung the burning brand down. The older men, their fathers I found out later, were less excited and appeared merely relieved that the youths had returned.

We had carried on our hurried rush through the city, over a precariously wobbling plank stretched between two roofs and then down into another dark building. From there we descended into a dank, dripping and foul-smelling tunnel. Torches were lit, casting flickering light on the slimy walls and on the sleek rats that slithered away from us. Our feet squelched in ordure, sending up powerful clouds of noxious vapours that made us all gag and choke.

"I cannot go on," Oslaf wheezed.

"It is not far now," said Hereward. He looked to Giso, hoping he might give some indication as to how far we had to go before reaching our destination. Giso ignored him, pressing on.

"I told you he wouldn't make it," he said over his shoulder.

"He'll make it, you nithing," growled Hereward.

But Giso was soon proven right. With a shuddering cry, Oslaf had fallen down and when Gamal and Hereward strained to lift him, they found he was dead.

"Leave him," Giso said, his tone brutal. "Or would you suffer the same wyrd?"

Gamal leapt up. "You whoreson," he shouted, his voice echoing in the tunnel. "I'll kill you."

"I am not your enemy, Gamal," said Giso, holding out his hands to show he was unarmed. "In fact, I am your saviour, along with Peleg here and his kin. Now," he went on, his voice softening, "you have done what you could for Oslaf. It is time to leave him, just as you left Ida. Surely it is better to live to fight again, no?"

Giso hurried on with the others, not waiting for a reply. The light from their torches dwindled quickly. The darkness had swelled around us until Runolf pushed Gamal on.

"I hate the little man," the Norseman said, "but in this he speaks true. The gods have smiled on us this morning, let us not spit in their faces now. Come, let's live to sing of Oslaf and Ida, to drink to their memory like war-brothers should."

Feeling ashamed, we left Oslaf to the rats and pressed on. After a dizzying number of turns, we finally climbed out into a narrow alleyway that was cluttered with crates and what appeared to be broken trestles.

From there, Giso, Peleg and the others led us to what looked like a storeroom.

We spent the next three days in that dingy room. There was only one small window, high up in the wall, and the air within the building was hot and stuffy during the day, stifling and clammy at night. There was little within the room to make our stay comfortable, but food and drink was brought to us regularly. Giso disappeared with Peleg, leaving the other three men to watch over us. We felt trapped there, like prisoners, but that these men had rescued us, and at great risk to themselves, could not be denied.

We sat, dejected and dazed in the darkness, in a space behind piled crates that seemed arranged for the purpose of concealment. We listened to the sounds of the city through the small window. After a long while, we heard the stamp of many boots in the alleyway outside and abruptly a hammering came on the door, followed by an angry command.

The three men guarding us held their fingers to their lips and quickly stacked boxes in the only gap of our hiding place, sealing us in. We sat in silence, breathing through our mouths and listening. I could make out Revna's eyes in the gloom, and I wished she sat nearer to me, but of course, we dared not move.

The wali's guards shouted at the men in the storeroom, demanding to know what they were doing and where they had been that morning. We sat tensely, clutching our weapons, ready for another fight. The guards pulled down one of the crates, spilling the contents of earthenware pots. The fragrant scent of sumac filled the warehouse. The men said the shipment was destined for Yafah and the Middle Sea beyond. After this, as if their anger had been spent with the wanton destruction of the clay vessels, the guards seemed content with the answers they received and went away.

It was shortly after that when Giso returned with three women carrying food and water. They also brought bandages and ointments. From the light of a small oil lamp they cleaned and dressed the cuts we had received. The long cut on my arm stung, but it was not the worst of the wounds among us. Drosten, always on the attack in battle, had suffered a deep gouge across his chest. He did not complain, but he was unable to keep from wincing when a short, frowning, matronly woman daubed some pungent-smelling unguent in the cut before sewing it up with a bronze needle and horsehair, and then winding a long bandage about his muscular tattooed torso. The women tended to all our wounds in silence, but when they learnt there was a young woman amongst us, they shook their heads and drew Revna away with them when they left.

"Do not fear," said Giso, "they will treat her well. They have daughters of their own and we will be here some time."

"How long?" asked Gwawrddur.

"Who can say? Two days? Three? As seems common for you, you have kicked the wasps' nest and now we must wait until the wasps settle down. It is too dangerous to attempt to leave now."

We had many questions for Giso, but once again he departed, following Revna and the women, and leaving us in the gloomy storeroom with our guards.

It was not till the following day, when he returned with the women, that Giso deigned to answer our queries. Hereward, Gamal, Pendrad and Sygbald were from Bebbanburg and had served with Ida and Oslaf for years under Lord Uhtric before joining *Brymsteda*'s crew. They were resentful of how their comrades had been treated. The rest of us didn't feel much better disposed towards the Frank. We knew he had helped to rescue us, but while we sat in that hot, dark room we had questioned his true motives. One question for which we had not reached a satisfactory conclusion was whether we would even have been in the wali's palace if Giso had not abandoned us at the Yafah Gate.

On that second day, after the women had carefully cleaned our wounds, applying more salves and bandaging them afresh, Giso perched himself on a crate and looked at us expectantly.

"I see that you burn with questions," he said, a slight smirk curling his lips. "We cannot leave here yet, so ask and I will answer what I am able."

"Who are these people?" said Hereward immediately. "And why do they help us?"

"All you need to know," Giso said, "is that they work for a man called Zakariya. He is…" – the briefest of hesitations – "…acquainted with Nu'man."

Hereward looked blank, not recalling the name.

"You mean the man in Bab al-Wadi?" said Gwawrddur. "Musa's uncle?"

"The same," replied Giso. "Nu'man told me how to contact

them. I had hoped they would aid us in our quest. I had not anticipated we would need quite so much help so soon after arriving in Ierusalem. As it is, without them, I think you would all now be wallowing in a cell, or perhaps hanging from the walls of the city." He chuckled and shook his head. "I know you have a certain set of skills when it comes to fighting, but the Almighty alone knows, you do so excel at getting yourselves into trouble. I have never known the like. I wonder if the Teacher sends you with me as a punishment for some infraction of which I am not aware. Either that, or it is a jest on his part, for surely you are more bother than benefit."

"You forget yourself, little man," said Runolf, lifting his axe and placing it across his knees.

"Aye," said Hereward, his voice as chill as winter bones. "The strife you think so amusing cost us the life of two good friends."

"Cumbra died on Kýpros too," snarled Arcenbryht. "He was a good man and brave. I will not hear you speak ill of him or any other of my shield-brothers." He pushed himself to his feet and drew his sword. "Let's see how funny you think it when I cause you some bother with my blade."

In the shadows, the men who guarded the door watched us with hooded eyes, but they did not seek to intervene. Giso did not move. He stared at Arcenbryht and said, "You are right, of course, brave Arcenbryht. I spoke out of turn and meant no offence. These days have been trying for me too and I am tired. Please accept my apology." He swept his gaze across the gathering. "All of you."

Beorn placed a hand on Arcenbryht's shoulder, pulling him down to sit once more. Hereward grunted. Runolf said nothing. Despite the heat in the room, there was a noticeable iciness between us.

"I almost forgot," said Giso, his face expressionless now. "I know how it pained you to leave Oslaf behind, so I had some of our friends retrieve his body."

"What of Ida?" Hereward asked.

"Alas, his body was taken by the guards. It was not possible."

"Can we see Oslaf?" asked Pendrad.

"No, no," said Giso with a sigh. "It would be too dangerous yet to show your faces in the city, but I have seen to it that a priest performs the funeral mass, and I myself sat vigil over his body." He made the sign of the cross. "Oslaf's mortal remains have been interred now. In the holy city no less."

"I give you thanks," said Pendrad, appearing mollified.

Hereward glowered at Giso for a long while. His distrust was palpable. I wondered whether Giso spoke the truth, but surely even he would not lie about such a thing.

"Let us talk no more of such sorrowful matters," said Giso. "You asked about our friends. It must suffice to say Zakariya and his people are no friends of the wali, which is a boon for us."

I had been thinking about their knowledge of the rooftops and tunnels, the relative ease with which they led us through the city; the hiding place behind the crates in the storeroom.

"They are thieves and brigands, no doubt," I said.

Giso feigned pain. "*Thief* is such an ugly word," he said. "Zakariya would simply take charge of his destiny. He trades in goods that the caliph and his wali would rather control. He prefers not to pay the taxes of the rulers he sees as oppressors in his land. Zakariya's world is in the shadows. It took much persuasion on my part to have him aid you so openly."

"We all know you can be persuasive," I said, thinking of Giso's interactions in the past. He was ruthless, threatening innocents if he believed it would further his, Alhwin's and Carolus' cause.

Giso grinned. "Indeed," he said. "But I do not think even my skills of persuasion would have convinced Zakariya to come to your rescue if it had not been for two things: the recommendation of Nu'man and our common enemy."

"You mean the wali?"

"The wali, yes, but we share another enemy, one who has wronged these people grievously."

He waited, his eyes flitting from one of us to the next, relishing our focused gazes, the power he held over us as he imparted his knowledge morsel by morsel.

"You speak of Theokleia and Artemis," I said, the realisation coming to me in a flash of inspiration.

Giso grinned. The expression looked predatory on his features.

"It would seem Eirene's agents now travel with several enemies of Zakariya's: men who are as ruthless as the women they now follow."

"Who are these men?" I asked. "And why have they joined Theokleia's cause?"

"Why does any man do anything?" Giso replied. "From what I hear, these men, to use your own words, are thieves and brigands. They will follow gold like a hound chases a hare. And the Empress of Byzantion has gold in plentiful supply."

"So the men who now follow Theokleia are foes of this Zakariya?" asked Drosten. "That is why he gives us aid and succour?"

Giso chuckled. "They are not friends of his, that is for certain, but that alone would not be enough for Zakariya to risk his people for us, even as persuasive as I am."

"Why then does he help us?" Runolf asked, his tone sharp. "Speak plain now. I tire of your tale-spinning, Frank."

Giso bowed his head. "I would not wish to anger you, Runolf Ragnarsson. And you are right, of course. We are all weary. I will tell you what I know."

The crunch of a footfall brought me back to the present. My thoughts had wandered, but despite the darkness and the weariness that clung to me following the escape from the city and the long walk that followed, I had remained alert. I had once drifted off to sleep when on guard duty, with devastating results. I vowed I would never again fail my friends in that way. I would not allow myself to sit, no matter how tired my legs or weary my feet. I knew all too well how easily slumber would take a hold of me if I permitted myself to grow comfortable.

I listened to the night. Silently drawing my sword, I stepped further into the moon shadow of the large rock at my back. Another scrape of stones and a figure stepped into the night's cool light. I instantly recognised the lithe movements and the slender form.

"Have you come to take the next watch?" I asked from the shadows.

An intake of breath, and she turned to look in my direction. "By Óðinn's one eye," Revna said, "you are getting as good as Giso at concealing yourself."

"It is not so difficult in the dark, especially wearing these clothes." I stepped out of the shade of the boulder.

"I can barely see you even now," she said. "You are a shadow among shadows."

I wore the black robes common to the *Badw*. My head was covered with a black cloth too, leaving not much more than my eyes visible.

"I still cannot believe we are free of the city," she said. She kept her voice low, for the night was very still and sound travelled far.

"Whatever else he may be," I said, "Giso is certainly a master at moving undetected. No wonder he is able to disappear so readily."

"He is not the only one with such skills, it seems."

"I am not so skilled."

"I was speaking of the men and women who got us out of Ierusalem." I could hear the smile in her voice.

I thought of how I had escaped the city, marvelling again at the audacity of those who had aided us. Knowing that the wali's guards were looking for more than a dozen warriors, all strangers to the city, we had been split into groups of two or three and each small group smuggled out of the walls by different means. None of us left at the same time or by the same route.

Revna had been placed on a cart with a noisy family and had left by the Lions' Gate. I had been paired with Gersine and a pair of taciturn traders. We rode camels and led several more behind us. Leaving from the northern Dimashq Gate, Gersine and I had struggled to hide our anxiety when the guardsmen had stopped our caravan and began to question its leader. Then I'd seen a glint of silver pass between the trader and the captain of the watch, and we had been waved through. The guards had barely looked at us. I had kept my eyes on the camel before me, not daring to breathe until we had left the gate behind us.

The others had been taken out of the city in similar ways, each group hidden in plain sight within larger bands of merchants, pilgrims or other travellers. Runolf and Drosten were the only two of our number who had left Ierusalem concealed from view. Deemed by Giso and our new friends to be too conspicuous, they were both secreted in a waggon beneath a pile of heavy sacks of grain. Just as in the warehouse where we had been screened behind crates in an existing hiding place, so our saviours already had a contraption built for the purpose of smuggling men or contraband without that cargo being crushed. Runolf and Drosten slid beneath a frame of timber that was then heaped with heavy sacks.

When we were all safely away from the city, our guides had led us to this remote spot where we were all reunited.

"How long do you think we will need to wait here?" Revna asked.

"Who can say? But I pray it is not too long." I stared out over the dappled, shaded ripples of the hills around us. "I had long dreamed of coming to the Holy Land. Now, I long to leave."

I had not been able to visit any of the sacred sites of Ierusalem and the events of the last days had soured the place for me. All I wanted now was to complete our quest and then leave this land of heat and dust behind.

Revna stepped close to me. I shivered at her proximity. I wished to reach out for her, but kept my hands at my sides.

"I am sorry," she said so quietly, I barely heard her.

"Do not lament your actions," I said, my tone harsher than I had intended.

"If I had not struck Kawthar..." Her words trailed off. "This is all my doing." Her voice cracked and she sniffed. I thought she was weeping, but I could not make out her face in the gloom.

I wanted to tell her I was glad she had hit the wali, that none of this was her fault. And yet I could not bring myself to utter the words. I could smell her skin in the darkness. Gone was the perfumed oil from the wali's palace, replaced by the familiar scent of her. I imagined what it would be like to take her in my arms, to press her against me, to kiss her... Without warning, the image of how she had smiled at Kawthar bubbled up in my mind, filling me with bitterness.

"There are many more things at work here," I said, unable to keep the ice from my tone and hating myself for it. "Giso. Theokleia. The search for the Blood of Christ. It does not do to think everything that occurs to us is caused by your actions."

She tensed. I glanced at her and noticed then the tears glimmering on her smooth cheeks. Immediately, I regretted speaking. I reached for her, but she pulled away.

"My words sounded harsh to my ears," I said. "I meant you should not blame yourself for the deaths of Ida and Oslaf. There is a battle raging between Carolus and Eirene, and we are caught between them, like iron twixt hammer and anvil."

She sniffed and cuffed at her cheeks. "You made yourself well understood, Hunlaf. Of all men, you are not one who can hide behind the misuse of his words. Even now with your apology you remind me that two of our friends are dead because of me. I know everyone is furious with me, but I had hoped that you at least would offer me some comfort."

"I would," I said, stepping close.

"No," she hissed. "Your thoughts are plain. You think I was a fool to be taken in by Kawthar's flattery."

"I didn't say that."

"No need. I have seen the look on your face. You may think me a fool, but at least I can see what is right before me, and I admit when I was wrong. It *was* foolish to allow Kawthar to believe he was wooing me. But Frigg alone knows he was the first man to spare me a moment of his attention in a long while."

"I give you attention," I said, weakly.

"Do you? And when is that, Hunlaf? When you need someone to spar with you? Someone to help you tend to the animals?" She sighed. "You are more of a fool than I."

Abruptly, she turned and began to walk back down the twisting path that led to the encampment in the gorge below.

"Wait," I said, hurrying after her.

"Why?" she replied, not slowing her pace. "So that you can once again tell me how I am a foolish girl? That I am to blame for Oslaf and Ida's deaths?"

My forearm throbbed and I recalled the sword cut I had received at the palace gatehouse.

"I did not say those things," I said, exasperation lending my voice volume.

"Perhaps not," she hissed, scrambling down one of the steepest stretches of the path. It was treacherous in the dark and I prayed that neither of us would slip. "But you thought them."

I skidded and scraped down after her, sending a spray of pebbles into the black darkness.

"Hey! Watch yourselves," came a strangled cry from below. I had not expected anyone to be so near. The camp lay far below still. I could not see the owner of the voice in the gloom, but I recognised it as belonging to Gersine. We were nearly at where the steep narrow track crossed the larger trail that we had followed into these hills.

"Sorry," I said softly, knowing my voice would carry to Gersine. "Revna, wait." I had caught up with her now and I grabbed a handful of her dress, pulling her to a halt.

"Let me go!"

"What do you want from me?" I asked, shaking her. "Why did you come to me?"

She struggled against my grip, but I held her firm.

"You really are a fool," she said. Something in her tone gave me pause.

"It's not Gersine's turn to be on guard," I said.

I sensed the shake of her head in the darkness. "No, but Gersine is a friend. He said he would whistle if anyone came." I could see the starlight twinkling in her eyes. "I thought…"

The unspoken meaning sunk in. I relaxed my hold on her and she shook my hands free.

"I was so angry with you," I whispered.

"That much was easy," she said. "And that was just what I wanted."

"What you wanted?"

She sighed. With a start I felt her fingers brush my stubbled cheek. My heart pounded. I could hear the rush of my blood in my ears.

"Perhaps we are both fools," she said, moving close. Her warmth and her scent were intoxicating.

"Anything is possible," I breathed, and reached for her. In that instant I wanted nothing more in the whole world than to press my lips to hers. The thought of it consumed me, my body taut and thrumming like a bowstring. She did not fight me now, yielding softly as I drew her into an embrace. I had dreamt of this moment countless times and I was barely able to register that it was finally happening. My mind was reeling, trying to make sense of everything. I was certain that in time she would explain to me all the ways I had been a fool, but right then I cared for nought but the soft curves of her body against me and the promise of her lips on mine, the anticipation of the taste of her.

Her breath was warm on my face as we moved closer. Our lips had not even brushed when Gersine's shout ripped the stillness of the night.

Twenty-Seven

For a heartbeat we froze. I wanted to rage at Gersine. He knew how much this meant to me, how long I had wished for just this moment. Was he not my friend, that he would interrupt us now when Revna was in my arms? This was his jealousy – I was sure of it.

He cried out again and I heard the terror in his voice.

My petty thoughts evaporated. Ashamed at my selfishness, I pushed away from Revna, dropping my hand to my sword and dragging it free.

"Are you armed?" I said.

She drew her sword. "I am not such a fool as you might think," she replied.

I peered into the darkness, searching for who might have come upon Gersine to scare him so. Had the wali's men found us here, despite all our efforts? Our guides had led us along winding tracks into these hills, and when we had finally taken the path that would take us up to this pass and the concealed ravine where we camped, there was nobody in sight. Could we have been tracked here?

I could hear Gersine moving about, the crunch of his feet on the gravelly path loud in the night. Far below came the shouts of the others, no doubt woken by Gersine's cries.

"By Christ's thorny crown!" Gersine called out in a

tremulous voice. There was real fear there. This was no jest, or attempt to disrupt my tryst with Revna.

I started down the last stretch of the steep path, hurrying, but careful not to lose my footing or twist my ankle in the pools of black shadow that dotted the track. Revna was at my back. Fleetingly I wished she would remain atop the hill, far from whatever danger awaited us, but as quickly as the thought came, so I dismissed it. Revna was a skilled warrior and I would be glad of her fast sword if it came to a fight.

"We're coming," I panted, deciding there was no need for stealth. Anyone on the track below would have surely heard our approach.

"Hurry," came Gersine's ragged reply.

Runolf's booming voice echoed up from the canyon. Judging from the clash and tumult that shattered the night, the rest of the men were readying themselves and already rushing up the narrow path to the main track through the hills where Gersine was located.

"Who is it?" I called out. "Who attacks us?"

I was just above the wider track now, and I paused for an instant, trying to make sense of what was happening. Gersine stood with his back to a boulder. His sword blade flickered dully, catching the silvery moon glimmer. His face was a pallid smudge in the gloom.

"Not who," Gersine gasped. "What!"

And then I saw the huge lion as it stepped into a patch of moonlight. My heart lurched. Surely this could not be the same creature we had fought before. And yet deep in my heart I knew it must be. The animal's powerful muscles bunched and rippled as it padded slowly towards Gersine. Its head was wreathed in dark fur and, in the cold, pale light of the night, I could make out the wound on its side where Arcenbryht's spear had cut a deep furrow along its ribs.

The lion was almost on Gersine now. It paused, lowering its haunches, readying to leap. I could not bear to see my friend torn apart by this devil, the beast that had stalked us, waiting outside the walls of Ierusalem only to pick up our scent once more when we left. But I was too far away to engage it.

"Hey!" I shouted, jumping down onto the path. "You ugly brute! Fight me!"

The lion halted, then spun about and fixed me in its baleful stare. It let out a deep, rumbling growl, and I felt my bowels loosen. Surely this was no normal lion. It must have been sent by the Devil himself to dog our steps so; in order to keep us from succeeding in our quest. For what animal would be so relentless in its stalking of human prey? I could not hope to stand against such a monster and live. I brandished my blade, but knew it would not be enough to stop the lion.

"Stay there," I called out to Revna, my fear for her more powerful than the certainty of my own death.

She ignored me, jumping down to stand by my side.

"We have fought worse than this old cat," she said. "Arcenbryht almost did for it before. It will regret crossing us again."

I was not as confident, but I raised my sword. I would not show Revna my fear. The sounds of the men climbing up from the ravine were strident, echoing from the sun-warmed rocks, but they would never reach us in time to save us from this demon creature.

Without warning, Gersine darted forward, jabbing at the lion's back. Faster than thought, the animal twisted, snarling. It swatted at Gersine and his sword clattered away, lost in the darkness. Gersine stumbled back with a yelp and a choking sob. It was too dark to see how badly he was wounded, but I would not stand by and allow my friend to be slain.

Running forward, I closed the gap quickly. Revna sprinted at my side. I pushed myself to run faster, forcing myself in front of her so that the lion would have no choice but to fight me.

I got what I wanted. The beast swung its great head back to face me, and my heart quailed.

I had only a fast heartbeat to take in its finger-long dagger-like teeth and the faint gleam of its eyes before it sprang at me. I was yet several paces distant and unprepared for its speed and strength. My sword was raised and without thinking I thrust it forward, but the lion batted it aside. In the same instant it hit me, toppling me as surely as if I had been struck by a boulder. I was young and strong, but I was no match for that beast's power. It would surely have killed me then, before Revna could react, and yet, God watched over me. In fending off my sword blade, one of the lion's paws, studded with deadly claws, missed their target. Still, I felt a stabbing agony as the sharp talons on one massive paw scratched at my chest.

I had lost hold of my sword and now, breathlessly battling for my life, I dug my fingers into the lion's mane, desperately struggling to keep its savage teeth from tearing into my flesh. Its breath engulfed me. It was hot and carried a charnel stench. Its jaws snapped together, narrowly missing my face. If I could free my hand and draw my seax I might yet stab the monster, but I could not risk relinquishing my grasp of his massive head. The creature bit the air above my face again. Spittle flecked my cheeks. I was weakening. There was no way I could hold the huge animal at bay much longer.

With a sudden roar of pain and frustration, the lion reared up, lessening its weight on me. Revna had cut into its side with her sword. Snarling, the beast swiped a paw at her. She skipped out of its reach.

Seizing the opportunity, I scrambled back, heels scraping in the stony dust. As I went, I tugged my seax from its scabbard. In the distance I could hear shouts, louder now, closer. Louder still I heard what sounded like the blare of a trumpet. I did not look away from the lion. I could not. Its eyes seemed to glow with an unnatural hatred and again I wondered if it was possessed by some evil spirit.

It was closing with Revna as she backed away towards Gersine's still form. She thrust her sword at the beast, keeping it at a distance, but it would not be held off for long. I could feel my blood running hot down my chest. I pushed aside the stinging pain and moved after the lion.

"Christ protect us!" I screamed, swallowing down my fear and launching myself once more at the animal. I would not allow Revna to come to harm while I yet breathed.

Sensing the danger, the lion turned to meet me.

"Come on!" I roared. "Come and taste the blade of my seax, Devil beast."

As if it understood my goading, it leapt at me. I was ready for it this time. I threw myself to the side, slicing at the animal's sleek, muscular body as it streaked past in the gloom. My seax blade connected and the lion yowled.

Falling painfully to the ground, I rolled, but the lion was quicker by far. Before I could spring to my feet, it was on me, knocking me back. It pinned my right hand to the ground with one paw, its claws digging into my skin. To this day, whenever I am writing, I can see the white scars on my scrawny wrist, reminding me of that night. And the young man I once was.

Still clutching my seax tightly, I struggled against the animal's bulk. It was no good; I was not strong enough. Again, I grasped its greasy mane in my left hand, trying to prevent it from biting me, but as it brought its dripping maw closer to my face, its foetid breath engulfing me in a stinking cloud, I was certain I would die. Revna was too far away. Gersine was unconscious, or worse. And the rest of our comrades would take too long to climb out of the canyon.

Closing my eyes, I prayed to the Lord, asking that He protect Revna and my friends, and forgive me my sins before I departed this earth.

In that instant, as I prepared myself to meet my doom, the weight of the monster was abruptly gone from me. The ground trembled beneath me and a rumble as of thunder filled my ears. Opening my eyes, I pushed myself up, ready to fight again.

My mind could make no sense of what I saw then. The

lion was flying through the air, and yet I could see it had not jumped. It had been flung somehow, yanked from atop my prostrate form and thrown high into the night. The darkness and mottled moon shadows made it difficult to comprehend what my eyes beheld, but later, in the light of day, I was able to piece together what I had seen.

A huge creature, much larger than a horse or a camel, lumbered out of the dark. Its flanks flashed past me, as solid and large as a house. It came on four legs, nimbly stepping over me and speeding after its quarry. On the creature's back sat a man. He was shouting out something as his massive steed thundered in pursuit of the lion.

The lion twisted in the air and landed deftly upright, snarling at this new threat. Without pause, it sprang at the huge animal, scratching at its leathery hide and great ears that flapped like wings on either side of its bulbous head.

The animal bellowed, and I recognised again that strange trumpeting sound that had echoed in the ravine's throat. I knew not what this new creature was, nor the identity of its rider, but I knew they had saved my life, so I staggered back into the fray.

As I drew close, the strange creature caught the spitting and growling lion in an appendage that appeared to be a rope-like snout. Lifting the lion up, it dashed it to the ground. Rearing up, it tried to crush the lion beneath its considerable weight. The lion, lithe and quick, rolled away.

Revna stabbed with her sword, piercing the lion's side. It spun about, maddened by the pain of its wounds. I ran at it, ramming my seax into its back, then leaping away. The lion roared and sprang for me. Slowed by the injuries I had sustained, my robes sodden with blood and sweat, I stumbled and the growling lion once more collided with me, knocking me down. This time though I did not lose hold of my seax. I plunged the blade deep into the animal's guts. It arched back, filling the night with ear-splitting fury.

Revna stepped close again, slashing at its side. The lion shook its shaggy head, for the first time seeming to sense the mortal danger it faced. Its flanks were streaming with blood from many cuts. Yet more blood gushed from the deep wound I had dealt in its belly. Wailing and crouching low, it pulled back from us, perhaps searching for a way out.

There was none.

Runolf surged up out of the ravine, followed by Drosten, Gwawrddur, Hereward and the others. They came carrying spears and swords and rapidly closed ranks, blocking the path. In the other direction stood the trumpeting creature with the cloaked rider. The lion turned this way and that, in the end deciding to attempt to scale the sheer rocks on one side of the path. It leapt, scrabbling for purchase. Its claws scratched at the boulder's surface, but it was exhausted now, bleeding and weakened. It fell to the gritty path, crouching and snarling at those who threatened it from all sides.

Runolf and the others stepped closer. Soon they would be upon the beast. There was nowhere for it to go now. It turned its hate-filled eyes on Revna and me, and for a hideous moment I thought it would throw itself at us again. Instead, it drew back, ears flat, teeth flashing beneath drawn-back lips. It was black with blood, its sides heaving as it laboured to breathe. Death would have taken it soon enough, but the massive creature that had saved me finished the lion with unexpected quickness. With another of its braying trumpets, it rushed forward and stamped on the lion's head.

The lion's body tensed and then it lay still. Its head was a bloody mess, burst like a ripe fruit beneath the weight of the huge creature.

The animal's rider said something in a soft voice. The leathery animal bent its knee, allowing him to step down from the saddle strapped to its back. Arcenbryht carried a torch, and he lifted it high now so that we could all see the man and his strange mount.

The creature was grey, its skin wrinkled and rough-looking like old leather. It had darkly intelligent eyes, framed by soft lashes. It seemed almost sad as it looked down at the destruction of the lion at its feet. It nudged the corpse with its snake-like nose. There were long scratch marks on its side and one of its stocky legs, the blood bright against its dusty skin. One of its leathery ears was torn too. The rider looked the beast over, whispering to it soothingly before turning to face us.

He was slender and of middling height. He had a long beard and rings glimmered on his fingers. His clothes looked expensive and there were silk slippers on his feet.

"Giso!" he said, his gaze picking out the small Frank standing someway off from the rest of the men. "I had not expected to see you here, so far from Frankia."

Giso stepped forward, a puzzled expression on his face. "I have to say, Isaac, I had not thought to see you here either. Our original mission was to meet you and travel with you as an escort, but our plans have changed. I thought you would be on the road from Dimashq."

So this was Isaac, the Iudeisc envoy we had been tasked with meeting. As Giso said, we had decided that with Kawthar knowing of our plans to meet Isaac on the road, we would have to avoid his route, which we had assumed would see him coming from Dimashq, for fear that the wali would set men to watch for the envoy's party and intercept us.

"It would seem my arrival here," said Isaac, "whilst a shock, could not have been more timely. Perhaps God Himself in all his wisdom sent me here. Whatever the reason, I am glad to have been of service." He looked down at the dead lion. "I have never seen a lion so close before. And I hope never to see one again if this beast was indicative of their ferocity. I have to say though, I have never heard of a lion being so determined to taste the flesh of men."

The clatter of hoofbeats made us all turn. At the sound, Gersine groaned and pushed himself into a sitting position.

My heart swelled to see he lived. Several mounted men cantered into the light. Behind them more riders and a line of pack animals came into view. We tensed, but Isaac held up his hand. "These are the men who accompany me. Those donkeys are laden with gifts for King Carolus. The caliph would never have allowed me to travel without protection."

"And which of these men is the emissary from the caliph?" Giso enquired.

"Emissary?"

"When Alhwin sent word for us to accompany you, he said you would be travelling with an emissary from the court of the caliph. A man by the name of Abul-Abbas."

Isaac grinned, then leaned back and laughed. The sound of his mirth was jarring on this rocky track that yet jangled with the aftermath of battle and was heavy with the metallic stench of blood.

"I do travel with one named Abul-Abbas," Isaac said when his laughter had subsided. "He is an emissary of sorts, I suppose, and is indeed sent by the caliph himself. But he is no man – he is another gift for our king."

"What do you mean?" Giso asked. His brow was furrowed in consternation. The Frank thrived on knowing more than his travel companions. How he must have hated not being in control of this situation.

Isaac stepped back and placed his hand on the side of the huge creature he had been riding. Its long snout lifted to caress his hand.

"Allow me to introduce you to Abul-Abbas," he said. "The elephant."

Twenty-Eight

I winced. The man applying the lamb fat to my cuts was not gentle. He hissed for me to be still. I forced myself to remain motionless, gritting my teeth as he finished his ministrations. He had already tended to Gersine's wound, a long gash along his sword arm. The blow to Gersine's head was more worrying. When he had fallen, he had banged it hard on a rock, knocking himself insensate. Now he sat, pale and shivering, complaining of a throbbing headache.

Guilt, curdled and bitter, churned in my guts. I should never have doubted Gersine's motives for calling out to Revna and me. He was brave to the point of foolhardy, and he was ever my friend. I would have to watch him, in case his head injury should grow any worse. I prayed for Gersine silently as the man worked on my cuts. An injury to the head was in God's hands. There was little any healer could do.

The lion had torn my clothes, slashing the skin across my chest. The cuts were long and ragged, but mercifully shallow, and while they stung terribly, once they were bound, I would be able to move quite freely. I would bear the scars for the rest of my long life, but I would live, if they did not become elf-shot. There was always a chance that wound rot would take hold, but I thought it unlikely. The healer had washed the wounds thoroughly with vinegar and I could see no indication of infection.

He was one of the men travelling with Isaac. In fact, he was Abul-Abbas' keeper and he had flown into a terrible rage when he had seen the wounds inflicted on the elephant. He had cleaned the animal's wounds first, then applied a thick layer of mutton grease to the gashes, before turning his attention to Gersine and me. He was no doubt highly skilled as a healer, but he treated us both with a disdainful annoyance, as if we had somehow been responsible for the lion's attack and the elephant's injuries.

"Do not mind Shafiq," said Isaac. "He loves Abul-Abbas more than I love my own children."

"Would you lead your children into danger?" Shafiq snapped. "Would you force them to fight a lion?"

"My children do not have the strength of Abul-Abbas," Isaac replied in a soft tone that evidenced his affection for the elephant's grumpy handler. "And what would you have me do, Shafiq? Allow these young men and this beautiful woman to be torn asunder by the beast?"

Shafiq waved his hand dismissively and hissed. Tying off the bandage he had wrapped about my chest, he slapped my back roughly and stood. Isaac watched him return to fuss over the elephant who stood unmoving in the gloom. The sky in the east was already paling. It would be day soon.

Isaac's party was too numerous, and the path down to the hidden encampment too treacherous for the horses and donkeys in the dark, so we had remained thronged along the widest part of the track. Come the dawn we would have to decide what we would do next. For now, I was content to sit back against a rock, resting my aching body.

The men who had guided us here from the city had melted into the night, wary of the warriors who bore the caliph's sigil upon their shields.

Giso drew Isaac away from us and they sat together sipping

from cups of wine filled by one of the servants who travelled in the envoy's retinue. I watched them for a time as they whispered. My curiosity prodded at me to rise and go to them, to hear what they spoke of. But my body was battered and weary, and I did not move.

"Once again you are lucky to live," Gwawrddur said, lowering himself down to sit beside me. "Lucky too that Revna and Gersine were there to help you." He raised his eyebrows suggestively.

"Lucky or blessed by God," I said, ignoring the bait in his words.

"I cannot believe that animal trailed us all this way," said Gersine.

Hereward had sent Pendrad up to where I had been on watch. He had posted Sygbald and Gamal some way down the track in each direction, with instructions to shout if anyone approached. Now the Northumbrian joined us. He handed me a skin of water as he sat.

"I said we should have turned back after Kýpros," Hereward said. "We have been cursed since arriving here."

"That lion was cursed," Revna whispered. "There was madness in its eyes. Evil."

I shuddered.

Runolf dragged the bloody carcass over to where we sat. It left a dark trail of blood in the dirt.

"Its pelt would make a good cloak or rug," he said. He looked at me. "As would the skin of any man who harms Revna."

My mouth was abruptly dry. I took a gulp of water from Hereward's waterskin.

Gwawrddur shook his head. "Revna has proven again and again that no man or beast can stand before her," he said. "She has been taught well, Runolf."

The massive Norseman sniffed. His eyes did not leave mine.

"Do not speak as if I was not here," Revna said without

warning, anger colouring her tone. As quickly as it came, so her anger evaporated and her shoulders slumped. "I am sorry for all of this... My foolishness has cost us dearly. If not for me..." She let out a trembling sigh. "I am sorry for my actions in the palace."

"Nonsense, girl," said Beorn, reaching for the waterskin. "The Lord above knows if that sweet-talking Kawthar had turned his attention to one of us, we would likely have gone willingly to his bed!"

Eadstan let out a guffaw and punched Beorn on his muscled arm.

"You would have taken little convincing," he said. "The rest of us are more choosy in our mates."

"As am I," said Revna, her tone frosty. "But if I had been wiser, I would not have allowed Kawthar to believe he could have me. It was foolish."

Gwawrddur placed his hand gently on Revna's shoulder. "The wali's actions are his and his alone," he said. "None of us blames you for what happened. Any one of us would have done the same."

"Apart from Beorn, it seems," said Eadstan, provoking laughter.

"Perhaps we should send Beorn back to Ierusalem to warm the wali's bed," Gwawrddur said.

"If I thought that would help," said Beorn, with a wink to Eadstan. Eadstan punched him again, this time hard enough to make him grunt in pain.

"Enough jesting," Gwawrddur said, holding up his hand for peace. He looked directly at Revna. "Oslaf and Ida willingly stood in your defence, just as any of us would. As you would fight for us. You are as kin to us all."

Beorn's expression was serious now. "The Welshman speaks true," he said. "You are dear to us, Revna."

"To some of us more than others," said Gersine with a

chuckle. I flashed him a sharp look. He grinned, despite the obvious pain he felt.

"I should have let that lion eat you," I said.

Another ripple of laughter from the men. Without a word Runolf pushed himself to his feet and stalked along the track until he was swallowed by the gloom. He left the bloody corpse of the lion behind him in the dust. I stared at its crushed skull, the mane matted black with gore.

Gwawrddur placed a hand on my bandaged arm. "Rest easy, Hunlaf," he whispered. "Runolf is not blind. Nor is he a fool. And yet he is a father, and some things are not easy for a man to accept."

I said nothing, but the meaning was clear. The change between Revna and I had been noted by all. I bit my lip. Staring at the dead lion, I wondered whether I would face a similar end if I openly declared my love for Revna to Runolf.

Drosten's thickly accented voice pulled me away from my worries. There were more pressing matters at hand.

"Do you think we will travel with Isaac towards the coast now?" he said, looking over at where Giso was still in deep discussion with the Iudeisc envoy.

"I pray so," said Hereward. "I would like to see us as far from this place as possible. But alas, after what Giso told us in Ierusalem, I think our path will take us further into this desert before we head homewards."

"Perhaps God guided Isaac and Abul-Abbas here," I said, "not only to save us from the lion, but that we would join his retinue."

"Maybe," said Hereward, "but I doubt Giso will see it that way. The Frank will praise the Lord for delivering us from that evil beast, but he will say the way has now been cleared for us to continue in search of the relic."

Hereward was probably right. Giso had been seized by the promise of finding the Blood of Christ. My mind still reeled at the prospect, but I could not deny I felt a thrill at the idea. Blood that had coursed through the veins of the Son of God! The Holy Land had proven as dangerous as any kingdom we had ever visited, and yet we knew now that somewhere out there in the dusty wastes of these hills, a relic of immense power lay hidden. To obtain it for King Carolus was our sacred duty. And if that meant we would snatch it away from that murderous whore Theokleia and the giant Artemis, so much the better.

In the warehouse where we had been hidden, Giso had told us what he had learnt from Zakariya. Shortly before our arrival in the city, two women matching the descriptions of Theokleia and Artemis had approached a priest in a small chapel.

The priest's broken body was left splayed over the altar, drenched in blood. His fingernails had been torn out, his limbs broken and his eyes gouged from his skull. He had put up a spirited fight, but in the end, before dying he had given up at least the direction of the relic, far out into the desert.

"If he was murdered," I'd asked, "how did Zakariya know what the priest had told his torturers?"

"That much is simple," Giso had said. "The priest was Zakariya's cousin, and Zakariya's young nephew was with him when Theokleia, Artemis and their mercenaries came to the church. The boy had been playing in a shadowed corner. Miraculously, neither the Byzantion bitches, nor the warriors with them, saw the child." Giso had made the sign of the rood, his face sombre. "When the priest and the nephew did not return for the evening meal, Zakariya sent some of his men to check on them, thinking perhaps someone had come demanding confession, or that his cousin had been detained by some other church business. What they found was a bloody mess on the altar and the boy huddled behind a pillar. The child could not speak. All he did was rock back and forth. And no wonder, after what he had witnessed. Still, his silence had surely saved him. If he had cried out, he would certainly have been slain too, just like his uncle."

"God be praised for that at least," I said. "The Almighty's hand must surely have protected the child. But I do not understand one thing: how did Theokleia know to question the priest?"

"The same way I knew to seek him out. Eirene's spies must have come across the same information as the Teacher. A thief, imprisoned in Attalea, was dying from the wounds he suffered during his capture. When he gave his final confession, he spoke of the Blood of Christ and said he had heard of its whereabouts from a priest in Ierusalem. The gaoler overheard everything and saw a way to fill his money pouch. He passed on the information. For a price. It would appear he was more avaricious than honourable, and he sold the information to agents of both the East and West. I had hoped to speak to the priest in Ierusalem and convince him to aid us. Theokleia reached him first, and she was –" he waved a hand in the air "– persuasive in a much more final way."

I had my doubts that Giso's way would have been any less cruel if left alone with the priest, but I said nothing. It mattered not now. And even if Giso would resort to such things, while we travelled with him the Frank would not dare. The crew of *Brymsteda* would never allow it.

Again I thought of the twists of fate and how we had come to be helped by the likes of Zakariya. If Theokleia and Artemis had gone to him with sweet words and promises of gold, we might not now be following them into the desert on the quest for the relic. Zakariya was a brigand, but he would know better than to double-cross the likes of Theokleia. He had told Giso as much.

"He has little love for me," Giso had said, "and he cares nothing for King Carolus. There is only one thing he values more than gold."

"Family," Runolf said, his face beaded in sweat in the sweltering heat of the storehouse. "I like this Zakariya."

Giso had shrugged. "He is not unlike you in some ways, I suppose," he said. "If you were smaller of build, fairer of face and sharper of wit." Runolf had snarled. Giso had grinned. "But yes, like you, Zakariya loves treasure, but places his kin above his wealth. When Theokleia had her brutes torture the priest for what he knew, she unwittingly turned one of the most powerful families in Ierusalem against her. Certainly the most dangerous."

"Another miracle of sorts," I said. "For you say Zakariya will send us a man who can guide us to where the relic is hidden."

"Yes," Giso replied. "It seems there are many tales of where this holiest of relics is located, but the men of the desert do not go near the place. They fear it. They say it is cursed. Until now it had seemed to Zakariya better to leave the relic there, rather than risk the wrath of God or the *jinn* of the desert."

"But now someone will guide us there?" Gwawrddur asked. "Are they no longer frightened of devils or God's ire?"

"They fear more the anger of Zakariya, it would seem."

"And he wants nothing in return for his help?" Gwawrddur looked incredulous.

"Oh no," Giso had said, "he wants plenty, but all you need to be concerned about is taking Theokleia's head from her shoulders. Artemis too must die, and the men who follow them."

"With all his power, why does he need us?" Drosten asked. "Why not send his own people to do this thing?"

"There is danger in this endeavour," said Giso. "There are several men with Theokleia and Artemis. Why risk the lives of his people when we will do the deed for him?"

"Perhaps," said Gwawrddur with a wry smile, "he is frightened of the tales of *jinn* and curses. Better that we strangers take his vengeance for him, than he should risk being cursed."

Arcenbryht had punched his fist into his palm then, his face hard with determination and a simmering anger.

"I for one will be happy to exact vengeance for Zakariya. No desert devil will stop me from getting revenge for Cumbra."

The men around me whispered quietly, discussing our options. I leaned back, staring up at the sky as my mind wandered. The stars were fading as dawn seeped into the east. My body ached, the bandaged cuts on my chest throbbing with the pulse of my heart. Revna was staring at me from where she sat. I longed to go to her, to draw her away from the men and to hold her in my arms.

I did not move. Weariness washed over me in waves and the prospect of Runolf's anger anchored me to the ground. I closed my eyes. My mind spun with images of flashing claws, dagger-like teeth and the echoes of the growling roars of the lion. I thought of the Blood of Christ, somewhere out in that desert waste. Had Theokleia already found it?

I had not meant to sleep, but exhaustion swept wakefulness aside and my thoughts transformed into dreams filled with Revna's shimmering hair, cornflower blue eyes, the scent of her skin and the feeling of her body pressed against mine.

Twenty-Nine

I awoke abruptly to the sound of animals and men moving. The crack of hoofbeats on the dusty track, the shouts of the riders, armed and mounted once more, the rattle and creak of harness. The bright sun-washed cleft in the hillside reverberated with noise.

The path was full of riders and pack animals, already moving past me. With a groan I pushed myself to my feet, wary that if I remained where I was, I might be trampled as the caravan moved along the narrow path.

Rubbing sleep from my eyes I looked at the sky, gauging how long I had slept. My body was stiff, my bruises and cuts screaming out as I moved. Judging from the shadows on the rocks, it was still early morning.

"Don't worry, we're not leaving just yet."

With a start I turned and saw Gwawrddur sitting on a boulder close by.

"I thought it best to let you sleep while you could," he said. "Though you looked none too comfortable."

Glancing about me I saw that the others were nowhere to be seen.

"They've gone back down to the camp," Gwawrddur said, reading my thoughts. "We still have to wait for the guide Zakariya promised us, and we thought we should remain hidden as much as possible. If the guide doesn't arrive soon, we'll have to move to another camp. The caliph's men know of this place now, something that Zakariya's men were furious about. Still, there is nothing for it now; the milk, once spilt, cannot be squeezed back into the teat."

Lumbering past us came Abul-Abbas. Isaac, perched on the huge creature's back, rocked from side to side. He waved as they passed.

"Godspeed," he called down. "I hope one day we will meet again. In Frankia, God willing."

I raised my hand, but said nothing. My head felt full of cobwebs, my thoughts slow.

"We do not go with Isaac then?" I asked Gwawrddur, watching the elephant trudge away, kicking up clouds of dust.

"You are sharp this morning," he said with a twisted smile. "And I thought it was Gersine who got the knock on the head." Seeing that I was still barely awake, he relented with his ribbing. "Giso and Isaac spoke at length," he said. "They decided we should continue after this relic. Hereward was not happy about it, but Isaac said he had protection enough, and he pointed out that if we were to travel with him, we would bring ourselves and him into more danger as we are being sought by the wali of Ierusalem."

Behind the elephant, Shafiq rode on a donkey. He halted before us and held out a small bundle to me.

"Clean bandages," he said gruffly, "and some more grease." He leaned down in the saddle and sniffed the air. Nodding, as if satisfied, he said, "See that you keep that wound washed and change the bandage tomorrow. With Allah's blessing you might yet live to be an old man like me."

"Thank you," I said, accepting the package. "May peace be upon you."

He waved away my gratitude and kicked his donkey into a trot. Half a dozen mounted warriors rode behind him. None of them seemed interested in Gwawrddur and me.

"How is Gersine?" I asked.

"Hurting," Gwawrddur replied. "But well enough, considering."

"Any vomiting?"

"Not when he left with the others."

"How is Runolf?"

"He will be fine," Gwawrddur said with a wink, "when he has had the chance to cleave someone with that axe of his."

"That is what I am afraid of."

The Welshman chuckled. "You have nothing to fear from Runolf," he said. "Unless you hurt Revna, of course."

"Never!" I said. "I would kill any man who harms her."

"So would any of us," Gwawrddur said, patting my arm. "You would do well to remember that, Hunlaf. If you hurt the girl, you will not only have Runolf to contend with."

We watched as the last of the riders passed. I felt a strange pang of loss as the swaying bulk of Abul-Abbas disappeared from view. There was something about the animal that spoke of a deeper intelligence than was normal in a beast. A depth to its long-lashed eyes, a softness wrapped within the immense strength of its form.

I thought of what Isaac had said and hoped that we would meet again. I would like to see how Abul-Abbas fared.

We picked our way down the steep path to where the water trickled and bushes grew around the rocky pool. One of Zakariya's men, a surly, scar-faced brigand called Qaid, was on watch on the path. He nodded to us silently.

Most of the men were sprawled out in the shade of rocks or plants, dozing. Runolf was not. He was stripped to the waist and standing before a timber frame fashioned out of the gnarled boughs of a thorn tree. To that frame he had lashed the carcass of the lion and was setting about gutting, skinning and butchering the beast. His arms and chest were smothered in gore. Flies buzzed above the offal and meat. Glancing at us, he nodded a terse greeting. Waving away flies with a massive, blood-smeared hand, he resumed his work.

Revna was with her father. She offered me a small smile and the subtlest shake of her head that said much without words. There was warmth in her expression, a welcome, but also a warning. I took her meaning and turned away from Runolf. Now was not the time to test that friendship. Gwawrddur patted me on the back.

"You'd do well to get more rest," he said. "When the guide arrives, Giso will not allow us to tarry. Theokleia and Artemis have four days' head start on us."

"You think we have any chance of beating them to the Blood of Christ when we are so far behind?"

The Welshman shrugged. "Giso thinks it is possible. I'm sure he has his reasons."

Without waiting for a response, he went to where his blanket was spread beneath the sparse canopy of the local pine trees. Lying down, he closed his eyes.

Gersine lay beside the pool. At my approach, he propped himself up on an elbow. His face was pale, but his eyes were bright and alert.

"How are you feeling?" I said, lowering myself down carefully to sit beside him.

"As if someone used my head to break rocks," he said.

"Thank the Lord it was not your head that burst."

"I am grateful for that, but my head aches too much to be praying. Can you do that for me? After all, I did save your life."

I grinned. "That blow has addled your memory," I said. "If Revna and I hadn't been there, you would have been that lion's meal."

"I wouldn't have even been there if not for you and Revna," Gersine said, raising an eyebrow.

I held up my hands in mock defeat.

"Very well," I said. "You win." He was right, of course. He

had risked much for us. His help had almost cost him his life. I watched as Runolf, with Revna's help, pulled the pelt of the beast away from its flesh, flensing it from sinew and bone with sharp knives, careful not to damage the skin further, though our sword blows had torn great gashes in it. "I'll pray for you," I said, not looking at Gersine. "And I'm glad your skull is thick." Ashamed, I recalled my petty thoughts when he had cried out in the night. "Thank you. For everything."

"What are friends for?" Gersine said easily.

"You had me worried when I saw you fall to the ground."

"I was plenty worried myself," he said, grinning.

"You were past worrying."

"True, but for a moment there I thought I had followed you one time too many." My guilt intensified. Gersine had always followed me. His limping gait, from an arrow in Hǫrðaland, reminded me of his loyalty. Perhaps sensing where my thoughts were heading and wishing to maintain the lightness between us, he changed the subject abruptly. "What do you think lion meat will taste like?"

Runolf was finishing the removal of the animal's hide and would soon begin to carve up its flesh. It was a large animal, heavily muscled and lean. There would be plenty of meat.

"I suppose we'll find out," I said.

"I imagine it will taste bad," Gersine said. "Like wolf meat, I'd wager."

"Perhaps," I said. "Meat-eating animals seldom have the most succulent of flesh. But it is meat all the same, and after all that work to butcher the thing, I won't be turning down a slice."

"If Runolf offers you any."

"I suppose that is doubtful at best."

"You can have some of mine," Gersine said with a lopsided smile. "Can't say I am looking forward to smelling that hide when we set off again. I doubt there'll be time to properly scrape and dry it."

"Anything is possible," I said, but he was probably right.

Runolf and Revna had barely finished with the lion carcass when Qaid whistled, alerting the camp.

The warmth of the day had worked its way into my bones, and I had just drifted off to sleep again. Now the shrill whistle brought me awake, blinking and drenched in sweat. I gasped at the sudden pain from my wounds as I sat up with a start.

"Be still," said Beorn, who sat nearby. "We are safe. These three are our guides, it seems. Though we will be lucky if they do not lead us into the desert and abandon us there to die."

"What do you mean?" I asked, pushing myself up to stand, so that I could get a better view of the newcomers. "What do you know of them?"

"Very little," said Beorn, "but I recall we made an impression on them, and you left your mark on the youngest in particular."

Frowning, unclear as to Beorn's meaning, I peered at the three men as they made their way into the camp. They came on foot, leading their camels behind them. They wore the dark robes of the *Badw* desert people. Their weathered faces were partly obscured by their scarves, their heads swaddled in cloth. We had seen countless such men since arriving in Yafah, and at first I saw nothing to distinguish these three from any of the others who had crossed our paths. Then I noted that each of their mounts bore a freshly scabbed wound on its rump and I looked back with renewed interest at the animals' owners.

Two of the men were older than me and paid me little heed. The youngest of the three was glowering, his eyes smouldering, jaw set. The flesh around his eyes was mottled and bruised – the many hues of storm clouds at sunset. My heart sank the instant I recognised him. Could it truly be that these men were to be our guides? We had stabbed their camels, and I had struck the youngest of this small band as we had fled from the wali's palace. The young man's fists were clenched at his sides and I knew without a doubt that, if he had the chance, he would kill me.

I walked towards them stiffly and bowed, touching my chest, lips and forehead in turn.

"Peace be upon you," I said in Al-Arabiyyah.

"And upon you," replied the leader of the band, returning my bow.

I swallowed, my mouth dry. I did not wish to speak further, but left unspoken, the wound I had caused, like an unwashed cut, could fester.

"I am sorry for my actions in Ierusalem," I said. "I meant you no harm, but we were running for our lives."

"I hear your words," the leader said, "and I thank you for them." His dark eyes did not leave mine and I saw that despite his politeness, just like the younger man, the leathery-faced *Badawi* remembered me well. And he too despised me.

The second *Badawi* bowed slightly, but said nothing. The youngest man halted before me. Slowly, deliberately, he sniffed and hawked, then spat a gobbet of phlegm and spittle into the dust at my feet. Without a word, he turned and led his camel down to the pool to drink.

Behind me, Runolf's deep voice boomed. "There's the Hunlaf we know so well," he said with a gravelly chuckle. "Making friends wherever he goes."

Thirty

No matter what they thought of us, and me in particular, the three *Badw* led us unerringly north-east into the dusty hills, following dry stream beds and hidden paths. The ground was fractured and broken but the secret tacks our guides followed allowed us to make good time.

Qaid and the rest of Zakariya's men had slipped away the previous afternoon after we had eaten some of the lion meat. As Gersine and I had expected, it was tough and gamey, but it was fresh and the Lord alone knew when we might find meat again in this desolate wasteland, and so we ate our fill.

I have eaten worse food many times in my life. I recall one memorable evening in the company of the Oguz il where I dined on pickled sheep eyeballs, a delicacy to the Türkmen clans. Even that was better than the stinking, rotten, fermented herring favoured by the tribes of Norrlanden. In comparison with that stomach-curdling delicacy, the seared lion's flesh was a feast. The *Badw* were particularly appreciative of it and asked if they might partake of the heart of the animal. Runolf obliged, and Nassif and Hamid, the older men, grinned at him, nodding as they chewed at slices of the rubbery organ. The youngest of them, whose name I had discovered was Jamal, scowled but I noticed that he too took a mouthful of the lion's heart.

We had set out as the shadows lengthened, travelling long into the moonlit night when the air was cooler. Eventually we had made camp in the shadow of a rocky outcrop, setting out once more when the dawn barely tinted the eastern horizon. The *Badw* spoke little but clearly understood the urgency of our quest, for we barely rested and they set a withering pace.

"I have told them to make all haste," Giso said, when I told him that we should halt for a time. Gersine was still pallid and, even though he did not complain, I could see from the tension in his jaw that his head still pained him. My own wounds were hurting too, and I would have welcomed some respite, but Giso would not hear of it.

"Those harlots of Eirene will not rest," he said, "of that you can be certain."

And so we had pressed on. The sun's rays scorched our skin. The hot wind buffeted us, peppering our faces with grains of sand. We rode with our eyes scrunched up, scarves wrapped tightly around our faces and pulled over our heads.

"Don't you think they will have found the relic by now?" I asked, riding my tired horse near to Giso's. "If the priest gave up the Blood of Christ's location, surely they will have it already and be far from here."

Giso had smiled at that. The sight of his grin was unnerving.

"Ah, yes," he said, "they may have found the Blood already. Time is of the utmost import now. But there is still reason to think the relic is yet within our reach."

"But they are days ahead of us."

"They are," Giso agreed. He was still smiling and I detected a slight madness in that expression. "But they do not have our guides." He turned in the saddle, his eyes twinkling from his tanned face. "And the priest died before he told them all he knew."

"How can you know this?"

"That much is simple," he said. "I questioned Zakariya's nephew." He shook his head at the memory. "The boy witnessed a terrible thing, but he has a sharp mind and recalled everything he had seen and heard. Theokleia and her servants revelled too much in the dealing of pain to the priest. In doing so, they slew him before he told them everything. They are going in the right direction, but they are missing a crucial piece of information. Eirene should be more careful to whom she trusts her future, but of course, the Empress of Byzantion is a bloodthirsty wench too." He smirked to himself, as if recollecting a fond memory. "I learnt long ago never to allow my emotions to take control. By relishing the torture and not focusing on her goal, this Theokleia has placed her mission in jeopardy. But God smiles on His own, don't you see? With the priest's early death, we are still in the race for Christ's blood."

I did not answer. I could not imagine the priest felt that God smiled on him as his nails were yanked out and his eyes plucked from their sockets. And yet Giso seemed capable of rationalising anything, even the priest's murder. I said nothing. Gritting my teeth, I squinted my eyes against the gusting sand and followed behind our *Badw* guides.

There was little talk as we travelled. Each of us lowered our heads and allowed our mounts to trudge along behind the animal in front. From time to time I looked over at Revna. She met my gaze and smiled, but it was as if the moment between us on the hill in the dark had never happened. Had I imagined the closeness between us? Had I somehow been mistaken? No, I had held her in my arms and she had leaned into me, lifting her face to mine, her lips parting. I ran over the events in my mind as we travelled, but try as I might, I could come to no other conclusion. We had been interrupted just before we kissed, but now, as if the wind had turned about at sea, it felt impossible that we should sail in that direction again.

When we camped, I had tried to speak to her, but Runolf glared at me, so instead I had checked how Gersine was feeling. His head still troubled him, but he was clearly feeling better than the previous morning in spite of the long ride.

Remembering Sadiq's advice, I peeled off my bloodstained bandages and set about applying more of the grease to the cuts across my chest. I was struggling to wrap the clean bandages around my midriff when hands took hold of mine. With a jolt I saw it was Revna. Her touch made my breath catch.

"Let me," she whispered.

"What about your father?" I asked, speaking so quietly only she would hear.

"Hush," she said, working expertly to bind the bandage tightly. "What sort of friend would I be if I did not help you?"

I was breathless as her deft fingers worked.

"We are friends then?"

"We are, Hunlaf," she said, tying off the bandage and offering my shoulder a squeeze.

I longed to reach for her, to finish what we had started in the darkness before the lion had attacked. She seemed to understand what I was thinking, for she held my shoulder firmly, keeping me where I was.

"There will be time enough for friendship when all this is done," she said.

"Just friendship?" I asked. "Not more?"

"Anything is possible," she whispered, her smile clear in her voice. "Now, get some rest. We will be riding again soon enough."

And with that, she was gone. I lay down, pulling my blanket about me, oblivious now of the pulsing pain from my injuries or the aches from the day's riding. All I could think of was Revna's touch, the scent of her and the sound of the smile in her voice.

Thirty-One

We saw the smoke rising like a goose feather quill above the horizon just after noon the following day. My spirits had been lifted by Revna's visit in the night. She was right that now was not the time to embrace our feelings for each other, but the promise of the future saw me riding into the dawn with a broad smile on my face.

Following the initial stiffness after waking, my body ached less too. My wounds were healing well and I was gladdened to see Gersine was feeling more his usual self too. Not even Runolf's dour glances, and Jamal's dark glowers, could dampen my good humour. I had ridden contentedly all that morning behind Nassif, the oldest of the *Badw* guides.

Hamid led the group. He was a man of middling years, strong and with a keen mind and a deep understanding of the land. Early that morning, as the first rays of the sun streaked the land with long shadows, he had dismounted from his camel and called a halt to our march while he examined the sand. He beckoned for Nassif, and the old man clambered stiffly down from his mount. Jamal trotted his own camel past us from where he rode at the rear of the party and leapt smoothly from the animal's high back. Crouching beside the older men, he listened as they conversed. He interjected something, but

Hamid shook his head, cutting him off. Jamal walked briskly back to his mount and climbed up into its saddle.

"Many riders passed this way," Hamid said. I translated his words for the others.

"How far ahead are they?" Giso asked.

Hamid shrugged. "I say a day, perhaps two. My father thinks less."

If Giso was as shocked as I to learn that Nassif was Hamid's father, he did not show it. Perhaps it was no revelation to him. The Frank always seemed to know more about what was transpiring around him than the rest of us.

"We must go with care," Nassif said.

When we saw the smoke in the distance, Hamid turned to us with a raised hand. We reined in our mounts.

"It seems my father was right," he said. "They are closer than I thought."

Giso was staring intently at the smudge of smoke as it was torn and tattered by the hot wind blowing across the barren land.

"What could be burning?" he asked. "Is there a settlement out here?"

Hamid and Nassif exchanged a dark look.

"There is no town there," Hamid said. "But our people wander where they will. We will not know the source of the smoke until we are near. There is a gully up ahead. We will take you there. Jamal and I will go on alone to find the cause of the fire."

Without waiting for a reply, they set off once more. We followed behind. I turned to look at where Jamal rode at the rear. He met my stare with open hostility.

"I don't trust them," said Drosten, when I translated what had been said.

"I am sure they would be glad to see us dead or lost out here," I said. "The Almighty alone knows what hold Zakariya has over them. But if they leave Nassif with us, I cannot believe they would abandon him, or lead our enemies to us."

The rest of the men joined in the conversation, each keen to voice their opinion, but when we reached the small gully Hamid had mentioned, we had not come to an agreement.

"Some of us should ride with you," I said to Hamid.

Jamal, sitting proudly on his camel, sneered at me and spat into the sand. Hamid hissed at the young man to be silent.

"Your horses cannot keep up with our steeds," Hamid said. "We know the ways of the desert, like a man knows the lines of his wife's face. We will approach unseen and return when we know what lies ahead. If we do not return, my father will guide you."

With a nod to Nassif, Hamid wheeled his camel around and kicked it into a lumbering run. Jamal let out a shout, slapping his goad to his camel's flank and set off after him.

Hereward frowned. "Eadstan, Pendrad, go up there and keep watch." He pointed to the top of the gully. "Don't let yourselves be seen. I will not have us ambushed here. And I am not sure I trust that having a hostage will keep us safe."

The two warriors scrambled up the slope, sending down a shower of pebbles. Nassif shook his head. He did not act like a hostage. Dismounting slowly, he led his camel deeper into the steep-sided ravine. There was some wispy grass and thin shrubs he called *Ghada* clinging to the rocks.

"Is there water here?" I asked the old man. "The horses are thirsty."

He laughed, a deep chuckle at the back of his throat. "Horses are always thirsty," he said. "They will have to wait."

We sought out what little shade there was, some of the men sitting beneath their mounts. Sipping from our waterskins, we nibbled on the tough lion meat. After a time, Hereward rose and began to pace. He kept looking up towards where

Eadstan and Pendrad were hidden in the rocks, but there was no movement and no sound.

The sun slid inexorably across the sky, the shadows moving and lengthening in the gully. We were all growing anxious now and with each passing heartbeat it felt as though we must have been betrayed, that at any moment our enemies would descend on us.

Eventually, the waiting became unbearable. Hereward called Gwawrddur and Drosten over to where he stood, staring anxiously up at the pale, cloudless sky.

"Ride after them and find out what that smoke is. Take no risks and hurry back at the first sign of trouble."

Drosten nodded. Gwawrddur seemed about to protest, but before he could speak, a shout came from above. It was Eadstan, his waving hand stark against the sky.

"They return!" he called down to us, his voice echoing in the ravine.

"Alone?" shouted Hereward.

"Alone," came Eadstan's reply.

We roused ourselves and readied the horses. Stiffly, Nassif rose and went to his camel.

The moment Hamid and Jamal rode into the gully, I could see that what they had found had marked them. Their expressions were bleak.

"What was it?" I asked, handing Hamid a waterskin.

Hamid accepted the skin and drank. His eyes were desolate and dark as he passed it back to me.

"Death," he said. "We found nothing but death."

Thirty-Two

What little smoke there had been on the horizon had all but completely dissipated by the time we arrived. The prints of Jamal and Hamid's camels were clear in the sand. The two *Badw* now rode out to either side of the path they had followed previously. They stared into the distance, searching for any sign of danger. Before we left the gully, Hamid had whispered quietly to Nassif. The old man's dark-skinned face was set now, as if carved in oak.

The smoke had come from the remains of the tents. There was little enough wood in the frames, and the hides that covered the timbers had not caught well. I recalled the smiles and laughter of Rabab and his people when we had sat in just such a tent near Yafah. I remembered the bitterness of the *marmaraya*, the greasy tang of the lamb, and the warmness of the *Badw* hospitality.

As we grew near, my horse shied away, snorting and stamping at the stink of blood. I dismounted and looped the reins on a spindly bush of *Ghada*.

"How many lived here, do you think?" Gersine asked, his voice startling me.

I looked about us at what was left of the camp. Bodies dotted the area, dark and unmoving against the sand. I could see the corpses of at least two children. Unbidden, the memory of the boys on the beach came to me. "Perhaps two families. Not more, I would say."

Runolf stood surrounded by the destruction. His chest heaved as he fought to control his emotions.

"What reason could they have for killing the children?" he growled.

I had no answer for him.

Nassif dismounted and knelt beside one of the bodies. Closing his eyes, he whispered something, then turned to me. "I know these people," he said, his voice cracking like old parchment. "This desert has been their home for generations. Now they are dust and ash." He pushed himself to his feet with a grunt. Sniffing, he wiped away tears. "This is madness," he hissed, pointing to several dark shapes scattered about the camp. For a dreadful moment I thought they were yet more children, but then I saw they were goats. There were perhaps a score of the animals. All of them had been hacked to death and left lying in their own gore in the dust. The carcasses were alive with flies. "Those we seek are devils," Nassif said, his voice hollow.

I could offer him no comfort.

"We will help you bury the dead," I said, not knowing what else to say. Nothing could make this right.

He stared at me, tears streaming from his dark eyes. There was fury beneath his grief and for an instant all I saw was a terrible hatred burning in his gaze. Then, with a sigh, he nodded, cuffing at his cheeks.

Giso had moved to stand nearby.

"They are close," he said. "There is no time. We cannot tarry here. We must hurry after our quarry." He spoke in Englisc so that the old *Badawi* would not understand.

"We will bury the dead first," I said firmly.

"We risk losing the chance of finding the relic before the agents of Eirene."

"And if we do not tend to the dead, we risk becoming as evil as them."

Runolf stood where two children lay beside one of the smouldering tents. The Norse giant stared down at their tiny forms, his expression murderous. "You will help us bury the dead, Frank," he said, his voice deep with menace, "or we will bury you along with them. The choice is yours."

Giso scowled. He looked from me to Runolf, then swept his gaze around the rest of the warriors. All of them were stony-faced.

"I suppose the relic can wait," Giso said.

We set about digging a grave. It was hot and tiring work. We did not have the tools for it, but using our hands, sticks, platters and pots we found in the wreckage of the camp, we were able to dig a hole large enough to accommodate the dead. There were fourteen in all: three men, four women and seven children. Those who had been partially burnt were twisted and charred, barely recognisable as human. The stink of roasted meat made my stomach twist and my gorge rise. After carrying a body from the ruin of the tents, Arcenbryht staggered away and puked loudly. None of us commented when he returned pale-faced, spitting and wiping the sweat from his forehead.

As we toiled, Giso stood off to one side, gazing into the distance. Runolf halted his digging, glowering at the man. Giso appeared not to notice, or perhaps he was deliberately ignoring the Norseman. Whatever the truth, it seemed foolhardy to me. Runolf looked as though he was about to launch himself at the Frank. His rage rolled off him like mist washing down a mountainside. But before the Norseman could move, Hereward shouted over to where Giso stood.

"The more hands that help to dig this grave, the sooner we can be on our way."

Giso nodded, but did not move.

"Come and help," Hereward urged, his voice taking on a hard edge.

Giso waved a hand. "Such work is not for me," he said. "You chose to dig, so dig."

Runolf growled and clenched his fists, but Drosten halted him with a hand on his arm. The Pict was stripped to the waist, bloodstained bandage tight about his bunching and bulging muscles, his tattoos writhing like serpents as he scraped at the sandy earth. Now, with a grunt of annoyance, he climbed out of the trench and strode towards Giso.

Seeing the violence in his eyes, the Frank took a nervous step backwards, raising his hands. "Hold your—"

Drosten's fist cut off his words. The Pict was a formidable brawler. He had been earning his keep as a fist-fighter when I first met him. Giso was a small man. Dangerous enough with a blade, no doubt, but he was certainly no match for Drosten with his hands. Drosten did not put his full strength into that punch. His hand lashed out with a straight jab that looked little more than a tap, but still Giso's head snapped back and he staggered. Falling hard, he sat down heavily in the sand and blinked up at Drosten. For a heartbeat the Frank was stunned, his vision dazed. Then his focus returned and he stared at Drosten with such venom that I feared for the Pict.

Drosten did not seem perturbed. Giso clambered to his feet, spitting blood. His lip was split, his teeth stained red. His hand dropped to the long knife he wore. Drosten stepped in quickly and slapped the hand away. Tugging the knife from its sheath, he tossed it aside.

"You going to pull a blade on me, little man?" he hissed. "Do it and you'll be joining those others in the pit."

Giso glowered at him, then shook his head. He spat more blood. "You should not have struck me, Pict," he said.

"You should have done as you were asked." Without waiting for a reply, Drosten took a handful of Giso's robe and shoved him hard towards the grave. "Now dig."

By the time we had finished digging the grave and laying the dead to rest, my limbs screamed from the exertion, and my wounds stung and prickled. We carried each of the bodies as carefully as we could, wrapping them in whatever remnants of clothing or hide we could find.

The last corpse I carried was a girl of perhaps ten summers. The thought of her life cut so senselessly short engulfed me without warning as completely as a breaking wave, smothering me and overwhelming me. Tears came then, and I sniffed as they rolled down my cheeks. Wiping them away on my grimy sleeve, I knelt beside the girl and covered her glazed eyes and innocent, unblemished face with the blanket I had wrapped her in. I prayed that God would have mercy on her soul and that we would be able to wreak vengeance on those who had done this. I could not believe they sought the same relic as us. We must do everything in our power to prevent them from obtaining a thing of such sacred power.

As I stood, looking about to see who would help me with this final burden, a shadow fell over me. Someone had already positioned themselves at the girl's feet. With a start, I saw that it was Jamal, his bruised face drawn, haggard and soot-streaked. He met my gaze and, for the first time, I did not see hatred there. He looked as desolate and sorrowful as I felt. A look of understanding passed between us and, setting aside our differences, we silently lifted the girl and bore her to the grave. There we set her down carefully beside the rest of her family.

We covered the dead with sand and such rocks as we could find. We were all exhausted, drenched in sweat and smeared with ash and dirt. I prayed silently, taking a mouthful of water from a skin and watching as Nassif, Hamid and Jamal knelt before the grave and prayed. The moment they had finished, rising to their feet, their expressions bleak, Giso strode over to his horse.

"Can we leave now?" He dabbed at his swollen lip with the

back of his hand, but it was no longer bleeding. "There is still daylight, and with each passing moment we are more likely to lose the relic we seek."

"Aye, little man," said Drosten, swinging himself into the saddle, "and those who did this thing are more likely to escape what is coming to them."

Without comment, the men mounted their horses. Revna jumped onto the back of her own mount, as keen as the others to be on the move once more.

Hamid and Jamal mounted their camels without a word. Nassif's camel knelt, and he climbed up into the saddle. He pointed to the tracks of many riders leading northward from the grave.

"Those who did this are making their way to the place you seek. The Cave of Tears."

The name the *Badw* tribesmen gave to the place, coupled with the death all about us, made me shudder.

"Can we reach it by nightfall?" I asked, looking up at the sky. The sun was already dipping towards the western horizon.

"If we ride hard," Nassif said. "But it is a place of death. Haunted by spirits. Too dangerous at night."

My skin prickled at his words. The day was blisteringly hot. I trudged over to my horse and pulled myself up onto its back. My shoulder throbbed and my chest ached dully.

"We cannot wait," I said, thinking of Theokleia and Artemis escaping with the Blood of Christ. "What of the horses? How hard can we push them?"

Nassif shrugged. "There may be water where we are going," he said.

"And if there is not?"

"Some of the horses will not live. Perhaps all of them." His eyes narrowed and a wolfish look came upon him. "But our enemies, the murderers of these people, have mounts. If we catch them, I think they will have no use for their animals where we plan to send them."

I translated the old *Badawi*'s words for the others. Runolf showed his teeth.

"I like the old man," he said. "And he's right. The dead can't ride. So let's ride while we live."

With that, he kicked his heels into his horse's flanks and set off at a gallop. With an ululating cry, Hamid and Jamal lashed their camels into a loping run. The rest of us spurred on after them, the dust thrown up from the other riders clouding around us and stinging our eyes.

Only Nassif did not immediately race off in pursuit. Shielding my eyes from the stinging grit from the galloping animals, I looked back and saw the old man still sitting there astride his camel, head bowed as he stared at the rock-piled grave. A moment later, he was lost to view in the swirling dust.

Thirty-Three

We rode out of the dusty desert hills and into a rockier area where tangled, low-lying shrubs grew in shadowed clefts. We had slowed our pace after the initial rush to be after our quarry. The horses were lathered and blowing, and even if we wished to push them to their limits, there was nothing to be gained from killing them before we reached our destination. And so we had maintained a steady trot that had soon seen Nassif catch up to us on his lumbering camel. The ungainly creatures ran in an awkward fashion with none of the grace of a horse, and yet there could be no denying they could eat up the distance more effectively in this arid, hostile wasteland.

After a time, Hamid – who had taken the lead once more – raised his hand and pulled his camel to a halt. We were in shadow now, a tall slope rising up to our left where the sun was setting, turning the sky a sickening, reddish hue.

"I do not like that sky," Hamid said.

"Storm?" I asked.

"Perhaps."

I wiped the sweat from my face. "I would welcome rain."

"Storms here do not always bring rain," Hamid said, staring up at the bruised-looking sky. "When they do, even the rain can be dangerous."

I looked about at the parched ground, the dry rocks and the scattered, wizened trees and shrubs.

"This gully can become a torrent," Hamid explained. "Let us press on. It is not far now, and if that is a storm, it is still a long way off."

We rode on and a short while later, Hamid reined in again. The shadows were darker now, the sky in the west growing purple and mottled.

"What now?" hissed Giso. "You said we were close. Why do you halt?"

Hamid ignored him, and slid from the saddle. He led his camel over to me.

"The place you seek is just beyond those rocks," he said. "The ground opens out and you will see an opening between two—" He said a word I did not comprehend.

"Boulders," snapped Giso from the gathering dusk.

"Translate for the others," I hissed at him, straining to hear Hamid as he continued to speak as if Giso was not present. The wind had picked up and was tugging at our robes, blowing billows of sand and dust down the canyon. As if frightened of being overheard, Hamid spoke in a hushed whisper now.

"We will go no further," he said. "Not at night. Spirits and devils lurk in that cave. Men who venture here are seldom seen again."

"How do we know you have not led us into a trap?" hissed Giso.

For the first time since we had buried the people at the burnt settlement, Hamid looked at him. His expression held a deeper chill perhaps than that desert canyon had ever witnessed before.

"You do not," he said, "but you have seen for yourself the trail of the people we follow. We promised Zakariya we would bring you here, and that is what we have done. But we will not approach that cave at night and we will not enter. We will guard your mounts and await your return. We might be able to find some water in the rocks. Perhaps enough to keep the horses alive."

Giso had stopped interpreting, so Hereward asked, "What is he saying?"

I translated Hamid's words.

"It pains me to say it," said Hereward, "but Giso is not wrong. We certainly cannot leave our mounts with them. They could ride off and abandon us. We had enough of walking through waterless mountains on Kýpros. I don't wish to repeat that experience and I don't imagine we would do as well walking out of this land."

I began to translate the gist of what Hereward had said. Hamid's face clouded.

"Do not doubt our honour," he said. "You helped us to bury our people, for that we thank you. You must trust me now. I have given you my word."

"Your word means little to me," said Giso.

Hamid took a step forward, slowly beginning to draw his sword from its long scabbard.

"I have had enough of you, Frank," he said. "The painted man bloodied your mouth; I will take your head."

Jamal had dismounted and now he stepped forward to place a hand on Hamid's arm, preventing him from fully unsheathing his sword's blade.

"I will go with them," Jamal said in response to the older man's surprised look.

Hamid was aghast. "No. Let the Christians risk their lives for what lies hidden beneath the earth. Your place is here, with me and your grandfather."

I saw then how closely Jamal resembled both men. How had I not seen sooner that they were three generations of the same blood?

"I am not afraid of the tales of ghosts and demons," Jamal said. "And if the men who killed our people are there, I would bathe my sword in their blood."

Hamid began to protest further, but Nassif shook his head.

"Hush, son," he said. "Jamal is a man and must choose his own path. This is the way of things. The young are always foolish. Or brave."

"What is the difference?" Hamid asked.

"That answer only comes later," said Nassif, his wrinkled features sad. "Those who survive are brave. Let him go. We were all young once."

Hamid looked first at his father, then at his son.

"Take care," he said to Jamal and embraced him fiercely. "And come back alive. I would like to tell your mother her son is brave, not foolish."

"Do not worry about me," Jamal said, handing his camel's rope to Hamid. "Watch the mounts until we return."

And with that, Jamal turned and walked out of the canyon, leaving his father and grandfather staring after him.

"Bring him back to me alive," Hamid said, his tone as sharp as splintered rock.

Thirty-Four

The shadows stretched long across the sand as we strode out from the ravine. The land about us was desolate, more dun hills rising up around us. There was nothing to mark this small patch of land as anything out of the ordinary. It resembled countless other valleys surrounded by rocky slopes and dotted with tough shrubs and bushes of *Ghada*.

But just as Hamid had described, two huge boulders loomed up from the sandy earth. A few smaller rocks were piled around them and they appeared to lean against a small rise. If we'd had no reason to believe those rocks hid what we were looking for, we would have surely ridden by without a second glance. But Jamal was already walking determinedly towards them.

"Wait," I called out, pitching my voice just above the bluster of the wind. I did not wish to alert anyone who might be lurking in wait for us.

Jamal turned, annoyance on his face. "What?" He swept his hand around to encompass the whole valley. Apart from the tall rocks there was nothing of interest. And nowhere to hide. "There is nobody here."

I hurried to reach him. The wind was stronger now, snatching the words from my mouth and sending threads of sand blowing from the peaks of the hills. The sky was dark and foreboding, but it appeared to glow with an unearthly light. I wondered if this was an omen. Had God forsaken us, or was his displeasure aimed at those who had passed this way before?

Reaching Jamal, I said, "Can you read the ground as well as your father?"

He sneered, but squared his shoulders with pride. "My eyes are sharper than his, and I have learnt at his side. Whoever walks this land cannot pass unseen or unnoticed."

"Before we go further, would you search for signs?"

He glowered at me for a few heartbeats, squinting at the dust that spiralled in the valley. He did not wish to take orders from me, but he could see the sense in what I asked. With a curt nod, he held up his hand for the others to halt their advance. "Keep them away until I have looked."

Without waiting for me to reply, he walked briskly away and began to circle the boulders, every now and then dropping down to examine the earth.

"Looks like Theokleia has already gone," said Hereward.

"I told him to check for tracks," I said. "Have you got the lamps?"

"Aye," Hereward replied. "Eadstan has them. Pendrad and Sygbald have the oil." Knowing we would be venturing beneath the earth, we had come prepared. "We'll need to get out of this damned wind if we are to light the things."

Drosten was staring up at the sky. A flicker of lightning stabbed the gloom in the west.

"I have a bad feeling about this storm," he said.

Giso scoffed. "That is the Almighty reminding us of his power. Perhaps the Lord will smite you for your insolence; for striking his servant."

"Perhaps He will," said Drosten, "but I think God would have wanted you to help us with the dead. Besides, if we come upon those who murdered and burnt those people you helped to bury, would you rather I was at your side to fight them, or slain by a bolt of lightning?"

Giso frowned, but said nothing further. Drosten scowled at him, as if daring the Frank to provoke him again. But I noticed that the moment Giso looked away, watching as Jamal made his way back to us, Drosten crossed himself and looked up nervously at the sky.

"Those we have followed were here," Jamal said. "They left a couple of men with their mounts. The rest went into the cave."

I translated his words.

"Is he certain?" Gwawrddur asked.

Jamal snorted. He pointed back at the rocks. "Do you see any horses or camels there?"

"Is it possible that some remained beneath the ground, awaiting our arrival?" asked Gwawrddur.

For the first time Jamal's self-assurance slipped. "Maybe," he said grudgingly. "But not likely. If they came in search of the same thing you seek, they would surely have taken it and left. Besides, to wait in ambush they would have to have known we were following them."

Lightning flickered in the clouds again, but I heard no sound of thunder, just the whistling of the wind as it scoured the broken land. All around me, the men's faces were drawn and anxious.

With a roar of challenge, Runolf abruptly lifted his axe and held it high above his head, as if tempting the lightning to find him. His shaggy hair and beard whipped about his face.

"Óðinn sends his son Þórr to rip the skies." He held his massive left hand next to his ear. "If you listen, you can hear his voice on the wind."

We fell silent. The fear that had gripped the others scratched its fingers down my back too. The air was thick with power. Was God speaking through the storm? Was that what Runolf heard? Or was it the thrumming energy of the sacred relic we sought that buzzed and crackled in the valley gloaming?

"I hear nothing but the wind," said Gwawrddur at last. "A lot of wind. Much like sharing a room with you, Runolf!"

The men chuckled at that and Runolf grinned. The tension lessened, torn apart by our laughter, as if the wind itself tattered it and blew it away. Revna caught my eye and offered me a small smile. My mood improved instantly.

"Perhaps that wind comes from Óðinn's arse," Runolf said, his voice booming, "but if it does, it is the All-Father's arse, and I can hear it speaking. You know what it says?"

Still laughing, Hereward shook his head. "Tell us what you hear in your god's farts."

"He says, 'Runolf Ragnarsson, there is nothing in that cave you cannot smite with the blade of your axe.'" He slapped the haft of the weapon into his left palm. "So, what are we waiting for? Jamal has told us our enemies are gone. Let us see what we can find. Even if we are too late, we will be out of this accursed wind."

Runolf strode towards the boulders, axe in hand. Behind him, Revna and the men fell into step, pulling their own weapons from their scabbards.

"What does the giant say?" asked Jamal, as we followed them.

"The Norseman speaks nothing but folly," Giso retorted.

Jamal ignored him and turned to me.

"He says his god has told him his axe can kill anything that is in the cave."

Jamal's expression grew serious. "Do you believe him?"

I weighed my words before answering. "I do not believe in his gods," I said, "but Runolf is afraid of nothing, and I have never met man or beast that he could not slay with that axe of his."

My words seemed to reassure Jamal. With a satisfied nod, he walked with renewed confidence towards the boulders. The rest of the group were already huddled about the stones, and

I peered past them. It was growing dark now. The setting sun had dipped below the horizon and the ominous cloud blocked much of the residual light that normally lingered at dusk. I had half expected to find a pile of rocks concealing the entrance similar to what we had encountered on Kýpros, but despite the gathering twilight, I saw at once the opening between the boulders. It would have been difficult to notice for anyone passing by the place, but on close inspection it was clear. It was like a door, with the leaning boulders forming the jambs and the lintel. The darkness beyond was dense and absolute.

Eadstan crouched in the wind shadow in the lee of the boulders. Beckoning for Pendrad to pour some of the oil from the flask he carried, he set about striking a spark. It took him some time while we watched on anxiously and the darkness crowded around us. Several times Eadstan believed the spark had caught in the bone-dry tinder, only for it to go out, leaving just the memory scent of smoke behind. But at last, the spark caught. Eadstan lifted the tinder to his lips and blew gently. When a flame flickered to life, he lit a taper that he had prepared, quickly putting the flame to the lamp's wick. Pendrad lit another lamp from Eadstan's and handed it to Revna.

Eadstan cupped his hand around his lamp, careful not to let the ever-strengthening wind extinguish it. Moving through the stone archway, he descended a couple of the carved steps that I could now see leading into the earth.

"Wait," said Jamal. His face was pale in the lamplight.

"What?" I asked.

"Tell him to go no further. Have him hold up the lamp that I might look at the steps."

I passed on what he had said and Hereward nodded. Beside him Giso was practically quivering with pent-up excitement and frustration.

"Hurry," he whispered. "Perhaps we are not too late." Nobody answered him. "Can you not feel it?" he went on, his voice trembling as if with cold. "There is power here."

He glanced at me and I knew he could see I felt it too. From the tight expressions on the faces of the others, we were not the only ones to sense it.

Jamal squeezed past Revna and Eadstan and crouched on the steps.

"Hold up the lights," he said, motioning with his hand what he wanted. Revna and Eadstan obliged, but the flames flickered and the shadows leapt around Jamal. After a while, he held out his hand to Eadstan. "Tell him to give me the lamp."

I told Eadstan what he wanted and he drew another lamp from his bag. Pendrad again filled it, and Eadstan lit it from the flame of the first, which he then handed to Jamal.

The young *Badawi* examined the steps for what seemed a long time, then nodded to himself.

"I cannot say surely, but it is clear that many descended and many left the same way. I know not what they found in the dark, but look." He pointed to a darker patch of sand on the stone step.

"What is that?" asked Giso.

Jamal dipped his finger into the stain and rubbed the sand between thumb and forefinger.

"Blood," he said.

Thirty-Five

We crowded inside the stone archway while the other lamps were lit. The wind blew great clouds of sand across the valley, but in the entrance we were sheltered enough that the flames were not snuffed out. We had six lamps in all. Revna, Jamal and Eadstan held one each. Pendrad and Sygbald carried two more. Giso took the last of the guttering lights.

Our enemies had left and it seemed highly improbable that any would have remained. And yet such was the tension in the air, the anticipation of violence coupled with discovering the blood on the step, that several of the men had drawn their weapons. I felt it too. My hand twitched and I fingered the hilt of my sword. And yet I did not unsheathe my blade. The passageway that descended into the earth was narrow; there would be little room for fighting.

"Keep your eyes open for snakes," said Hereward.

This reminder of what we had faced in Kýpros gave us pause and we jostled uneasily for position on the steps, anxiously looking into the darkness and the shifting shadows there. I could detect no serpents; no movement at all. But there was no telling how many steps there were, or what we would find in that underground passage. Hereward took command, quickly placing us in an order that saw the lamps spaced between us.

I found myself beside Revna. She did not look at me, but

without a word her hand took mine. She gave it a squeeze, then released it. My heart beat faster still and I instantly felt the loss of her touch.

Giso shoved brusquely past, placing himself in the lead.

"If what we seek is in there," he said, "it would be best not to trample it under your warrior boots." The energy of the swelling storm and the thrum of power in the air appeared to energise him, giving him renewed confidence. It was as if, stepping out of the dusk and into darkness, Giso was moving into a realm he understood. The rest of us were of the light, fighters who battled with blade and shield. Down here in the shadows was Giso's world. Holding his lamp high, he began to descend the steps.

Hereward shrugged and signalled for Drosten to follow behind.

"Stay close," he said. "Don't allow yourselves to get separated. We don't know how big this place is."

We followed Giso down into the earth, leaving the rush of the wind and the fading twilight behind. Soon the storm was nothing more than a whisper, and the passageway closed about us. Beyond the pool of light cast by the lamps there was only blackness. Our steps echoed in the gloom and the sound of our breath was loud. As we shuffled down the carved stairs, I searched the rock walls and floor for snakes or any other threat, but I saw none. The steps were clean, as if they had been swept. The lamplight picked out carvings on the walls: symbols I did not at first recognise. Sigils, patterns and images.

I recalled the steps in the Serpent's Maw. That echoing darkness had been similar and yet something was different here. The air was less stale. The entrance was open to the elements, allowing fresh air in, but there was something else. The cavern in Kýpros had been lost for centuries. Dead. Despite the remoteness of this place, it felt used, lived in somehow.

The light spilt out into a larger area and Giso halted, allowing us all to reach him. The sound of our footfalls reverberated into the dark, giving the impression of a much larger area. Our lamps illuminated the shapes of broad columns. Their rounded, chiselled stone bore more carvings like those on the stairway walls. I had imagined this place might be like the cave where we had found the Spear of Longinus, but I saw the ghosts of more pillars further off in the dark. There was no telling how vast the chamber was, but it was much bigger than I had expected.

"Where now, little man?" hissed Drosten.

"Let me see better," replied Giso. "Hold all the lamps aloft."

Beside me Revna raised her lamp. The others did the same, and the warm light shone further into the cavernous room, pushing the darkness back and displaying yet more thick columns, stretching off as far as we could see. Giso peered up at the stone ceiling of the vault, perhaps searching for a sign.

Jamal moved past him, stepping into the chamber, the light from his lamp tumbling into the gloom around him. It gleamed on metal. He stooped and held up an object for us all to see.

It was a long curved knife. Dark blood was smeared on its blade.

"There," Jamal said, pointing towards the next row of pillars. Revna let out a small gasp. I felt my chest tighten.

At the base of one of the columns sat a figure. The lamplight glimmered in his eyes, but it was immediately clear that he was dead. Jamal dropped down beside him and touched his hand. Checking the shadows for signs of danger, I followed the others as we moved close, looking down at the corpse.

Jamal rose, his face grim. "I know this man," he said. "Bad man. Deadly fighter."

The dead man wore the robes of the *Badw*. His bearded face was dark from the sun, lined with age. An old scar ran down his left cheek.

"Perhaps my father was right," Jamal went on, shaken by what he had seen. "There are devils here. This is the home of *jinn*. I can feel their dark magic."

I made the sign of the cross, but chose not to interpret Jamal's words. Giso handed his lamp to Gamal, then stooped and placed his hand on the dead man's neck.

"Still warm," he said. Tearing away the man's robes, he exposed a deep wound in his chest. Blood had pooled in his lap, drenching his clothes and smothering his belly. "But this wound is not the work of any devil or *jinni*. This is a sword thrust."

Runolf stepped close, glancing down at the body and then squinting into the shadowy darkness. "Look," he said, his voice rumbling in the cavernous space like a rockfall, "there was a fight here."

On the edge of the light, I could just make out two more dark shapes slumped on the stony floor.

Without realising I had drawn my weapon, I found my sword reassuringly in my hand. Cautiously, all the while looking about us, we made our way to these new bodies. Both of them were young men, dressed in white robes, similar to the habit of a monk. The two of them were dead, blood staining their robes and puddling around their still forms. Short, broad-bladed swords lay near their bodies. Both weapons were dark with drying blood.

The stink of death, the acrid scent of spilt bowels and the metallic tang of blood, was heavy in the still air. As we reached the corpses, our expanding light fell on two more bodies sprawled between the pillars.

"What happened here?" asked Hereward.

Gwawrddur looked down at the white-robed bodies and then at the two dark-garbed corpses that lay further into the chamber.

"It would seem that those young men put up a sterner resistance than the families we buried."

I pictured the white-robed men hiding in the shadows of the columns and springing out to confront Theokleia and her mercenaries. If they had not expected resistance, it would have been simple enough to kill some of their foe before being overwhelmed by superior numbers. I gripped my sword tightly, wondering if there were more defenders lurking in the gloom.

The two furthest corpses were rough-looking men, much like the first man we had found, wrapped in the cloaks and scarves of the *Badw*. And quite dead.

The throat of one had been torn open by a sharp blade. He lay on his front, his face caked in blood. When Runolf rolled him over the man's head flopped back obscenely, showing the deep gash like a wide grin beneath his chin. I could imagine one of the defenders stepping from his hiding place and delivering the blow before the dead man even knew he was being attacked.

The other warrior had managed to fight before he was killed. The vicious-looking blade near him was gore-smeared and blood splattered his face. The blow that had killed him was a slashing cut to his inner thigh that had severed the thick artery there. Such a wound killed in moments. There was blood all around the two men. Some of it had splashed the pillars, drying in rivulets and congealing in the lines of the carvings. There were footprints leading from the blood. The line of them went further into the cave.

Following the bloody prints with my gaze, I noticed that our lights shone further than before. Squinting, I stared into the gloom beneath the columns. For a moment I was not certain of what I was seeing. Then it struck me. "There is a light there!"

Gwawrddur clapped me on the back. "You have the eyesight of an owl," he said.

Runolf scrunched up his eyes, staring hard into the darkness. "I see nothing. Just our lamps reflecting from the stone."

"Hunlaf's eyes are younger," said Gwawrddur. "And sharper. He is right. There is a flame burning back there."

By some unspoken agreement, a hush fell over us and we moved ahead stealthily. I barely breathed, straining to hear anything that might give away a threat. As we passed each stout column I quickly peeked around, but there was no hidden assailant waiting for us with sharpened blade.

I could see now that we were coming to the end of the rows of pillars. Now there was no doubt, a light burnt at the end of the chamber where steps rose up to a raised area that was hidden from view. As we drew closer, step by step, I fixed my gaze on the thin light that rippled at the top of those stone steps.

Reaching the bottom of the short flight of stairs, a small chamber was visible beyond. There were drapes or curtains hanging over the walls, perhaps hiding exits or alcoves. In the centre of the rear wall was a stone altar. The light emanated from a lamp that rested on the altar's smooth surface.

Giso was ahead of me. Placing his foot on the lowest step, he started up. My fear had been overcome now by my curiosity and I followed just behind the Frank.

"Can you feel it?" he whispered.

I nodded, in truth unsure what I felt. And yet there could be no denying the air felt charged, throbbing with unspent energy, like the tension on a summer's day before a storm. I pondered whether the tempest outside might be responsible for the feeling. Whatever the cause, the hairs on my arms and the back of my neck prickled with excitement.

Giso began to utter the words of the paternoster quietly in Latin. Without thinking, I joined him and together we mounted the steps, both intoning the Lord's Prayer. The others climbed silently behind us.

"Are you angels?"

The thin, tremulous voice spoke in Greek. It seemed to come from the altar. The prayer died on my lips and my steps faltered.

"We are not angels," said Giso, "but we are friends."

"Friends, you say?" replied the voice before breaking into a fit of coughing. "She said she was a friend too. But she was a devil."

My initial fear at this voice vanished. Climbing the last of the steps, I saw a man sitting with his back to the stone altar. The single flame of the lamp was above and behind him, throwing his face into shadow, but there was enough light to see he wore similar white robes to those of the dead men we had found. As first Jamal, then Eadstan and Revna stepped into the chamber, the light from their lamps washed over the man and I saw that, unlike the dead men, his face was lined by age, his hair and beard white and wispy. And yet, like them, his robe was stained with blood.

Gamal and Pendrad reached the top of the steps and the old man blinked at the sudden light, looking up at us as we approached.

"You do not look like devils," he said. He suppressed another cough, wincing in pain. "But neither did she."

I dropped down to kneel beside him. Giso squatted on the other side.

"We mean you no harm," I said, still speaking in Latin.

"That is what she said." The old man looked down at his bloody robes. "But look at me. And my boys…" He fell silent and a tear trickled down his cheek.

"She is our enemy too," Giso said. "We followed her here to stop her from stealing something."

The old man's eyes narrowed. "Stealing what?" he asked.

Giso gave me a warning look. I knew he believed it always best to keep secrets, for he said you never knew what they might be worth.

"Something of great value," I said, ignoring Giso's silent warning and his sharp intake of breath. "The Blood of Christ."

The old man turned his gaze on me. His eyes were glazed with pain, but there was a sharp intellect there.

"Someone who speaks the truth at last," he said, his voice wheezing. "Who are you?"

I sensed he would see through any lie, so I kept to the truth.

"I am Hunlaf. I was once a novice monk, but now I am a warrior serving a good Christian king."

The man smiled, then grimaced and let out a grunt of pain.

"I am not sure how many kings are good, young Hunlaf," he said. "But you have given me your name, so I will give you mine." He dragged in a long, rasping breath. "I am Shomer."

"And what are you doing here?" asked Giso, unable to contain his impatience any longer.

"I thought that much would have been clear to you," Shomer said. "I am the Guardian of the Sacred Blood of Jesus Christ, the Son of God."

Thirty-Six

I made to pull back Shomer's blood-sodden robe to examine his wound, but he pushed my hands away.

"I have some skill at healing," I said. "Let me help you."

"No, no," he said. "My time to leave this earth is close. I am in God's hands now. There is nothing you can do."

I held his feverish gaze for a moment, seeing the truth in what he said.

"Would you like us to pray with you?" I asked, thinking that might bring him some comfort.

"I thank you," he said. "I think I would like that." He blew out a long breath, steeling himself. "But first I must tell you what happened here. The Lord has seen fit to keep me alive until your arrival. This must be in His plan." He looked up at Runolf, Drosten, Hereward and the other warriors. They were nervously pulling back the wall hangings and looking furtively down the steps, as if expecting attack at any moment. "Tell them there is nothing to fear. Those who did this to me and my sons left long before you came."

I relayed this to the others. Hereward nodded, but none of them truly relaxed. I did not blame them. I still felt the strange thrill of energy in the air and we were far underground. I imagined the incalculable weight of stone and earth above us and shuddered.

"Is it here?" Hereward asked. "I wish to be gone from this place. I feel as if we might be buried alive at any moment." He looked about him and sucked his teeth. "We should have headed homeward when we had the chance."

"I sense your impatience," said Shomer, "and I understand it. I would be impatient too in your position, waiting for an old, dying man to tell you the location of the holiest relic in Christendom."

Giso leaned forward. "You have it still?" he snapped.

"I did not say that," said Shomer. "But all in good time. I will tell you what you wish to know." He looked at Giso and smiled. "I see the fear in your eyes. You think I will die without giving up my secrets. Have faith, my friend. God may have allowed those who came here to murder my sons and me, for there can be no doubt the sword that pierced me will take my life. But I have enough time yet to tell you what you need. I have always heard that stomach wounds are painful and I can now attest to the truth of it." He winced, his face beaded with sweat. "I have never felt such agony, but I accept this pain as penance for my sins. My wound is deadly, but I will linger yet a time in the land of the living. The Almighty has brought us together. He will let me live a while yet."

Taking a deep breath to calm himself, Giso sat beside Shomer and nodded.

"Very well," he said. "Tell us your tale."

Shomer gave a thin smile. "Have you some water?" he asked.

I called to Arcenbryht who carried a skin. He handed it to me and I unstoppered it. I held it to Shomer's lips. He drank sparingly and sighed.

"You will think me foolish that I believed I could protect the Holy Blood with only my sons to help me," he said. "It may seem unwise now, but a small number of guardians has served us well for generations."

"How long has the relic resided here?" Giso asked.

"Centuries. The Blood was soaked in a cloth used to clean Christ's body at the very moment of his Passion. It has been hidden away by my forebears ever since. They knew they could never let it fall into the hands of evil men, for this was the very bodily essence of the Son of God. And so it remained hidden by my family until one day, perhaps a century after Christ's ascension, the then Guardian of the Blood discovered this place."

I looked at the stone walls, the altar and the steps leading down to the pillared chamber.

"It was not built to house the relic?" I said.

"Nobody knows why it was built, but there were remnants of soldiers from Roma here when they found it, or so the tale passed down to us goes. But as soon as they set foot within these stone walls, the guardians knew this cavern had been ordained by God Himself that we might preserve His son's blood. Perhaps the Almighty had commanded that others construct it, for to delve so deeply into the rock would surely be beyond my people's ken. However it came to be here, since that day, the Blood of Christ has remained within these walls, far from the greed and evil of man. My great-grandfather brought me here to worship, and my grandfather after him. When my father passed into the realm of the Lord, it fell to me to continue as Guardian. I had two sons, but alas my wife gave me no more children before joining Our Father in heaven, and my sons' wives are barren."

Giso's eyes shone in the lamplight as he listened to the old man. "If the line of guardians would have died with your sons," he said, "what of the future?"

Shomer let out a long sigh. It rattled in his throat and he coughed. Reaching out I steadied him, clasping his hand as the coughs shook him. When the fit abated, he nodded his thanks. Leaning back, he groaned at the pain.

"I prayed for guidance," he said, shaking his head at the memory. "I thought I had been cursed, but the Lord places these trials in our path to test our faith. Now I see I made a mistake. It was my actions that brought about our end. When that devil woman arrived, I knew my fears had come to pass. For the first time in seven centuries I had allowed one into this shrine who was not of my blood. We had managed to keep the Blood safe all this time with tales of *jinn* and curses. The shrine is far from any settlement, and if any traveller should stray into the cavern, we had ways of removing them, and making them so terrified they would never return. But I knew my sons alone would not be able to protect Christ's Blood forever, and so, like a shepherd ushering a lion into his flock, I welcomed Oren into our fold."

He fell silent, lost in memories. Pressing his left hand over his belly, he moaned in the back of his throat.

"Water," he croaked. "I will finish my tale quickly now. The Lord grows weary of the sound of my voice, I fear. He will call me to His side soon."

Giso flashed me a look that said he too was tired of listening to the old man. I was as anxious as he to learn the whereabouts of the Blood of Christ, but I was enraptured by the story; the picture that Shomer drew for us with his words was vivid and captivating.

I held the waterskin for the old man again and he took a mouthful, before sinking back against the altar. His eyes closed and for a moment I thought perhaps he had drifted to sleep, or even death.

Giso shook his shoulder gently. "Who was this Oren?" he prompted.

Shomer's eyes fluttered open. "A thief and a liar," he said. "I should have slain him, but I could not bring myself to. He had been a friend for a long while, or so I thought. Then one day I found him taking the Blood of Christ. He was going to steal it. To sell it to the highest bidder." He closed his eyes again, looking back into his memories, and sighed. His eyes flicked open and he stared at me. There was a hardness there now that

I had not seen before. "He left without the relic. And without his right hand. I took it so that all would know the manner of man he was. I told him if I ever saw him again, I would take his life."

"What happened to him?" I asked.

"I did not know until yesterday. Until these murderers came here and snatched the cloth from the altar. Oren vanished from my life more than five years ago. I thought I would never see or hear from him again. But he must have somehow reached Attalea, for it was there that the woman, Theokleia, said he had been imprisoned. He had been arrested for stealing, so she said. I suppose he thought he might sell the information he had, or perhaps there was a promise to free him if he gave up the hiding place of the relic. I know not, but I bemoan the day I met him and hope his soul burns for all eternity for what he has done."

I recalled Giso's tale of how he had come to hear of the Blood of Christ.

"Oren was no doubt an evil man, but for this crime at least perhaps he is innocent."

"Never has a man been more guilty," said Shomer. "Oren is venal and measures everything in terms of the profit he can make."

"Perhaps," I said, "but he is avaricious no longer."

"I cannot believe he has changed."

"He is dead," I replied. "And he did not sell the location of the Blood of Christ."

"Then how did that demon Theokleia know him by name?"

"Oren was indeed imprisoned, but he was dying in captivity. He spoke of this place, and the Blood of Christ in his final confession. At the end he sought absolution for his sins. It was his gaoler who saw profit in the knowledge he overheard."

Shomer sighed. "Absolution," he said, his voice scarcely above a whisper. "Ours is a merciful God. And just. And yet I cannot imagine meeting Oren in heaven. I am merely a poor sinner and I cannot find it within my heart to forgive him for what he did. My sons..." He squeezed his eyes shut and tears rolled down his dust-streaked cheeks.

I grasped his hand. His fingers dug into my flesh like talons, like a drowning man clutching to the last splintered spar of a wrecked ship.

"I am sorry we did not reach you sooner," I said.

"So am I," he said, and a glimmer of sour humour touched his eyes. "I much prefer conversing with you than with those women from Byzantion and their Godless hounds. Judging from your companions, you would have given them a good account of yourselves."

"We would not have allowed this to happen to you," said Giso fervently. "Or your sons. But as you said, the Lord puts obstacles in our paths for reasons only He can comprehend. We will find the Blood of Christ, and we will make Theokleia and her servants pay for what they have done to you and your kin. If anyone can make this right, it is us. I give you my word that we will avenge you and reclaim what you have lost."

"I do not seek revenge," Shomer croaked.

Giso appeared not to have heard him for he continued without pause.

"We serve the king of the Franks. He is a pious man. One day, with God's blessing, he will be the Holy Emperor of Roma. Carolus will see that the Blood will be guarded for as long as the sun shall shine." He reached out and took Shomer's other hand in his. "Your time is growing short. Let us pray with you before the end, that you might feel peace and not the anguish that engulfs your soul. You and your sons have been God's best, most faithful of servants. The Almighty knows this well and will welcome you into His host to sit at His right hand. He knows you did your best to protect the blood of His son."

Shomer began to shake and I thought his end had come. Then I realised these were not the throes of death. He was chuckling, the sound of his laughter crackling in his dry throat.

His mirth dissipated quickly, as he was gripped by a sudden bout of coughing. He pulled his hand free of Giso's grip and wiped his mouth. With a groan of pain, he let his hand fall to his lap. There was fresh, dark blood on his bony fingers.

"You think I failed to protect the Blood," he said at last. "You did not let me finish my tale."

"You said Theokleia took the cloth from the altar." Giso's confused tone matched my thoughts.

"And so she did," Shomer said, a sly glint in his eye. "Upon the altar there was a gilded casket, fronted with fine crystal, which allows the viewer to see the bloodstained cloth within. It is this reliquary that the she-devil took."

"The cloth within does not hold the Blood of Jesus Christ," I said, seeing the simple truth.

"It was my grandfather's idea. If ever someone should try to take the relic by force, they would see the gold and the crystal and decide that the cloth within must be holy. But it was the blood of a goat Theokleia took. Not the Lamb of God. You know, I still recall the taste of that animal. It must be sixty years since we ate its flesh. Strange how some things remain in your memory while others drift away."

Giso grinned. "Your grandfather was cunning."

"And he was right," Shomer replied. "Theokleia came with evil in her heart, only thinking of the value of what she stole." He shook his head, smiling sadly. "Just as my grandfather had said would happen with an unholy pilgrim. She chose poorly."

"If it was not the relic that she took," said Giso, his voice sharp and urgent now, "where is the true Blood of Christ?"

Shomer scrunched his eyes shut, tensing as pain rippled through him. "Yes," he said, breathless. "I should tell you that before the Lord welcomes me to his side." He gripped my hand with a savage, desperate strength. "Do you swear that this Carolus that you serve is a God-fearing king? That he will protect the sacred blood from evil?"

"He is the scourge of God's enemies," I said. "He has defeated the pagans in the north, burning their sacred trees and their devilish idols. In the south, he has fought against the Al-Muslimun of al-Andalus."

Giso leaned forward, his eyes piercing and bright in the shadowed chamber. "King Carolus is blessed by the very Pontifex Maximus himself. We are his trusted servants and seek the Blood of Christ. With it Carolus will prevail against the idolatry and false prophets that threaten to snuff out the light of Christ in this dark age."

Shomer held Giso's gaze.

"If I would not give it to you, did you mean to steal it, just as Theokleia did?"

"Never," said Giso, his tone smooth as melted butter. "We planned to beseech you in the name of all that is holy."

"And if I refused to give it up?"

"We brought silver and gold too."

Shomer shook his head. "Treasure cannot buy the favour of the Almighty." He sighed. He was visibly weaker than just moments before. His skin was as pale as his beard and hair, his lips blue-tinged. "There are none left to watch over the blood of our Lord now. God has brought you here and you have prayed with me. I am not sure I trust you fully, but I trust in the Almighty. Open your eyes. The Blood of Christ is there for the faithful to see."

A shudder ran through him and he closed his eyes against the pain that racked his body. Releasing his hand, I pushed myself to my feet and scanned the chamber once more. The single lamp flickered on the altar, but there was nothing else there. Could the relic be hidden behind one of the wall hangings? Had Theokleia been so sure she had found the object of her quest in the gilded reliquary that she had not searched beyond the obvious? I moved towards the nearest curtain, reaching out my hand to pull it back.

"There is nothing there," Hereward said. "We have searched

the place while you talked to the old man. None of the tapestries hide anything. No doors, or passageways. Nothing."

I hesitated, thinking of the implication of what Hereward said and repeating Shomer's words in my mind. The truth of it hit me abruptly like a physical blow. I stepped back involuntarily.

All the wall hangings were old; smoke-stained and worn by time. Most of them bore embroidered designs, images that I assumed were of Christ and his apostles. One was covered in visual depictions of Jesus' miracles. Another had Christ crucified, golden thread symbolising rays of power emanating from His head. Yet another told the tale of Jesus' birth and the slaughter of the innocents. Only one of the cloths hanging from the walls had no such decorations. Like the others, it was dusty and old, but apart from the large, brown stains upon it, the cloth was plain. It was no tapestry sewn with gold. It might once have been used to dry hands or feet.

Or to wipe blood from a wound.

I pointed at the cloth, not daring to touch it.

"This is the Blood of Jesus Christ?" I said, my voice trembling.

Shomer opened his eyes and smiled. "Mopped from his wounds on Calvary," he said. "My family has guarded it for centuries, but it seems its time here is over. Take it to your King Carolus and see that it is kept safe from the likes of those devils who killed my sons." He winced. "And me."

Giso sprang up and pushed me aside. He appeared to harbour none of the qualms I felt about touching the holy artefact, for he reached for the old cloth and took it down from where it had been hung from two hooks. He held it close to the light of the lamp, though careful not to get it near enough to burn.

"Can it be true?" he whispered. "The blood of the Son of God."

"It is true," croaked Shomer. "Can you not feel its power?"

Giso's eyes were wide. The light from the lamp made them glow. "I can feel it," he said.

The thrumming energy in the air was more noticeable than ever. I longed to reach out and touch the cloth, but I was scared at what I might feel.

After their initial search of the chamber, the men and Revna had lounged on the steps, sipping from waterskins and whispering to one another as Giso and I conversed with Shomer. Now, Pendrad, who must have wandered down the steps into the larger, pillared hall below came running up towards us, the flame from the lamp he held flickering as he ran.

"Someone is coming," he hissed.

Thirty-Seven

"Could it be your father and grandfather?" I asked Jamal.

"They believe the place to be cursed," he said, shaking his head. "Perhaps if the storm is bad enough…"

Pendrad might not have understood my words in Al-Arabiyyah, but he guessed my meaning.

"It's not them," he said. "There are many more than two."

"How many?" snapped Hereward.

Pendrad bit his lip. "A score?" he ventured, lifting his shoulders. "More?"

Gwawrddur cursed. "Whoever they are," he said, "I doubt they are friendly."

The small chamber was suddenly filled with movement as the warriors stood, drawing their blades once more, ready to face this new threat. Hereward turned to me. His face was grim, but there was no sign of fear there.

"Ask the old man if there are any other ways out of this place."

I dropped to my haunches beside Shomer, taking his hand in mine once more. Gone was the furious strength in that grip. His hand was limp. He was utterly still, sitting with his back against the altar, his head slumped forward. I touched his throat but knew the truth before my fingers confirmed there was no pulse.

"He's gone," I said, placing his hand gently in his lap and making the sign of the cross over him.

Behind Shomer, indifferent to his death, Giso was quickly folding the cloth on the altar. When it was small enough, he stuffed it inside his leather bag.

From the shadowed opening beyond the steps the sound of many men was clear now. Perhaps they had meant to move stealthily, but judging from the echoed noise their boots made on the stone floor, the creak of leather, the clank of armour and the rasp of whispered commands, there were too many of them to sneak anywhere.

Runolf spat and lifted his axe. "Can your god's blood get us out of this, Hunlaf? If not, I am willing to spill some blood for Óðinn."

He moved towards the steps, Drosten and Gwawrddur by his side. Hereward called them back.

"Hold," he said. "We know not who awaits us."

"Whoever is down there," snarled Runolf, "the less time they have to ready themselves, the better."

"Perhaps," conceded Hereward. "But listen to the din they make. There must be many more of them than us. Attack is not always the best option, my friend."

"Since when did we concern ourselves with the odds against us?" Runolf growled.

Giso moved to join them, his hand resting on the leather bag slung over his shoulder. "Whatever we decide now," he said. "We must protect the Blood of Christ. It is more valuable than anyone's life."

"Even yours?" asked Drosten, stepping close and baring his teeth. "If it comes to it, do not fear, I will gladly kill you to save the relic."

Giso did not flinch. He patted the bag. "Nothing is more important than getting this back to Alhwin and the king."

Before anyone could answer him, a shout came from below. The voice was harsh, the clipped words of Al-Arabiyyah slapping against the stone walls of the chamber. This was the voice of a man accustomed to issuing orders.

"I know you are up there," snapped the voice. "Your lights are bright and we can hear the babble of your infidel tongue."

The voice was familiar, but at first I could not place it.

"Aziz," Revna hissed.

The instant she said the name, I could picture the vicious captain of Kawthar's guard, sneering below in the gloom.

"How has he followed us here?" I asked.

"Betrayal, no doubt," said Gwawrddur. "Though whose, I cannot say."

Aziz grew impatient waiting for a response. His voice was louder when he called out again.

"I have orders to bring you back to the city to face the wali's justice. You are outnumbered and trapped. Give yourselves up and you will not be harmed."

I translated his words quickly.

"Tell him to go swive a camel," snarled Runolf. "We cannot surrender. If they take us back to Ierusalem, we will never leave."

"He is right," said Giso. "We must fight. With God's grace we have a chance. To give ourselves up means certain death. Those are our only choices."

I glanced at Revna. Her face was pale, her eyes glimmering. Her fear was plain, but she held her sword ready at her side. She would not go quietly.

"To die quickly," said Hereward. "Or to die slowly. Those are our choices?"

"I know which choice I will make," said Runolf. "I will not be thrown in a cell to be tortured. And while we fight, there is yet a chance we can escape. We have got out of worse places."

I thought of the reckoning in the shadow of Aljany's fortress in the mountains of al-Andalus, the blood-soaked night of flames at the hall of Ljósberari. It was true we had survived against dreadful odds, but I could see no way out of this.

"Come down," shouted Aziz. "You will be treated well. I give you my word."

"Do not answer," whispered Hereward. "If we are to fight, there is no need to talk. Let us listen and ready ourselves instead."

Moving away from the steps, Hereward quickly marshalled the warriors, putting them into positions that would best allow us to defend the chamber. There were enough of us to line the top of the steps, two warriors deep. Still, we carried no shields and wore no armour. Strong and skilled as we were, we could not hope to stand against a much larger force for any length of time.

Aziz screamed at us, growing increasingly angry. After a while, he saw we had no intention of responding to his threats and insults, and he fell silent.

"Soon they will come," said Gwawrddur.

"Why attack when they could wait us out?" I asked. "We have the higher ground and they will surely lose many men."

Gwawrddur narrowed his eyes. "Aziz does not strike me as a patient man," he said. "Nor do I think he cares how many men he sacrifices to get what he wants."

The hall below us was hushed now, save for the muffled conversations of the guardsmen and the echoed sounds of their movements. Their shadows danced and leapt on the steps, lit by their own lamps or torches.

"How much oil do we have?" I asked Sygbald.

He held up his flask and shook it. Liquid sloshed hollowly within it.

"Not much," he said. "If they do not attack soon, we will be fighting in the dark."

Hereward sniffed. "If the oil runs dry, it is true we will have no light up here, but we will not have to fight them blind. They can no more see in the dark than we can."

The sense of what he said settled on us, but I knew I was not alone in the worry that gnawed at my guts. We were trapped in this underground chamber, and before us I could see only death.

Revna made her way to my side and offered me water. I took a sip, smiling my thanks. Her fingers brushed mine as she retrieved the waterskin. Her eyes met mine and I could see the fear threatening to engulf her.

"I will not let them take me," she hissed, her words barely audible. "I will not."

The sharp horror in her voice stabbed me like a blade.

"Do not say such things," I said, grasping her arm. "Whatever happens, you must stay alive. While we live, there is a chance."

Her eyes were bleak. "Some things are worse than death."

"We will live," I said, squeezing her arm tight enough to make her wince. "We will get out of this. We will." I spoke with force, as if my conviction alone could make it so.

Revna nodded, perhaps reassured, or just wishing to placate me. Without another word, she pulled away, and moved to her father's side. She handed him the waterskin, rubbing her forearm as he drank. She did not look in my direction. My heart twisted. My words had given her no comfort. Even to my own ears they sounded false and hollow.

Jamal's voice dragged my attention away from Revna. "Do you think they are dead?" he said.

Momentarily confused, I looked at him. In his bruised features I saw a reflection of my own fears. Understanding billowed in me like blood spilt in water. He was terrified that his kin had been slain outside in the sand-blown night. It seemed likely to me. Scared as I was for myself and my own loved ones, I had no solace to offer him. Instead, I chose the truth, brutal as that was.

"I don't know," I said. "I hope not."

He nodded, setting his jaw. Taking a deep breath, he stood

straight. "They live yet," he said forcefully, more to himself than me, I thought. Again, I saw myself in him.

"I hope so," I murmured, but he had turned away and was no longer listening.

Thirty-Eight

Gwawrddur was right. Aziz did not wait long before he sent his men up the stairs. They came surging up without warning, and it was only Gwawrddur's acute hearing and focus that prevented us from being surprised, which is what Aziz had no doubt intended.

The Welshman held up his hand and hissed for silence.

"They've ceased speaking," he said. Remaining motionless for a heartbeat, he listened, straining to hear any sign of what our enemy was about. Then, with an urgent cry, he had shouted, "To arms. To arms."

We had thrown down the waterskins and snatched up our weapons. Already dozens of feet stamped up the stone stairs, the sound reverberating in the lamp-licked gloom. We had barely enough time to take the positions Hereward had assigned to us.

Realising we were aware of their attack, the guardsmen let out their howling battle cry of "*Allahu Akbar!*" as they swarmed up to meet us. They came in what they hoped would be overwhelming force, and as the dim light of our lamps fell on the hard faces of our enemies, fear gripped my heart. There were so many of them. Surely there was no way we could endure such an onslaught.

But even as I faltered, fearing that Revna had been right,

so Runolf let out his booming chant of "Óðinn," his voice louder than a dozen guardsmen. His axe flashed as he stepped forward to meet our foe-men and blood sprayed. Gwawrddur and Drosten were at his side, and each of them fought like heroes from legend, their blades glimmering as they cut down the men before them like ripe barley at harvest.

"Fight!" came Hereward's bellowing roar, and I felt my spirit lifted by that of my sword-brothers. We were the crew of Brymsteda. We would not so easily be killed. I welcomed the rage I felt bubbling up within me and sliced my sword into the throat of the nearest guardsman.

Twisting the blade, I tugged it free, showering blood over enemies and friends alike. Kicking the man into the path of the guards on the steps, I jumped down towards them, hacking and stabbing, relying on my sword skill, the endless days of training under Gwawrddur's tutelage and God's grace to keep me alive.

After the fight, I found several cuts on my arms and legs, but I felt nothing in those moments of furious abandon on the steps. Runolf, Gwawrddur and Drosten had cleared a swathe of stairs, and the stone before them was piled with dead and dying. I slipped in the blood that slicked the steps, stumbling and falling painfully on my back against the hard stone. Springing up, I parried a blow from a snarling, bearded guardsman, before cutting so deeply into his sword arm that his hand hung by a thread of skin. His sword clattered away and I punched him with my left hand, spinning him into his comrades. They shoved him away, desperate not to have their view hampered. Hereward and Gersine were near to me, but I was lost to the battle lust, wallowing in the sheer joy of slaying those who would harm me and my friends.

But no matter how many guards we slew, yet more clambered over their corpses and climbed up to meet us. The biting aroma of smoke reached my senses then. A glance over my shoulder showed me that the wall hangings had somehow caught fire.

Tinder-dry from the years stored here in the desert dark, the fabric crackled and blazed. Thick clouds of pungent smoke already hid the ceiling of the chamber.

We fought on. I was dimly aware of both Arcenbryht and Sygbald taking injuries. I could not see how badly they had been hurt, but their wounds were severe enough for them to retreat towards the altar. They returned stumbling and coughing a moment later, driven back by the heat and smoke from the burning tapestries.

Panic fluttered in the smoky air like bat wings. A score of guardsmen lay at the base of the steps, but with our wounded, our defensive line was close to being sundered and there was nowhere for us to retreat. Smoke half filled the chamber now. Tears streamed from my eyes and my throat burnt.

"We must fight our way down," shouted Hereward. "There is clearer air there."

He was right, but the idea of advancing on the superior numbers of the guards was madness. But what alternative was there?

More guardsmen crowded the lowest steps, but we forced our way down. Hereward cut at one, sending him tumbling away to whimper against the wall. The men before me seemed too scared to approach, despite their shields and armour. But even through the fog of my fury, I could sense the tide of the battle shifting. There were more enemies remaining than we had defeated, and with the smoke pushing us from behind, when we reached the larger hall, we would easily be surrounded.

Fingers of fear worked their way into my soul, clenching around my heart in dread. We would all die here.

A man slashed at me. Without thinking, I caught his blade on mine, knocking it off line, then brought my own sword slicing down across his face. He fell back in a welter of crimson, screaming like a pig at slaughter.

I cast a glance about me. Where was Revna? I could not see

her in the confused smoke and the writhing shadows of the fighting men. I thought of the Blood of Christ then, the holiest of relics, the ancient stained cloth safely hidden within Giso's bag. *Please, Lord,* I prayed, *even if I should die here, spare Revna. Keep her safe, I beseech you.*

As if in answer to my prayer, a scream cut through the cacophony of the subterranean chamber. A tremor ran through the men, the fighting faltering. Hesitating, I turned towards the sound of the scream and locked eyes with Revna. She was alive!

My hope fell away as I saw who stood behind her. Aziz had her long hair wrapped about his fist, and as I watched helplessly, he yanked her head back savagely to expose her slender, flawless throat. Against her smooth pale skin, he placed a curved dagger. Its blade was lambent in the flame flicker.

"Drop your weapons," shouted Aziz, his voice slicing through the tumult of fighting. "Do it or she dies now!"

I was caught in an agony of indecision. The stairs were redolent of smoke, blood, piss and shit; clogged with death. And I had seen all too well what Aziz was capable of when crossed. But if we surrendered, what would stop him from killing Revna and the rest of us?

Some of the men yet fought on, perhaps oblivious of Revna's capture. But Aziz's shouted command had pierced Runolf's frenzied fighting, or the Norseman had perhaps sensed his daughter was in danger. However he knew, he shoved the man he was facing down the steps and took two quick paces back. Seeing Revna in Aziz's grasp, Runolf blanched. If he was torn as I was, he did not show it. With a roar of frustration, he threw his axe down and held up his bloody hands.

"Tell him not to harm her, Hunlaf," he snarled.

I repeated his words in Al-Arabiyyah.

Aziz sneered. "She will be unharmed, if you all put down your weapons at once."

"Drop your weapons," I shouted, my voice hoarse.

Hereward and the men around him had advanced into the large hall; now they retreated towards the steps. I followed them, pulling Gersine with me, careful not to lose my footing on the slippery stones where the blood had run from the stairs. The guardsmen before us did not move. They glowered, holding their shields high, blades ready to strike if the battle should recommence.

On the other side of the entrance to the chamber steps, where Runolf had led the defence, Drosten and Gwawrddur still fought, locked in a savage battle with half a dozen men before them.

"Drop your swords!" Runolf cried.

Drosten heard him at last. He did not lay down his sword, but he disengaged, moving back towards the Norseman.

"Gwawrddur!" he called. "Pull back."

The Welshman made no move to retreat from the fray. He held a seax in his left hand, his sword in his right. Both blades dripped with blood. As I watched, his sword licked out and took one man in the eye. With the long knife in his left hand, he parried a stabbing blow aimed at his groin. With the grace of a dancer, he spun on the balls of his feet and brought his sword around to slice through the second attacker's throat. The man fell to his knees, a torrent of blood washing over his chin to mix with the puddling gore on the flagstones.

"Tell him to halt now!" screamed Aziz. "My patience is gone."

"Gwawrddur," I shouted. "Surrender! He will kill Revna if you do not."

One of the guards before the Welshman directed a scything blade at his shins. With the agility of a cat, Gwawrddur jumped over the sword. He landed sure-footed and punched forward with a lunge of almost impossible speed. The guard was off balance, overextended. Gwawrddur's sword pierced the man's armour just beneath his armpit. With a shudder, the guardsman collapsed atop his fallen comrades.

"Gwawrddur!" I cried again. "Put up your weapons!"

At last the Welshman heard me. Breathing heavily, lathered in sweat and blood, his kirtle soaking and dark, he stepped away from the men.

Aziz pressed his blade into Revna's throat, making her gasp. I tensed, calculating my chances of reaching them before he slit her throat. It was no use. None of us could hope to rescue Revna from the captain's grasp while he had his steel at her neck.

"Good," he said, nodding at me as if he could read my thoughts. "Now tell your friends to place their weapons on the floor, unless you want to see whether this pretty one can breathe with her throat cut."

The hall was hushed now. The echo-memory clash of metal on metal lingered on the edge of hearing. Some of the wounded moaned. Men panted from their exertions and coughed from the smoke that drifted down from the altar room. We were surrounded by guardsmen, many of whom had yet to test their weapons. They scowled, leaving me in no doubt how much they longed to kill us all. If Aziz gave the order, we would share this tomb with Shomer and his sons.

"He says to put your weapons down," I said. I could see no alternative, so – not taking my eyes from Revna's – I stooped and placed my blood-smeared sword on the flagstones.

Gwawrddur shook his head. He had split his lip at some point in the fight and now he spat blood at the feet of the guards in front of him.

"This is wrong," he said. "It is as Giso said. We fight now and die quickly, or we surrender and die slowly."

"He has my daughter," said Runolf.

One of the guards jabbed his sword at Hereward. The Northumbrian slapped the blade away. Aziz snapped something angrily at the guardsman, who stepped back from the huddled mass of warriors.

"Hunlaf," said Hereward, "does he give his word not to harm the girl, or us?"

I relayed the question. Aziz did not relinquish his grip on Revna, but he lowered his dagger, holding it out away from her body.

"I give you my word as a servant of the wali, the caliph, the Prophet and Allah," he said. "Tell him I will not harm the girl or any of you, if you surrender now. But I am finished with this conversation. Make your decision quickly or face the consequences."

I interpreted his words. Hereward held Aziz's gaze, then, his shoulders slumping, he dropped his sword with a clatter. "Do as he says, lads," he said.

All around him, the warriors of *Brymsteda* put their weapons on the stone floor. Drosten was the last to comply, but eventually, he too – his tattooed face like thunder – dropped his blade.

Only Gwawrddur remained, knife in one hand, long-bladed sword in the other. Runolf stared at him.

"Please, brother," the Norseman murmured.

With a sigh, Gwawrddur bent down and gently placed his blades on the flagstones. "This is a mistake," he said.

At a barked command from Aziz, guards moved forward and removed our weapons. There was no going back. The flickering light from the room at the top of the steps was dimming. With nothing more than the wall hangings for fuel, the fire had burnt brightly and quickly. Now, the smoke above our heads was thinning as it drifted towards the entrance, finding its way out into the windswept desert valley. The only other light in the hall came from torches that the guardsmen had brought. The flames showed the twisted sneer on Aziz's features, his forked beard jutting, as he snapped another order.

Before I could shout out a warning, the guards nearest to Runolf, Drosten and Gwawrddur rushed forward. Runolf roared, throwing a man away from him as he saw the threat. But two more guards were behind him. They hit the back of his head with the pommels of their swords, knocking the Norseman to his knees.

Drosten cracked a savage punch into the jaw of one man and sent a second spinning away with blood spurting from a broken nose. But more guardsmen overpowered him. While a couple held Drosten's arms, others pummelled him with their fists. One man kicked him hard in the groin, leaving the Pict gasping and retching on the ground.

Of the three, Gwawrddur alone did not resist the guards. The time to fight back had passed and, having set aside his weapons, the Welshman grimly allowed the guardsmen to restrain him. He spat more blood from his bleeding lip.

Hereward hurried forward to go to our comrades' defence, but several blades jabbed at him, holding him where he was. "You gave your word," he shouted at Aziz.

"Silence him," Aziz said. A guard stepped forward and punched Hereward hard in the gut. Winded, he doubled over. Beorn and Eadstan snarled and spat beside him. I thought they too might launch themselves at our captors, but Hereward held up a hand for them to halt.

Revna was staring at me, wide-eyed with shock. I looked from her to the hard features of the man who still held a fistful of her golden hair. I thought in that moment that my hatred for Aziz could not burn any hotter.

I was wrong. "You said nobody would be hurt." I spat the words at him. They had no effect.

He merely smiled. "I don't think I did." He cocked his head to one side, as if replaying his words in his mind. "No, I am quite sure I did not say that. I am many things, but I am no liar. I said I would harm none of you, and that is true." He leaned in close to Revna and sniffed her hair. He smiled and licked his lips. "What my men do though…" He left the words hanging in the smoke-hazed air for a moment, then, with a leering grin he turned to the guards holding Gwawrddur. "Kill him," he said.

Thirty-Nine

It happened so fast I didn't even have time to scream.

Later, I would relive the moment over and again in my nightmares. I would probe all the decisions I had taken, scrutinise every word I had spoken in that shadowy chamber beneath the desert. Even now, as the end of my own long life approaches, my thoughts frequently turn to that night and whether there was anything I could have done differently. Anything that might have saved Gwawrddur.

Across all these years I can almost hear the lilt of his Welsh accent counselling me not to dwell on the past. It is sound advice I know. Advice that I have often offered others, yet, as anyone with regrets knows well, such wisdom – no matter how sensible – is impossible to follow.

Gwawrddur was the most gifted swordsman I have ever witnessed. He strove every day to improve his sword skill and taught me most of what prowess I once possessed. He was keen to fight strong adversaries, always seeking worthy foes. He lived by the sword and I had supposed that one day he would meet his match. I had never imagined he would be cut down in cold blood, a sword thrust through his back to protrude from his chest, tenting the sweat-dark fabric of his kirtle, before tearing through the linen. The sword's steel glistened in the torchlight, barely a smear of blood on the metal.

Gwawrddur grimaced. "A mistake," he said through gritted teeth. "Told you." The guard tugged his sword free of the Welshman's flesh. Gwawrddur shuddered. Blood bubbled and gushed from the wounds in his chest and back. Falling to his knees, he groaned. "Giso was wrong," he said, his voice tight with pain, "they have given me a quick death."

"No!" I yelled, finally finding my voice. "No! No!" I could find no other words to describe my horror. This could not be happening. Gwawrddur should not die like this.

Gwawrddur slumped, his right hand pressed to his chest, the fingers slick with fresh blood. He caught himself with his left hand on the flagstones, holding him upright for a moment. Our eyes met. "Don't worry about me, Killer," he said. "There is no pain."

With a sigh his breath left him and he toppled forward. He made no effort to halt his fall. His face cracked into a flagstone and he lay, eyes unblinking, in an expanding pool of his lifeblood.

My vision blurred. The world tilted around me. Dimly, I was aware of Hereward's wailing cry. Drosten bellowed, trying to force himself up, but he was struck repeatedly. Runolf howled like a wolf, using his prodigious strength to shake off the men who held him. He punched one guard so hard that the man fell to the floor beside Gwawrddur, instantly insensate. Oblivious or uncaring that he was unarmed, Runolf launched himself at the guardsman who had slain our friend.

Revna's shriek brought him up short. The sound of her scream also cut through the despair that threatened to swallow me. I dragged my gaze away from Gwawrddur's corpse. Revna was on tiptoes as Aziz once again pressed his dagger into the soft flesh beneath her chin. Her eyes were wide with fear and I saw a trickle of blood on her perfect skin.

Runolf snarled, his meaty hands balled into fists. Drosten glowered. Hereward and the others shouted furiously, hurling insults at Aziz and his guardsmen. For a few heartbeats our future balanced on a sword's edge. I could see in the eyes of my shield-brothers that they were ready to throw themselves at our captors, weapons or no. The wali's guards had killed Gwawrddur and, if Hereward gave the order, I would gladly follow him and the others, though our death would be assured.

Even as I thought this, so the sharp fury of violence leaked from us. None of us could bring ourselves to put Revna at greater risk. To attack would be to see her killed before our eyes just as Gwawrddur had been. My comrades' shouted imprecations slowly turned to dark, muttered curses and promises of vengeance.

Aziz swept his gaze across us all, nodding as if content with what he saw. At his command, his men began to lash our wrists together. Runolf and Drosten were bound first. Aziz dragged Revna with him to stand against one of the thick stone columns. He did not relax his hold on her. Nor did he lower his wicked-looking knife from her throat.

When the Norseman and the Pict were secured, the guards moved on to Hereward and the others. Aziz relaxed slightly, but still kept a tight hold on Revna's hair.

Christ said we should forgive those who sin against us. Decades have passed since that terrible night and I am not ashamed to admit that I have never forgiven Aziz. Glowering at him then, I could think of nothing I wanted more than to see him choking on his own blood. And I have prayed countless times that his soul will never find peace and, if I could return to that shadow-flickered, death-filled subterranean hall, I would gladly exact the blood price for Gwawrddur with a blade or my bare hands.

"Why?" I asked him, as a guard pulled my hands roughly behind me.

"Why what?" Aziz asked, raising an eyebrow.

"You did not need to kill him," I hissed. The guard lashed my wrists together with a leather thong, tugging the bond tight enough to make me wince.

"Perhaps not," said Aziz, "but nor did I need to allow him to live." He took in the numerous dead and wounded who lay scattered about Gwawrddur's corpse. "He was a dangerous man. He killed some of my finest warriors after I commanded him to surrender. Such insolence must be punished."

"You were his enemy," I said. "It is not insolence to fight against one who means to take your life, one who threatens women rather than standing and fighting."

Aziz laughed. "I am no fool, young Hunlaf. You cannot goad me into fighting you or one of your number."

"Mayhap not a fool," I said, "but perhaps a craven."

He laughed again. "Your words wash from me like water from a duck's feather. You lost. You are my prisoners."

I scowled at him, imagining what it would be like to stab my sword into his body, just as the guard had done to Gwawrddur.

"You should have killed us all," I warned him.

"I would like nothing better," he said, his tone harsh and cool, "but I am a servant of the wali, and I have my orders. And unlike your friend there –" he gestured to Gwawrddur's still form "– I know how to follow commands. The wali wishes to see the painted one again and he has plans for you too, warrior monk. It is a long way back to Ierusalem, and food and water is limited. Tell the others that if they give me cause, I will not hesitate to kill them."

A thought permeated my grief-stricken mind. "How did you find us here?" I asked.

Aziz thought for a moment, then raised his shoulders, deciding there was no reason not to tell me. "I knew you had slipped out of the city," he said. Seeing the surprise on my face, he grinned. "Even rats have their price. For enough silver, or the right threat, there are men of Zakariya's who will tell me anything."

I tried not to react at the mention of the name. "But we are far from the city."

"True. And we would never have found you if not for the help of a woman we met on the road."

"A woman?" I said, my breath catching.

"A rich widow, on her way to Ierusalem to visit family. Allah smiled on me, for some of her men had spotted you out here. One of them, a huge man, as big as that one –" he pointed at Runolf "– but much fatter by far, knew of this place. Said you were surely travelling here. Even so, if we had not found your mounts, we might have missed the place in the storm."

"You found our animals?"

"Indeed." He sneered. "You are fools indeed to leave them with no shelter on a night like this."

I flicked a glance at Jamal. He was sombre-faced, but his eyes were sharp. The significance of what Aziz had said was not lost on him. Before I could ask Aziz more, we were shoved and herded towards the steps that led to the entrance of the cavernous hall.

As we grew closer, the air became sweeter, the smell of smoke replaced with the scent of hot sand and dust. A droning buzz, as of a swarm of bees, filled the shadowed darkness. My head still spun from seeing Gwawrddur cut down and it took me some time to realise the sound came from outside. No moonlight filtered into the darkness, and the torches and lamps flickered terribly as wind gusted and billowed down the steps. Sand lay thick on the stairs. Any sign of our passing, and that of the wali's guards, had been obliterated, buried under a thick layer of dust falling from the storm-heavy sky.

The night was a churning chaos of howling wind and skin-ripping sand. There was no way we could venture out into that storm, so the guards dragged the corpses we had found away from the entrance and commanded us to rest in the space between two columns and a wall.

We were bound and weaponless, but Aziz was no fool. We had killed enough of his men, both in the city and here, under the rocky floor of the desert hills, that he would not underestimate us. He kept Revna close to his side, a rope tied about her neck. Her hands were also bound behind her back. There was nothing we could do, but Runolf did not remove his eyes from Aziz and his daughter. I too watched them, in an agony of self-pity and remorse. Would Gwawrddur yet live if I had not told him to drop his blades?

Aziz ignored us, leaving his guards to watch over us sullenly. Arcenbryht and Sygbald sat stiffly, for both had taken deep cuts in the fighting and had only had a moment to bind their wounds. I had asked if my hands could be untied so that I might tend to them, but Aziz had laughed.

"If they die, two fewer men for me to worry about. They must be able to ride come morning…"

He did not need to voice the implied threat. I did not translate his words, merely saying that he had refused to allow me to aid them. But I thought Hereward might have understood more than he let on. He was grim and silent as we sat in despondent dejection, waiting for the storm to blow itself out.

Jamal sat close by, his bruised face gaunt, his eyes filled with fear and hatred, whether for me and the men of *Brymsteda*, or for Aziz and the wali's guards, I could not be certain. Most likely he loathed us equally.

"I am sorry about your friend," he whispered, jolting me awake from a doze. My shoulder ached from the awkward position my tied hands forced upon it. I rolled my neck in an attempt to loosen the stiffness there.

"And I am sorry we got you into this," I said.

"I am a man," he said gruffly. "I make my own choices."

He had the right of it. He was not much younger than me. I thought of my own choices, the decisions that had led to this point, all the dead that littered the path behind me.

"I hope your father and grandfather escaped."

Jamal fell silent for a while. "I do not think these sons of dogs saw them," he said at last. "If they had, Aziz would have said something. He isn't a man to miss a chance to gloat."

I nodded, but said nothing. He might have been right, but I found my heart empty of comfort for him. It was a barren waste and all I could think was that we would be dragged before the wali and then we would be tortured, and no doubt slain. We were already dead. Giso was right. We should have fought on and been killed quickly.

A sudden thought came to me and I peered around the shadowed faces of the others. Hereward looked over at me, alerted by my change in demeanour.

"It took you long enough," he said, with a shrug.

He was right. While my mind had been occupied with grief and fear for our future, I had failed to realise that Giso had vanished.

Forty

I awoke stiff and aching, and surprised I had slept at all. My mind had buzzed and thrummed like the whirling storm outside, and yet the tribulations of the day exacted their toll, and slumber overcame my roiling thoughts, smothering them and bringing me brief respite from my anguish.

My eyes were crusted with dust that had blown down from the entrance and my throat was as dry as ashes. I longed for water, but none of the guards offered us any and I was not about to beg.

Daylight filtered down the sandy steps. Gone was the tumult of the storm. The only sounds now were those of the men rousing themselves. I pushed myself to my feet, groaning as my muscles protested. Sygbald and Arcenbryht were both awake. Sygbald nodded to me and Arcenbryht raised a hand. I was gladdened to see they were no worse. I offered up a prayer that God would watch over them and keep the rot from their wounds.

I searched the shadows and for a terrible moment I could not see Revna. My stomach twisted as I imagined what Aziz might have done to her deep within the seclusion of the cavernous chamber while I slept. As panic gripped me, her hair caught the thin light from the cave's entrance and Revna walked out from behind a column. Aziz still had her tethered, his rope tied about her neck, but she met my gaze and offered me a nod of reassurance. Revna was not the only thing of beauty to have caught Aziz's attention, it seemed. I noticed he wore on his belt the fine dagger Arcenbryht had been gifted by Nu'man. The rest of our weapons had been bundled into sacks.

"No sign of Giso?" I whispered to Runolf, who had risen and was stretching his back and arms.

"That weasel disappears the moment danger is near," he said.

Drosten twisted his head to one side then the other until there was an audible crack. He grunted, a mixture of pleasure and pain.

"That little man will be halfway back to Yafah by now," he said.

I was not so sure Giso would have fled. He could have abandoned us in Ierusalem, but he had returned. It was possible though. He had the Blood of Christ in his possession and nothing else mattered to him, it seemed.

"Have you got any ideas how we might escape before we reach Ierusalem?" I asked. I could not imagine anything good awaited us in the Holy City.

"Pray to your god, Killer," said Runolf. His use of Gwawrddur's name for me stabbed like a knife blade.

I opened my mouth to reply, but a spear butt cracked into my ribs, driving the air from my lungs.

"No talking," snarled a tall, lean man with a scarred nose that looked as though it might have been burnt. I glowered at him, but fell silent, struggling to draw breath.

The guards pushed us up the steps, using their spears liberally and none too gently. We stumbled out beneath the stone lintel and stood blinking in the bright sunshine of the early morning. The valley was partially in shadow. There were no clouds in the sky, but it was a hazy, reddish hue, the sun struggling to force its rays through dust so thick it looked like fog in the east.

When Aziz stepped into the daylight, he snapped an order and one of his men took a silver-decorated horn from his belt. Putting it to his lips, he blew a series of short, sharp notes. The guards all turned to look in the direction of the valley where we had left Hamid and Nassif with our mounts. Nothing happened for a long time. Aziz barked at the horn-blower and the man repeated his blatting call.

More time passed. The guards were growing restless, murmuring and nervously looking about the dun-coloured slopes, when finally a dozen guards rode out of the valley's cleft, leading a line of horses behind them. They did not push the mounts, and it took them some time to reach us. The guards' heads and faces were covered in scarves, and dust came off them in clouds as they jostled in their saddles. The mounts they were leading were all dust-covered. Many of them looked as if they were on the verge of collapse. Among them, I spotted the chestnut mare I had been riding. I recognised a few of the other men's horses too. But some of the animals we had ridden into the desert were clearly missing.

I glanced at Jamal. He was stony-faced as he took in the collection of horses trailing the guardsmen. He caught my eye and frowned. I looked at the mounts again and understood what he had seen. There were no camels within the group.

"Where are the rest of the animals?" asked Aziz to the weary, dust-streaked officer who halted his steed before the captain. The horseman gave a slow salute, exhaustion oozing from his every movement. The noise of the storm had been terrible from within the safety of the underground chamber. I could barely imagine what it must have been like to endure the full force of it outside.

"Some ran off during the night," said the officer.

"Ran off?" said Aziz with a sneer. "Did they untie their ropes? Did they fly away?"

The officer looked at his feet, but seemed too tired to protest. "We fashioned a pen before the worst of the storm struck. It blew apart in the night and some of the horses fled before we saw what was happening."

"I do not wish to hear your excuses," snarled Aziz. "Your poor leadership has cost us dearly. If there are not enough mounts, you and your men will walk. And when we reach Ierusalem, you will be punished. Now, see that the prisoners are mounted and tied to their horses."

Skins were passed around, but none of us had more than a couple of mouthfuls before the flasks were pulled away. Our hands were untied, then retied in front of us so that we could ride. When we were in the saddle, guards tied our feet together beneath the horses' bellies.

The sombre-faced officer who had been in charge of the horses would still face his punishment when we reached our destination, but there were enough mounts for him and his men to ride.

Jamal grinned savagely to see them all mounted. "We spared them a long walk by killing so many," he said.

The guard with the burnt nose heard Jamal and nudged his horse close. The instant he was within reach, he lashed out and cuffed the young man across the face. Jamal rocked in the saddle, but did not lose his seat. Shaking his head, he spat into the sand, scowling at the guard.

"Jest again about my friends' deaths and you will join them before we reach Ierusalem. I do not think Aziz or the wali will miss the likes of you, *Badawi* rat."

Jamal was wise enough to keep his mouth closed after that, but when the guard rode away, he grinned at me. His teeth were scarlet with blood.

The day was long and hot. We wound our way along the narrow ravines and paths we had followed before. There was little left of the *Badw* camp that Theokleia and her band had destroyed. Sand was banked against the rocks we had piled over the dead. A few scraps of hide and clothing were strewn far across the land, half buried by the storm.

We did not stop to rest. Aziz was eager for us to return to the city as quickly as possible and he pushed us on. We rode with our heads down, the sun beating from the remorseless sky. For a time I thought perhaps I could kick my horse into a gallop, somehow evading capture long enough to lose myself in the twisting ravines and gullies. The truth was that few of the horses were strong enough to gallop anywhere. I had been placed on an old grey nag that Beorn had ridden previously. Nassif and Hamid, or perhaps the guardsmen, must have found some water for the animals, for without any, I did not believe they would have lasted until midday. As it was, the sun was barely past its zenith when Runolf's horse stumbled and slowly sank to its knees. The Norseman was lucky the beast did not roll, for, tied as he was, it might have crushed him.

They cut Runolf's bonds and allowed him to walk beside the horse after that. Shortly after, Pendrad's mount, a bony mare with prominent ribs and hips, halted and refused to walk on. There were no spare mounts, and Aziz's face was dark with anger as he gave the order to dismount and rest.

My back ached and my legs quivered as I lowered myself down cautiously onto the sand. Jamal joined me. I had seen him watching the horizon all that long morning, but if he had seen any sign of his father and grandfather, he did not say. Now he scanned the land in every direction. I followed his sweeping gaze, but saw no movement save the languid circling of a couple of carrion birds far off to the east. I wondered if Jamal imagined his kin to be lying dead or dying on the blanched sand beneath those birds, prey for vultures and jackals. He said nothing for a time, stroking the side of his horse, running his tanned fingers along the animal's jutting ribcage.

"Without water," he said at last, "most of these horses will not make it to sunset."

"Shut your mouth," said the guard who had struck him, whose name we had learnt was Fawzan.

Looking at the horses, I thought Jamal was right, but neither of us spoke further.

After a short break and another sip of water for each of us, Aziz ordered us once more into the saddle. We trudged on. Like Jamal, I took to watching the hills, but I saw nothing of interest. The vultures had vanished from the sky. I pictured their long necks probing hooked beaks deep into Hamid and Nassif's flesh. I imagined the birds tearing meat from the *Badw* tribesmen's camels' carcasses and shivered, despite the blistering heat.

The sun was low in the sky, painting the western horizon the red of forge coals, when another horse collapsed. The guards' horseflesh was stronger than the animals we had ridden into the desert, and Aziz cursed as Drosten's saw-backed mount halted, swollen tongue dangling from its slack mouth. A guard untied the Pict's feet so that he could dismount. Drosten tugged on the animal's bridle, but the horse merely rolled its eyes, shaking and panting. Drosten heaved, but after two faltering steps, the animal let out a pathetic whinny and rolled onto its side, chest heaving. No coaxing would get it on its feet again.

We were close to the higher hills now and the hidden location of the cistern where we had rested and waited for our guides. Aziz stared at the slopes, rubbing his hand through his beard. There were no extra horses. We could walk, but it would be dark long before we reached the water, assuming the wali's guards knew of its location. Eventually, Aziz summoned the disgraced officer who had guarded the horses the night before.

The man dismounted stiffly. His eyes were glazed, his grimy face haggard.

"This is your doing," Aziz said. "You will rectify it."

The officer said nothing.

"Take your men and ride to those hills. Return with water enough for the horses. In the morning, we will ride to the nearest river and water the mounts before continuing on to Ierusalem."

The officer looked as if he was going to say something, but instead, he pulled himself to his full height, straightened his shoulders and offered a crisp salute. Turning on his heel, he rounded up men and horses, and as many waterskins as they could carry.

The remainder of the guards began to prepare a camp for the night. They created a pen for the mounts, while others erected a tent for the captain. Runolf, Drosten, Hereward and the others had their hands bound behind their backs again. Jamal and I, the youngest of the band, must have looked less dangerous, for the guards did not replace our bonds after we dismounted. Instead, we were each given a small wooden shovel and ordered to dig a midden ditch some way from the campsite.

We dug in silence. My shoulder ached dreadfully as I stooped to dig in the hard, crusty earth. In the distance, their shadows long and stark on the dry land, the figures of the riders sent to fetch water stood out clearly against the brown hillside.

The guards assigned to watch us paid us little heed, and after a time Jamal whispered to me as we laboured.

"We could run," he muttered, his voice barely audible.

I glanced at the sky. It would be night soon. Perhaps we could escape into the darkness. Aziz's tent had been erected now, and the captain of the guard was ushering Revna inside. She did not look at me as she ducked under the tent flap. The thought of what might happen within made my stomach churn.

"I cannot leave my friends," I said.

Jamal nodded.

As if they imagined what we had been discussing, the guards called us back and quickly tied our hands again.

With all of us securely bound, the guards were free to pray. Taking turns and always leaving some of their number to watch us, they knelt, bowing and muttering their chanted prayers towards the south-east.

Runolf sat in brooding silence. He stared at the praying guards, then swung his gaze to Aziz's tent. No sound came from within. Runolf's eyes blazed. I bit my lip, knowing just how he felt. Impotent rage boiled within me too.

"I will not die like this," growled Drosten. "We should have fought with Gwawrddur."

"Then we too would be dead," said Hereward.

"Better that than what awaits us in Kawthar's palace."

Hereward stared into the gathering twilight. "Perhaps, but while we live, there is yet hope."

"Giso is still out there," I said, forcing myself to look away from the tent in an attempt to put it out of my mind. "Perhaps he will save us."

Drosten spat. "That worm has saved himself, no doubt. We will not be seeing him again, I'd wager."

The rest of the men grumbled. They were despondent and seemed to reserve a portion of their anger for the secretive Frank. They held him responsible for our predicament. I supposed in a way he was. If we had not gone in search of the Blood of Christ, we might well have left the Holy Land safely. But Giso had not been alone. I had spoken in favour of seeking the relic. I wondered if my friends blamed me too.

The wiry guard, Fawzan, strode over to where we were huddled together. He raised his spear menacingly. "No talking," he said.

Most of the guards were gruff, but seemed more focused on getting through the heat of the long day than tormenting us. Fawzan seemed to revel in his position of power over us. We had all received blows from him since our capture, so now we quickly fell silent. Our rapid compliance did not assuage Fawzan's viciousness though, and he cracked the butt of his spear hard against Drosten's head.

One of the other guards called Fawzan away. Drosten

glowered after him, rubbing his head. We did not speak further. I stared out into the dusk and prayed silently for a miracle.

When I awoke from a troubled sleep, I thought the Lord had answered my prayers. The sky was as black as if God had spilt ink across the firmament. Against that ink-dark sky, bright stars glittered, and a waxing moon silvered the land with its chill light. My breath steamed the air before me as I listened to the sounds that had brought me out of my sleep.

The stamp of horses. The nickering welcome from the mounts in the pen. Men's voices, low and resonant in the gloom. A night bird screeched somewhere far off. Beside me, Jamal jerked awake.

"What is it?" he whispered.

The dim light from the stars and moon showed me enough to cause my initial excitement to ebb away.

"The guards who were sent for water."

We sat in silence, listening as the guards dismounted and carried waterskins to their comrades and the horses. Only when the animals had been watered did a guardsman bring a waterskin to us captives.

"Drink your fill," he said, and I recognised the weary voice of the officer. "Tomorrow we will refill the skins in the hills."

I took the waterskin and drank deeply, before handing it to Jamal.

"Make sure everyone gets some," I whispered to Hereward. "There will be more water on the morrow."

Hereward murmured his thanks, and I listened as the skin was passed between my friends. I wondered whether Revna had been fed more than the dry crust of bread we had received, but thoughts of her threatened to overwhelm me, so I stared up at the stars and thanked the Almighty that we yet lived. Silently, fervently, I prayed that He would deliver us.

We had not been rescued, but at least we were no longer thirsty and, as Hereward had said, while we yet lived, there was hope. I rolled onto my side so that I might sleep once more. The night was cold and I shivered on the hard ground. A stone was pressing into my hip and my shoulder throbbed. I could not get comfortable and I was certain I would not find sleep again that night.

I was wrong.

When I awoke, it felt as if only moments had passed, but the moon had slid far across the sky. The hushed chatter of the guards and the quiet stamp and whinnies of the horses had been replaced with the thrum of galloping hooves, and the stillness of the darkness was ripped asunder by shouts of alarm.

Forty-One

"The horses have broken free," hissed Hereward.

Peering into the night I saw the shadowed shapes of the animals streaking past us, their bodies shimmering in the moonlight. Men shouted, waving their arms in an attempt to halt the rushing horses, but to no effect. One guard was struck and fell twisting to the ground with a cry.

I could just make out Drosten and Hereward nearby. Runolf's bulk rose up from the earth. Beorn and Eadstan were already on their feet.

"We need to get out of these bonds," Drosten gnarred. "They will give up chasing those horses soon."

I searched about us in the gloom. My gaze fell on the guard who had been knocked down. If he was hurt badly enough, I might be able to take a knife or sword from him. I moved tentatively towards him. I held my breath, though the night was strident with the clamour of horses and men. If the guard had any of his wits and strength about him, I would be no match for him, hands tied behind my back as they were. Still, I could think of no other option, so I increased my pace, keeping myself hunched over and shuffling towards him.

Over the thunder of the hoofbeats and the shouts of the guards, I heard again the sound of the night bird from earlier, its shriek surprisingly loud. Had we made camp on its nest?

I had ever been interested in birds, spending long days on the shores of Northumbria watching the redshanks and oystercatchers on the mudflats. Part of my mind wondered what species of fowl produced the call, but there was no time for such thoughts.

Just before I reached the fallen guard, he stirred. With a groan, he pushed himself up onto his knees. The horses had all fled now, the sound of their hooves pounding away into the darkness. Someone had thrown dry kindling onto the fire and a sudden flare of flames lit the night, making me blink.

The guard, halfway up, stared straight at me. The light shone in his eyes. His mouth was a dark circle of surprise. Just as I had hoped, he had a short sword hanging from his belt. I had prayed I might be able to steal it from him while he was dazed. Instead, he climbed to his feet and pulled the blade from its scabbard. Its edge caught the firelight. It looked viciously sharp. My hands were tied and I was helpless. Retreating, I shook my head.

"Trying to escape, are you?" he hissed, moving towards me.

In the flickering light from the fire I recognised Fawzan's scarred nose and sneering lips. My guts turned to water. He had so enjoyed hitting us with his spear butt. The gleam in his eyes showed me he would relish cutting me with his sword much more.

Licking his lips, Fawzan advanced on me. I was defenceless. I thought of running, but he would catch me quickly. All I could do was watch his deadly approach and pray. Behind me, closer even than before came the strange bird's piercing cry. In the same instant, Fawzan sprang forward. I side-stepped, narrowly avoiding his swiping sword. He spun to face me again, furious that I had thwarted his attack.

"You can't escape," he said. "Death is coming for you."

Unseen by the guard, a shadow rose up from the darkness behind him. Fawzan stiffened, his back arching. Collapsing to his knees, he gasped for breath, his eyes pleading, mouth working. The figure behind him leaned in and dragged a knife across his throat.

"Never make the mistake of talking too much," Giso said, stepping into the light. "Turn around."

I could scarcely believe what I had witnessed.

"You came back for us," I stammered.

"Were you not listening? Turn around. There is no time."

I did as he asked and felt him sawing at the leather thongs that bound my wrists. The moment I was free, he placed the dead guard's sword in my hand.

"Help free the others. There are horses beyond those rocks." He waved a hand vaguely towards the east. My mind was spinning, but I did not stop to ask him further questions. Turning back towards the other prisoners, I almost collided with someone. I raised my blade, thinking it was one of the guards.

But a glance showed me they were all still occupied with the horses. The dim firelight picked out Jamal's bruised face, and I lowered my sword. His hands were already free and a dark-garbed figure ran beside him. Instantly, I recognised Hamid. The *Badawi* warrior did not slow his pace. In his right hand he gripped a dagger. In his left he grasped his son's robe, pulling him along with him. At my shocked expression, Jamal grinned and let out the shrill cry of the night bird. Then, father and son were swallowed by the darkness.

Hurrying to the others, I cut Hereward's bonds. He tore his hands free and set about untying Drosten.

"Giso says there are horses beyond the rocks to the east."

"Giso?" asked Drosten, his tone incredulous.

"There is no time," I said, running to Runolf and leaving the rest of the men to free themselves.

Without a word, the giant Norseman turned his back to me and held out his wrists. I severed his ties just as two guardsmen saw what we were about and ran at us from the dark. Runolf bellowed, swaying past the first man's slicing sword, then lifting him bodily into the air. Using his prodigious strength, he twisted the writhing man, then slammed him head-first into the ground. The guard's neck made a sickening cracking sound and he lay still.

The second guard swung at me. I stepped inside his guard, slapping his sword arm away with my left hand and punching my short sword into his belly. Twisting the blade, I tugged it free and shoved him away.

Without speaking, Runolf and I knew where we were heading. The tent loomed before us. There had been no movement from the shelter. If there had been sounds from within, they had been lost in the tumult of the night. Runolf was ahead of me. He held the short sword of the guard he had killed. It was dwarfed in his massive hand.

When we were still a dozen paces from the tent, the flap was thrown open and Aziz stepped out. Beside him, hands secured behind her, stood Revna. Her face was pale. She was still clad in her dusty travel clothes.

"Guards!" he shouted. "To me."

"Let her go," I said.

He bared his teeth wolfishly. "You cannot win, you fools."

His eyes flicked to his left, giving me a warning. Several guards were running towards us. Runolf and I spun to meet them. Runolf cut one down, but there were too many for us. More guards were rallying now and as Runolf and I stood side by side, I realised that Aziz was right. We could not hope to win against these odds.

That was the moment when Drosten, Hereward, Beorn and the others crashed into the guards' flank. They had snatched up whatever they could find to use as weapons and were laying about them with a savage ferocity that saw the guards stumble back. Beorn swung a flaming torch like a club, sparks flying as he smashed it into a guard's face. Hereward brandished a knife he had found somewhere. Gersine even had a spear that he rammed into the ribs of the guard nearest me.

Eadstan, Gamal, Arcenbryht, Sygbald and Pendrad used their fists and rocks. But as the guards before them fell, so they were able to better arm themselves. In moments, the tide had shifted and the guards were in rout.

Leaving the guardsmen to Hereward and *Brymsteda*'s crew, Runolf and I turned back to face Aziz. Two more guards stood before him, swords drawn. Seeing that the fight was not going well, he stepped out to join them, pulling his blade from its ornate tooled leather scabbard with its glittering silver chape.

At his barked order his guards moved to intercept Runolf. Aziz crouched into the warrior stance and moved smoothly towards me. The sword I held was short-bladed and clumsy, no match for his whip-fast thin blade. I could see from his movements that he was a master swordsman. With a pang I thought that it should be Gwawrddur standing before Aziz, not me. But there was no time for remorse or regrets. I dropped into a defensive stance and prayed that Gwawrddur had taught me well enough to survive this encounter.

Beside me, Runolf battled the two guardsmen, but I could not look away from Aziz. He stamped forward, aiming a thrust at my chest. He was fast and I parried late. I leapt back, his blade missing me by a hair's breadth. Deciding there was no time for finesse, I sprang forward, swiping at his face. He parried my attack easily, twisting his wrist and slicing at my exposed arm. With difficulty, I avoided the blow, spinning away. He pressed his attack and it was all I could do to parry the flurry of strikes.

I was retreating, soaking up his blows. Then, without warning, I changed the direction of my movement, powering myself forward on the balls of my feet. I lunged with my blade, attempting to grasp his sword arm at the same moment. He shook off my attacks as if I was a child. With a leering grin of victory, he caught my wrist in his left hand, using the very move I had attempted. He twisted my wrist savagely. With a gasp, I dropped my sword.

He smiled as he raised his blade for the killing thrust. I saw Death then.

And yet it was not coming for me, not there in that desert night. Before he could bring his sword down, Aziz's eyes opened impossibly wide and a terrible, shocked horror washed over him. He looked down at his side in amazement. Arcenbryht's dagger jutted there. Revna, hands unfettered, had pulled the weapon from Aziz's belt and stabbed it into his side, burying the blade up to the bejewelled hilt.

Behind her, a shadow within the shadows, Giso stepped from the tent. The knife in his hand glimmered.

The gleam of triumph on Aziz's face was instantly replaced with the terror of defeat and certain death. He looked from the knife in his side to me, comprehension slowly dawning. Rage and horror contorted his face, and he howled like an animal. There was such hatred in his eyes. I could see there was only one thing in his mind in that moment: if he was to die, he would take me with him.

Wrenching my wrist free, I snatched up my weapon from the earth and, warding off his sword with my forearm, I surged up with a roar of fear and fury, ramming my short blade deep into his heart.

The moment Aziz fell, Hereward called the men to close up around us. The guards were rallying, more of their number running out of the gloom as they gave up on chasing the horses and returned to fight us.

"Fetch our weapons!" shouted Hereward.

As if woken from a dream, Revna spun around and hurried into the tent. I followed her, ducking under the leather flap. There was little inside save for a rug, a bedroll, an oil lamp hanging from a chain, saddle bags and a couple of large sacks. These Revna dragged into the centre of the space. Tugging the jute cloth open, she revealed our swords, seaxes, throwing axes and Runolf's great war axe. I helped her heave the sacks outside, shouting for the men to take up their arms.

With our aid, soon everyone had a familiar weapon in their hand once more.

While we were inside the tent, the guards had attempted to rush our shield-brothers, but Hereward, Runolf, Drosten and the others repelled them. Several of the *Brymsteda* men were bloodied, but it was too dark to see if they were badly injured. Not that it would matter for long. We were still outnumbered and the guards eyed us balefully.

They would attack again soon and I could see no way we could withstand a concerted onslaught.

Forty-Two

It was then that I heard Jamal's bird call again.

"Ready yourselves," I shouted, understanding the significance of the sound. "The *Badw* come for us."

A few heartbeats later the rumble of hooves reached us. Hamid, Nassif and Jamal burst out of the night, mounted on their camels and leading a string of horses in their wake.

If the wali's guards had been disciplined, they might have taken us then, in the confusion that followed. But they were shaken and disorganised. They made a paltry show at attempting to prevent us escaping, but Hereward led Gamal, Beorn, Eadstan, Pendrad and Drosten in a counter-attack, while the rest of us climbed onto the horses.

As Hereward and the others fell back to the mounts, Hamid, Nassif and Jamal turned their camels and raised their hands high above their heads. There was a whooshing sound, and I saw they carried leather slings that they spun fast in the air before loosing them with a snap. Stones clattered into the advancing guards. One man fell, his forehead split and bloody. Others cursed. But at this range the slingers could not miss and the guards retreated from the stinging projectiles.

Hamid and Nassif had managed to spirit away several mounts the night before, but there were not enough for us to ride one each. As one of the lighter men in the group, it fell to me to ride with another. Revna was slight of build and was the obvious choice to share a horse with me. My heart thrilled when she held out her hand so that I could pull her up behind me.

Runolf helped propel Revna up onto the rump of my horse and our eyes met. He gave the briefest of nods before turning and leaping onto his own steed. I felt as though something had changed between us, but the night was still fraught with danger and I could not dwell on a possibly imagined understanding with the Norseman.

The last of the *Brymsteda* men leapt onto the remaining horses and we galloped into the darkness.

We rode hard for a time, but the horses would never make it if we pushed them for too long. The animals had benefited from not having been ridden the previous day and, after stealing them from the unlucky guardsmen during the sandstorm, it transpired that Hamid and Nassif had led these horses to water. But we were heading back into the desert again, and even with water and rest, the horses laboured under their loads.

The animal I rode with Revna was tiring more quickly than most.

We slowed our pace. The sky was dark, the shadows black, impenetrable. The thought that our mount might step in a hole, breaking its leg and throwing Revna and me onto the hard, stony ground, plagued my mind. Imagining the guards in pursuit worried me also. And yet, as I rode, despite the grief and concerns that plagued me, I was smiling as the sun finally rose, bright and pure as a new promise. We had escaped what had seemed certain death and Revna rode behind me, her arms gripping tightly about my chest. I relished the sensation of her closeness, the warm weight of her against my back. Briefly, I wondered whether she felt the same elation. Was she smiling in the gloom as our horse carried us away from the camp, or was she perhaps crying, silent tears streaking her cheeks in the darkness?

I pushed aside such thoughts. We were free and alive, that was all that mattered, and I revelled in the joy of the wind on my face and Revna's body pressed against mine.

Forty-Three

I stared out across the rolling hills of the desert, squinting at the glare. The shadows were long, the sun low in the sky. Dawn was still fresh, the air not yet the scorching dry that it would be in the sun-baked midday.

I ached from the recent fights and the ride through the darkness. I reflected on my fight with Aziz. He had bested me easily. It had only been a matter of luck that Giso had freed Revna in that moment and that she had stabbed the captain of the guards.

I could hear Gwawrddur's voice as I gazed out at the lightening land. *A warrior makes his own luck.* Perhaps, or maybe the Almighty had intervened on my behalf. Whether luck, chance or divine intervention, one thing was certain: it was not my sword-skill that had carried me to victory. Gwawrddur had taught me well and I was no novice when it came to combat, but standing before Aziz, watching the lithe fluidity of his movements, I realised how little I understood of the art of swordsmanship and how much more I had to learn.

I closed my eyes, feeling afresh the loss of the Welshman, like a scab being torn from a wound.

Revna's voice made me start. I had been so lost in my thoughts I had not heard her approach.

"Strange how the dawn can make you feel like a different

person," she said. "As if the world has changed from the one it was in the dark."

The rising sun made her skin glow and her hair gleam. Her beauty caused my throat to tighten.

"Much can change in a single night," I said, wondering at her words. "But some things are not so easily altered."

She had brought a waterskin, which she handed to me. I drank, looking at where Nassif had turned over some rocks at the base of the bluff and was scratching at the ground with a wooden bowl. He said that with the dawn some dew would collect in the depression, but I could not imagine there would be enough water to make any difference to us.

Most of our band lay sprawled on the sand. Hereward had set Gersine and Gamal some distance away on a rocky bluff to watch our back trail. Jamal, tired as he must be, was tending to the animals with Pendrad. Giso, Hereward, Runolf, Drosten and Hamid were huddled together talking.

Exhaustion fell over me like a bearskin cloak, but I knew I would need to go to them soon. They would be deciding our future and I should lend my voice to such discussions.

"And what things are those?" Revna asked.

I thought for a moment. Her closeness made me nervous and unsure. "God's love," I said awkwardly.

She laughed and my face grew hot. "What cannot be seen is indeed hard to change."

"True," I said, struggling to find the words I wanted to say. "I do not speak only of God. What is in someone's heart, cannot be changed…" I bit my lip. "Cannot be changed by what others do to us."

She stiffened. "And what do you think has been done to me?" she said, her voice brittle.

"Nothing." I sighed. Words were inadequate to express my sorrow and regret. "I am sorry."

"What for?"

"That I could not save you from Aziz."

Her smile was bitter. "Oh, Hunlaf. You truly believe I need saving?"

"No... I'm sorry. I didn't mean—"

She cut me off, her tone as sharp as a knife now. "What did you mean?"

My head pounded. I was dismayed at where this conversation was taking me.

"When Aziz took you, I felt powerless. I wanted nothing more than to help you." I rubbed at my wrists where the leather thongs had marked my skin. "But I was bound..." My voice trailed off. Everything I said sounded like an excuse for my actions. I wanted to tell her of the pain deep in my chest at the thought of her suffering. Of the sinful, soaring, boundless joy I felt as Aziz's hot blood pumped over my hand. The savage elation that gripped me as I watched the life-light ebb from his eyes. But I could not compose my thoughts clearly. I have ever been more adept at explaining my mind with quill and ink than speaking. And of course, I could not write down my feelings for Revna. She was standing directly before me, sadness in her eyes.

"You do not need to explain yourself, Hunlaf," she said. "I see well enough what thoughts eat at you and my father." She placed a hand gently on my arm. "Know this. Aziz did not harm me."

Relief flooded through me. In the same instant, I saw the disappointment in her eyes at my reaction. I took hold of her hand, urgent that she should know the depth of my feelings for her.

"I meant it. What I said before. What is in a person's heart cannot easily be changed. Whatever happened, how I feel for you in here –" I tapped my chest "– would not have changed."

"Perhaps that is so," she said, sadly, pulling her hand away. "I hope we will never know."

Her words stung me.

"It is true," I said, my tone bleak and pained.

But Revna was done with this conversation. Turning away from me, she looked back to where Giso was gesticulating angrily.

"Of all the surprises this night," she said, "Giso's return shocked me the most. Do you think we can trust him?"

I took a deep breath of the morning air. I was glad of the change of subject, though I did not wish to admit it.

"I do not know. That he came back for us must count for something."

"Maybe. And yet I always feel there is another reason for everything he does. One that is shown and one that is hidden. It is the same when he talks; for every thing he says clearly, there is a different, secret meaning."

She might as well have been describing how it felt for a foolish young man to converse with a lovely young woman who had stolen his heart, but I did not say as much.

"He cut your bonds," I said. "For that I will be forever thankful."

"As will I." Her hand went to her throat, as if she could still feel the rough fibres of Aziz's rope. "And yet even in that, perhaps Giso had another motive."

"What reason could he have for freeing you beyond saving you from that nithing Aziz?"

"Who can say? But think. In doing so, does he not make friends of you, and my father?"

"Nonsense," I said. "He came back with the *Badw*. For all of us." And yet, now that she had uttered the words, I could not shake the idea that Giso might have used Revna's rescue as a means to manipulate our opinion of him.

I could hear the Frank's voice now, louder than his usual sibilant speech. Hereward raised his voice too. Hamid shook his head. Nassif, finished with his digging, sat on a rock and looked as though he was in a doze. Runolf towered over them all. He stood stiffly, his hands bunched into fists, but I noticed he was saying nothing.

"Let us see what they are arguing about," I said, walking towards them.

"That is a good idea," Revna said, her words somehow making me feel foolish. "Especially as, besides Giso, you are the only other one of our number who can translate the words of the *Badw*, and ours to them."

Surely Giso would not twist the meaning of his translations. Even as I thought this, I knew the truth of it. I had seen him kill men in cold blood to gain what he desired. He would lie without a second thought if he believed it might gain him an advantage.

When I reached the group, I bowed to Hamid. Giso fell silent.

"Peace be upon you," I said.

Hamid returned my bow and touched his chest and lips. "And upon you."

"I give you thanks for coming to our aid."

Hamid's expression was grave. "I came for my fool of a son," he said.

"Then I am glad you saw fit to bring enough horses for us too."

He smiled at that. "They were your horses."

"In truth, they are Zakariya's," I replied. "But whoever's horses they are, I give you thanks. And perhaps Jamal is not such a fool."

Hamid did not look convinced. "To enter the Cave of Tears and then to be captured by the wali's guards. These are foolish things."

"He fought bravely. And most importantly, he yet lives."

Hamid snorted at that. "Still, he is a fool. But you should thank him. Not me. My father and I were going to take the horses as payment for our trouble. Jamal made me return for you and your friends."

I was surprised at that. Revna caught my eye and shrugged. "Much can change in one night," she said.

Giso had grown increasingly impatient as we spoke. His tone now was sharp.

"We cannot tarry here," he snapped. "If you have finished offering thanks, perhaps you can help me to get through this Northumbrian's thick skull."

Revna raised an eyebrow at me.

"What is it you are trying to explain?" I asked.

"Giso here," said Hereward, "believes we should flee from this land with all haste and hurry back to Alhwin at Tours."

"Isn't that what you want also?" I said. "You have been saying as much ever since we left Kýpros."

Hereward frowned and scratched at his beard. "I see things differently now."

"What would you have us do?" I asked.

"I will not be able to rest knowing that bitch Theokleia is alive. I stand by what I said before. I still think it was a mistake to come here. I don't need to list the reasons why. But we cannot change the past. The future, however, is ours to bend to our will, and I would live in a future that sees us feed Theokleia, and that monster Artemis, to the ravens and wolves."

Drosten growled his assent. Beorn and Eadstan sat nearby and added their voices in support of Hereward's cause. Runolf paced back and forth, clenching and unclenching his fists.

"What say you, Runolf?" I asked, flicking a glance at Revna.

Runolf ceased his pacing. His skin was reddened from the sun. He rubbed his hands through his unruly beard and hair, the sun catching in the resulting cloud of dust.

"I want vengeance for Cumbra, Oslaf, Ida and Gwawrddur," he said. "If it had not been for Theokleia, we would surely not have been cornered in that cave by Aziz. The blood price for our fallen must be paid by those who have wronged us." Hereward and the others grinned, but Runolf held up a huge hand. "Giso has earned the right to say his piece. He came back for us and, if not for him, we would still be Aziz's captives."

"My thanks, Runolf," Giso said. Runolf's lip curled as if

he had tasted something sour. Giso did not appear to notice. "Revenge is an earthly passion," he went on. "You can seek it at any time, but the Blood of Christ is unique. We cannot risk losing it. I say we head to the coast and then sail for Frankia, as quickly as we are able. When the relic is safely with Alhwin and King Carolus, I will help you track down Theokleia and her minion, that you might exact your vengeance."

Drosten began to protest, but I silenced him with a gesture.

"One thing is certain," I said. "We cannot stay here any longer. Isn't that so, Hamid?" I spoke the words to him in Al-Arabiyyah.

He nodded. "We are not safe here," he said. "Our tracks are fresh. The guards who lived are near."

"We cannot remain here," I repeated. "And it seems to me that any course we take will lead us in the same direction. For surely Theokleia herself is heading towards the coast, almost certainly Yafah, where she landed shortly before us." I looked about at the faces of those around me. "I say we make all haste to the sea and decide on our course of action when we reach *Brymsteda*."

"The boy speaks sense," Hereward said. The rest of the men nodded in agreement. Runolf looked relieved. Giso frowned, fixing me with a dark scowl, but he said nothing more. Turning on his heel, he stalked away towards where the horses stood in the shade of some great boulders.

Turning to Hamid, I said, "We have agreed we must return to Yafah and our ship. Will you guide us from these desert hills? We have little to offer you, but I fear we do not know this land well."

"Truly? I never would have guessed," Hamid said with a twisted grin. "I thought perhaps you were secretly *Badw* and had spent all your lives in the desert."

I returned his smile. "You will guide us then?"

He grew serious. "Do you mean to hunt the people who killed my kin?"

I looked over to where Giso was checking the cinch of his mount. He was well out of earshot, but even so, I lowered my voice to barely a whisper.

"We will hunt them down and slay them if we are able. They have caused us much strife and the death of our friends."

Hamid stared at me, weighing my words. His eyes were dark and cold in the bright desert sunlight. "Then we will guide you out of the desert and help you avoid the guards of Ierusalem. You say Aziz spoke of meeting this Theokleia on the road to the city?"

I nodded.

"If she remains on the road and heads to Yafah as you say, with us leading you, we may be able to reach the coast before her." He reached out and grasped my shoulder. His grip was painfully strong. "A devil such as she should not be able to leave these lands with her life."

I thanked him, and he shouted at his father and son to round up the rest of the men and get them mounted. Walking to his camel, he climbed up into its saddle.

"There is no time to waste," he said. He looked down at me with a wistful gleam in his eye. "My people have long feared the Cave of Tears, saying that *jinn* resided there. It is strange to discover the only devil found there came from far away."

Forty-Four

Hamid said that, Allah willing, we could make the coast in three days, but on the morning of the second day, while we were still in the scabrous terrain of the desert, the horse I shared with Revna pulled up lame. The *Badw* men had guided us to water the evening before and there was even some scrubby grass and weeds growing along the stony stream bed. The horses cropped at the scant vegetation while we rested. We had been making good time and our spirits were high. All that day we had looked nervously at the horizon behind us, but we had seen no sign of the wali's guards. Giso thought they had decided against chasing us. I hoped he was right.

It was early the next morning, soon after we set off, when my horse stumbled. We were picking our way down a rocky hill when the beast momentarily lost its footing, its hooves scuffing the loose stones. For a dreadful moment it seemed it might tumble, sending us careening down the hillside. Revna clung to me to avoid falling and, as always, I felt a flutter of excitement at her closeness. During the previous day, she had talked frequently to me, her voice soft in my ear, and as much as her touch, I welcomed the warming in her humour towards me. I chose to ignore any further thoughts about what might have happened to her in Aziz's tent. She said he had not harmed her and she had no reason to lie to me. We rode on, the horse's hooves sliding and scraping on the loose gravel of the path we followed.

For a time I thought nothing more about the animal's earlier lurching slip. But when we reached a relatively flat portion of the path Hamid was leading us along, the horse slowed. It had developed a noticeable limp. Very soon, it became clear the animal had damaged its foreleg enough that it could not bear our weight.

Hamid dismounted and walked back along the line of travellers. Dropping to his knees, he examined the animal's hoof. Standing, he looked at me and shook his head. I knew what he was going to do, but blessedly the poor horse had no idea. With a fluid motion, Hamid drew his knife and cut the creature's throat. Clutching tightly to its reins, careful to avoid its hooves as it kicked out, he hauled it down to the sand as its strength left it.

"We will have meat for the journey now," he said. "But we will travel more slowly."

During our travels, Gamal and Oslaf had always taken on the duty of butchers. Gamal did not need to be told what to do now. With Gersine's help, he set about quartering the animal, then slicing the choice cuts from the carcass. I was surprised to see Lord Mancas' son involved in such gruelling, bloody work, but this journey had been full of surprises. The haunches of meat were distributed amongst the men and soon we were ready to ride again.

Jamal had dismounted too. He was good with the animals and, by unspoken agreement, he had become the group's hostler. Now, after an inspection of the remaining horses, he shook his head. "None of them is strong enough to carry two riders over this terrain," he said.

I looked at the larger animals the *Badw* rode. "What about the camels?" I asked.

Again he shook his head. "The men from your land are all tall and heavy. The camels cannot carry two such men."

"Revna is light," I offered, though disliking the idea that she might ride with one of the *Badw*, particularly Jamal.

Behind his tan and bruises, I thought I saw his face blush. "The lady is indeed slight," he said, not looking at her. "But we cannot share a mount with a woman. It is *haraam*. Forbidden by the Prophet," he added on seeing my confusion. His face brightened as he came up with a solution. "She can ride. I will walk."

"What are you talking about?" asked Revna.

I explained and she sighed.

"I can walk as well as any man," she said.

And so it was that Revna and I trudged on through the heat and the thick dust kicked up by the camels and horses.

At midday, when the sun was directly overhead and there was scant shade to be found, Hamid shouted something to Jamal that I could not make out. Without waiting for a reply, Hamid lashed his camel into a loping run, guiding the animal up a nearby rise. There was an unusual but welcome splash of green at the base of the hill. Jamal steered his own mount towards it.

Dust blossomed in the hot air behind Hamid. He was already halfway to the crest of the slope.

"Where is he going?" I asked Jamal.

"To see what he can see from up there."

We rested beneath a date palm next to a small pond of still water. Nassif filled his goatskin from the pool.

"The people dug beside these trees many years ago so that travellers would have water," he said. "It flows close to the sun here. Fill your skins before letting the beasts drink."

My feet ached and I removed my shoes, looking at the blisters there. Gersine sat down beside me.

"Why don't you ride for a while?" he said. "I can walk."

I pulled my shoes back on over my swollen feet with a grimace. "I'll walk," I said, stubbornly. I would not ride while Revna walked.

Gersine knew me well enough not to attempt to convince me otherwise. Rising, he began to collect twigs and spiky dry leaves that had fallen from the palm. "I can make a fire," he said. "Cook some of the meat."

Seeing what he was about, Nassif shook his head. "No fire," he said. "We ride on."

I was about to reply, when Hamid returned, his camel trotting into the frondy shade beneath the date palm.

"We will eat soon," he said. "But not here."

"What have you seen?" I asked. "Is it not safe?"

"Safe enough," he said, taking a sip from a waterskin. "But we will eat better if we ride on a ways. A large band of our people are camped to the south and west of here."

We could see the smoke from their cooking fires as soon as we passed the hill. And yet the *Badw* settlement was still deceptively far away. I was hobbling on bleeding feet by the time we reached the large flock of sheep and goats in the mid-afternoon heat.

A group of men were watching the flock. On seeing us approaching, they rode out to meet us. They were mounted on camels. The leader's saddle was adorned with silver trinkets that glittered in the glaring sun. I was surprised to recognise him.

"Bachir, son of Rabab," I said, bowing. Straightening my back, I pulled myself to my full height. I placed my hand on the pommel of my sword, puffing out my chest. "Peace be upon you."

"And upon you," he said.

Hamid offered him greetings and told him of our situation. Bachir listened courteously enough, but when Hamid had finished recounting our tale, the young man sneered down at me.

"You seem very careless of your mounts," he said. "But my father has many more and he is always ready to welcome men with silver in their purses. Even infidels like you."

"You forget yourself, Bachir," said Giso, nudging his scrawny horse forward.

I knew not what history there was between the two men, but Bachir paled to see the small Frank.

"Shabah," he murmured, inclining his head. "Peace be upon you. My father will be pleased to see you."

"It is always a pleasure to drink *marmaraya* with Rabab of the Hukuk," Giso said, kicking his horse into a trot and riding past Bachir without another look. The goats and sheep parted before him. Bachir watched him go, then swung back to me, his distaste plain on his features.

"Hamid says you have walked far," he said. "You must be weary. Would you care to ride to my father's tent?"

I bristled. My feet hurt terribly, but I would never show weakness before Bachir.

"I will walk."

"And what of the lovely lady?" Bachir grinned at Revna, his teeth bright in his sun-dark, handsome face. "Would she care for a ride?" He licked his lips lasciviously.

Taking hold of Revna's arm, I pulled her with me and began to walk after Giso, hiding the pain that lanced through my feet with each step.

"She too will walk," I replied, my tone icy.

Revna may not have comprehended the words, but the meaning of the exchange was clear enough.

"Did he offer me his camel to ride?" she asked when we had passed Bachir and the other *Badw* riders who sat their camels, staring down at us imperiously.

"I said we would walk," I replied curtly.

"I'm not so sure," she whispered. "My feet do ache."

I looked at her sharply, ready to snap a retort. She was smiling and I felt my anger dissipating. Revna took my arm and gave it a reassuring squeeze.

"I didn't want him when he offered five camels and a flock

of goats, Hunlaf. Do you think I would go with him just for a ride... on his camel, however nice it might be?"

As Runolf rode by, he glowered at Bachir. Bachir muttered something to his companions. The sound of their laughter drifted after us. I glanced back, suddenly afraid that the wali's men might be on our trail, but there was no sign of movement in the distance.

Everyone from *Brymsteda* had passed the *Badw* now, leaving just Hamid, Nassif and Jamal. Hamid spoke with Bachir briefly, then, with a whooping shout, the son of Rabab lashed his camel into a run, easily overtaking our tired band. His companions joined him, scattering the sheep and goats before them.

Hamid rode his camel close to Revna and me.

"I see you have met Bachir before," he said.

"I have had that pleasure," I replied.

He smiled at that. "Rabab is a good man," he said. "He will give us hospitality. But he is cursed, like so many men, with a foolish son."

With that, he let out a barking laugh and clapped a hand on Jamal's shoulder. Jamal laughed and together they rode off towards the tents, leaving only Nassif behind, staring after them and shaking his head.

"It is a curse indeed," said the elderly man, his features flat and expressionless. As he trotted past I saw that his eyes glimmered with mirth in his seamed, weathered face.

Forty-Five

Hamid was not wrong about the reception we would receive. Just as when we had met him near the beach of Yafah, Shaikh Rabab was a most hospitable host. The womenfolk brought us bitter *marmaraya* tea to drink and platters heaped with dates and cheese. Knowing that the meat we carried would not keep in this heat, we offered Rabab the great haunches of horseflesh. He accepted with a broad smile, and the women cut it up and roasted it so that the air was thick with the aroma of cooking.

That night we sat in the cool of the desert, the land draped in shadows and the great expanse of stars soaring above us, and we feasted until we could do little more than sprawl out on the sand and stare up at the dark heavens, our bellies full to bursting.

I had worried that Bachir would cause problems, but Rabab was as wise as he was generous. Despite his son's protests, Rabab sent him out to watch the flock. After a brief confrontation between father and son, Bachir stormed off cursing. The slight to him was clear, as was his fury at his father. I wondered how long Rabab would be able to maintain his control over his unruly young son.

The gathering fell quiet, listening as Bachir spat epithets and imprecations in the darkness, before mounting his camel and riding off into the night.

Jamal leaned in close to me. "You would do well not to wander far from the tents tonight," he said. "Lest Bachir should find you."

"Why?" I replied, feigning innocence. "Do you think he does not have enough with the goats and sheep?"

Jamal sniggered at that, earning himself a cuff around his ear from his father. Hamid glowered at me.

"The lad is right," whispered Giso in Englisc, "and you would do well to remember it. Bachir does not like you."

"I do not like him much either," I said.

"That is as may be," said Giso, "but we need his father, and it does not do to insult the son of one's host."

I swallowed any further comments. Giso was right. As the night drew on, I ate and drank more, but spoke little, instead watching my friends' faces in the flame flicker of torches and lamps. Rabab appeared to know Giso well. After watching their interactions for some time I noticed how Rabab would defer to the Frank, allowing him to lead the conversation. And when the moment arrived for them to haggle over the cost of donkeys for Revna and me, Rabab put up only the most perfunctory resistance in the negotiation, parting with the animals for much less than he could have demanded given our precarious predicament. Rabab was master over his people and accustomed to being obeyed in all things. From his dealings with Giso I could not decide whether he liked the Frank or feared him. Perhaps a little of both, I concluded.

In the morning, we rode into the west, our shadows ranging long ahead of us as the sun warmed our backs. It felt good to be mounted again, though my donkey was saw-backed and its gait uncomfortable and ungainly. I missed having Revna riding behind me, but I was glad to be able to rest my blistered feet. Rabab had ordered one of his women to give me a greasy salve to rub on them. Sniffing the concoction, I detected garlic and ginger, both of which would help with the pain and the swelling. There were other herbs in the ointment, but the overwhelming smell of the stuff was goat grease. As if I didn't smell bad enough after days of travel, I now reeked of rancid fat.

Revna rode her donkey up to mine and wrinkled her nose. "If you did not wish to ride with me any longer," she said, "you could have said so. You did not need to smother yourself in sheep tallow."

She had walked as far as me, but inexplicably her feet were unscathed.

"It was not for your benefit," I said. "I thought it was the best way to be rid of Bachir."

She laughed. "A dubious plan at best," she said. "He might have a weakness for sheep."

"My plan was a sound one even so," I said with a smirk. "For this ointment is not made from sheep fat, but goat grease. Besides, I heard he lusts after beautiful girls from the north."

"Is that so?" Her eyes sparkled in the early morning sun. "And what about fierce Norse warrior women?" She pulled her lips back in a parody of a snarl.

"Luckily for me he has no interest in those. Prefers sheep and camels. Much less trouble."

There was a lightness about us all as we rode away from the *Badw* settlement. We had obtained provisions and mounts, rested well, and I had avoided any trouble with Bachir. We had even learnt something of our quarries' movements.

A wizened man, travelling north on some errand of his own, had also been a guest at Rabab's fire that night. He spoke little, keeping his own counsel. When Giso had enquired who he was, Rabab had introduced him as Mahna, saying he was his uncle's cousin and a man to be trusted. That had seemed to satisfy Giso, but I watched the man as the night drew on. He ate and drank in silence, but when he heard mention that we pursued a woman, he spoke up, his gruff voice surprisingly strident after so long being hushed.

"Is she a stranger to these lands, this woman?" he asked. "A stranger like you?"

Giso eyed him for a time before answering, perhaps assessing him.

Rabab nodded. "Speak freely," he said. "Mahna is kin. He has my trust."

Giso thought on that, perhaps thinking, as I did, that not all kin were trustworthy. But we were Rabab's guests and there had already been embarrassment with Bachir. It would not do to insult his hospitality by refusing to speak to this man he vouched for.

"Not like me," said Giso. "But a stranger, yes. This woman is from Byzantion."

"Travels with some bad men?" Mahna said. "Men who would cut out your kidneys as soon as drink *marmaraya* with you?"

"That sounds like her," Giso said. "There is another woman with her too. Tall and brutish, so I am told."

"Huge and ugly as a bear," I added.

The old man's brow furrowed. "A woman, you say? I don't think so. There was a big warrior though. Head and face covered, but that could have been no woman."

"This woman is almost as tall as him," I said, pointing to Runolf.

Mahna's eyes widened. "Perhaps I saw her then," he said, his tone doubtful. "But if that monster was a woman, I would not wish to be her husband."

"Where did you see them?" Giso asked.

"The road to Yafah, near Ierusalem."

"When was that?"

"Yesterday. They might be at the coast on the morrow. The next day if they do not hurry."

Giso glanced at me.

"She thinks we are dead or captured," I said. "She has no reason for haste."

Giso pursed his lips. "Perhaps that is so," he said. "But I do not imagine Theokleia to be an incautious woman." He turned back to Rabab and Mahna. "Can we catch her?"

Mahna shrugged. "Hard to say. With fair weather, strong mounts and good guides, you might."

"Hamid and Nassif are guiding them," Rabab interjected.

Mahna sniffed the air. "And I smell no more storms on the wind. How about their mounts?"

Rabab puffed out his cheeks and held out his hands as if weighing something.

"They are alive," he said. "And they have legs."

Mahna grinned. "Then two out of three is not bad. With Allah's blessing, you will reach the woman you seek. But you must know she is not travelling with that name."

"Theokleia?" said Giso. "What name is she using then?"

"I heard her men call her Salome of Clopas."

Forty-Six

Giso rode close to me the morning we left Rabab's tents behind.

"She is a clever one, this Theokleia," he said, "Or perhaps I should call her Salome."

"You sound admiring of her," I said. "She is a murderer."

"None of us is without sin." He shrugged. "And yet I cannot deny I feel admiration for her. She has outsmarted us at every turn. And now this new name. There is a poetry there, don't you think?" He looked at me sidelong. "You understood the reference in the name, I take it?"

That he should admire such a woman was no surprise to me. I had seen Giso kill readily enough to further his own ends. But his tone, and the implication that he was sharper than me, infuriated me.

"It is not so complex for anyone who has studied the Scriptures," I answered coldly. In truth, though the name had carried the ring of familiarity to me the night before, my mind and body had been too tired to land on the answer. I had lain awake listening to Runolf's snoring and the distant bleating of the goats. All the while I had turned the name over in my mind. In the end, sleep had taken me. It was only in the light of the morning that the solution presented itself. Of course, I did not mention any of this to Giso.

"Salome and Maria of Clopas were two of the women who tended to Christ's body after the crucifixion," I said. "They are both named as being among the first to witness the empty tomb." I felt a pang that I had been so close and had not been able to visit the place where our Lord's body had been laid to rest for three days. "I imagine," I went on, "Theokleia thought it amusing to adopt a name made up of women who wiped the very blood from Jesus' wounds."

"No doubt," said Giso. He patted the leather bag that never left his side. "She is not as clever as she believes though."

"She does not have the Blood," I said, "but she still has the Holy Lance, and is responsible for Gwawrddur's death. Artemis killed Cumbra and almost killed me too."

We rode on in silence. The day was warming around us, the sun hot on my head and back. Sweat trickled down my spine like a caress. I shivered. The horizon was dotted with palms and olive trees – a welcome sight after the days of dry sand and heat-cracked rocks.

"You believe we should chase after her," Giso said after a time. "You seek revenge like the others."

I said nothing.

"You are brighter than that, Hunlaf. They are brutes. You are a thinker."

"I am a warrior," I said. "And Gwawrddur was my friend. Cumbra too."

"We should not risk losing the Blood of Christ. Carolus must have the relic's power."

"I *do* want vengeance," I admitted. "And yet I know you are right. What you carry in that bag is beyond value."

"When the time comes then, you will speak up for returning to Frankia as quickly as possible?"

I thought for a moment before replying. "I will pray on it," I said at last. I meant it too. The decision weighed heavily upon me. And yet deep down, I knew the warrior within me had already defeated the studious monk I once was. Giso gave me a stern look. I suppose he knew the truth too. If he did, or suspected it, he chose not to discuss it further.

The land was more fertile as we approached the coast and came down out of the rocky wastes of the desert. Olive groves dotted the hillsides and though we travelled across open country and were not riding along the large roads left by the Romans, we saw many more people than we had of late. Farmers, shepherds, drovers and pedlars all crossed our path.

Everyone we passed looked at us with open interest, taking in Runolf's size, pale skin and flame-red hair, Drosten's ink-lined face and the procession of hard-faced warriors who, despite wearing the dusty robes of the *Badw*, were evidently far from home.

Hamid and Giso asked for news of other travellers or sightings of guardsmen from Ierusalem, but the people shook their heads. Travellers used the road to Yafah, not these paths, and Ierusalem was far off. The wali's guards seldom bothered anyone out here.

We camped that night in the shadow of a collection of ruined buildings. The golden light of the setting sun picked out the shape of a large settlement that must have once been home to many. Now all that remained were stone walls jutting from the dusty earth. There were the remnants of fires in some of the collapsed buildings where others had sheltered. Charred streaks of soot partially obscured the ghosts of ancient paintings that had once adorned the whitewashed walls, and I marvelled to see forms of people and animals depicted with great skill by long-dead, unknown artists.

Goat and sheep dung, dried and flaky, dotted the place. In one room, surrounded by broken columns, the colourful stones of a mosaic glimmered from the dust, the cunning image of swimming fish brilliant in the last rays of the day.

"My people use this place when passing," said Jamal, leading the horses into the largest area that must have once been a great hall. Now it only had walls on two sides. "Last year, I found this in the dust."

He extracted a small object from a pouch and handed it to me. It was a disc of silver, polished and shiny. Embossed on one side was the image of a man's head, wreathed in laurels, on the other a woman bearing what looked like a cornucopia. Letters were inscribed around it.

I traced the text with my finger. Many words were abbreviated, but one was clear enough. "This is a coin from the age of Emperor Traiano. During his rule, the Empire of Rome ruled all the world. I wonder what happened to the Romans who lived here."

"The same thing that happens to all flesh," Giso said. "Those who once resided here are now dust."

I looked about at the sand that coated everything and suppressed a shudder.

We left before dawn. Hamid said we would reach Yafah by midday. Our nervous anticipation grew. The sun had not long risen behind us when we caught our first glimpse of the sea. It was still a long way off, and when we rode down from the crest of the hill, we could no longer see it. But the vision of our destination caused us to pick up our pace.

We passed through an orchard of fig trees, following the course of a stream, along which were planted beans and barley, and then – as we rode out from the shade of a stand of tall, swaying date palms – Yafah came into view. I recalled well the roof of Simon the Tanner's house, and though the pale buildings were yet far in the distance, I fancied I could pick out the blue and white tiles where I had knelt to pray. The sea gleamed beyond the town, its surface glistening like countless gems.

"I give you thanks," I said to Hamid. "You have guided us well."

He acknowledged my praise with a taciturn nod. "What kind of desert men would we be if the sea eluded us?"

I chuckled. "You make a valid point, and yet still I offer you thanks."

We were all in high spirits. No matter Hamid's humility, he had led us unerringly through the broken desert hills, and then across the dusty farmland that sloped down to the Middle Sea. In spite of my lame horse, we had made good time, and there was even yet a possibility we might reach Yafah ahead of Theokleia.

On seeing our destination, a shimmer of excitement ran through us. I noticed Drosten, Hereward and the others loosening their swords in their scabbards. I did the same, wondering whether we would have to fight again before leaving the Holy Land.

Close by, there was a stand of cypress trees. The land was green there, where a small stream flowed, irrigating the fields nearby. Riding into the shade of the trees, we dismounted and led the horses to the water for a drink before the final stage of our journey down to the coast.

Before we mounted once more to continue on to Yafah, Giso addressed us all. He had spoken little since the previous disagreement, but now he set his shoulders and spoke in a clear, calm voice.

"I should go on alone," he said. "I can check the town for danger."

Drosten's face darkened. "What treachery is this?" he said. "We are so close now. I say we ride on. There is no time to waste."

"You are brave and stalwart to be sure, Drosten mac Galanan," Giso said. "But you should use that thick head of yours for more than battering your enemies."

The Pict snarled, but Hereward restrained him with a hand on his shoulder.

"We should at least listen to the Frank," he said.

Drosten scowled. Giso nodded his thanks to Hereward.

"Think for a moment," he said. "We have ridden to Yafah as

quickly as we were able in the hope of intercepting Theokleia. We have assumed this was her destination, as this was where she arrived in the Holy Land."

"We know this, little man," said Runolf. "So why not ride on with haste to meet her? Every moment we tarry, there is more chance of her escaping. But then that is what you want, is it not?"

Giso let out a long breath. "Are you all such thunder-heads? Do none of you understand?" Annoyance coloured his tone now. "As *we* have assumed Theokleia's destination, so others might assume ours."

I glanced at Revna. Her face paled as she comprehended the meaning of Giso's words. I understood too, and cursed myself for not thinking the obvious earlier.

"The wali knows where our ship is," I said.

Giso clapped his hands together slowly in mock celebration.

"Finally!" he said, his tone oozing with exasperation. "We think his guards gave up the chase. They may well have done. After all, we killed many of them and finished off their captain too." He bowed slightly to Revna and me. "But do you think that when Kawthar heard of our escape he would so easily forgo his pursuit of us? Do you believe that such a proud man would allow us to leave his lands with impunity after the shame Revna inflicted on him? We have slain many of his men too. He will never forgive us."

He looked at each of us in turn, gauging our response to his words.

"I can pass unnoticed in Yafah," he went on. "You know this to be true. If you ride in," he waved a hand vaguely in the direction of Runolf and Drosten, "our presence will be known to everyone in as long as it takes to boil an egg. If an ambush awaits us, it would be better not to stumble into it without warning."

Hereward was nodding. The sense in what Giso said was plain. I was furious with myself for not having thought we might find more enemies than Theokleia and her warriors in Yafah. Drosten, however, was not prepared to drop his objection.

"What is to stop you finding another ship and leaving without us?" he said, his tone sharp with disdain.

Giso stared at Drosten for a time. His expression was that of a man who is struggling to believe the stupidity of others. With a sigh and a shake of his head, he replied at last.

"Have you forgotten so quickly all the times I have come to your rescue? I find your lack of faith in me disturbing, and yet I have grown accustomed to these insults. We have been in this position before, or have you already forgotten al-Andalus? You did not trust me then and yet I returned, did I not?"

"We do not trust you now, Frank," growled Drosten.

Giso smiled at that. "That you despise me is almost soothing to me. I find constants in life comforting. It is good to know I can count on you, Drosten, even as you can count on me to do what is best for my master and the men who serve him. Do not forget we all serve Alhwin and King Carolus. And this is what is best for all of us. I can pass unnoticed, so I will go into Yafah, and you will await me here."

"I do not think—" said Drosten.

"No," said Giso, cutting him off, "you do not, and I do not hold that against you, for you are a mighty warrior and each must serve in his own fashion." Drosten made to reply, but Giso ploughed ahead without pause. "There is no time for debate. I will head into Yafah and ensure the way is clear for us, and – so that you do not suspect I will flee, abandoning you to your fate – I will leave with you the Blood of Christ."

Without waiting for an answer, he took his bag from his shoulder and handed it to me. Solemnly, I looped the leather strap over my head and across my shoulder, but not before I had checked that the relic was indeed within. My display of distrust earned a snort of derision from Giso.

Drosten was not happy with the plan, but the rest of us agreed with Giso. The Frank held his horse's reins out to me.

"Let me ride your donkey," he said. "The animal is less memorable than a horse." Nodding, I handed him the donkey's reins. Giso climbed onto the animal's sharp back with a wince. I could not hide my smile at his discomfort.

After the mounts had drunk, we tied them in the warm shadows of the trees. I looked after Giso. He was already in the distance, a dark shape swaying astride the dusty donkey. There was nothing to distinguish him from the countless *Badw* we had encountered. I watched him until he was lost to sight, swallowed by a dip in the land. I patted the bag slung over my shoulder. It felt suddenly heavier than it had only moments before.

Forty-Seven

The sun slid slowly across the pallid sky towards the sea. On the eastern horizon, wispy clouds formed over higher ground. The shadows of the trees moved around us. The stream provided water for the animals, and we filled our skins.

Walking a short way downstream from where the others drank and rested, I removed my shoes beside the rivulet. Lush rushes grew in abundance on the bank, and I had to push the leaves apart to make room. Almost completely hidden from view, I lowered myself down, groaning with pleasure as I dipped my aching feet into the cool water.

"Careful now," said Revna, who had come quietly through the trees. "If the others hear you, they might get the wrong idea about what we are doing."

I felt my face grow hot. I had been praying that we would be successful in finding Theokleia and returning with the Blood of Christ to Frankia. Watching Revna untying her own shoes and exposing her pale legs, my mind leapt to much less noble thoughts.

Shoving aside the rushes that grew thick by the water, Revna made room to sit beside me. I could not take my eyes from her shapely calves and slender ankles. I longed to reach for her, but I kept my hands at my sides. Giso's bag was heavy on my shoulder. Since he had given it to me, I could think of little else. I was painfully aware that I held close to my chest a cloth dipped in the very blood of the son of God. Surely it must be blasphemous to entertain such thoughts of Revna while in the presence of the holy relic.

"We should get back to the others," I said, making to rise. "If your father—"

She pulled me back down. "Sit a while. Do not concern yourself with my father."

I swallowed, my mouth dry. "Does he know you are here?"

She shrugged. "I did not hide myself and he is not blind." Her tone was light, but I could not shake my anxiety. "Rest easy, Hunlaf. Runolf is not my keeper."

Not her keeper, no. But Revna was Runolf's sole surviving child and he was ferociously protective of her. I took a deep breath, relishing the scent of her hair and skin. The air was redolent of damp earth, the broken stems of verdant rushes. Taking several more long breaths, I forced myself to relax.

From beneath the trees came the voices of Runolf, Drosten, Hereward and the others. I watched as a damselfly flitted low over the trickle of water. Revna leaned her head on my shoulder. My breath caught in my throat.

"Do you think Giso will return?" she asked.

I needed no time to think of my answer. I had made up my mind about that question before he had left. I patted the leather bag. "He would not leave without the Blood. Besides," I said with a wink, "I think he likes Drosten."

She laughed. "Do you think perhaps they feel something deeper than friendship?"

I looked at her sidelong. She stared at the water and the dancing flies, but she knew I was watching her face. Her eyes twinkled.

"Anything is possible," I said.

We both laughed, then fell into a comfortable silence, listening to the murmur of the men's voices, and the drone of insects in the afternoon heat.

As the day grew old, our friends' voices became jagged and fractious. Nerves were frayed and Drosten berated the others, saying they had been wrong to trust the Frank. The sun was low over the sea now, turning the water to molten bronze. Despite my own initial certainty that Giso would return, fingers of doubt began to scratch at the edges of my mind.

I stood and offered a hand to pull Revna to her feet.

"It will be dark soon enough," Drosten was saying as we walked back to the main group. "Just as I said, the little bastard has vanished."

Runolf eyed Revna and me with a frown, but thankfully, he said nothing. I hoped Revna was right, that I had no need to worry about him, but I was still unsure on that score.

"If he has not returned by nightfall," said Hereward, "I say we head into Yafah and see what we can find."

They began to argue the merits of waiting till dark, or heading out immediately. Gersine put forward the option of camping beneath the trees and going into Yafah in the morning.

"At least then we will be able to see what is happening," he said.

The others all had their own opinions and soon the small stand of trees was noisy with raised voices.

Hamid had been on the edge of the trees and now came striding back. The *Badw* had remained with us, despite Hereward thanking them and saying that they could leave now that they had seen us to the sea.

Hamid had sniffed at that. "We will leave when we wish," he had said. "But for now, we await to see vengeance dealt on the devil woman who killed our kin."

Now, not comprehending the words of the arguing men, but clearly disturbed by the volume of their disagreement, Hamid hissed for quiet. Everyone turned to him, their angry voices trailing off.

"Someone approaches," he said.

I translated his words. We fell silent, turning to look in the direction Hamid had indicated. Beorn had been sitting with Eadstan on the west of the glade. They both now rose quickly, pulling their swords from their scabbards. The sound of hooves on the dusty earth was clear. A moment later, a donkey and rider came into view.

It was Giso.

"No need for your swords," he said, slipping down from the saddle. "The little bastard has returned. And you are lucky I am not an enemy. I could hear you almost as soon as I left Yafah!" He pushed his hands into the small of his back and grunted. "And whatever pain you might wish upon me, this beast's spine has already inflicted worse. I do not know how you have ridden on this creature, Hunlaf. Any further and I think it might have cut me in twain."

Despite Giso's complaints, there was a bounce to his step as he led the donkey into the shade and tossed me the reins.

"What tidings?" Hereward asked.

"Direct, as ever," said Giso. "But you are right. There is no time for chatter. As I suspected, Yafah is awash with the wali's men."

"How many?"

"Hard to say. I would guess somewhere close to a hundred." Gersine whistled.

"You were not seen?" asked Hereward.

Giso looked affronted. "Of course I was seen," he said. "I am not a spirit." At Hereward's look of horror, Giso grinned. "I said I was seen, not that I was noticed. To Kawthar's guards I appeared to be a lone *Badawi* herdsman about some business or other. They paid me no heed."

Jamal tugged at my sleeve. "What does he say?" he asked. Hamid and Nassif also looked at me expectantly.

I conveyed Giso's news, and they scowled.

"If there are so many," Drosten said, "what are we to do now?"

"That, my painted friend, is a good question and one that I

can answer easily enough. There is a cove to the north of here beyond a tall rock on which a sole palm grows." Turning to the three *Badw* men, Giso relayed the description of the place in Al-Arabiyyah. "Do you know it?" he asked.

After a short discussion with his father, Hamid nodded.

"Good," replied Giso, reverting to Englisc. "There is no time to lose. Hamid will lead us to the beach with all haste. *Brymsteda* will be waiting for us there." Looking at our surprised faces, Giso chuckled. "Do not look so shocked. I said I would return and I have. But what did you think I had been doing all this while? Did you imagine I had slept all afternoon."

"We thought you had run," said Drosten, though without his previous vitriol, I noted.

"I know what *you* thought," said Giso. "But I gave my word. While you have been lounging in the shade, cooling your feet in the stream and –" he looked at where I stood with Revna and smiled "– whispering to one another, I have been busy. I sent a fisherman out to *Brymsteda*. Alf and Nicetos are not fools. Seeing so many of the wali's men arrive recently in Yafah, they decided to move far from shore. While I awaited the fisherman's return, I listened to what people were saying and I learnt much." He tapped his head and grinned at Drosten. "This little bastard has more than turds in his head. You really should doubt me no longer. I have proven myself many times over on this voyage. We serve the same masters and, whether you like it or not, our wyrds are intertwined. I go where you go."

Drosten sniffed. "Even if that means chasing after Theokleia, rather than heading straight for Frankia?"

Giso scooped up one of the waterskins from the ground. After rinsing his mouth, he spat into the dirt, then took a deep swallow of water. "Even then," he said. "I have thought much on this and prayed for guidance these last days. And I believe that perhaps you are right. It would be best if Theokleia were not allowed to escape. She is a murderer and much too dangerous an enemy to leave at one's back. Besides," he said, with a twisted smirk that looked out of place on his usually sour face, "she has the Spear of Longinus. The Almighty does not deal in coincidence. I can only believe that in His infinite wisdom, God had good reason to place Theokleia in our path, first on Kýpros, and now in Yafah."

Runolf took a step forward. Excitement stirred through the rest of the men. "She is in Yafah then?" the Norseman said.

"We beat her after all?" added Hereward.

Giso held out his hands palm up. "Alas," he said, "we did not. She arrived in Yafah yesterday."

The winds of hope that had so quickly billowed the sails of our anticipation were just as rapidly snuffed out, leaving us becalmed on an ocean of despondency.

"Then we have failed," said Arcenbryht. He was recovering well from his wounds and he burnt with his desire to avenge Cumbra. Now, his strength appeared to leave him. His shoulders slumped and he gazed down at the dusty soil.

"Not yet, my friend," said Giso. His tone was jovial. His demeanour angered me. It seemed that he relished holding power over our emotions; eking out the knowledge he held. "A ship left this morning from Yafah on the early tide. I spoke to a seaman on the wharf who watched several wealthy passengers board. It was a merchant ship that usually sails this coast. He said it sometimes travels as far afield as Kýpros. This voyage though will be much further. For the ship was commissioned to carry its passengers all the way to Constantinopolis itself. And it was a woman who paid the skipper. In gold coins no less, freshly minted. I imagine they bore the face of the Empress Eirene."

The excitement of the chase returned, the subtle shift in the men's humour like a wind rustling the leaves of a forest. Taking up the reins of the donkey that Giso had left trailing in the dirt, I swung myself up into the saddle. I was done with this.

"You told us we had no time to waste," I said, "and yet

you draw out this tale like a gossiping goodwife. I take it the woman was Theokleia."

"No," he said, his face expressionless.

"No?" I was incredulous. "The ship was not paid for by Theokleia?"

"It was not." The ghost of a smile touched his lips. "It was paid for by Salome of Clopas."

Forty-Eight

"Pull!" shouted Runolf from where he stood at the steerboard. "Your time ashore has softened you."

I dragged the long oar back, the blade cutting into the dark surf. Beorn and Eadstan flung retorts at the massive Norsemen. Runolf laughed and roared at us to row harder.

I did not speak. Conserving my breath, I gritted my teeth and settled into the rhythm that had become so natural to me over recent years. Fixing my eyes on Gersine's back, I matched his motion. It was dark, but the sky was clear of clouds. The moon and stars illuminated the pale sand of the beach and the thin lines of the waves breaking there.

We had not been ashore long enough for my hands to lose their calluses. My shoulder ached with each pull on the oar's loom, and the scabs on my chest and arm stretched painfully, threatening to tear my cuts open, a stinging reminder that our time in the Holy Land had been anything but soft. Runolf knew this well enough of course, but just as I and the rest of the warriors had fallen back into the routine of following orders, the moment we had clambered aboard *Brymsteda*, Runolf too had reverted to his role of gruff skipper.

As Giso had promised, the stallion-prowed ship had been waiting for us north of Yafah. The sun had already dropped behind the horizon, leaving only a ghost of fire in the darkening sky. Alf and the rest of the crew had welcomed us warmly, and my heart had swelled at the sight of the ship and our friends. But there had been no time for tender reunions.

"The tide is already on the turn," Alf had shouted as we arrived, anxiety in his tone. "If we do not wish to be stranded here come dawn, we must leave at once."

Seeing that the water lapping at the strakes was barely keeping the keel afloat, Runolf began barking orders. I noticed the rueful smile on Alf's lips as the Norseman took control without acknowledgement of the seaman who had maintained both vessel and crew safe these past weeks.

"You have done well," I said to Alf, giving his arm a squeeze. "Runolf will thank you too. In time."

Alf grinned. "We have little enough of that," he said. "He can thank me when we are safely to sea, if he wishes. I would hear all about your time in the Holy Land too." He glanced about at the men who had dismounted and even now were wading into the water to lend their strength to the task of heaving *Brymsteda* into deeper water. "And," he added, "how so many of our friends came to be left behind." His face was sombre in the dusk and my mood darkened. He was right. There, on the beach with the tide receding, was not the time for chatter. For lengthy greetings. Or farewells.

I set about helping Eadstan, Gamal and Pendrad to remove what few possessions we had on our horses and donkeys, throwing the sacks, saddlebags and waterskins up to hands on the deck. Then, unable to put it off further, I turned to the three *Badw* men who waited patiently beside their camels. I could make out little of their features in the gloom, but I knew each one well enough to imagine their expressions. The sorrow of parting struck me without warning, sharper and harder than I would have believed possible only a day before.

"We must hurry," I said, my words clipped. "The tide does not wait."

Nassif bowed. "We are but men. It is for Allah to control the sea, the sky and the sand. All we can do is journey where He wills it and do His bidding with an honest heart."

"I will try to do that," I said, my throat tight with emotion. "We cannot take these mounts where we are going. Please accept them as payment for your help. I know you did not wish to guide us, but without you, we would be at the wali's mercy. Or most likely dead."

Nassif nodded gravely.

"Zakariya ordered us to aid you. We had little appetite for it, it is true. But you have shown yourselves to be men of honour. Thank you for the gift of these mounts. Peace be upon you."

"And upon you," I replied, returning his bow.

Hamid stepped forward and clasped my arm in the warrior grip.

"Find this Theokleia," he said. "May Allah rub her luck with soot." His eyes gleamed in the gathering gloom. "And when you find her, tell her Hamid ibn Nassif of the Dhullam tribe of the Badwu an-Naqab curses her. Then send her to the fires of *Jahannam*, where she belongs."

"If we find her, she will know before the end that Hamid ibn Nassif wished for her death."

He inclined his head. "Now go," he said. "Your ship is afloat and with each moment that passes, Theokleia draws further away."

I saw he was correct. *Brymsteda* rose slightly as the waves rolled towards the beach, breaking along the sleek sides of the ship. As I watched, the last of the men in the waist-deep water were hauled aboard. Beside me, the only other one of our number left on the strand was Runolf, standing sentinel with his arms folded across his broad chest.

"Come on, Killer," he said. "The hunt is afoot and the gods despise a dawdler."

Turning to say my final farewell, I was surprised as Jamal enfolded me in an embrace.

"May Allah watch over you," he said. Pushing me away, he squirmed sheepishly, apparently embarrassed at his display of emotion.

His face was hidden in the gloaming, but I knew his bruises had almost completely vanished now. What marks remained blended with his dark tan.

"I am sorry for punching you," I said.

"No, you are not," he said, laughter in his voice. "But I am. Now go and travel safe."

I hurried over the damp sand to where Runolf waited. The strength of feeling at leaving Jamal and the others shocked me. There were tears in my eyes and I was glad that it was too dark for Runolf to see. We waded into the sea. The water was warm and pleasant, nothing like the chill North Sea, where it is cold enough to make you gasp, even in the height of summer.

"You made a new friend," Runolf said as we splashed towards the waiting ship.

I thought of Jamal's farewell and my reaction. With a jolt of surprise, I realised Runolf was right.

"It is strange how friendships can form where we least expect them."

Runolf had reached *Brymsteda*. The fine stallion prow reared up against the twilit sky. Drosten stood there, one hand on the beast he had carved, the other reaching down to us.

"True," Runolf said. "I can hardly believe I befriended a young man who now sniffs around my daughter. But of course, anything is possible."

Without waiting for my reply, he reached up and accepted Drosten's hand. Beorn took his other arm, and together they heaved him up and over the side. By the time Beorn and Drosten had pulled me aboard, Runolf was already at the stern and shouting orders for the oars to be unshipped.

My muscles strained and my wounds ached from the exertion of rowing, but I found the wing-beat rhythm of the rise and fall of the oars comforting. My shipmates and I had lost none of our sea-skill, and the blades lifted and dipped with barely a splash, pulling the wave-steed smoothly out into deeper water.

As soon as we were clear of the beach, we had turned the ship about, sitting on our sea chests and settling into the familiar exercise at the oars. Off to the right, a smattering of lights shone in what must have been Yafah. The night sky gave just enough light to make out Runolf's looming bulk at the stern.

I pondered what he had said, turning over his words in my mind, looking for signs of anger or disappointment. I could find none, and prayed that Runolf would give me his blessing. Though what that would mean, I could not be sure. If Runolf was indeed agreeable to Revna and me being together, that could only mean one thing: we would need to be wed. Runolf's daughter was not one of the whores on the docks of Quentovic or Xiphonia. To lie with her would require a vow, not silver. The thought of marriage terrified me. Was this what I desired? Did Revna want it? *Brymsteda*'s hull shivered as the keel cut through each rolling swell, the water churning along the strakes, as my thoughts tumbled through my troubled mind.

The tide pulled us away from the coast and we sped out into cooler, deeper waters. A wind picked up from the south. Runolf bellowed for the sail to be unfurled. We shipped the oars and set about heaving the heavy woollen sail aloft, hauling the halliard hand over hand to the rhythm of Beorn's chanting voice. The wind bellied out the cloth. The timbers and rigging creaked. We trimmed the sheets and soon *Brymsteda* was flying across the waves.

Sailing at night was dangerous. There could be other vessels in our path. Sandbanks and rocks could shatter the oaken planks of our hull. I thought of the great leviathan we had seen in the far north and wondered with a shudder whether such huge whales swam in these warm oceans and might come surging up from beneath us, splintering strakes and sending us tumbling into the black sea.

But Nicetos knew these waters well and said the risks were small. It was deep enough that rocks would not pose a problem, and the moon and stars gave sufficient light that Mantat, who stood at the prow and peered out into the night, should see anything untoward before it was too late.

After a brief debate, Runolf, Alf and Nicetos had decided that Theokleia's ship would most likely have dropped anchor in the shallows of one of the coves to the north. They had no reason to believe they were being followed and therefore no need to risk voyaging in the dark. Pushing on through the night would give us the best chance of catching up with them.

Wrapping my cloak about me against the cold of the sea and the night breeze, I sat with my back against the ship's wale. I listened to the water rushing along the strakes and tried to sleep. I longed to be able to talk with Revna, but she was in the Drag crew before the mast and I was in the Aft. We had returned to our positions on the ship without comment. The sailors who had remained aboard whispered to us, asking after the men who were missing. We told them in murmured voices how they had fallen, but none of us wished to retell those sad stories in the darkness.

Oslaf, Ida and Gwawrddur were all mourned and their absence, added to the recent death of Cumbra, meant that several of the crew sections were short-handed. We were experienced enough that we could function without them, and the only change Runolf made to the sections was to order Gamal from the Foreship to the Midship, where the loss of both Gwawrddur and Ida had left Alf struggling.

When making the alteration to the crews, Runolf strode down the length of the ship, stepping nimbly over sacks and coils of rope, and around barrels, chests and snoozing men. I watched as he went close to Alf, who had returned to his Midship section without complaint. Runolf leaned close, speaking quietly into Alf's ear so that only he might hear the Norseman. Alf nodded. Runolf gripped his arm and clapped him on the back before returning to the Lifting at the rear of the ship, where Beorn had briefly taken the tiller.

Runolf offered a few words of encouragement to some of the others as he passed. He did not look in my direction, or say a word to me. Closing my eyes, I tried to block out the turmoil of thoughts that assailed me, but my mind was uneasy and the rolling motion of the ship made me queasy as I had not been since we had first sailed years before.

Standing, I took hold of a brace and leaned out to watch the wine-dark sea sliding by, the pale tracery of *Brymsteda*'s wake trailing away into the blackness. The wind was chill and I took a deep breath, forcing down the nausea that had momentarily turned my stomach.

I had thought Gersine to be asleep, but he rose to stand beside me.

"How do you feel?" he asked.

"Sicker than normal, but I am sure that will pass."

He sniffed, and I knew he had not been speaking of my stomach.

"You had such dreams of coming to the Holy Land," he said. "So much has come to pass and little enough of what you had hoped for."

"That is the danger with dreams," I said, recalling how I had felt a few weeks earlier at the prospect of walking in the footsteps of Jesus and his Apostles. "They are often better left as fantasies."

"You may not have been able to pray in the Church of the Holy Sepulchre or walked along the paths of the Garden of Gethsemane, but you have touched the very Blood of Christ Himself. And," Gersine went on, keeping his voice low, "some other dreams might have come true. No? I saw Runolf speak to you on the beach. Has he given you his blessing?"

"I know not," I replied truthfully.

Sensing that I was in no mood to talk, Gersine fell silent. We stood together, staring out at the night sea. The moon and stars glistened on the dark water. I breathed deep of the cool air. My stomach settled. Gersine was right. The Holy Land had not been what I had expected. What I had hoped would be a dream had descended into nightmare. In the shimmering reflection of the waning moon I saw the faces of the friends who had fallen. I relived the horror of the moment Gwawrddur's body was pierced by the guard's blade. In my mind's eye, the Welsh swordsman's face blurred and merged with that of the monk, Leofstan, cruelly murdered in Ljósberari's hall far away and years earlier. Both men had guided me in their own way. In the murmur and plash of the waves against the hull, I could hear their whispered voices. Leofstan would tell me to turn away from the path of vengeance, to take the relic to safety and continue with my life. I had found love with Revna; now I should seek peace.

Gwawrddur would have been less forgiving. He was a warrior, and yet he was ever pragmatic. The man who had slain him was dead, as was Aziz, who had given the order. *Take the spoils and live*, Gwawrddur whispered to me from the night.

With an effort, I shut out the ghost-voices of the dead. I thought of praying, but could not bring myself to utter any words to God. The Lord was love and in that moment, plunging through a dark sea, I felt nothing but fury and hatred.

It was too late for doubts. My decision was made and the crew of *Brymsteda* was set on a course for revenge. We had suffered much defeat and needed to wash away the bitter taste of it with the blood of our enemies.

My heart and resolve hardening like the rocks of the desert mountains, I turned my back on Gersine and gazed northward, waiting for the lightening of the sky.

Forty-Nine

Tiredness overcame me for a time and I slumbered fitfully, wrapped in my cloak and a blanket taken from my sea chest. I woke, stiff and aching, as the dawn tinged the sky in the east. Rising, I saw Runolf still at the steerboard, resolute and unmoving. The land beyond was dark beneath a gilded glow of sun. To larboard the sea was vast, its emerald expanse unfathomable. Between *Brymsteda* and the shore, the dawn light picked out the sails of three vessels. My heart leapt at the sight.

"Fishing boats," said Scurfa, his taciturn tone dousing my excitement. The dour sailor was sitting quietly in the shadows of the ship's wale. I had thought he was asleep, but now I saw the glisten of his eyes as the sun crested the world, bathing land and sea in warm light.

I peered at the boats, shielding my eyes and squinting. Scurfa was right. Each of the vessels was small, and carried no more than half a dozen men.

"Do you think we might have passed them in the night?" I asked.

He shrugged, offering me a twisted smile. "Anything is possible," he said. "But I doubt it. Alf will tell us soon enough if we are still on the right course."

Turning towards the Midship section I saw that Alf was

already halfway up the mast. I had seen him and some of the other men do this several times before, but it never ceased to shock me to watch the apparent effortless ease with which they shimmied up the thick, smooth oak. To fall would mean broken bones or death. Or, if they fell overboard, disappearing into the unforgiving deep. Alf seemed to give no thought to the dangers as he clambered past the shrouds and onto the yard. There, atop the mast, he grasped the taut forestay with one hand and held the other over his eyes against the rising sun's glare.

It didn't take him long to see what he was looking for.

"Sail ahoy!" he shouted, pointing in the direction we were travelling.

"Is it the merchant ship from Yafah?" Runolf called back.

Alf took stock, staring intently into the distance. "Aye, Runolf," he said. "I recognise the cut of that sail and the rise of its stern. It is already underway, sailing with the wind. But *Brymsteda* is faster."

"There is none quicker," Runolf said. "There is no chase this stallion cannot win." He began to bark orders, rousing the men with his booming voice. Soon the ship was alive with activity as we adjusted the rigging.

I looked back at Runolf and he grinned at me with such impetuous joy I couldn't help but laugh out loud. The rising sun caught in his fiery hair and beard, and he seemed to glow. Perhaps he had forgotten his previous annoyance, or maybe he was merely overcome with the elation of the rocking deck beneath his feet, the wind in his beard, trembling steerboard in his hand and an enemy to pursue. Whatever the truth of it, his excitement was infectious and there was none of the usual griping from the men as they hauled on halliards, trimmed the sheets and tightened braces.

The dawn saw the wind shift into the west, and with the corrections to the rigging Runolf had ordered, *Brymsteda* charged forward. The carvings on the stallion prow-beast were stark in the morning sun and the whole ship thrummed beneath our feet as it plunged over a wave with a shower of spray that swept over us all like spring rain.

I licked the salt from my lips and pulled myself up on the wale, peering ahead for a sight of our quarry. There was yet no sign, the sail still hidden behind the line of the horizon. But Alf's eyes were sharp and we all knew it was only a matter of time before we would see the ship we chased.

Revna turned and smiled at me. I grinned back. She was radiant in the golden light of the dawn. I was conscious of Runolf looming at the stern behind me, but I did not dare turn to look.

"Best ready ourselves for battle," I said to Gersine, turning away from Revna. There was certain to be a fight. I could not allow myself to be distracted by thoughts of Runolf's daughter. Gwawrddur and Leofstan would both have agreed on that.

Gersine gave me a strange look, but – following my lead – he took a whetstone and sat with me to sharpen his blade. My sword had taken several nicks in our recent fights and it was soothing to scrape the stone along its length, smoothing the jagged edges that might catch and tear, and honing the sword's edge to deadly sharpness. I could picture Gwawrddur nodding his approval. I sighed, forcing myself to concentrate and focus. When the sword was as sharp as possible, I worked on my seax for a time. My fingers gripped the familiar ivory handle and I recalled winning the blade in Orkneyjar. I thought of Thurid, the girl I had met there, and how, for a fleeting moment, I had toyed with the idea of marrying her and settling down. Another dream shattered beneath the weight of reality. Would Revna prove to be another such fragile delusion?

With *Brymsteda*'s speed, I had assumed we would catch the merchant vessel quickly. But, as Leofstan and Gwawrddur had both been keen to remind me frequently, as is so often the way, I was wrong. After a time, Alf shouted down from his precarious perch that we were gaining on the ship. Slowly. Too slowly for Runolf's liking.

"The bastard must have seen us," Runolf snarled, shouting for minor alterations to the sail. "He is running."

There was little else Runolf, Nicetos, Alf or anyone else could do to eke more speed out of *Brymsteda*. The sail was full, the braces and sheets taut. We seemed to skim across the water, the sea burbling in a rush along the strakes.

Despite our pace, it was after the sun reached its zenith when Mantat shouted from where he stood at the prow. He had been there for some time, clasping the stallion's wooden mane and staring out patiently ahead of us.

"Sail!" he yelled.

I had almost begun to believe there was no ship just beyond the horizon, but now we could all see our quarry. Like many of the traders along this coast, its sail was triangular, but this vessel was larger than most. Its distinctive stern was steeply sloped up from the water.

The consensus among the men was that the merchantman must be captained by a skilled seaman for, though his ship was heavier and more cumbersome, he gave us a good chase. In the end though, the broad-beamed bark was no match for *Brymsteda*'s sleek speed. The sun was lowering over the western sea by the time we got close enough to shout at the other ship. We could see the tanned faces of the crew staring back at us over the water. Some had bows in their hands and Runolf gave me the order to offer them terms. He wanted to avoid unnecessary bloodshed. He also didn't want them to escape us after the long day's pursuit.

"If we allow them to run for much longer," he snarled, "we could lose them in the dark. If night falls, there will be little hope. Their skipper is no fool. He knows this too, so make it good, Hunlaf." Runolf's face was drawn, his skin raw from the sun, his eyes red after a night and day at the tiller. But despite his weariness, he had that savage glee about him that I had not once seen while ashore.

I made my way to the bow and climbed up to stand beside the stallion prow-beast, wrapping my left arm around the forestay. Mantat stood behind me, a strong hand gripping my belt in case of sudden waves. Cupping my hands to my mouth, I shouted across the distance. The other ship was still several spear throws away. I hoped my voice would carry and not be torn away by the wind.

"I would speak with the captain of your ship!" I shouted, forming the words in Al-Arabiyyah as clearly as I was able.

There was no reply. A gull swooped between the two vessels. Its shrieking cry sounded like laughter.

"Who speaks for you?" I bellowed, loud enough that it hurt my throat.

A dark, bearded face appeared at the stern. I saw his lips move and a heartbeat later, I heard the sound of his voice, thinned by distance, but clear enough.

"I am Shams al-Din Abu'Abdallah ibn Lawati," he shouted, "and this is my ship. You are stubborn for pirates, but know this: if you try to board us, it will not go well for you. I have two dozen armed warriors aboard. And my archers are skilled. There are fatter and softer fish in the sea for you to hunt."

I relayed his words to my shipmates.

"He is bluffing," said Giso, who had made his way down the length of Brymsteda and now stood near the prow. "He does not have such numbers of warriors aboard."

"It matters not," said Hereward. "If it comes to a fight, we will take them. Hunlaf, let him know we do not want his ship, or his cargo, just the women and their mercenaries."

"We are not pirates," I yelled across the water. The wind strained our sail, the mast creaking and the rigging humming. Almost imperceptibly, we grew closer to the merchant vessel. Brymsteda surged over a wave, sending up a plume of spray.

I would have lost my footing, if not for Mantat's grasp on my belt.

"Then why do you chase us?" came the reply. "You have been in our wake since sunrise."

"Since Yafah," I called back, correcting him. "We wish you no harm and have no interest in your cargo. All we want are the women who boarded at Yafah. And their guards too. If you hand them over to us, we will leave you to continue on your way unharmed."

Shams al-Din did not reply immediately. Perhaps he was mulling over my words, or debating his options with his crew. We crested another wave. The spray glistened like flakes of gold in the light of the setting sun.

"A pirate would say he meant us no harm," Shams al-Din shouted. "How can I trust you?"

I sighed. Dragging this out did not benefit us.

"All I can do is tell you how it will be if you do not give us what we seek," I shouted. "We will board you and we will slay every last one of you. I do not believe you have a dozen warriors, but even if you are not lying, we are men of the far north; we have waded through the blood of our enemies and fought in shieldwalls against armies. Your sailors hold no fear for us. But if you allow us to pull alongside peacefully and give us those we seek, we will not harm you or your ship. The choice is yours, but it has been a long day and I have run out of patience. Decide now and face your fate."

There was a longer pause. While we waited, I told the crew what I had said.

"Do you think they will accept these terms?" Gersine asked.

"If they do not," growled Runolf from the stern, "we will catch them and kill them all just as Hunlaf said. The best threat is the one that is truthful."

We were drawing inexorably closer. I squinted over the bright water, gauging our relative speeds and the distance between the ships. At this rate we would reach them before nightfall, I thought.

A movement on their deck drew my attention. Shams al-Din stepped up once again to the stern rail of his ship.

"You will come alongside," he shouted, "but keep your distance. We will give you what you are looking for. Any attempt to board us, and my archers will fill your ship with your blood."

Even as he spoke, I saw the merchant crew adjusting the sail, allowing it to luff and lose wind. Instantly, *Brymsteda* seemed to leap forward, closing the gap as the merchant slowed. Runolf snapped orders, so that we would not sail past the slowing ship. Leaning on the steerboard, he took us veering off to the right so that if the merchant ship kept its course, we would come alongside it on our port side.

I stepped down from my perch, relaying what Shams al-Din had said.

Drosten smiled broadly, the tattoos on his face stretching. "For once something comes easily to us," he said.

In the instant that he spoke, I knew this thing would not be easy, for the unmistakable sound of blade against blade reached us. A fight had broken out on the merchant ship. Swords, knives and axes flashed in the distance. Shouts of anger and pain echoed over the water. Shams al-Din appeared again at the stern, but this time he did not speak. His mouth was working, but I could not make out any sound beyond the slap of the waves against *Brymsteda*'s hull, the cries of the fighting men and the clash of metal on metal.

The figure of a massive warrior loomed behind Shams al-Din. Dark-garbed, with head covered, the warrior was more than a head taller than the bearded skipper. Aghast, I watched as a sword slashed. Blood spurted, brilliant red in the golden sunset. Shams al-Din mouthed silent agonies and seemed to fly into the air. I blinked, trying to make sense of what I was witnessing. Then with a stomach-curdling memory of being thrown from the cliff in Kýpros, recognition hit me. The huge warrior was no man. It was Artemis. She had lifted Shams al-Din bodily above her head. And now, without a moment's hesitation, she flung him overboard. Shams al-Din's blood coloured the ship's wake pink for a heartbeat as he floundered, splashing weakly. Then he was gone, dragged down into the dark waters of the sea.

The speed with which Artemis had killed the ship's captain shocked me. My shoulder ached and I recalled the sickening feeling of my own impending death as she had thrown me into the ravine.

"Artemis!" I screamed. "Death is coming for you!" Staring across the water, my hatred for her flared. And yet, even as I bellowed with fury, imagining the vengeance I would wreak on her, she spared me no more than a glance before turning away. The merchant ship was in chaos and she leapt into the fray, her bloody sword flashing.

"Hooks! Hooks!" shouted Hereward. The men rushed to do his bidding. We were well trained in boarding other craft. Using iron hooks attached to long ropes, we would drag *Brymsteda* alongside, allowing us to climb over the strakes and into our enemy's vessel.

"To arms!" Drosten roared. The men raised their shields and drew their weapons, ready for combat.

Already we were sliding near to the merchant ship. Its crew had abandoned the rigging and the tiller, and the ship wallowed, rocking in the swell. Clambering aboard would be treacherous, as the two vessels rose and fell on the waves. I had not expected us to join in combat so quickly. My sword and shield were back in the Aft section. Staggering along the deck, I hurried for them. Gersine was already wearing his byrnie and was holding mine out for me. I shook my head.

"No time for that," I said.

Already Drosten had thrown the first of the hook ropes. As

we slid closer, Beorn made a prodigious throw, his rope snaking out behind the heavy hook. The iron bit into the merchant's deck and *Brymsteda*'s crew began heaving on the ropes.

Gersine dropped my byrnie back into my sea chest. Snatching up my sword and shield, I watched as Gamal threw the third grappling hook. His first throw fell short, splashing into the water. The Midship rope had been Gwawrddur's. The Welshman had never missed. Gamal cursed, pulling back the wet rope as quickly as he could.

His second attempt flew true and the hook snagged in the trader's rigging. *Brymsteda* matched the merchant's speed now and the deck rocked and yawed terribly. At least not wearing the iron-knit shirt would make the jump over the side easier. But watching the raging battle on the merchant's deck, I thought I would miss the byrnie's protection soon enough.

Several men were already dead or dying, the deck slippery with blood. The opposing sides of the conflict were clear enough. Towering over all others, Artemis stood surrounded by around a dozen armed men. Facing them were the ship's crew. They carried daggers and small hand axes. It looked as though the archers had been the first to fall. Those who remained were panicked and frightened, shaken by the loss of their captain and the sudden death of their comrades. Lambs before wolves.

But if Artemis, Theokleia and their mercenaries were wolves, the crew of *Brymsteda* were lions. With a roar, Runolf led the charge, leaping atop the sheer strakes and hauling himself over the side of the merchant ship. Whatever weariness he might have felt had fled, replaced by a savage lust for death. His great axe hacked down, splitting the head of the nearest warrior.

"Óðinn!" he shouted.

His invocation of his pagan god would have angered me, but there was no time for such thoughts. Screaming my own battle cry of "*Pro Christo*", I hauled myself over the side and joined my shield-brothers in the mad glee of bloodletting.

Our enemies on the merchant ship had known we would attack, but the speed with which we were able to board appeared to catch them by surprise. In those first few heartbeats, half a dozen dark-robed warriors were cut down.

A bow-legged brute with a forked beard slashed at me. I caught his sword on my shield and sent a slicing blow to his face. My blade did not connect. The man was already falling to the deck, blood fountaining from his torn throat. Drosten grinned savagely at me, raising in salute the gore-smeared dagger that had opened the warrior's neck.

After the initial shock of our attack, Theokleia's men had rallied. The fighting was furious, but a group of them had locked shields and were holding off Runolf, Hereward and a knot of Northumbrian warriors.

A shout of triumph drew my attention and I turned to the far side of the deck. Arcenbryht, with one other warrior, had somehow managed to fight his way to where a slender warrior fought beside Artemis' hulking form.

Beyond them, at the prow of the ship, the merchant crew cowered.

"For Cumbra!" Arcenbryht screamed, hacking and slashing with his sword. He cut down a swarthy warrior and turned on the slim figure that could only be Theokleia. Their swords sang, clashing with a flurry of parries and ripostes, but neither was able to land a telling blow.

Artemis scythed her heavy sword at the warrior who fought beside Arcenbryht.

My heart twisted and I sprinted forward. The warrior Artemis faced was Revna! Revna was a gifted fighter, lithe, skilled and fast. But speed and training were no match for Artemis' raw power. As I rushed to close the gap, Artemis caught Revna's sword arm in her meaty fist, twisting it savagely. Revna's sword clattered to the deck. She cried out in pain. Artemis chuckled.

For a sickening moment, time seemed to halt and I thought

I would see Artemis bring her sword crashing down on Revna. Instead, she pulled Revna towards her and at the same time snapped her own head forward and down. Her forehead hit Revna's nose like a hammer. Revna went limp, sagging in Artemis' grasp.

In that instant, I reached them. Artemis shoved Revna into my path. I pushed Revna aside with my shield, but in doing so, I was momentarily unable to defend myself against the giant woman. Artemis swung her sword like a cleaver, with no finesse, but with such power that if she struck me a solid blow, I knew I would die. Her sword flashed for my head. There was no time to think. All I could do was throw myself down onto my knees. Her great height aided me then and Artemis' sword whistled in the air above me.

I stabbed up at her, trying to push myself to my feet. She batted my blade away, punching me hard in the face with her left hand. The blow stunned me. My vision blurred and I lost my footing. My sword was gone, fallen from my weak grasp. Revna's unmoving weight was atop my shield. I tried to roll away from the killing blow that would follow, but deep down I knew it was too late.

Above me, Artemis grunted.

"That is for Cumbra, you slut," shouted Arcenbryht.

He had killed Theokleia and now turned his rage on Artemis. The blade of his sword had broken and he had tossed it aside. Pulling the dagger he had received from Nu'man from its dark leather sheath, he buried it deep in Artemis' back. She shuddered, but did not fall. Her sword was still in her hand and she raised it high, her eyes burning with hatred. Spinning quickly, she faced Arcenbryht. Such was her strength that the dagger was tugged from his hand and remained jutting from her flesh. Arcenbryht stood before her empty-handed, gaping at the sudden reversal to his fortunes.

Abandoning my shield beneath Revna's still form, I summoned all of my strength, and sprang up with a roar.

Catching Artemis around the midriff with both arms, I propelled myself forward, driving my feet against the blood-wet deck. Artemis tried to fight against me, but she was off balance and Arcenbryht's knife was already sapping her strength.

She staggered backwards as I yelled, pushing her to the ship's rail. Her legs hit the wood and I heaved, but it was no use. I was no match for her bulk, even injured as she was. I scrabbled for purchase against the slippery deck, trying in vain to lift her over the railing, but she might as well have been carved from granite.

With a bestial growl she swung the pommel of her sword down into the back of my head. Agony exploded in my skull and my sight clouded. And yet I stubbornly refused to release her. She struck me again. My legs buckled, but somehow I remained on my feet. My mind was filled with fog, but I knew there was no way I could survive much longer.

As she raised her sword again, I released my hold on her, throwing myself backwards and drawing my seax. My only hope now was that I could land a thrust with my own knife before I succumbed to my wounds.

But before she could bring her sword down on me, or I was able to stab her with my seax, Arcenbryht came running. He hit Artemis low, his shoulder striking her ample stomach, his arms wrapping around one of her tree-like thighs. With a cry of fury, he lifted her from her feet. For an instant she teetered on the edge of the railing, clawing at the air, or perhaps trying to scratch Arcenbryht's eyes from his face.

Then, without uttering another sound, she fell with a great splash.

I pulled myself up beside Arcenbryht and looked over the side.

"For Cumbra," he panted, his chest heaving. "You nithing bitch." He spat into the surf. There was no sign of Artemis. She had been swallowed by the waters as surely as if a whale had swum up from the deep and devoured her.

My head throbbed. I clung to the railing to avoid falling. The ship seemed to be rolling with the swell more than ever, or perhaps it was my head that was spinning. Hawking, I spat blood and phlegm over the side. I could barely believe we had beaten her. I slapped Arcenbryht on the back.

"You said you would get revenge," I said. "Cumbra would have been proud. You killed them both for him." Arcenbryht shook his head.

"Just that giant, Artemis."

"What happened to Theokleia?" I asked. "I saw her fall to your blade."

"That was not Theokleia," he said.

Turning away from the ship's side, I looked down at the corpse of the slender warrior Arcenbryht had been fighting and saw he was right. It was not even a woman. No doubt one of Theokleia's mercenaries, the face that stared up at me was a man, wiry, slim and clean-shaven.

Fifty

"She is not here," Giso said, shaking his head. After the fighting had finished, he had made his way onto the merchant ship.

"You trust the word of these scum?" Hereward asked, indicating the three warriors tied to the mast. Two of them had suffered wounds and were pale in the growing gloom of the dusk. The third had thrown down his sword and had been spared any more than a couple of punches from Beorn while he was bound with his comrades. The moment Artemis had been defeated, the resistance of the mercenaries had crumbled and they had been quickly overrun.

"I trust them no further than I could throw them," Giso said, his hand stroking the leather bag that contained the Blood of Christ. The strap was looped over his head and across his chest. There was no way he was going to lose the bag or the relic it held, but I had noticed how he touched the leather compulsively, as if he feared it would disappear without him noticing. "But you have searched the ship and she is nowhere to be found. And the crew all say the same thing."

Before Giso had come aboard, I had questioned the surviving warriors as they were lashed to the mast. The throbbing in my head was dreadful and with each beat of my heart, my vision pulsed and blurred. My pain and the sight of Revna's bloody face had filled me with an unholy fury and I had struck the uninjured warrior. Seeing him whole while Revna's nose had been broken, caused something to snap within me. The man was defenceless, his arms secured behind his back, but that did not cause me to stay my hand. I punched him hard in the belly, doubling him over, then slapped him across the face, splitting his lip. I was glad to see blood welling up from the cut.

"Where is Theokleia?" I had shouted at him. "Where is she?"

He had shaken his head, and when I'd raised my hands to his companions, they too had denied knowing anything of the woman.

"Don't lie to me," I had screamed, pulling my seax from its sheath and stepping close. The man's eyes widened in fear. And well might he be afraid, for my anger had seared away all restraint and I was ready to begin cutting him to get at the truth.

As if from far away, in the back of my mind I thought I heard Leofstan's disappointed whisper. I pushed his voice savagely down, hiding it in the darkness where it could be ignored. Now was not the time for mercy. Theokleia, like Artemis, must die, and I would know of her whereabouts. Her actions had caused several of my friends to be killed. I could not suffer her to live.

And yet, I could see the truth in the warriors' eyes. They were not lying. They truly did not know where Theokleia was. It was then that Giso had arrived. He touched my arm and I spun around to confront him.

"Easy, Hunlaf," said Runolf, moving close. His face was spattered with gore, his golden-red hair dark with the stuff. "The fight is won."

"Allow me," Giso had said, stepping past Runolf and me. He looked down at the warrior I had struck. Using the edge of his robe, he dabbed at the man's bleeding lip. "Where is Salome?" Giso asked. The man's eyes widened in recognition of the name. I cursed. I should have remembered the name Theokleia had been using in the Holy Land.

"Salome did not board the ship," the warrior said.

"Why?" I snapped.

The man's eyes flicked to the seax in my hand.

"I don't know," he said, swallowing his fear.

Giso crouched down beside him and placed a conciliatory hand on his shoulder.

"You must know something," he said. "Think back to what happened in Yafah. Why did Salome not board with you? Think carefully now. If you help me, I can help you."

The man licked his lips.

"I truly do not know why she did not come with us. She spoke to the big woman, Ruqayyah. But she did not tell us her plans. All we knew was she had other business to attend to. Ruqayyah was not pleased about it – I can tell you that."

"Well," said Giso, his tone soft and friendly, "she is beyond caring now. Where did she have her belongings?"

"We brought a chest with us."

I shouted over to the crewmen to fetch the chest. They were terrified of us, but had seen we had not bound them or caused them any harm. Without a word, two of them carried a metal-bound coffer out into the twilight.

Hereward opened it. Inside were a couple of pouches of silver coins, a golden goblet and a gilded casket. The front of the box was fashioned of cut crystal. Opening the casket, Hereward pulled out a cloth. It was plain and frayed at the edges. In its centre was an old, dark stain of blood.

"That reliquary will do well to hold the true Blood of Christ," Giso said. Turning back to the man he was questioning, he said, "You say you know nothing more of this Salome, or where she was heading?"

"Nothing," the man said.

Giso leaned in close to him, staring into his eyes for a long while. The wind ruffled the sails. The ships creaked against the rope fenders the crew of *Brymsteda* had placed between them. At last, Giso rose and nodded.

"He is telling the truth," he said brusquely. "He is no more use to us. Kill them all."

My stomach curdled. A moment earlier I had wanted to harm these men, to vent my fury on them, make them pay for what had been done to Revna, as if I believed that inflicting pain on them would somehow lessen the hurt I felt. Now, I turned away, disgusted with myself and horrified at Giso's casual pronouncement of death for the prisoners.

Staggering away, I went to where Revna was leaning on the rail. The last vestiges of the setting sun lingered in the sky, the red of the sunset making the blood and blossoming bruises stand out starkly on her freckled face. Her nose was swollen and it was clear it would never be straight again.

"Can you ever love me now?" she whispered. "I am ugly."

"You could never be ugly," I said. "Artemis was ugly inside and out. Seeing you must have made her angrier than anything else in this world. But even if she had hit you a hundred times, you would look beautiful to me."

"I am glad she only hit me once," Revna said, a ghost of a smile on her lips. "I don't think I could have stood another blow like that."

I touched the back of my head gingerly. It was swollen and painful. Back at the mast, I could hear Pendrad, Sygbald and Eadstan killing the prisoners. I did not look. The men's cries were loud for a moment before they were silenced.

"Let's go back to *Brymsteda*," I said.

Revna nodded and took my hand. Her touch anchored me, her warm fingers imparting strength. I walked close to her, not caring who saw us. Together, we went to the side of the ship, carefully stepping over the bodies of the fallen warriors and crewmen. I climbed over the railing, clambering into *Brymsteda,* then helping Revna down. We were both groggy and aching from the fight, and yet I knew she too felt that strange elation that comes after a hard-won battle. Accepting a waterskin from Mantat, we sank down with our backs to the steerboard strakes and listened to the sounds of the sea and the ships, content for the moment to be alive.

Fifty-One

It was full dark by the time the rest of the crew returned to *Brymsteda*. The sky was clear, the moon's light cool on the water. I pushed myself to my feet, pulling Revna up too. We had sat quietly enjoying the closeness between us for long enough. Now we would have to help our section crews as we set off once more.

The merchant crew unhooked our ropes and dropped the iron grapples into the sea. I helped pull in the dripping fenders, then took up the Midship rope and hauled it in, looping the wet hemp neatly and handing it to Gamal. He nodded his thanks.

Runolf paused beside Revna, touching her face gently, turning her head to better see her bruises in the gloom.

"That Artemis is lucky Arcenbryht killed her," he growled. He glanced at me. Was there an accusation there? "I would not have done it so quickly."

Turning towards the Lifting, he strode down the deck, barking out orders as he went.

"Where now?" I asked Hereward.

"Frankia," he replied. "We have all the vengeance we are likely to find, I fear. Some treasure too."

Beorn and Eadstan had carried Artemis' chest from the merchant ship; the others had collected the mercenaries' belongings and weapons. Runolf had wanted to enslave the merchant sailors and take their ship too, but I had heard the discussions and raised my head over the side of the ship.

"I gave their captain my word," I said.

"I didn't," Runolf grumbled. "Besides, their captain is dead."

"Yes, he died doing what I asked." I'd said, readying myself for a heated dispute. "We will let the crew keep the ship."

Runolf had scowled at me, but his heart wasn't really in the argument. We had exacted the blood price after the long chase, and now we were sated and tired, like lions after the hunt.

Mantat and Beorn were using oars now to shove *Brymsteda* away from the merchant ship. Runolf was shouting for the sail to be raised once more. I went to join Gersine in the Aft section. He patted me on the shoulder.

"Glad to see you up and about," he said. "I thought perhaps that giant had split your skull."

"I think she might have," I said with a grimace. "But I am better off than her." My head was pounding. All I truly wanted was to curl up and sleep, preferably with Revna gently stroking my hair. Instead, I took my place behind Gersine and grasped hold of the halliard, ready to haul up the heavy sail.

I took up the slack, waiting for everyone else to take their position, and for Beorn to begin the chant that would give us the rhythm of the labour. The ship rocked from side to side, turning my stomach. Waves lapped against the hull and splashed over the sheer strake. What was Beorn waiting for? I glanced over my shoulder, trying to make him out in the darkness. The tall warrior was not sitting as he should be, instead he was standing beside Runolf. Both of them were staring at Giso. He was standing with another figure. In the gloom, I thought it was Arcenbryht, for since Ahmad had left the ship in al-Andalus, Arcenbryht had served in the Lifting section.

Then, in a splintered instant I realised two things. The figure was much taller than Arcenbryht, and Arcenbryht was already

seated with his hands wrapped about the halliard to lift the
sail.

Giso gasped, his eyes wide in shock.

I blinked, unable to make sense of what I saw. It could
not be. A wave of giddiness washed over me, but there could
be no denying what I beheld. The tall figure with Giso was
none other than Artemis! Her clothes and hair were plastered
against her, dark from the sea and blood, her face as pale as
the moon. In her hand she held Arcenbryht's dagger. Somehow
she had plucked it from her body. Her own blood stained the
blade she now pressed to Giso's throat.

Nobody moved. A stillness had fallen over the crew, all
eyes turning towards the diminutive Frank and his giant
assailant.

Artemis bellowed; the sound like a stag at rut, booming and
full of challenge.

"Take me to shore," she shouted.

Nobody spoke.

"Now!" she screamed, wrapping her left fist in Giso's bag
strap and shaking him. Grievously wounded as Artemis was,
Giso still looked puny and defenceless beside her. "I will kill
him!"

"Take her to land," Giso hissed. I had never before heard
such terror in his voice. "If you do not, she says she will kill
me."

Runolf shrugged.

"I don't think I will," he said. "I care nought if she kills you,
little man. But that woman," he spat the word as if it was an
insult, "is not leaving here alive."

Artemis may not have understood the words, but she knew
there was some debate as to what to do. In an effort to help
Runolf make up his mind, she pushed the dagger blade against
Giso's neck. It broke the skin and he let out a whimper.

"Runolf," I said.

He ignored me. He did not take his eyes from Artemis. In

turn she glared back at the Norseman, her eyes glimmering coldly.

"Hey! Over here!" The voice was loud, the Pictish lilt strong.

Turning towards the sound, I sensed movement. Something flashed past me in the darkness. Drosten stood, his right hand outstretched as if pointing at Artemis. Looking back, I saw a knife hilt had appeared in her right eye. As I watched, she collapsed, toppling back and over *Brymsteda*'s side. Giso went with her, tumbling backwards, pulled by her weight and the fist she had tangled in the leather strap of his bag. He clattered against the strakes, the strap pulling taut around his throat. He clawed at the leather. Strangled gurgling squeezed past his protruding tongue. His eyes bulged. All of Artemis' bulk was pulling on that strap. There was no way he could remove it. Giso was suffocating, being hanged by Artemis' dead weight. He would die in moments.

Without thought, while the others watched on in awe, I was already jumping across the thwarts. Arcenbryht's dagger lay on the deck where Artemis had dropped it. I snatched it up and set about sawing at the strap that was choking the life from Giso. I looked over the side of the ship into the dead face of Artemis. Water sloshed into her open mouth, washing over her unblinking eyes as the waves tugged at her corpse.

Giso clawed at me now, scratching in blind panic. I hacked at the taut leather, ignoring him. His struggles grew weaker and I thought I would be too late. Then, without warning, the strap parted and as fast as thought, for the second time, I saw Artemis disappear into the deep.

Vainly, I shot a hand out in an attempt to catch hold of the bag, but it vanished, pulled beneath the dark sea's surface.

Artemis was gone, and the Blood of Christ went with her.

Fifty-Two

Giso gasped and gagged. Collapsed at my feet, he coughed and choked, dragging in ragged lungfuls of air. Runolf was shouting for calm as the crew leapt to their feet. Slowly, at his insistence, they returned to their places.

"We have not yet raised that sail," he shouted. "We will make better time now we do not have a Byzantion barnacle hanging from the hull."

Laughter rippled through the men, alleviating the tension of the chase, the battle on the merchant ship, and the sudden reappearance of Artemis from the sea.

I had not noticed her approaching, but Revna was at my side. Without thinking, I took her in an embrace. I was shaking now, sharp pains reminding me of the many wounds I had suffered.

"See," I said, "I told you Drosten likes Giso."

More laughter from the crew. Drosten came and peered over the side into the dark waters.

"*Like* Giso?" he scoffed. "I was aiming at the whoreson. My poor throw lost me a good knife."

"A knife?" spluttered Giso, pushing himself up. His voice rasped and speaking was clearly painful. Still, he continued, his face crimson, blood trickling down his neck. "A knife! You

Pictish fool! We have lost the most wondrous relic! What will we take back to Carolus now?"

"Well, little man," Drosten said, looming over Giso, "if you are not careful, we will not be returning with a certain Frankish emissary. There is room in the sea for you to join Artemis and your precious relic."

Giso looked at the hard faces of the crew. He swallowed. Forcing a deep breath, he coughed again, then turned back to Drosten.

"You are right," he said, his voice small. "I owe you my life. You have my thanks."

Drosten spat over the side.

"I don't want your thanks," he said. "I want a new knife."

"Well, you're not having this one," said Arcenbryht, taking his dagger from me and pushing it back into its sheath.

When we had hoisted the sail and were underway, I went to where Giso stood dejectedly at the stern. I felt strangely sorry for him. I thought that I, more than anyone else aboard *Brymsteda*, understood his sorrow and sense of loss. My body was stiff and aching, and I walked with the gait of an old man, hesitant and trembling. My recent exertions had torn open the scab of the cut across my chest. I could feel blood oozing from it.

Of course, I was young then. Within a few days I would be fit and able once more. Now, what feels like only moments later, I am old; I know what it is to face each day weaker than the last. I would give almost anything to feel again the energy and certainty of youth.

Giso stared out at the moonlit expanse of the sea. We did not speak for a time. Runolf had ordered Nicetos to guide us in closer to shore where we would take a well-earned rest before heading back across the Middle Sea towards Frankia. The breeze was light, and we were no longer pushing the ship for speed, so *Brymsteda* rolled sedately over the swell. Absently, I hoped there would be enough wind to take us all the way to shore. I was not sure I could face another stint at the oars.

Giso spoke without warning, startling me out of my thoughts.

"We have lost everything we sought." His voice was bleak.

"Not everything," I said. "Most of us yet live."

He sighed. "The deaths of the men weigh heavily on me." His admission shocked me.

"I thought you cared nothing for the lives of others."

"How can you say such a thing?" he said, anger flaring. His swollen throat made his voice hoarse. He sounded like a different person. "What value is there to anything without life?"

"You often seem uncaring," I said, softening my tone somewhat. Perhaps I had misjudged him.

"Sacrifices must be made at times," he acknowledged. "But to lose men and still return empty-handed. This is worse than pointless. I have failed completely. Drosten and the others are right to despise me."

"Without you, we would not have escaped Ierusalem, or from Aziz, and we would have stumbled into a trap at Yafah."

"Perhaps," he said, "but still we return with nothing to show after months of travel."

We had been speaking not much above a whisper, but the night was quiet and sound travelled easily. Beorn had replaced Runolf at the steerboard. The Norseman was wrapped in a blanket and huddled nearby. I had thought him to be sleeping, but he had evidently been listening. He rose with a grunt and made his way over to us.

"Every voyage is full of danger," he said. "Men have died, Giso, it is true, but such is the wyrd of those who go a-viking. I do not like you, Frank. But those who have fallen are not for you to mourn alone. Their deaths are not for you to bear." I stared at Runolf, open-mouthed. He ignored me. "And we do not return empty-handed."

"We have lost the Holy Lance of Longinus," croaked Giso. "And the Blood of Christ."

Runolf ran his fingers through his unruly thatch of beard, scratching at something he found there. "Perhaps one day we will find Theokleia and retrieve the spear," he said. "But we have some silver and you are wrong. We have not lost the Blood of Christ."

"It is at the bottom of the sea," Giso said. "Perhaps the Lord in His wisdom did not wish for us to take it from the Holy Land."

The moonlight shone on Runolf's face. He was staring at Giso, eyebrows raised.

"We have not lost the Blood of Christ," he repeated.

Giso looked at him, mouth agape. "You mean—? No." He shook his head. "That is not the true Blood of Christ."

Runolf shrugged. "Who is to say? Theokleia believed it to be the true relic. It is in a fine reliquary. I am sure Alhwin and King Carolus will reward handsomely those men who return with such a prize."

"But we know the truth of it."

"The truth? There is nobody aboard *Brymsteda* who will speak out against the relic in that chest being real."

"But it is sacrilege," I said, speaking up for the first time. "That is not the cloth that touched the skin of the Son of God. The blood on it is that of a goat."

"Hear the man out," said Giso, placing a hand on my shoulder. "We are Christians. Our belief must surely be more important to us than any earthly artefact."

Runolf was nodding. I could see his grin in the pallid light from the moon. "Yes," he said. "Are you not always saying that your faith is what gives Christians their strength? So have faith. If you do, Carolus will too."

Giso was also smiling now, his previous morose mood dispelled by the prospect of success and perhaps, I thought bitterly, riches.

"If we can provide the king a powerful relic," he said, "it is surely our duty to do so. Is that not so, Hunlaf?"

They each fixed me in their gaze, unusual allies in this strange, unexpected deception. I was too tired to fight them, my body and mind exhausted. So I merely nodded and returned stiffly to my blankets. I was uneasy, my conscience screaming that this was wrong. In the soft sounds of the ship's rigging and the sigh of the water along the strakes, I fancied I heard Leofstan's whispered condemnation.

I closed my eyes, pushed the dead monk's disapproving voice away, and slept.

Fifty-Three

And so it was that we returned to Frankia and were welcomed as heroes. First Alhwin and then King Carolus, the man who would be emperor, gazed in awe at the bejewelled reliquary and the bloodstained cloth within. They listened in a reverent hush as we recounted the tales of our many exploits. To my great surprise they were almost more excited by the golden goblet we had found in the chest. Giso told how we had come by it, telling the story truthfully and emphasising that we did not know of its provenance or what significance the object might have. And yet somehow in the telling, a masterful pause here, a catch in his breath there, Giso managed to give the impression that the cup might well be the chalice used by Jesus and his apostles at the Last Supper and that, just perhaps, it was the very grail that had caught the Blood of Christ as he lay dying on the cross.

As a young man I worried at our deception, ashamed at what we had done. I thought of the countless miracles the faithful had prayed for, invoking the holy power they believed to reside within the bloody cloth, and the secret almost became too much for me to keep. I imagined telling the truth of it all to Alhwin and the king; unburdening myself from the shame of my sin.

And yet I did not speak up, and over time I have decided

there are worse crimes, many of which I myself have committed. And, while Leofstan's voice often troubled me in the still of long nights, as the years sped by, I found it increasingly easy to drown out his recriminations and judgements. Now, though I miss him still, the sound of his voice is but a distant memory.

Of course, I have my own voice to taunt me. It whispers to me that I am a terrible sinner, doomed to burn in the fires of hell for all eternity. Try as I might, I cannot silence this harsh, hissing voice. It awakens me from my fitful sleep when my guts gnaw at me, bringing tears to my eyes and making me whimper for relief. At such times, I bear the agony for as long as I am able before reaching for the cunning woman's draught. I deserve for my flesh to be chastised, and yet I am but weak, and so, in the end I always swallow down the bitter potion, blunting the ache in the pit of my stomach and dulling my senses too, enough that I am able to sleep again.

Despite still making use of the witch's brew, I have not fallen back into the spiral of self-pity that gripped me after Coenric's death. Godstan or one of the other brothers only bring me a small flask of the medicine every evening after Vespers. Many days I do not touch it, so that when the abbot or a monk visits in the morning after Prime, they take away the flask still brimming with foul liquid.

They nod to me then, as if I am brave to endure the pain without aid. They do not understand. To spend a night with a clear head and then to sit through each day reliving the time I spent with Runolf, Gwawrddur, Hereward, Drosten and the others, is a punishment more acute than any other. To picture Revna's beauty, to conjure her words in my memory, her warmth, the sweetness of her breath, is worse than any torture.

And yet each dawn I awaken filled with excitement for the day ahead. God has given me this time and Godstan was right to encourage me to continue my writing. It may have started as an act of pride and rebellion, but there is more value in it than that. I can see that now, and I do not believe it is merely my own ego speaking.

Outside, the year is turning. Yesterday, a storm lashed the coast, tearing leaves from the alders that grow by the river. Soon the snows will come, the ground will turn to rock and the land will slumber. Winter will bring peace, for no Norse or Danes will take to the Whale Road when the year is old. Ever since the attack in the spring we have been spared, but tidings reach us of other raids. Only a month past we heard of the sack of a minster in Wessex, in which they say all the brethren were put to the sword or taken as thralls. The Norse grow in strength and there is talk that they plan to descend upon Britain with a great horde.

I do not know if this will come to pass, or how much longer my body will continue to win the fight against whatever ailment is inside me, but Gwawrddur once told me he had never met a more stubborn man. Perhaps he was right. I see the surprise on the faces of the brothers who bring me food each day. They expect to find me dead in my cell, and each morning, my continued life is a shock. One day they will enter my room to find me cold and unbreathing. But until the Lord claims me, I will continue scribing these tales. I am fatigued, my fingers stiff and painful, but I will not rest. I have asked for more vellum and Abbot Godstan has agreed to my request. Tomorrow, I will take up a fresh quill and begin writing more of the adventures of the *Leones Imperatoris*, the Lions of the Emperor, as the crew of *Brymsteda* became known.

If the Almighty grants me enough time I may write of how my love for Revna blossomed like a rose and then, like a thorn in winter, withered and died. I will tell of our part in the crowning of Carolus, Emperor of the Holy Roman Empire, how Popes and kings bowed to us. Mayhap I will even tell of the time I fought alongside Dunston, the one they call "The Bold", for that is a tale that has oft been told in the mead halls of the kingdoms of Britain, and yet, never by one who witnessed the events.

I pray that the Lord Almighty will give this sinner enough time to put pen to parchment and record all these things and more, but for now, I hear the brethren singing the psalms of Vespers. I have not joined them in prayer for many days. Today I feel stronger than I have of late. I crave the company of my brothers, and so I will put aside my pen until tomorrow.

And so it remains for me to commend my soul to the Lord. May His blessings be upon all who read this tome.

And thus ends the fourth volume of the Annals of the life of Hunlaf of Ubbanford.

Author's Note

While the battle between spies working for King Carolus (aka Charlemagne) and Eirene (aka Irene of Athens), the Empress of Byzantium, may be my own fanciful creation, the rivalry and the struggle for supremacy over what was left of the Roman Empire at the end of the eighth century was very real.

Eirene was almost unbelievably ruthless in her pursuit of power, and the lengths to which she would go to keep hold of the influence she had were astounding. She did not come from aristocracy but was chosen to marry the sickly Leo IV in a sort of beauty pageant called a "bride show".

Her husband was sickly, suffering from tuberculosis, from which he died five years into his reign at the age of thirty. He left his nine-year-old son and heir, Constantine VI, in the care of his regent mother. Little could he have imagined Eirene's potent mixture of ambition and cruelty that would colour the next two decades of the empire's history.

During the 780s, Constantine VI ruled in name only. Eirene exercised full control over all manners of state. When he was just sixteen, Constantine VI was made to hold the Second Council of Nicaea, which saw the condemnation of Iconoclasm and sanctioned the veneration of icons. This was the work of Eirene and was popular with the people and the church. She also decided her son should marry Rotrude, the second daughter of King Carolus of the Franks. This diplomatic match would have helped unite the two halves of the Christian empire. However, the engagement was called off, probably on the initiative of the Frankish side, and instead, Constantine was married to a young woman named Maria, who, like his mother, was chosen in a bride show, plucked from obscurity because of her beauty.

Constantine though was unhappy with his new wife and, growing ever more difficult for his mother to control, he took to consorting with a lady-in-waiting called Theodote. He sent Maria to a monastery and married Theodote instead. This was a dreadful controversy as it was seen as a form of bigamy by the Orthodox clergy. Ever scheming for her own power, Eirene sided with the church and condemned her son for his actions, weakening even further his standing with the populace.

There followed years in which Constantine's popularity continued to wane. He led several failed military campaigns and developed a penchant for increasingly cruel punishments for anyone who stood against him. In 797, Eirene had Constantine arrested and his eyes put out. Reportedly he was to be confined to a small chamber in the palace where he was born. His wife Theodote allegedly volunteered to be incarcerated along with him. Whatever the truth of the plans for the emperor, after his blinding, Constantine VI was never heard of again. Eirene became the first woman to rule the empire in her own right.

Often choosing to call herself the masculine name for emperor, *basileus*, rather than the feminine, *basilissa*, Eirene governed for only five years. She was a disastrous ruler and was eventually the victim of a coup herself, and exiled to the island of Lesbos, where she lived out the last of her days in poverty, but mercifully escaping the torture she had inflicted on her son.

The Roman Empire was effectively split into east and west, separated by language, interpretations of Christianity and geography, each side coalescing around the separate religious centres of Rome and Constantinople. Carolus ruled in the west, Eirene in the east. In a bid to combine these two factions into a single, all-powerful empire, it is said that Eirene even offered her own hand to the king of the Franks. If she could unite the empire in marriage as her son had failed to do, nothing and nobody could stand in her way. Charlemagne declined the offer. For a woman capable of torturing and murdering her own son to further her ambitions, I imagine Eirene did not take the rejection well.

This led to me imagining a conflict between the two rulers, carried out by their agents and proxies in all corners of the known world. And, as the war between the two halves of the empire was governed by religion and differing beliefs of Christianity, what better target for the players in this cold war than holy relics? I could envisage a religious arms race playing out in the shadows, each side doing whatever they could to secure the most desirable and powerful relics. And there could be no more powerful relic than flesh or blood taken from Jesus Christ – a corporeal remnant of the Son of God made man.

When researching this novel, I discovered that according to legend Charlemagne actually presented one such relic to the Pope on the day of his coronation as the Holy Roman Emperor. This relic – the Holy Prepuce – was to be the initial focus of this novel. But when I told my wife that my characters were going to fight to the death over Jesus' foreskin, she laughed and said it would read more like a Monty Python script than a tale of action and adventure. No matter that it was a real relic that features in Charlemagne's story, and that over the centuries there have been up to eighteen such holy prepuces recorded in different churches across Europe; in the end I realised my wife, as is usually the case, was right. Sometimes, fact is just too strange to be used in fiction, at least if you want anyone to keep a straight face while reading!

A true fact that made it into the novel is that Alhwin (aka Alcuin), Carolus' counsellor and teacher, was made abbot of

Marmoutier Abbey at Tours in 796. It is also a fact that Alhwin had a wonderful library at York. This library has since been lost and what happened to the fabulous tomes it contained is a mystery to this day. My own theory is he had it moved to his new abbey.

Alhwin wrote letters widely and had many contacts all over the world. Whether he was also a spy master is another matter, but while unlikely, it is not completely unfeasible.

You may think it another flight of fancy of mine that there were lions in Palestine at this time, but again, this is true. Asiatic lions were once common in the Holy Land and lions are mentioned over 150 times in the Bible. Ancient civilisations such as the Assyrians and Egyptians carried out royal lion hunts, and wild lions could be found in Palestine until about AD 1400.

When I read this, I could not pass up the chance for Hunlaf and his friends to have a frightening encounter (or two) with one of the beasts. It is unusual for lions to kill humans, but when they do, they can be tenacious and seemingly bloodthirsty, as if they get a taste for human blood, or at least relish the weakness of human prey and the ease with which they can be killed. There are many documented cases of such man-eaters, with one of the most famous accounts being that of two lions, named by their hunters as Ghost and Darkness, the so-called "Man-eaters of Tsavo".

These two maneless male Tsavo lions preyed on the construction crews of the Kenya-Uganda Railway in 1898. Between March and December of that year, the two animals killed dozens of workers, often seemingly for sport. Railway records attribute twenty-eight worker deaths to the lions, but the predators were reported to have killed many local people of which no official record was ever kept. This led to the original estimate of people killed by the pair to be in excess of one hundred. Whatever the true number of casualties, the lions were eventually shot and killed by Lieutenant-Colonel John

Henry Patterson. Their stuffed skins are now on display in the Field Museum of Natural History in Chicago.

To this day, in many countries of Africa, where humans encroach on their natural habitat, lion attacks are relatively common. When such attacks occur, there is no recourse for the local human population but to hunt down and kill the predator, even though it is only following its natural instincts.

The *Badw* people who befriend Hunlaf and his comrades are more traditionally known as Bedouin. These are the nomadic Arab tribes who originated in the Syrian Desert and the Arabian Desert, later spreading across the rest of the Arab world in West Asia and North Africa after the spread of Islam. Today the Bedouin population numbers approximately twenty-five million.

As so often during its long history, Jerusalem in the late eighth century was a place of contention. Revered by Christians as the location of Christ's death, it was at this time under the control of the Abbasid Caliph Abu Ja'far Harun ibn Muhammad al-Mahdi, known as Harun al-Rashid, who followed the newer religion of Islam. Despite being a sacred place for three religions and the conflict that brings, at this point in history Jerusalem was relatively peaceful, with the Islamic rulers tolerating Jews and allowing Christian pilgrims to visit.

One might imagine that the Christian Franks would wish to have nothing to do with the Islamic Caliphate, especially when taking into account the war over land and ideology raging between King Carolus and the Islamic Moors of the Iberian Peninsula in al-Andalus. However, the best rulers are ever pragmatic, and trade – often with one's enemies – is always a necessity.

Such trade was facilitated by diplomatic envoys travelling between the different kingdoms. One such emissary was the diplomat known as Isaac Judaeus, or Isaac the Jew, who Carolus sent to the court of Harun al-Rashid in Baghdad in

797. Isaac returned with a rather unusual gift from the caliph in the form of an Asian elephant, called Abul-Abbas. Isaac and Abul-Abbas the elephant finally reached Aachen in modern-day Germany in July 802. Abul-Abbas was paraded around Frankia and admired by all. He eventually died suddenly in 810.

When I read about Isaac and Abul-Abbas, I knew I had to include them in the story. Their encounter with Hunlaf and the lion is purely fictional.

The Blood of Christ, as depicted in the story, is fictional too, but of course there are many relics purporting to be remnants of Jesus' blood. The strange cavern where the adventurers find the relic and its guardians has some obvious nods to a certain whip-wielding archaeologist, but it is based on a real location.

In 2009 an enormous artificial underground cave was exposed in the Jordan Valley some 4 kilometres north of Jericho. The cave covers an area of approximately 1 acre, measuring approximately 100 metres long by 40 metres wide. It was uncovered during the course of an archaeological survey being carried out by the University of Haifa, and, according to Professor Adam Zertal, head of the excavating team, when they arrived at the opening of the cave, "two Bedouins approached and told us not to go in as the cave is bewitched and inhabited by wolves and hyenas".

Ignoring the warning, the archaeologists entered and found an impressive underground structure supported by twenty-two giant pillars. There were cross markings on the pillars, an engraving resembling a zodiacal symbol, Roman letters and an etching that looks like a Roman Legion's pennant. There were also recesses in the pillars, which would have been used for oil lamps.

Ceramics found within the cave and the engravings on the pillars date it to the first six centuries AD. The cave's primary use was probably as a quarry, but other findings indicate that the place was also used for other purposes, such as a monastery and possibly as a hiding place. What, or who, might have been hiding there, Prof. Zertal did not hazard a guess.

Hunlaf certainly had an eventful life and, luckily for us, he managed to write at least some of his adventures down. At the end of *Dominion of Dust*, he is all set to continue recounting his tale and that of those who travelled with him. I for one hope he was able to survive his ailments and the increasingly frequent Viking attacks on the shores of Britain to pen at least one more story before death claimed him.

If he did, we shall find out another day.

And in other books.

Acknowledgements

A while back, my youngest daughter read the acknowledgements in a book of mine and made fun of me for addressing my thanks to "dear reader". However, as I do not know your name, and you are truly dear to me, I will stand by my choice of words, pretentious or not!

So, *dear reader*, let me thank you for taking the time (and perhaps spending your well-earned money) to read this book. I really appreciate it. I know how difficult it is to carve out a slice of time large enough to allow yourself to get lost in a book. And when you have managed that, you have then chosen this book over all others, so I am genuinely thankful for your faith in me. I hope you do not regret your decision. If you do, you don't need to tell me about it. If you have enjoyed the book though, feel free to tell me all about it, please mention it to others too, and consider leaving a review online at your store of choice. A few words are enough. Reviews really do help readers find new authors.

I must give extra special thanks to Jon McAfee for his ongoing generous patronage. To find out more about becoming a patron, and what different tiers of rewards you can receive for doing so, please go to www.matthewharffy.com.

Thanks to my friends and test readers, Gareth Jones, Alex Forbes, Shane Smart and Simon Blunsdon. As always, they were the first to read the book and their input was extremely helpful.

Thanks too to Steven A. McKay, friend, fellow author, and co-host of *Rock, Paper, Swords! The Historical Action and Adventure Podcast*. It is great to have someone who will listen to me moan about my latest manuscript on a regular basis. Steven is a great guy and a wonderful writer. Go and read his books after finishing all of mine!

Thank you to my editors, Nicolas Cheetham and Greg Rees, for polishing the story, and thanks to all of the wonderful team at Aries and Head of Zeus for designing and producing the finished product.

Thanks to the online community of authors and readers who connect with me regularly on social media. It is always wonderful to hear from like-minded individuals.

And finally, but never least, my undying love and gratitude go to my family. To my daughters, Elora and Iona, for keeping me young even when making me feel old, and to my wife, Maite, for her steadfast guidance, unwavering support and, above all, love.

Matthew Harffy
Wiltshire, January 2025

About the Author

Matthew Harffy grew up in Northumberland where the rugged terrain, ruined castles and rocky coastline had a huge impact on him. He now lives in Wiltshire, England, with his wife and their two daughters. Matthew is the author of the critically acclaimed Bernicia Chronicles and A Time for Swords series, and he also co-hosts the popular podcast *Rock, Paper, Swords!*

Follow Matthew at @MatthewHarffy and www.matthewharffy.com.

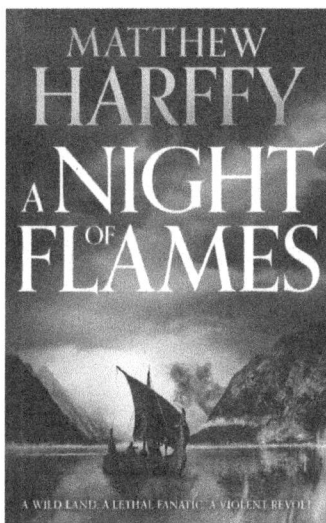

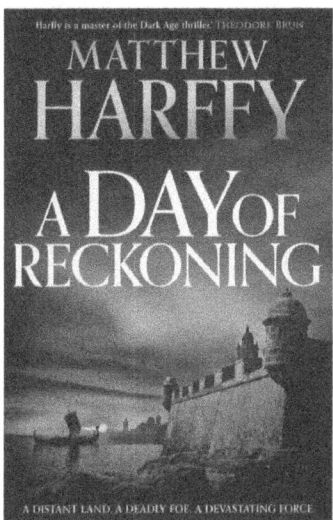

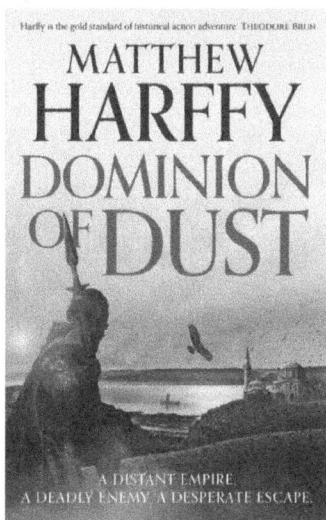